WEIRD TALES INSPIRED BY H. P. LOVECRAFT

CTHULHU FHTAGN!

EDITED BY ROSS E. LOCKHART

Other books by Ross E. Lockhart

Anthologies:

The Book of Cthulhu
The Book of Cthulhu II
Tales of Jack the Ripper
The Children of Old Leech: A Tribute to the Carnivorous Cosmos of Laird Barron (with Justin Steele)
Giallo Fantastique
Dead Suns (with Justin Steele) (forthcoming)
Eternal Frankenstein (forthcoming)

Novels:

Chick Bassist

Critical Acclaim for *Giallo Fantastique,*
edited by Ross E. Lockhart

"Lockhart translates giallo fantastique as weird crime, and each story, while very different in style and tone, melds crime and supernatural horror with panache and verve. [...] The stories' conclusions are never definitive, leaving the reader with a delicious sense of lingering unease."

—*Publishers Weekly*

"A lavish, sumptuous tapestry of luxurious surrealism and strangeness."

—*The Horror Fiction Review*

"...ultimately satisfying, with a few tales that skirt tantalizingly close to brilliance."

—Mer Whinery, Muzzleland Press

Critical Acclaim for *The Children of Old Leech: A Tribute to the Carnivorous Cosmos of Laird Barron,*
edited by Ross E. Lockhart and Justin Steele

"Lockhart and Steele collect 17 original stories from some of the shining stars of modern horror, constructing a worm-riddled literary playground from elements of the fiction of horror maestro Laird Barron. The results come across with a coherent feeling of dread, without feeling derivative of the source. [...] Hopefully Barron will enjoy this tribute; his fans certainly will."

—*Publishers Weekly*

"This multifaceted grimoire, and the talent associated with it, is staggering to behold. [...] The tales, while sometimes recalling certain tropes or characters from his fiction, can be enjoyed in their own right; and, I must say, the range of styles on display is consistently impressive."

—C. M. Muller, *Chthonic Matter*

"A reader new to the whole Barron cosmos won't feel excluded at all, though familiarity with those totems obviously will help. What they will feel is entertained, shocked, stimulated, rewarded, upset, disturbed, and sometimes very scared."

—*TeleRead*

Critical Acclaim for *Tales of Jack the Ripper*,
edited by Ross E. Lockhart

"*Tales of Jack the Ripper* manages to walk that fine line between entertainment and exploitation with real finesse. It's a gripping group of stories about one of our most enduring mysteries, and well worth your time."

—*FEARnet.com*

"...there are enough original and inventive approaches to this most bedeviling of true-crime mysteries to suggest that Jack the Ripper and the Whitechapel Murders of 1888 will continue to inspire imaginative speculations for some time to come."

—Stefan Dziemianowicz, *Locus*

"You need to get up off your lazy duff and buy this collection."

—*Shock Totem*

"…there's enough variation of theme and style here to interest almost any crime or horror reader…"

—*The Big Click*

"Readers interested in Jack the Ripper will love this anthology. Horror fans in general should be quite pleased."

—*Tangent*

"Most of the authors explore the Ripper's mind, and it is indeed a place of grue and madness. [...] Yet, taken one by one, the stories show a remarkable level of skill and power."

—Richard A. Lupoff, *Locus*

"*Tales of Jack the Ripper* marks a strong debut for Word Horde. Lockhart, in usual fashion, has managed to put together a strong, multifaceted anthology that explores the Ripper legend at length. If this book is indicative of what's to be expected from his new press, than readers have much to look forward to."

—*The Arkham Digest*

"Judging from the author lineup in this book, Word Horde will not have time for your Mickey Mouse bullshit."

—*HorrorTalk.com*

"The bottom line is these are all excellent stories, all about Jack."

—*Hellnotes*

WORD HORDE

PETALUMA, CA

Cover Illustration by Adolfo Navarro
Cover design by MMP

Edited by Ross E. Lockhart

An extension of this copyright page appears on page 314

First Edition

ISBN: 978-1-939905-13-0

A Word Horde Book
http://www.WordHorde.com

This one is dedicated to those who seek out, collect, buy, sell,
and, most importantly, *read*
strange books filled with stranger tales.

And in particular, my friends at Copperfield's Books in Petaluma, CA.

TABLE OF CONTENTS

INTRODUCTION: IN HIS HOUSE AT R'LYEH...

Ross E. Lockhart

My nightmares fascinate me. Most are the usual anxious dreams: driving an unknown suburb on a foggy night, all the houses alike. Unanticipated public nudity, or invisibility, or ghoulishness (shades of "The Outsider"). The padlocked impossibility of loosing a scream. Sometimes I get movie monsters, but since my subconscious has long been steeping in the stuff of horror, most monsters come through in my dreams as too-familiar camp or titillating kink (or some combination of the two). Nothing to truly shock or scare. The most intense, effective nightmares are the ones that act on your most buried impulses, that primordial soup of wants and hopes and desires and fears that might just make Clive Barker blush. Fears that root in the most animal places in our collective unconscious. After all, we are animals. Animals with language, imagination, and houses.

Speaking of houses, when I have nightmares, they are most often set in houses. Familiar houses. Places I've lived. The leaking beach storefront where damaged floor tiles had been partially removed, giving way to constant foot-high duststorms of asbestos and mites. The Victorian basement where effulgent fungus quickly grew on food left out to cool and the walkway flooded, ankle deep, during power outages. The apartment building where chittering conversations echoed up through a garbage chute. The parsonage with the shrouded baby's room and the unfinished closet that opens upon an earthen pit. My parents' house.

That last one may be the most common setting for my nightmares of all. A three-level Southern California stucco-covered home, pale green, with a two-car garage, quite-climbable roof, and fruit trees beside it. I grew up in that house. My parents still live there.

The funny thing is that it's never the house as it is now. My parents have changed quite a few things over the years. Multiple kitchen remodels. Adding skylights. Converting a screened patio into a proper room. Covering concrete stairs with wooden ones. No, in my dreams it's the house, circa 1972. Or '78. Or '87. Nightmares built around the small traumas of childhood and adolescence. Times when the house felt big, and permanent, and full of secrets. And because dreams are weird, they can trigger off the tiniest memories, say digging though one of my father's drawers, and finding a pocketwatch, a switchblade knife, a pistol. Discovering the hashpipe my cousin hid in a box of old country-western records in a closet. Digging through the dead man's toolbox that Dad brought home from a swap meet.

As storytellers in the dark, fantastic realm of horror fiction, we take our nightmares, hew them into lumber, and build haunted houses. And what a neighborhood it is! Walpole's *The Castle of Otranto* next door to Ann Radcliffe's Gothic manse from *The Mysteries of Udolpho.* Poe's ramshackle House of Usher across the street beside Hawthorne's *The House of Seven Gables.* Down at the cul-de-sac sits William Hope Hodgson's *The House on the Borderland.* And up the way Shirley Jackson's *Hill House* and Richard Matheson's *Hell House.*

But the architect I'd like for you to contemplate today is none other than H. P. Lovecraft, whose haunted houses could populate an entire subdivision. Consider just the ones with "house" in the title: "The Shunned House." "The Strange High House in the Mist." "The Picture in the House." "The Dreams in the Witch House." The titles alone conjure all sorts of Gothic effects, set the hair on the back on one's neck upright, invoking a wonderful shiver of fear. Of strangeness. Of the Weird.

And speaking of the Weird, listen to the chant that echoes through one of Lovecraft's best-known haunted houses, his 1926 story "The Call of Cthulhu." Something canted by "Esquimaux wizards" and degenerate Louisiana swamp dwellers alike. Say it with me: "*Ph'nglui mglw'nafh Cthulhu R'lyeh wgah'nagl fhtagn.*"

"In his house at R'lyeh dead Cthulhu waits dreaming."

Aklo, the incomprehensible alien occult language Lovecraft uses here, is deliberately imprecise. Vocal ululations impossible to form with human mouths, partially remembered transliterations, rough soundings of mind-bending calligraphies. Tongue-twisters. Lovecraft borrows the idea of Aklo from Arthur Machen's "The White People," and runs with it, adding his own vocabulary to it, creating an impressive array of occult language and arcane quotes, but never coming close to the meticulous worldbuilding inherent in, say, Tolkien's Elvish. Or Klingon. Or Dothraki.

Most Lovecraftian scholars look at the famous chant above and take the heart of it, "Cthulhu fhtagn," to mean "Cthulhu sleeps." Or "Cthulhu waits." Or even "Cthulhu dreams."

I disagree. Because it was explained to me in a dream.

"Cthulhu fhtagn" means "Cthulhu's house." Or "House of Cthulhu." Which makes me think of campy monster movies, *House of Frankenstein* and *House of Dracula.* I might have called this anthology *House of Cthulhu,* but it invoked the funhouse, more so than the haunted house.

So I went with the title you hold in your hands: *Cthulhu Fhtagn!*

In the aforementioned dream, I also learned that if you slightly rasp the final syllable, it means "Cthulhu's home."

Think about it for a moment. We're waiting that time when stars grow right. When Old Gods return. When Cthulhu comes home. That is the core cosmic terror in Lovecraft's oeuvre, millenarian angst writ large: an advent is coming; the chickens are coming home to roost, bringing in the sheaves. And by "chickens," I mean of course terrifying, ravenous god-things.

Good thing we're safe as houses.

Haunted houses, that is.

When I began assembling this anthology, I quickly noticed a theme emerging. Of hundreds of stories I read, the stories I loved, the stories I found myself drawn to re-read, to reconsider, all shared a common thread.

Houses—and the expectations and definitions of home—figure loomingly in these stories.

Perhaps I was drawn to these stories in particular because my wife and I have been house hunting. Considering neighborhoods, histories. Examining architecture, excavating public records. Making discoveries. Oh, someone died in this one. Where does that weird door go? What's underneath that trapdoor? Are those rats… in the walls? Houses can be such strange and sinister spaces when one looks below the surface. And there is little more terrifying that making an offer on a home, knowing everything that could go wrong.

And imagining worse.

Regardless, I'd like to welcome you to this haunted house, *Cthulhu's house*, its nineteen stories built by some of the finest writers working in dark fiction today. Herein you will find tales of tentacles, terror, and madness. And houses. And dreams. And stranger things. Please, feel free to show yourself around.

But don't wake the sleeper, whatever you do.

Cthulhu Fhtagn!

Ross E. Lockhart
Word Horde

THE LIGHTNING SPLITTER

Walter Greatshell

"Good morning! We're from the Rhode Island Historical Society, and we were hoping to speak to the owner of this charming house."

"Well…that's me."

"Oh, it's a pleasure to meet you, sir. We've always loved this little place and we are so happy to see that it was bought by someone who wants to preserve it. We were terrified that the new owners would turn it into a student rental and pave the backyard for a parking lot. Are you aware of the colorful history of your home?"

"Mm, not really, no."

"Did you know that George M. Cohan used to practice the piano in your living room?"

"Is that right? The *Yankee Doodle Dandy* guy?"

"Yes! And the famous author H.P. Lovecraft was a frequent visitor as well. His mother was of very old New England stock, and her family had some connection to the original owners. They also had a house next door, but it was destroyed in a fire. Rumor has it that superstitious locals burned it down because the family was believed to commune with evil spirits, which is rather exciting."

"No kidding. Didn't they all wind up at Butler Hospital?"

"Well, it's a tragic story: Lovecraft's childhood was quite privileged until his father suffered a mental collapse and died in the asylum, probably of syphilis. The family lost their home, lost everything, and eventually his mother had a similar breakdown, although her death is attributed to complications from surgery. Again, probably syphilis...or perhaps suicide. Doctors at the time were expected to protect the public reputations of their patients, so who knows? The point is, Lovecraft was plagued with nightmares for the rest of his life—terrible, ghastly nightmares he channeled through his classic stories. Sadly, his genius was not acknowledged in his lifetime; he died in poverty and obscurity, never knowing that his name would soon become famous."

We talked a little longer about the house, until the two elderly ladies thanked me for my time and left me with an envelope of Xeroxed historical documents. Reassured that they weren't trying to sell me anything, I belatedly invited them in for a cup of tea, but they suddenly remembered a pressing engagement and hurried away, calling back, "Enjoy your lovely house!"

Interesting. Getting my reading glasses, I sat down and opened the packet. The top sheet was a photocopied page from Homes section of the *Providence Sunday Journal*, dated October 13th, 1982. The headline read:

LIKE LIVING IN A CHURCH

But owners say Victorian cottage is also 'cozy as a treehouse'

The article that followed was basic real estate puffery, describing the house's physical charms without mentioning any of the curious history I had just been told. I was more interested in the accompanying photos, which showed how little the place had changed in the last thirty years.

My wife and I had only bought it a few months back, our first home. We had been living abroad for the previous eleven years as civilian employees of the military; our son was born overseas and had never lived in the States; we decided it was time to return. Having saved enough for a down payment on a house, all we needed was the house—and we found the perfect one.

It was a Lightning Splitter, a type of Victorian cottage with a tall, steep-sided roof, sharp as a ship's upturned keel—a perfect wedge against the elements. Amid the ranks of triple-decker apartments, it stood out like something from a fairytale, a tiny witch's den in the working-class neighborhood of Fox Point. Though less prestigious than homes in nearby College Hill, it was walkable to downtown, a stone's throw from the bay, and (most importantly) within our price range. After being shown around some really scary properties, we knew we had to take it. What really got us was that it was a "plaque house"—a building officially designated as historic, with a plaque listing its original owner and the date it was built. Ours read: Comfort Horton, 1861. Yet because it was not located in the historic district, the price was not commensurate with the plaque.

Inside, the ceilings were surprisingly high for such a tiny house—we had browsed other houses seemingly designed by gnomes, with ceiling fans and chandeliers at eye level—and the two upstairs bedrooms were the highest of all, their angled walls rising some twelve feet before meeting at the peak of the roof. Downstairs, the house was divided between living and dining spaces, with a woodstove on one side and a fireplace on the other. Kitchen and bathroom were in a newer part of the house, a small additional wing obviously tacked on with the advent of indoor plumbing.

The house had certain problems. There was virtually no closet space, and very little extra room to store anything. The wiring was a mess; we were forever resetting clocks and replacing lightbulbs. There was no access to the basement from inside the house, so that in order to get at the fuse box or do laundry it was necessary to go out the back door to a separate basement door, unlock it, and descend a treacherous stair of uneven stone slabs to the ancient, rock-lined cellar. It was like a cave down there, damp and earthy, with colonies of black mushrooms sprouting from the walls and cobwebs that grew back as fast as I could sweep them away.

Clearly, the house had not been cared for properly in years, and we were not the ones to start. We hadn't bought a house to practice our handyman skills, nor did we have extra money to hire professionals. I was willing to mow the lawn and paint the place, if necessary to keep up appearances, but that was about it. So of course God couldn't resist punishing me with a little practical joke.

Our tiny bathroom had no room for a tub, barely managing a shower stall, which the former owner had lined with wood in the style of a Japanese or Swedish sauna. We liked this a lot, but almost as soon as we signed the paperwork, the house was invaded by huge black carpenter ants, which I soon traced to the bathroom. They seemed to be coming from the walls of the shower.

Examining the wood, I could feel that the boards had rotted at the bottom, crumbling between my fingers like moldy cheese. Crazy drunken ants sprinkled out of the cracks. I pried off the first few slats and could immediately see the source of the trouble: the plaster wall behind the newer wood was slimy and soft, black with mold. Having been soaked for months or years, it fell apart under its own sagging weight the minute I exposed it to the light of day. It smelled like an open grave.

Revolted, I spent the next two days cramped in that shower, digging out foul debris and dozens of huge gray-green slugs. Once the rot was all gone, I could see that the ants had eaten through the wall joists, nearly severing the big four-by-four corner post that supported the roof. The whole thing could have collapsed any second. Having missed a bullet, I learned my lesson—it was actually a pleasure putting that shower back together...this time the right way.

The experience gave me a connection to the house; I had taken responsibility and thus felt the pride of ownership. I had fixed it. The downside was that there was so much more to fix. Well, I would have to get to it later. I had books to write!

***

When my wife came home from work, I told her about the visit from the Historical Society, and the interesting factoids they had shared with me.

"That's so cool!" she said. "We should put up a sign: 'George M. Cohan slept here!'"

"I don't think they said anything about him sleeping..."

"And H.P. Lovecraft—wow! You know what we should do? We should go to Swan Point right now and get a grave-rubbing off his headstone. We can frame it and hang it over the fireplace!"

"Who's H.P. Lovecraft?" asked our son, Max.

Racing the winter sunset, we drove to Swan Point Cemetery before it closed. We liked to do things like this, nonsense errands just to break the routine. Having met at the back of an old movie theater during intermission, we were both suckers for romance and foreign films. Max grumbled and I stood watch while Cindy got a good charcoal print off Lovecraft's marker. It was nearly dark. Spraying it with fixative, she kissed me and said, "We should do this more often."

I kissed her back, longer. "Absolutely," I said.

"Can we just *go*?" Max said.

The wind was picking up as we returned home, shaking the huge maple tree in the backyard. I always had trouble sleeping on windy nights, imagining that tree falling on us. I made dinner while Cindy mounted the print in an ornate old picture frame she had picked up at the Salvation Army.

"Beautiful," I said, giving her a taste of the sauce. "Yummy," she agreed.

Eating dinner beneath our new work of art, we drank a toast to Lovecraft, and afterward decamped to the living room couch for a showing of the movie "Re-Animator." Max left to play videogames in his room. We finished the movie and read for a while before going to bed. Our last day together.

We never should have returned to Providence. That was my big mistake—come to think of it, the same mistake Lovecraft made after things didn't work out for him in New York. A lot of people try to leave Providence, but most eventually come back. In our case it took eleven years for the curse to get us.

I woke in the middle of the night, my heart racing. My impression was that there had been a jarringly loud noise, but the more my wits returned, the more I realized I had probably dreamed it. Cindy was not in bed with me, and I assumed she had gone downstairs to the bathroom, or possibly to make herself a cup of warm milk and meditate on the couch. Max was snoring in the next bedroom. I stared at the ceiling for a few minutes before deciding to go down and sit with my wife. We both had learned to like such moments of unscheduled quality time in the wee hours—they seemed to exist outside the fuss of normal reality.

Cindy was not downstairs. I could practically see the whole house at a glance; there was nowhere to hide. Feeling a worm of panic in my stomach, I called, "Honey?" The sound of my anxious voice was worse than the silence, and I didn't want to wake Max. Where the hell was she? The car was still in the driveway, so she hadn't taken it for a joyride.

The only place I hadn't checked was the basement—but why would she go down there? She wouldn't, certainly not in the middle of the night. Not without telling me. Unless...unless maybe she realized she had left something in the washer or dryer, something she needed to wear for work in the morning? But no—I could see through the floor vent that the basement light was off.

I suddenly realized it wasn't even possible for her to have left the house. The security alarm was still set; she would have had to turn it off to go outside. Which meant she was still in here...somewhere.

Channeling my growing worry into motion, I turned on all the lights and searched every cubbyhole, every cabinet, looking under furniture and behind appliances. Nothing. The cat was freaking out, and I was losing it myself. On the verge of calling 911, I stumbled upon what I was looking for: not my wife, but an answer to the mystery.

The shower. It was literally the first thing I checked, and I had missed it. In the dark, I had not looked carefully enough at the floor. Re-checking it in the light, I realized at once what must have happened to my wife, and it wasn't good.

The floor of the shower was gone. Where there had been a solid stone slab with a drain in its center was now a square black hole, a bottomless pit.

Oh my God—my worst fears realized. All the time I had been rebuilding that shower, I was nervous that the floor might collapse under me. I pictured myself trapped there, pinned against the wall by the heavy slab, my flailing hands grabbing for the faucet and inadvertently spinning it to the hottest setting so that I was boiled alive under the searing spray. Despite these fantasies, I had not pulled up the slab to check the supports—it would have been a big job, requiring plumbing and masonry expertise. It seemed solidly placed in its corner of the foundation, so I left it alone. My hair stood on end at the sickening thought: Had I killed my wife with my stupidity?

But maybe she was alive! The hot water wasn't running, so at least she couldn't have been poached to death! She might be okay down there, just a bit shaken up!

Grabbing for this flimsy straw of hope, I called down the hole, "Honey! Are you okay?" Not waiting for her answer—and there was none—I got down on my belly and leaned as far as I could into the dark opening. I couldn't see a thing, and cursed myself for not replacing the batteries in the flashlight. "Honey, can you hear me? Try to make a sound if you can!"

There was a sound, or maybe I imagined one, a kind of faint gurgle which could have been the sewer pipe under the toilet, but which in my terror I heard as the cry of my injured wife. "I'm coming, baby, hold on!" Wedging my right foot between the toilet and the wall, I thrust my upper body into the hole, reaching as far down as I could with my arms. I wasn't sure how deep it was, since the area beneath the addition was separated from the main basement by the original stone foundation; I had always assumed it was little more than a crawlspace. But as I dangled my searching hands in that clammy well, I could not find anything within reach. "Take my hand," I begged her. "Can you see me? I'm right above you."

Without warning, my wife's ice-cold hand grabbed mine—and suddenly I was slipping, yanked face-first into the pit by her claw-like grip. I landed hard on a pile of concrete rubble, but the pain meant nothing to me—my wife was alive! Crawling to my feet in my robe and slippers, I said, "Oh my God, honey—" but she was not there. "Honey?"

My eyes adjusted enough to see that I was standing in a circle of greenish light from the shower above, but otherwise the darkness was total, thick with the smell of must and decay. The hole was barely out of reach. I might be able to jump up and catch hold of the rim, but I knew I was nowhere near strong enough to hoist myself back inside the house. *Shit.*

Trying to sound calm, I said, "Well, now we're both stuck down here." Why didn't she answer?

I tried to find her, venturing away from the light and feeling my way along the damp walls of the foundation. Nothing! Flinching from imagined spiders, my fumbling hands almost missed the opening—a narrow tunnel. A sound of pure incredulity escaped my lips, echoing in the fathomless dark. *A tunnel, sure, why not?*

Careful not to bump my head, I ventured under the low brick archway and down the passage. It was wetter in there, the walls slick with moss, and my slippers were soon soaked. Squish-squishing along, I thought I heard the murky tinkling of a piano, but when I stopped to listen it went silent.

"Honey!" I yelled. "Cindy!" I was beginning to wonder if that had even been her hand that grabbed mine—maybe she had been grabbed too. The thought was too unnerving to contemplate.

My fears were interrupted by the pain of stubbing my toe against a flight of stone stairs. By my reckoning I was somewhere under the backyard, so I knew the stairs had to be a dead end. But as I climbed them, they just kept going and going as if ascending a tower, far beyond what was even remotely possible. My body shuddered involuntarily, my legs turning to jelly so that I had to sit down for a minute. Could I be dreaming? I often thought I was awake when I was dreaming, but never the opposite. This was definitely real…yet how could it be? I dearly wished it were not.

Gradually I became aware that I could see. Light was coming from somewhere above, and as I kept climbing it got brighter, illuminating the steep passage so I could make out the weird greenish-gray stone of which it was built. It was the same translucent mucous color as the slugs in the shower. At last I reached the source of the light, a square opening atop the last flight of stairs. It looked like bright daylight, although I knew sunrise was still hours away—but I was far past such quibbles. I just wanted to get out of there and find my wife.

Shading my eyes against the orange glare, I emerged to a sight so impossible that I couldn't even be shocked, merely blank. My dullness morphed into sick fascination: *Welcome to Mars.*

For it really looked something like Mars, or maybe an artist's conception of Mars from a lurid old pulp magazine: a red desert of low hills and jagged rocks as far as the eye could see. The sky was something else again. It seemed almost liquid, like an inverted sea of molten lava, rolling and heaving above the planet as if with a life of its own—a mind of its own. It had an eye, a half-eclipsed monster sun whose radiant menace was palpable on my skin, cancerous, and I knew that if it turned the full light of its gaze on me I would die.

As my eyes adjusted, I could make out human figures scattered across the landscape. They were all kneeling in the same direction, their rapt faces turned upward and their mouths hanging open in frozen awe. I could also see more doorways like the one I had come through, each on its own little hill. Hoping and fearing to find my wife, I walked towards the nearest people, three of them sitting together holding hands, two men and a woman. All were wearing vintage formal clothes—costumes reminiscent of old photos and silent movies. One of the men looked familiar, though I wouldn't have recognized him if not for my recent Google search. He was H.P. Lovecraft. I supposed the other two were his parents…or maybe the second man was George M. Cohan. I didn't care.

They all seemed to be dead, inert as fossilized tree stumps, their fogged eyes wide to the heavens and their dry mouths full of sand. Passing them by, I searched further, scanning the alien wasteland for the only one I cared about.

And there she was. I choked, "Cindy."

Running to my wife down the slope of the hill, I tripped over my slippers and tumbled in the sand. I was babbling like an idiot. *It's her, yes it's really her, thank God it's her.* I was terrified she would be like the others, and she was…but her eyes were still clear, her skin pliant, her lips soft and moist. She was still warm. Grabbing her by the shoulders, I shook her and shouted in her face, "Honey! Come back to me! You hear me? You have to come back!"

For what felt like forever she didn't move, and I broke down then, falling beside her and sobbing into her hair. I wrapped my robe around her, making hopeless sweet-talk under the sleeping eye of that black sun. I wanted to be beside her when it woke up, so it could take me too. We would worship it together, forever, like the family Lovecraft.

"Dad?"

Holy shit, it was Max. He had followed me! The last person I wanted to see right now was my nine-year-old son. Jumping to my feet, I cried, "Max! What the hell are you doing here? You're supposed to be in bed!"

"I had to pee. I couldn't find you guys. Where are we?"

"That's none of your business! You shouldn't even be here! Go back!"

He wasn't listening to me, agog at all the strange sights. "What's wrong with Mom?"

"She's just…I don't know, but we have to get her out of here! God damn it, grab her legs!" Cindy was stiff in her kneeling position, but I got my hands under her arms and we lifted her between us as best we could.

As we lugged her back toward the door in the sand, she began to loosen up. The sight of her coming to life made me sob with relief, but then she started getting difficult, rubbing her eyes and moaning, "Mmm*no*! Leggo! Put me down!" She kicked and squirmed like a madwoman, but we kept dragging her all the way up the hill. No way I was going to let go of her now.

"Dad, look."

Something was happening to all the other frozen bodies—they were waking up and moving. Toward us. Not slow but fast. The Lovecraft trio had already hustled to intercept us at the doorway. Nearing them, I could see that they were drooling sand, their white eyes bugging out of their sockets like the eyestalks of slugs, their pinpoint black pupils fixed on the sky as their animated bodies scrambled to stop us.

"Stay with your mother," I told Max. "I'll keep these guys busy while you get her to the stairs." She had stopped fighting us and was actually wobbling along with minimal support, mumbling incoherently.

Struggling to control her, Max said, "I can't carry her there all by myself!"

"Yes you can! Just guide her in the right direction!"

Wearing nothing but my boxer shorts, I charged straight at the Lovecrafts, intending to bowl them over with my sheer momentum. I'm a pretty big guy. But when I hit them, they exploded—it was like hitting three mummies. Their bodies burst in a cloud of dust and brittle dry bones; their clothes fell apart in shreds. What was inside their heads, though, was more substantial. Lively as Mexican jumping beans, their disembodied skulls danced around me on the sand, jaws clattering, and I made the mistake of kicking one. It shattered like a clay pot, unleashing a whirling monstrosity resembling a thorny black starfish with a vile mouth at its center. An instant later the other skulls burst open as well, hatching two more grotesque, gnashing maws surrounded by tentacle-like petals that flapped and spun, flinging greenish slime. All three dervishes screamed like rabid pigs as they came for me.

And now the Sky-God was waking up.

The sun was coming out, the red desert turning gold. In that awesome and awful light, all the sleepwalkers were falling to their knees again, faces canted to heaven. The three black whirligigs froze in their attack and dropped quivering to the sand, their putrid mouths prolapsing in orgiastic bliss...and I too felt the hideous ecstasy stealing my will, prostrating my body to its unearthly purpose.

With my last strength, I wrenched my burning eyeballs away from the sky toward my wife and son. They had just reached the stairs and were climbing down. Good. I didn't want them waiting for me. I might be awhile.

DEAD CANYONS

Ann K. Schwader

Darkness. Lifeless, thirsting darkness. Layer upon layer of alien history bled out, worn down to a depth unmatched in the solar system. An open wound in a dying world.

And at the bottom, scrabbling like a beetle in the shadow of a boot, one small machine intelligence twists its wheels toward retreat—

"Are we disturbing you, Susan?"

Dr. Susan Barnard flinches in her seat. Flash dream. Another damn flash dream, in the middle of a meeting—and in front of the mission director, always a plus. Inez's crow-bright eyes are merciless.

"Sorry. Haven't gotten a lot of sleep lately."

Truer to say she's been avoiding sleep, but Inez probably doesn't want that truth. Or the explanation behind it. Or, indeed, her presence on the *Clementine II* team.

Nikolai should be here instead, offering his tenured analysis of Clem's recent behavior. He could make Inez listen. Maybe even understand the rover's...reluctance?...*panic*?...in the face of what infuses Melas Chasma. Clem's "mind" was his baby, the field test of the Sarkov Process.

A test he hadn't survived.

Eleven months ago, she'd been sitting beside him in the control room, watching Clem plunge toward the Martian surface. Only she had noticed her supervisor's sweat-slicked forehead, his grunt of shock and pain as he slumped over. By the time she'd started CPR, it was already too late: decades of nicotine and chronic overwork had spoken.

When Nikolai's records proved to be (a) in longhand, (b) in Cyrillic, and (c) illegible even to the native speaker Susan located, Inez nearly had her own cardiac event. Recruiting Sarkov had been the gamble of her career. Determined to upstage Clem's predecessor *Curiosity* on a fraction of its budget—"Cheaper and Deeper!"—she had moved the whole mission from California to his Colorado home campus. She'd even hired his postdoc assistant for the team.

Sarkov insisted that she was essential. The look Inez gave Susan that day said she'd misunderstood completely—

But Inez is speaking again. Something about the rapidly approaching solar conjunction, and getting Clem under control before she's out of contact with Earth for two weeks. The team's engineers enumerate the fixes they've tried.

Few make much sense to Susan, who knows better.

Inez cuts them off. "So you're saying it's not the hardware."

When they nod, her glance turns to Clem's chief programmer.

"Or the software?"

He glares. More than anyone else here, he distrusts the secret sauce Clem's "mind" holds. Piggybacked onto a perfectly adequate operating system, rigged to overrule and overthink it, Sarkov's little box is the bane of his existence.

"The software I know about."

The mission director's mouth tightens. Her glance shifts to the far end of the table.

"Three days left." She exhales sharply. "Maybe. And this rover's suddenly got a mind of its own."

But wasn't that what you paid for?

As Susan's exhaustion tests her mind/mouth barrier, she reminds herself how much she needs this job. Robot behaviorists aren't exactly in demand. With Nikolai gone, only Inez can write her a recommendation.

It's a good thing Nikolai's notes were unreadable. Despite Inez's fervent expectations, his Process did not create near-AI, but something stranger. Something Susan is paying for every day—and night—of her life.

"So what exactly *is* going on, anyhow?"

When Susan doesn't answer at once, Inez slams down her metal coffee mug. It rings into silence—

Annihilation flavors the powdery dirt, the flecks of stone peppered with useless microfossils. No life here again, ever. A hunger beyond understanding, beyond the primitive corporeal, has claimed it all and found it not enough—

Susan sucks in her breath. "She's scared."

This is not science. Not anything Inez was wanting, or expecting. Her thin eyebrows threaten her hairline. "Repeat that, please."

The whole team is watching now.

"Clem is scared."

***

Hours afterwards, Susan cuts through campus on the way to her car, pulling her collar high against encroaching night. The sunken footpath turns the buildings into sandstone canyon walls, dotted here and there with small lights—*lives?*—abruptly winking out as she passes.

The cold dark itself is a hunger. A presence. A chasm that cannot be filled, not by all the warmth of her flesh or the nerve-fires of her mind. Just as the deep heart of Mars came to know its own death, billions of years ago, so her own core feels that first flickering—

Layers of anonymous time. Time and flowing water, weather and wind and beginnings. Sparks in the water carving down into stone. Possibilities. Deeper and faster the flowing water, the miniscule kindlings of life. Higher and thicker the atmosphere pushing out against void.

Then from that void, the banished Other.

Bodiless. Formless. Insatiable—

"Susan!"

She whirls. One hand jerks up with her defense spray, then drops as the speaker steps into a rare pool of campus lighting.

"Good God, Ryan." She exhales. "Please tell me Inez didn't send you to find me."

"Nope. I'm here on my own recognizance."

She wants to believe him. Ryan is one of Clem's engineers—and her former hope for a lasting relationship. Until the Sarkov Process complicated things. Since Nikolai's death, they've barely seen each other outside of work.

So why now?

"But Inez has something to do with it." It isn't a question. "Hell, maybe the whole team does."

"Do you blame them?"

Oh, yes. From the beginning of this mission, Inez and the others have tiptoed around the Process's deep weirdness. The fudge factor Nikolai sold them. All they ask for is data, and *Clementine II* spews that to the orbiters like a fire hose. Her capacity for independent action lets her accomplish more in a few sols than *Curiosity* did in months of mission time.

Only now, when that capacity has become a problem, is anyone taking a real interest.

"Inez wanted the truth." She shrugs. "I gave it to her."

"You do know you're in trouble, right?"

In ways you can't even imagine.

"I know Clem is. She's found something in the chasma that she has no way of investigating, sampling, or analyzing. The deeper she goes, the more of it she finds." *The more of it finds her.* "She can't handle it, so she's trying to leave."

"Because she's scared."

He can barely get his mouth around the concept, let alone his mind.

"Yes."

Dark silence closes around them both, filling the canyon of classrooms and offices and labs. One of those labs is—was—Nikolai's. Three very secure rooms, with a retinal scanner on the single outside door. That scanner recognizes only two patterns, one of them ashes now. No one else has even applied for recognition.

"Susan...how can you know that?"

Not *you're nuts.* Not *that's ridiculous.* Just an honest admission of ignorance, perhaps even willingness to understand.

A lifting of the dark lonesome silence.

"It's going to take some explaining," she finally says. "And a lot of coffee."

***

Even at this hour, the student center café is stainless steel bright, holding back chaos with French roast and fresh pastries. Aside from one study group at a corner table, it is also vacant.

Something Susan is appreciating more and more as their own conversation goes on.

"So Clem thinks the way it...she...does because her 'mind' was modeled on yours?" Ryan's hands tighten around his mug. He's on his second refill.

Susan nods. She's considering her third, though replacing fatigue with hyper-caffeination holds its own perils.

"It's an emulation. Like a template, but more specific."

And more complex. And far more painful to create, even with drugs blurring the worst. Her memories of those twelve-hour days and locked-in lab weekends have significant gaps. Nikolai was careful to record everything—and show her those vids before he deleted them—but after a while it hadn't mattered. She wanted his Process as much as he did.

Maybe more.

The dreams had started during mock-up testing, when Clem's "mind" first rolled around the lab in its framework. Once she'd checked it out on the simple stuff—turn left, turn right, extend drill—Susan had headed home for a desperately needed few hours' sleep. Nikolai and his bottomless coffee urn remained behind.

Next morning, he'd asked her which room the rover mock-up had finally lost battery power in. And she had known. She had felt it in her sleep, like a tiny death.

Nikolai seemed pleased, but not surprised. The Process was complete: they were ready to move forward. Once it reached Melas Chasma, Clem's new intelligence would deliver more than Inez or her team could imagine.

When she finishes the story, Ryan frowns at her across the table.

"Sounds a *lot* more specific." *Like true AI*, but he does not say it. That particular grail is no part of his faith, if engineers have faith. "Did Nikolai put any of this in his reports?"

"Hell, no."

They both know what she has just given is not an explanation. Only Nikolai might have provided that.

"Okay, " he finally says, though his eyes don't. "Clem is scared. The further it travels into the chasma, the more scared it becomes. The more it tries to change direction without orders from us."

He exhales audibly.

"Susan, what is Clem scared *of*?"

Only recently, the dreams have begun to show her—though she is no longer certain whose dreams they are. Not Clem's glimpses of steep walls and eroded materials on the chasma floor, that's for sure. Not her own nightmares. Something new has tapped into the Process's uncanny feed, leaving images she can neither explain nor forget.

Rifts in the substance of space itself, torn by the passage of something…somethings…her mind's eye veers away from.

Whiteout storms savaging a city of oddly angled cubes and twisted towers.

Tall figures gliding from caverns deep beneath that city.

War.

She reaches for her mug. Ryan has refilled it, though she can't remember when.

"I'm still figuring that out." Her throat clenches. "But I already know Inez isn't going to like it."

"Because…?"

Glancing past him, she sees the study group is gone now. Good.

"Because this mission—her whole career—is about finding Martian life, right? Recent evidence, anyhow. *Curiosity* didn't do it. The Europeans didn't. Inez convinced JPL to give up the surface stuff and go deep, where it's obvious there was water once."

Ryan nods cautiously.

"Just one problem, though." She takes a long sip of coffee. "Mars is dead."

The words fall into silence as Ryan's gaze shifts away.

"It's been dead a long time, now, from the core on out. No magnetic field. Practically no atmosphere. No protection from the solar wind. Maybe water locked up in the soil or the rocks, but that's disappearing faster than anybody will admit."

When she pauses for breath, Ryan glances over his shoulder at the student baristas tending their equipment.

Okay, fine. Susan's voice drops to a hiss.

"We aren't going to find anything. There is nothing to find. A catastrophe happened over three billion years ago, and the planet never recovered."

Her next mouthful of coffee is void cold.

"Mars didn't just die, Ryan. It was killed." Her voice drops even further. "And I think Clem's found what killed it."

She was expecting his reaction, but the familiar pain still comes.

"This is what I'm supposed to tell Inez?"

Nothing to lose now. "No. You're supposed to tell her to put Clem into safe mode, tonight. Immediately." She hesitates. "Whatever's going on in the chasma needs to stay there. If Clem's 'mind' stops talking to the orbiters—"

"That's not going to happen."

Ryan reaches across the table. It is the first time he's touched her since Nikolai's memorial.

"Susan, you've got to get some sleep. Get yourself straightened out. In three days—more like two, now—the sun cuts us off. Inez isn't about to waste that time."

Desperation. Formless black roiling in the farthest depths. Rage against the pure inferno's encroachment, blocking bluegreen deliverance from this drained husk forever.

Deliverance and return—

She pulls away from him, shaking her head.

"We haven't got that long." Her breath catches in her throat. "Maybe a day."

In the café's well-lit silence, she watches him swallow half a dozen questions.

"That's what tomorrow's meeting is about," he finally says. "That and Nikolai's Process notes. After that Belarusian TA you found gave up, Inez sent them to some linguistics institute in St. Petersburg. She's supposed to get the results later tonight."

And this helps Clem how?

Before Ryan can say anything else, she pushes back her chair and grabs her coat. By the time he's on his feet, she's already halfway to the door, back to the sandstone canyon walls with their fragile lights.

"Just get Clem into safe mode," she says over her shoulder.

She does not wait for a reply.

***

No choice. No control. Only inexorable motion, blindly into the dark. Forward and downward and downward. Deeper into the heart of what her instruments could not analyze when they still spoke to her, what her wheels could not avoid even when they responded.

Nothing responds now. She is fully awake and paralyzed, fight or flight alike denied by the severing of some vital connection.

The pressure of thoughts not her own increases with each moment. Each centimeter forward. Her thin-shelled consciousness cracks, and cracks again, until shadow tongues seep inside to whisper their hunger.

There is nothing left here. Even this planet's life-fire is guttering, drained by insatiate darkness through aeons of exile. Defeated, disembodied, that darkness can sustain itself no longer...yet it cannot die. Will not die.

Not so long as deliverance awaits—

Raw sound tears at her, clawing her from the void. Fighting one arm free of tangled sheets, Susan gropes for her phone.

"Ryan?"

He doesn't answer right away.

"Glad you finally got some sleep." Another pause. "Should I tell Inez you'll be in soon?"

Wiping sweat from her eyes, she checks the time on her screen and swears.

"I'll take that as Yes."

There's something in his voice she can't read. Something he's trying hard not to mention.

"Ryan, what happened about safe mode?"

The silence thickens perceptibly. "Inez wouldn't go for it," he finally says. "Not until the last possible minute. With that conjunction coming up fast, she wants Clem as far into the chasma as possible. No samples, no side trips, and no more attitude."

Suspicion knots in Susan's stomach.

"So what *did* she decide to do?"

"Got Programming to disconnect Clem's 'mind' from the rest of its operating system, pronto. Turns out they'd written the code weeks ago."

"Damn weasels."

Ryan's breath whistles through his teeth. "Knew you wouldn't like it." He hesitates. "You don't sound too surprised."

Forward and downward and downward—

"Did you think I would be?"

He says nothing. As clearly as a flash dream, she sees that he never meant to convince their mission director of anything. His only goal last night—after the first few minutes, anyhow—had been to end their conversation as quickly as possible.

Her grip tightens white on the phone. "Inez has got to get those instructions reversed—"

"You can tell her yourself at the meeting. Two o'clock." Something in his voice changes. "I wouldn't miss this one, Susan."

It is her turn now to say nothing.

"Inez finally heard from St. Petersburg last night. She won't say any more until the meeting—but she *really* needs to talk to you."

***

Three screens of flickering data surround her, ones and zeroes raining down as she swivels between touchboards. Aside from the squeak of her chair, the lab is utterly silent. Her hands are already trembling, but Susan washes down two more caffeine tabs with the last of her coffee before returning her attention to Clem's feed.

Anything to stave off another flash dream.

She's running raw feed because she no longer trusts her station's conversion filter. When she switched it on this morning, expecting a running log of Clem's location, direction, and speed, her screens filled with gibberish. Worse than gibberish. The words, if that's what they were, gave her a headache when she tried reading them. And when the filter's text-to-audio cut in—

Wind from the void beyond failing stars. A chittering of mouthparts never meant for speech. Death-cries at the cellular level of existence. Entropy articulate and inexorable, pronouncing itself to a thousand ruined worlds—

There's a fresh crack in one of the touchboards.

This data downpour offers no useful information, but she can't stop watching. It is her last safe contact with Clem's "mind"—and a time-delayed reminder that the rover's consciousness is still under attack. Whatever its six wheels are carrying it toward—*into*?—is desperate. The solar conjunction is an encroaching barrier of fire to it, an agony she has already awakened from screaming.

Sweat slicks her forehead. The ones and zeroes are coming down in clumps now, clotting like blood on the screen.

Clem's programmers might have severed her consciousness from her propulsion system, but they couldn't shut it down. Nikolai's design made sure of that. Susan wonders if he'd considered what that might mean for her: flesh played a part in his Process, but never the determining one. He'd worried far more about that little box's design than he had about her headaches or her dreams.

At the time, she'd hardly noticed—

Ping.

The bright block of a priority message-screen displaces her data. Inez is in the team's usual conference room, with a pile of hard copy and a haggard expression.

"It's two-oh-five," she says, without preamble.

Susan already knows this. On any other afternoon, she'd be tearing out of here with visions of termination Totentanzing in her head.

"Clem's in trouble, Inez. She needs to go into safe mode *now.*"

It wouldn't really be now, but even fourteen-plus minutes later might not be too late. Not if the Programming weasels do their jobs this time. Among other things, safe mode will put Clem's "mind" into a coma—or the AI equivalent—for the next couple of weeks, until the solar conjunction is safely past.

No data. No thoughts. No connection to her. Nothing the rover's implacable, intangible attacker can use.

She doesn't think it can wait that long.

"We've already had that discussion." Inez's hands tighten on the pile of paper. "Your input's needed on another issue, immediately."

Susan can take a good guess.

"Nikolai's notes?"

Several voices off-screen confirm this before Inez's expression can.

"The script was Cyrillic. The handwriting was nothing a rudimentary program couldn't handle." She hesitates. "It was the language itself that caused problems."

More off-screen comments, the chief programmer's the loudest.

"Nikolai was apparently using one of his own devising. At least, that's what St. Petersburg suspects. Their algorithms found no match to any known language—living or dead."

Susan forces herself to ask the next logical question.

"So it's like a code?"

"Not according to them. They weren't even sure it was a constructed language."

Ask the next one, damnit.

"Then what?"

"Natural language. One they'd never heard of, never included in their algorithms." Inez's voice goes flat. "Which they claim is impossible."

Entropy articulate and inexorable, pronouncing itself to a thousand ruined worlds—

"Can you send me some of that transcript?"

The priority-message screen vanishes, replaced by a page of text. Susan's stomach clenches. So do the small muscles in her temples. Glancing away fast, she dry-swallows another headache capsule. Then she pulls up this morning's output from her conversion filter, fits it opposite Inez's sample, and starts scrolling.

"Susan?"

She ignores the disembodied voice. These jagged clumps of lines—paragraphs? formulae?—demand all her attention, even as the painkiller takes its sweet time. In two minutes, her head is pounding.

In three, she no longer cares.

Highlighting passages on either side of the screen, she asks her station to confirm what her nerves already know. Then she flips the results back to Inez and the team in their cozy conference room.

"I assume you have some explanation for this?"

None you'd believe. None that I want to. She can feel the next flash dream coming on, darkening her vision with images she has no words to describe.

"I think we all need to discuss this in person, Susan. Now." Inez takes a long, audible breath. "These are Nikolai's notes. You were his assistant. You are the last connection to his Process, his intentions—"

The reverberation of Susan's chair against the floor cuts off the rest.

***

White agony encroaching upon the last path to deliverance...this frail not-flesh link already failing. Shadows upon shadows in the last deepest refuge, but none deep enough. There can be no further downward. There is only outward, soon, or the unthinkable—

Susan gropes for the wastebasket between her feet, but only dry heaves come. The flash dreams are nearly uncontrollable now, each more vivid and incomprehensible than the last.

Clem's crippled perceptions of Melas Chasma have shattered into madness, a babble of images cached from other mission instructions. These at least do not sicken her. Though fragmented, they are familiar: these are the behaviors she imprinted on Clem's "mind," the muscle memories Nikolai's damned Process let her share.

And then there are other dreams—

Shriek of wind and snow against skin-wings already torn by rough passage through the void. The swarm as one. The swarm as hunger. The stranger city glowing at the limits of...taste/scent/ sight...rich with warmth and lives. Attack. Spatter of stranger fluids into the wind, staining wings and...hand/claws—

Her mind convulses as a thread of sunfire severs the connection. Gasping, she stares at her own extended fingers contorted into weapons still rending the air.

The solar conjunction is very close now.

But not close enough. And Clem still hasn't gone into safe mode, despite several calls from Ryan trying to calm her down, assuring her that Inez is "just about" to order it.

Just about, she suspects, is already too late.

Her phone is buzzing again beside her, Ryan's ID flashing onscreen. This time, there's a voice-override icon: this call is coming through whether she answers or not. Just as well. Her hands are useless things, knots of pain lying in her lap.

"Susan, if you're there, please listen. Please don't...do anything."

His voice is cracking. Or is that the engineering veneer? Either way, it no longer matters.

"Programming just sent the safe mode command. Clem's going to be fine. Just hang on, will you?" His voice drops to a hiss. "Inez is threatening to call 911 if you don't pick up. If the Regents even hear—"

She finally manages to swat the phone onto the floor.

When she can flex her hands again, Susan forces herself off the couch and back into the kitchen. She has placed one last solution on the scarred dinette table. One final hope of severing Clem's connection to whatever dominates her "mind," shrieking its craving for survival—and its determination to return.

Dead canyons. Not Martian chasmata, but the steel and concrete and sandstone canyons of this world, desolate beneath a mocking star. This world's deep heart cooling toward oblivion, drained by a life-thirst once defeated...disembodied...and driven back into its native void.

But those victors are dust now, particles entombed in Antarctic ice. Their strange angled city has returned to its elements.

As perhaps they intended, or at least could not prevent—

This flash dream is the clearest yet, with a certainty that drains her strength and darkens her mind. Almost too late to act. Sinking into the nearest chair, Susan takes several deep breaths, focusing. The snub-nosed .38 she bought for protection after Ryan moved out lies inches away.

It's not a software problem now. It's a hardware problem.

Maybe the Sarkov Process had always been intended to do what it has done. Or maybe Nikolai, like Inez, was a victim of impossible temptation. Given his chance at true AI—after a lifetime sacrificed to dreams and failures—he'd offered up one last sacrifice to the dark beyond human understanding.

And the dark had answered in its own language. In formulae tested by a million habitable zones, on thousands of worlds Kepler never got the chance to find. All islands afloat in the same pitiless vacuum sea, awaiting—

Lives shining ripe through the narrowing passage. Dissolution of not-flesh link imminent. This host paralyzed, its strange mind slowing...soon useless. Only one route left to survival.

To deliverance and return—

Through a haze of neural anguish, Susan reaches for the .38. Its weight is nearly too much for her damaged hands. It takes precious seconds to tighten her grip on the weapon and pivot it into position, then carefully cock the hammer.

Then lift toward her open mouth.

These actions require every bit of her shattering consciousness. There is none left for the snick of her apartment door, unlocked by a key she does not recall Ryan keeping after their breakup. None for the pounding of his feet on the living-room carpet, for the kitchen's doorway suddenly filled with his form.

None for his terrified grip on her wrists as he twists the gun away.

"Oh, God, Susan—I thought I was already too late."

Her eyes are inches from his, bloodshot blue clearing to ice. Then to crystalline void as her hands reach up, fastening on his face and the fragile shell beneath. Its pulse beacon of life.

"Not at all," she breathes. "You're just in time."

DELIRIUM SINGS AT THE MAELSTROM WINDOW

Michael Griffin

A woman calls, says she's FBI. My daughter's been found. So many years I expected this call. Eventually, I stopped waiting.

First I think it's a joke. She goes on about transfer protocols, cooperation with Interpol, that kind of thing. My daughter's no longer a minor, but my presence is requested. One thing that zaps me right in the heart, she says the girl asked for me.

Thoughts and feelings, all kinds, unsorted. Eagerness. Fear.

I rush downtown, envisioning a reunion with the eleven-year-old I last saw. Maybe slightly grown, but I'll recognize her. Sure, I know the math. She'll be nineteen now. Somehow that part doesn't register.

I check in, someone guides me to Interview Room B. Observation mirrors, microphones, video cameras. There's this woman sitting there waiting, platinum blond, exotic, maybe twenty-five. She stares, expectant, trying to puzzle me out. At first I take her for the agent who called, but she's wearing an outfit more suited to a fashion runway. In her smile, I recognize something of my wife when she was young. It's her, my little girl, a glammed-up version of her mother.

No time for any big reunion. The female agent arrives, black suit, straight brown hair, dangling plastic badge. My daughter's not suspected of any crimes. The agency's interested in what her mother did, anything she remembers. Questions fly.

Can't believe I'm sitting here beside her. I try to pinpoint her accent. French, maybe Belgian or Swiss? There's this superior, unimpressed manner. Insists on being called Bettine, not her birth name, Elizabeth. We called her Betty when she was little. At least the name's in the ballpark of what I know. The girl herself, totally unfamiliar.

Black suit's interested in that other Elizabeth, my wife. The questions are old news to me. Scars heal tougher than the skin they replace.

"Did you observe your mother assaulting your father?"

Sliding across the table, photos I've never seen. I wonder why she's making us look at some corpse, poor guy chalk-white, twenty stab wounds over his chest and shoulders. Then I see the right hand dangling, half-severed.

It's me.

"What reasons did your mother offer, after the attack, for what she'd done?"

"Where did your mother take you, after she fled the country?"

Lots more questions. Few answers. Don't know. Can't remember. Her accent fades out, returns. They landed in France, crossed into Belgium. Moved a lot, especially at first. Always old towns, out of the way. Five years ago, her mother took off. Some unspecified drug problem. This left the girl alone with an older man they'd been living with.

There's a revelation.

"The last five years," she says, "his home was mine." Claims she never knew his name, doesn't know how to find him. Can't name the town.

I can see the secrets, withheld behind her eyes. Just not sure what she's saving them for. Her self-possession seems alien, especially in someone so young. She's the same age as Elizabeth and I, when we met. Now I'm forty-four, a quarter century older than my daughter, and still less in control. I've grown adept at redirection, the way a magician hides whatever he doesn't want you to see. After Elizabeth tried to kill me and took our daughter, I entered a bad spiral of self-pity and solitude. Self-prescription: a river of

Black Velvet. Pills for pain, prescription at first, then the real trips. Any pleasure I could taste without breaking seclusion. Even after my anger faded, everything felt so broken.

Rehab saved my life. I'm clean, and plan to hold onto that. The hard part's knowing I'll never feel pleasure again. Not without the drink, and the white powder. Too many scars to cover. Not just stab wounds, and the useless, dead hand.

Black suit decides we can go. My daughter throws me this purposeful look. My inference is she's promising to let me in on whatever this is. She's my girl, I realize, but it feels more like my wife is finally ready to explain.

On the way to the car I notice she's tall, probably taller than me even without the heels. Just like her mother. Makes me wonder about her upbringing. How down and out could things have been, if she grew up looking like this?

A question coalesces. *Is it really you?* I almost say this aloud.

Maybe a scam artist? Someone sent by my wife, working some angle.

All I really know is I'm supposed to call her Bettine.

This narrow, angular creature follows me into the house, carrying her glossy black leather bag. Charcoal couture dress, oversized sunglasses, that regal platinum mane. Like a poised starlet, strutting out of a Fellini picture.

She greets her old room like a houseguest seeing it for the first time. A half smile at the little girl decoration. Shit, embarrassing. I kept washing the sheets, changing the bed, just in case. Drifted way out of touch. So many years.

She sits, knees together on the little bed, seems to shrink, drawing herself in, as if imagining how she might cram herself into this tiny space she once occupied. Her eyes flit to the space beside her on the bed. Wondering if I'll sit down? Hoping I won't, or that I will?

"No FBI here now." I try for casual, feeling awkward, nervous. "You must remember something." I expect her shell to crack. Show some vulnerability, at least let me in on the secret.

She shrugs. "I thought I was born there, speaking French. Mother and I, first we lived alone, always moving. Then we settled, this very old town, living in the gentleman's house. Mother said she belonged to him." She pauses, looking around. "This house, it's not familiar. If you say I was here before, I believe you. I remember this couvre-lit, this bedspread. Speaking English, that must come from somewhere. I took no lessons."

"Where were you trying to go, when they stopped you at the airport?"

She sighs as if tired. "I told them my passport was false, so they would deliver me to you."

This doesn't make sense. So many questions. It's torture, holding back. "You said you don't know where your mother is," I venture. "We might try looking for her. With or without cops—"

"Elise?" She makes a face, as if remembering something unpleasant. "You and FBI, you call her Elizabeth. Mother never called herself that."

From the interview, I knew their aliases. The only surprise is how little she remembers.

"Elizabeth Dahut Nix was your mother's maiden name. You're Elizabeth Melusine Sky. We called you Betty until you were ten. You asked us to start calling you Elizabeth."

Bettine leans back, propped by thin arms.

"It's Okay," I say. "I'll get used to calling you Bettine."

She sits forward, darts one hand into her bag, produces a silver case and a lighter. Withdraws a black cigarette, lights it. I'm shocked, about to protest, but stop myself. What right do I have?

"There's no need, looking for Mother." She exhales. Clove smoke drifts, unexpectedly pleasant. Burning sugar overpowers the tobacco aspect.

"What?" Distracted, I missed her point. The sweet, spicy smell. Wondering how it tastes.

"Her problems I mentioned. She was lost to addiction, victim of unrestrained craving. I should have told you. Many in our circle succumb the same way."

What's she saying? My head spins, dizziness, panic. "Did I understand… You're saying your mother's dead?"

She nods, resting her hand on the glossy black leather case.

Everything seems far away, clouded. My head buzzes, tingles. Must be the clove smoke. I can taste the sweet burning paper on my lips. It reminds me of something else I smoked, some high barely recalled. Nothing else explains this feeling. I crave numbness, escape. Want to run.

"I'll let you sleep." I back out, shut Bettine's bedroom door.

From the dark hallway, I hear leather rustling, and the click of steel fasteners.

***

Two thousand black midnights alone. Now this. How long have I wavered, not existing, merely remembering? I sprawl atop the bed, still dressed, in frustrated wakefulness.

Music intrudes at the lowest reaches of my awareness.

I rise, open my door. A song from another room, something I don't recognize. I work in the listening room at the University music department. I've heard everything. Not this. The scratch of an old record, classical strings. Voice distinct from the music. She sings along, tentative, slightly out of sync. In that hesitation, something familiar. A hint of the girl I recognize.

I cross the hall, touch the door, trace fingertips along the wood. I want to knock, but still feel a stranger in my own house. It's Elizabeth's ancestral place. Probably I'll always feel unsettled, like a visitor imposing on hospitality.

Eight years.

She took everything. Lots of men say that, meaning the house, the 401K. Mine took our daughter, left me bleeding to death, riddled with stab wounds, hand almost severed. Punctures became scars. Healing floated away the pain, left behind a brittle shell. Not a man, just a bloodstream pumping a prescription cocktail so powerful it prevented me from caring about the one miserable truth I was sure of: I was done living, at least in the real meaning of the word.

The University held my job longer than I'd expected. After ninety days, someone in HR finally said, now or never.

I decided on never.

To the rest of the world, I was lucky to be alive. Is everyone really unaware there are worse things? Do they only pretend? Despair so bottomless. Each breath, agony. Every morning, the most sickening hangover. Of course, whiskey played a part.

This house is the only thing Elizabeth left me. Now that I'm sober, I don't want it. If I can stay clean, hold onto this job, maybe I'll climb out.

Something like Bettine coming along, that's a potential trigger for relapse. Recovery 101.

My knuckles strike the door.

Singing stops. The door swings open.

"Oh, I woke you."

She's wearing a white sleepshirt so diaphanous, I have to look away. Smell of burning candles. Warmth. On the bed, scattered ancient records in brown paper sleeves. Without makeup, she looks like the Elizabeth I first met.

"Those look like 78s," I say. The library collection has rooms full of these.

"That's all I kept, from over there," she murmurs.

"Where'd you find the old Victrola? I've never seen it around."

"There's so much here." She points beyond the east wall, toward the storage rooms. "I think you never explored."

"This house must seem…humble. You're accustomed to being kept with money."

"You don't mean Mother. You mean—"

"Yes, this man. She…left you to him." Trying to remain neutral. Can't seem judgmental.

"I never knew his name." She looks down. "He asked me to call him Daddy."

I manage not to flinch. No response at all.

She shrugs. Her gaze flits to the ceiling. "He owned the tallest house on Rue d'Auseil, the oldest block of the district. A gigantic house, like a looming range of mountains, seeming to lean out over the road."

"You describe it like a fairy tale." Can't help frowning. "You were too young."

Her persistent half-smile flares into stubbornness, something like awareness of advantage. "It was not what you imagine. Not at all. More like being mistress and paid research assistant to a brilliant scholar of the arcane."

The word mistress sticks. I try to move past. Instead: "Scholar…arcane?"

"An eminent occult experimentalist, founder of Maîtres de l'autel de verre, that is, Knights of the Glass Altar." She nods. "One of Europe's wealthiest men, yet anonymous, exerting power in stealth, within his secret society. I learned much. Took these records, and many secrets."

I move closer, seeking angles against her inscrutability. "Tell me about your mother. What you said about her addiction."

She holds my gaze, then looks away. "Yes, the white smoke. Within our circle, the Glass Altar, of course we all experience it."

"White smoke? What is that? A plant, or—"

"It's not a drug, not something you buy. Like so many pleasures, the aim is to approach as near as possible, while avoiding the harm of too great proximity."

My heart, a blunt hammering in my chest. Seeing her smile this way, talking so casually about this strange high. She has no idea all I've been through. The horrible depths, recovery, relapse. I don't want to tell her, but she has to understand how dangerous this is.

"The high used to be all I had," I begin. "I can't do that anymore."

"This smoke is different." Her gaze intensifies. "Better than anything you've known."

I shake my head. "I'm in recovery. It's fragile. You need to respect that certain things are dangerous for me."

Her lip curls into a teasing smile. "I do understand."

Though I'd like to remain, try to draw more out of her, I feel uneasy. Smiling vacantly, I wish her good night, and back out of the room.

Sleep, that's my intention. I lie atop the still-made bed, mind rushing, hyper-sensitized.

There's no mistaking the sound of the needle drop. So attuned to solitude and quiet, the slightest noise pierces my attention. Bettine's singing elevates, flits delicately, a white butterfly in the aggrieved blackness. The vocal line entangles with high jagged-edged strings, I think solo viola. My daughter's voice, accompanying a song recorded before she was born. Before I was.

Eyes close. Jagged lysergic colors swirl, worse than ever. In our twenties, Elizabeth and I pursued such kaleidoscopic stimuli, found pleasure in them. Finally I was the one who insisted we had to stop. It was her leaving that plunged me back in. Now my gut churns, and I'm filled with fear of the depthless vacancy I feel, tugging.

The song ends. Scratchy background noise repeats, the needle stuck in a run-out loop.

The record restarts from the beginning. This seems familiar, the scenario if not the voice. Perhaps her mother. Did Elizabeth sing along with records while I tried to sleep?

I'm out of bed again. Outside her bedroom, ear pressed to the door.

The voice pursues a more ethereal, almost angelic line than the main thrust of the recorded song, which is more aggressive, raw-edged and strident.

I drop to one knee, fit my eye to the keyhole.

In the center of her room, she stands looking up, arms raised in the same delicate nightshirt. Her orderly hair and intact makeup tell me she hasn't yet been to bed. I can't see what's overhead, attracting her attention. Our bedrooms match, mirror images. Must be the skylight. In my own room, the glass is a black rectangle framing a few scattered stars. A million hours I stared up through that portal while the world slept.

Straining upward, she sings as if rhapsodizing some beauty unseen to me. The melody she weaves is strange, angular and swerving, yet beautiful. Beneath the startling bluish moonlight penetrating from above, her skin is radiant, her garment transparent.

Look away. I'm curious, fascinated, yet overcome with the exhaustion of many sleepless nights. Better to return to my room before she catches me watching. Close my eyes, try to dream.

***

By the time I'm ready to leave for work in the morning, there's no sign of Bettine waking. I leave a note on the kitchen counter.

My boss knows my history, my scars, and the right hand I drag around like cold meat attached to my wrist. When she hears about Bettine, she suggests I head home early, catch up tomorrow. I think she feels sorry for me. A lifetime ago, I was a teaching assistant in the Music school, hoped to become a professor. I lost all that, lost everything. Can't be bitter, though. They didn't have to let me back in the department at all.

Anyway, I don't mind playing sympathy for a few extra hours at home. Maybe Bettine and I will reconnect. Whether I need it more, or she does, I'm not sure.

At home, everything downstairs is exactly as I left it. The only sound, hardwoods creaking under my feet. My note sits untouched on the counter.

Then I hear the record playing.

As I climb the stairs, music clarifies. From the upper landing, I see her door standing open. I don't want to burst in, frighten her. Having an adult daughter, I don't know where to begin. No point of reference. Technically she's still a teen, but I'm out of my depth, have no idea how to approach. Should I leave her alone? Who knows what she might be doing. I want to help, but I'm afraid she might be dangerous. All her talk of ecstasy, and white smoke.

Outside the open door I stop. I should announce myself.

Bettine's standing next to the bed, just where I saw her last night, through the keyhole. This time, she's surrounded by a white, whirling cloud. I expect a druggy smell, pungent like weed, or the plastic tang of a sizzling boulder, but what I get is airy, light and sweet, like a puff of powdered sugar inhaled off a donut.

"Is that..." I step into the room. Of course it is. "You can't, Bettine! Not here." I think to hold my breath, back away. Already the taste on my tongue is incredibly sweet. I should spit it out, but can't. The intense, unexpected sensation brings me up short. I feel an urge to open my mouth, to take it in. I want more.

Only a man's unbuttoned dress shirt and panties cover a model-thin body, legs impossibly long, the crest of hipbones visible through her flesh. Arms aloft, head tilted back, as if she hasn't heard me, still thinks she's alone. No paraphernalia visible. Just the music, and a girl gathering clouds to herself. Reveling in it.

I want to forbid this, drive it away, but there's nothing tangible here. Nothing to prevent.

She notices me, turns. Upraised hands flutter, as if playing with something invisible, trying to catch butterflies I can't see. Lowering her arms, she smiles like she knows I'm wondering what to make of this. As the cloud dissipates, she moves the needle back to the beginning of the 78. She drops playfully onto the bed, then reaches for something behind her on the mattress. Her hand goes between the old records, produces a black leather book. Not the black polish of her luggage, but aged and worn.

She pulls me down next to her, and scoots up close. It's strange, touching her for the first time, feeling her warmth. I want to put my arms around her, squeeze her to me. I'm afraid of how that would feel.

"Within these pages," she says slowly, dreamily, "all the secrets."

"What..."

She flashes the book's cover, illegibly titled. "Mother found the book here. In this house."

"You said you didn't remember, before."

"She told me, as we departed Liège. Said she found it in her ancestral home, in Oregon, in America. Here. This book ignited her search, our trek to Europe. It fired her great hunger."

Bettine doesn't open the book, but allows a closer view of the florid script, waxy metallic ink the color of molten lead on the cover. *Chansons de l'extase lumineuse*. A scent, pleasantly earthy, almost pungent. As I reach, she withdraws the book to its hiding place, between records in brittle sleeves.

"I'll be careful," I venture. "It's part of my job, repairing old books and records."

"You said before. At a library." She shifts slightly, hiding the book behind her.

I try another approach. "How did your mother really die?"

"Why should you want to hear about her?"

I don't answer.

"You should hate her." She looks up. "This book was all she cared about. Until the smoke."

"I've never seen it before." I regain eye contact, see she's holding something back.

She hesitates. "She suffered. Those of us most susceptible to pleasure, we suffer most."

That was me, before. Don't want to remember. "You mentioned this man." Despite all she's experienced, I feel I should protect her. My stronger impulse, though, is the desire to know. I have to look away. "You called him Daddy."

I glance back, catch her looking with pity at her poor father, scarred and broken. Carmine lips a recurve bow, her mother's mocking smile. Maybe she wishes she found this place empty, enjoyed a solitary homecoming, free to pursue whatever inspired her return.

"It's not answers you need." Her accent thickens. "You have so much pain."

"I'm glad you're here. But you seem fully formed by your life over there."

"It did offer many rewards." Her eyes focus far away.

"So, why return?"

She exhales slowly. "Daddy decided Mother was right. He gave himself over to bliss."

"What do you mean? He overdosed, thinking he'd be with your mother?"

"Something like that. Perhaps an accident. Some believe everyone who gives themselves to the smoke does so willingly. I had to leave while the Gendarmerie sorted things out. I thought I could return, that his house would become mine. I retained a lawyer to fight for me, but Daddy's secrecy had been absolute. He had no public identity, no will. I could never return to the house on the Rue d'Auseil. I was homeless, and possessed only the essentials I carried with me that day, expecting within weeks I would return."

"How lucky you took the records with you. And this book, something about songs."

"As I said, some believe every seeming accident disguises secret intent." She chews her bottom lip, eyes darting up, to the corner of the ceiling. "Perhaps I knew this was my journey's next stage."

"Your mother's ancestral home." I stand, shrugging off suspicions, feeling more settled than I can remember. Do I have a part to play? "Are you hungry? I'll make dinner."

She looks surprised. "I don't need food."

In the doorway, I stop. "I'll make enough for two."

After it's clear she's not coming down, I eat alone. What's left, I put in the refrigerator.

In solitude my mind settles. The house is dark enough, quiet enough. I might sleep.

***

Distant music shoves me sideways, from cramped sleep into sweat-drenched wakefulness. Such a song echoes in and out of uncomfortable dreams, carrying into black delirium the dizzy significance of half-forgotten mad hallucination.

I'm out of bed before I know it, standing in the hall, searching for recognition within the tune drifting from Bettine's open door. A restless song, sharp thrusts and tension-fraught lunges.

Though the room seems empty, I'm hesitant to enter. Recently I'm always up late, listening at her door to the sounds within. I creep as far as the doorway. Bettine hasn't left the bedroom since she arrived. Where could she have gone?

The Victrola spins unwatched under the pewter lamp's glow. The old leather book amid lacquer records spilled across the bed evoke an age when Elizabeth's forebears built this place.

Shadows shift on mahogany floorboards, the quality of light altered as if the lamp has moved. Stepping inside, I see at once what's changed. It's the skylight, not transparent to the dark sky, but full of milky liquid. What I'm seeing makes no sense, this glass portal filled like a shallow pool, contents held up by inverse gravity. A shimmering, seething maelstrom. Out of the surface—liquid, yet weightless as air—a white tendril reaches down, wavering like ivy growing at time-lapse speed.

My hand extends, against my will. The right hand, the dead one. This pale, wavering finger strains toward me from overhead. I want to touch it, despite knowing my dead nerves will feel nothing. I raise my left as well, strain on tiptoes toward the ceiling.

Pleasure tingles all my fingertips, hyper-stimulation that makes me suck in breath. Both hands are alive with sizzling, electric sensitivity. It's too much. It's wonderful. Dead nerves, thrillingly alive.

"I didn't bring that in." A woman's voice, behind me. "This time, it was you."

I spin.

My wife in a towel, wet skin flushed from a hot bath. Years spin past in reverse, before my eyes. Elizabeth, as I first knew her.

No. Memory is a filter, overlaying what I see.

It's Bettine.

She approaches. "Now you've felt it. You understand."

My heart pounds, fingers tremble. "You can't have this in the house."

"It's always been here, and it's sublime." She stands beside me, rises on tiptoes, one hand grasping my shoulder as the other reaches. Her towel slips from her breasts. She reaches to catch it, but not before I smell her skin's hot dampness, fragrant of gardenia. "What must change is your perception."

She strains upward and the wet surface above her breaks. A misty hint of white reaches toward her, solidifying.

"What is this stuff? How'd you bring it with you?" I remember that sensation, desire to feel it again. I'm more afraid than ever, yet the temptation has also grown. I'm hungry to know that feeling again. "We have to stop. Otherwise…I'll go."

I turn away.

"Wait." Her voice, softer. She reaches down, adjusts the Victrola. The strange music clarifies. "Every pain can be soothed. Nothing need trouble us, ever again."

I try to flex my right hand, already deadening again. I crave that dazzling tingle, remember it clearly. "I'm an addict. Pills, powders, everything. I have to be afraid."

"We've learned to approach the danger." Bettine sits on the edge of the bed, daring me. Her eyes go to the skylight, where the gelatinous substance is now settled, motionless. "Reach, once again. I want you to breathe it in."

My hands tremble. I mean to refuse, but no words will come. The strange wet surface shimmers into gaseous drift, subtly glowing.

"Inhale." Her towel slips again. She starts to reach for it, then with a half-smile, allows it to fall. "Let it penetrate your lungs, gentle as a whisper. Let another reality shift into place, superimposed onto this one, like a slow film crossfade."

"It's dangerous," I whisper. "You said it killed your mother."

"It's not the smoke that kills, but the ancient beings behind it. They use the smoke, a conduit to rapture, to tempt you nearer. It's accessible only at certain windows, in a few houses in all the world. This is such a window. You only have to open yourself. Take from them their pleasures. Use the music as your shield."

I force myself to look down, away.

She takes up the black book, broad and thin like an artist's folio, perhaps fifty pages.

"Chansons de l'extase lumineuse." Fingertips trace words standing out in thick relief. "The name, it means Songs of Luminous Ecstasy. It's our instruction."

I lean in, tentatively reach for the book, expecting her to snatch it away. She moves it just beyond my reach, and opens the cover to reveal pages lined like musical score. Some sheets are scrawled with dots and loops like alien musical notation. Others are handwritten in a mix of styles and colors, or annotated with diagrams.

"The only copy," she says. "The work of many hands."

"You helped write this?" I ask.

She laughs, surprised. "No. It's very old."

The words seem plain enough when I glance at an entire page. When I focus on individual lines, try to follow the thread, they shimmer out of focus. A smell of rotting flowers and incense, perhaps memory again. I rub my eyes, shake my head. "What does this say?"

Her finger traces a line, the hand's proximity focusing my attention. Vague letterforms clarify, resolve into words, punctuation. Violet English cursive, needle thin, precise. Sky blue French, looping and textural. Inky black German, fraught with blotches and smears.

"Entice them," Bettine reads, "take their sweet fruit, but beware, they would devour."

The words on the page come clear.

"Desire of mind to bring them. Music of Reich to sooth them. Songs of Zann to drive them away." She turns the page, hands the book to me.

I read where she left off. "We feed of their fruit, they feed of our worship. Such is the ecstasy of the Glass Altar."

"For years uncounted, this music, has kept at bay the harm approaching the callers of the white smoke." She kneels naked at the phonograph. Though the song isn't finished, she lifts the needle back to the beginning. "Some, like Mother, believe it possible to ascend. To become a higher being, dwelling forever within bliss."

"I'm not going that far," I whisper. "I just want to feel good. Just for one minute."

"I know what you need," she sings, voice light as the mist. "I'll protect you."

I crave something I barely understand. I'm tired, weak from lack of sleep. Too much worry. Not enough happiness. I stand, raise my face to the glass. Let it come to me.

Beside me, Bettine looks up at the skylight, filled with liquid clouds. A pale, barely tangible finger extends. She sings a brief, urgent melody, and the snaking tendril withdraws, leaving behind an airy puff of floating powder. She flicks out her tongue. I taste what she tastes, sweetness like powdered sugar inhaled. The flavor of her mouth, like a kiss. I can't help swallowing. A rush of pleasure floods my body, the swirling embrace like a warm opiate cloud, but more energetic. The perfect balance of peace and stimulation.

Against this, I have no defense. I desire nothing more.

***

What paradise would I choose? A shimmering ecstasy of safety, comfort, belonging. Blackness of night transformed to a limitless, accepting universe.

Swallow deep. Again. Who could ever want anything else?

I wander hallways, explore an infinitude that has always existed, all around. Every time I think I'm dead-ended, new doors swing open. Unfamiliar rooms, passageways to my past, my future. I thrill at possibilities, certain this wondrous potential will remain, available to me after my head clears. My bitterness no longer matters. Without it, I'm weightless. All the pain, memories of blood, acid rage. All set aside. A lifetime of unmet desires and cumulative defeats. Unwind years of struggle. Vanilla self-help books. Endless platitudes of diversion, rehab.

Inhale sweetness, that's all. Can't stop myself. Smoke is solid, spun sugar in my lungs.

Pinned and wriggling, mouth agape, breathing helpless in white delirium. A mind-reeling, spinning cinema, of a scale vastly beyond the human.

Anxiety feels distant, benign awareness of risks behind my pleasurable veneer. Remember, the smoke doesn't kill. It's the ancient things behind. That's what got Elizabeth. Dangers unknowable to us, except by their beautiful creation. The loving smoke.

We just have to remember the music. Our book tells us so. A soundtrack, far away, reminds me. Climb again. Here Elizabeth glows, a slow motion drift. Her smile tells me she knows my thoughts.

I drop to the floor beside the bed, out of range of the smoke. Lying on my back on the polished hardwoods, head clearing as lungs gasp flavorless air.

Bettine leans down, grabs my right hand. "Come on!"

She pulls, but my sweat-slick hands slip loose. She takes my wrist two-handed, pulls.

I'm up again, beneath the skylight, pressing my face into a warm, blissful dessert.

"I want you to see it up close. Not just the outer smoke. Delve inside, to the heart of it."

Together we enter a whirling other-realm, throb with impulses triggering every sense, amplified. A cycle of mad hunger and feeding, only to feel greater need, a desire where attainment merely heightens craving. Everything escalates. There is no limit. I press deeper into the whiteness, sensing power, concentrated and profound. My eyes see a darker core within.

A hand on my shoulder surprises me. I'm still here, tangible. So long since I lost track. I remember, I'm standing in Bettine's bedroom.

Grinning wildly, she shakes me. "Isn't it the utmost?"

"I decided to give in." I'm breathing hard. "Stopped fighting."

She embraces me. "You took the smallest taste, went flying."

The way she holds me feels wrong. Her body pressed against mine, nudging me away from the Victrola.

"What are you doing?" Insinuations flash, a flash recap of memory. Abduction, life on the run, used and objectified too young, exposed to who knows what kind of occult madness? Of course she's damaged. Is that why she came to me? Trembling, I pull back. "Bettine, no."

She grips me by the shoulders, pushes my face into the miasma's seething depths. I try to pull back, against her wrestling my body, half of me wanting to give in to whatever she plans. For a moment I stop struggling. That's enough. I've lost control, perspective.

I don't care. All I feel is my wanting.

"Don't fight. Come with me." Her hands release.

I pull back, inhaling fresh air. I want to say something. It's hard to remember.

She looks at me strangely, possessed of some overpowering intention. "That's why I came here, to jump into heaven. Like Mother, like Daddy." Her eyes lit with fervent desire. "These windows are gateways to that infinite paradise where they dwell. I knew you'd want it too."

Bettine lunges, knocks the Victrola off its stand. The record bounces off the platter, shatters on the floor. She turns back and for the first time without music, opens herself to the cloud, arms wide in acceptance. One hand grips my wrist, tugging me along.

"They left me behind," she says. "Then I knew it would be you."

I try to pull away.

Translucent white strands, like ghostly ropes or smoke tentacles, reach into her mouth, penetrate her eyes, her ears, her nose.

Her grip loosens. I pull free, scramble on the floor by the bed, trying to right the Victrola. The record lies shattered, jagged shards of brittle lacquer.

More tendrils lash out from above. A pale cord whips around her neck, and lifts.

Bettine's eyes are wild, anticipating her greatest desire. Lips trying to form words, she pulls the cord free of her neck and rasps, "Don't let me…go alone."

As it lifts her away I pull back, turn to the bed, find an intact record labeled, "Music of Zann." Remember the book's words, Songs of Zann to drive them away.

The white membranous lump fully encompasses my daughter's motionless shape as I place the record on the platter, set it spinning and drop the needle mid-song. I inhale a surge of ecstatic pleasure, a sensation both welcome and horrifying.

There's a visceral tearing as the music bursts forth, shrill in such proximity. Malevolent heat, not the sweet warmth of before. Tangy acidity, the unmistakable smell of burning. No screams. The veil covering my daughter smokes as it lifts her away. Flailing tendrils reach for me, only to withdraw from the music.

The white membranous surface resounds, like a struck drum. The vibration dissipates, leaving only the music. No more struggle, no anguish. I delve my hand into the soft warmth, feel the familiar tingle. Taste the sweetness. My hands grope for anything solid, find nothing.

Clouds thin, particles sucked quickly away, as if the glass is open to the sky.

Alone. Just me, and the jarring music. Bettine's gone, again.

I drop to the floor, watch the record spin. When it's almost over, I start it from the beginning. After some hours, I dare brief outings to check the rest of the house. Calling in anguish, knowing I won't find her. Always I return, start the music again, at the beginning.

The smoke can return, any time, night or day. I know I'll feel more secure in daylight. As long as it remains dark, my resolve may slip. I might decide to jump. What did Bettine say? To leap in, give myself over to bliss. To follow, and never come back up.

All night I sit by the player, starting the record over and over. This Zann's music spinning, spinning. Well past sunrise, I remain within the music. Only when I'm sure I won't break, in a room morning bright and growing warm, I finally stand and leave the Victrola behind. Across the hall, I pack the things I'll carry away from here.

INTO YE SMOKE-WREATH'D WORLD OF DREAM

W. H. Pugmire

I.

Morning mist engulfed the magnificent structure of the First Baptist Church so that I could not behold its stupendous steeple; and yet the clinging fog enhanced, in an eerie way, the aura of the venerable house of god, which has stood on College Hill since 1638. That was but twenty-nine years after Shakespeare's sonnets had first been published, and only twenty-two years after the Immortal Bard's death, the man who was my own God of Literature. This was one of the glorious aspects that overwhelmed me whenever I visited Providence—one could almost taste the hoary past. Finally, I turned away from the mist-enshrouded church, crossed Thomas Street, and walked slowly past the gaudy Fleur-de-Lys Building, pausing for one brief moment to touch that structure in which artists such as me lived and worked. I had been guided through the building once, on my first visit to Providence four years earlier, and the memory of the dusky lower rooms filled with implements of art, framed paintings, and so forth was like some happy enchantment, some pleasant dream. Perhaps Jacob could get me inside the building a second time.

I had returned to Providence to spend time with the mad poet, Jacob Grall. Frankly, I was concerned about him, for his behavior—always odd—was becoming severely lunatic. He had sent me sheets of his newest poetry, which he had composed for a collection he planned on calling *Sunken Dreams*, and they were far more morbid than his usual gloomy work. How can I describe what bothered me? It seemed to me that the poems exuded a subdued hysteria that threatened to explode as screams of diabolic nonsense. It wasn't just the dark undertone of the poems, but the way his handwriting had altered, as if the poems had been penned by one who suffered from delirium tremens, sonnets composed during fits of seizure. Jacob had refused to greet me at the train station, requesting that we meet at the Providence Art Club. I moved away from the Fleur-de-Lys and stalked up the hill until coming to the door of the lower Dodge House Gallery, opened the door and entered in.

I was surprised to be greeted by a stern-faced security guard, to whom I nodded and said "Howdy." He seemed especially interested in the two individuals who stood some ways from the door before an artifact that rested on a white pedestal and was encased inside a block of clear plastic or glass. I approached the couple and touched my hand to Jacob's shoulder. He glanced at me with eyes that seemed on fire, and then returned his gaze to the sculpture inside its protective block. I read the card attached to the wall just above the artifact, and saw that the bas-relief was the work of one Henry Anthony Wilcox and was on loan from Miskatonic University in Arkham.

Suddenly, Jacob began to speak. "The exhibit is dedicated to the work of students and others who once lived and labored at the Fleur-de-Lys. This particular beauty was fashioned in late February of 1925. Isn't it fascinating, the way one's eyes can't quite *fix* onto the thing? It's like the image isn't solidly rooted to our own dimension. If I gaze on the thing too steadily, I feel as if I may lose my foothold on this terrestrial plane—the earth seems to tremble beneath me, and I am filled with a delicious dread that the ground will crack open and release some rising *thing*." Although his language was so wild, Jacob spoke in a calm and quiet voice, as if in reverence.

The woman standing near him bent so as to take in the contours of the idol. I saw that she was very young, and perhaps of Native American or Eskimo heritage. She was one of those Goth kids, attired in somber black and with a small hoop of metal piercing her lower lip. When, at last, she spoke, there was no mistaking the fervor of her emotions. "It shouldn't be here, trapped beneath this fucking plastic or whatever it is. It should be elevated on a high pillar in some secluded place beneath the stars! Beneath the shifting stars where we can worship it with spilled blood and sweaty orgasm! We will be naked, braying and bellowing and writhing like the beasts we are! Murder and mayhem will be our religion, as we slaughter the world for the glory of Cthulhu! Ia! Ia!" Then, violently, she clutched at the block of heavy plastic and tried to move it from where it had been secured. I was pushed away by the security guard, who grabbed the woman by her wrists and roughly escorted her from the gallery.

Jacob's mouth pressed against my ear. "She's right," he sighed. He leaned away from me and spoke in a whisper. "It doesn't belong there, trapped within walls of plastic or whatever that stuff is. I know the legend of Cthulhu means nothing to you, but you can't deny the *effect* of this dream-image. Yes, Nathan, this rectangular artifact was inspired by a dream. Indeed, Wilcox actually stated that he *made* the thing 'in a dream of strange cities.' You look bewildered, but it's quite true. Those new poems that I sent you, on which you refuse to comment: *I made them in a dream of strange cities that rose from depths of ocean beneath a red sun that turned water into blood.* Do you see that suggestion of Cyclopean architecture that serves as vague background behind the horror in clay? That's what I beheld through the crimson mists of nightmare. How could it not inspire verse?"

I studied the "horror in clay," as Jacob named it, as if through looking at it carefully I could comprehend its meaning. But, no, the thing was meaningless. The object was a bas-relief about an inch thick and six inches in area, carved on red-green clay. Bizarre hieroglyphics had been etched onto the bottom of the thing, and above them, in sharp relief, was what seemed an impressionistic portrait of a kind of monster. The creature's strangest aspect was its pulpy, tentacled head, that might almost suggest some creature from the ocean if it wasn't so damn *wrong*. The grotesque and scaly body had a pair of wings extending from its back, but they weren't the wings of any earthly creature. That was it, actually—the thing was absolutely unearthly, like some mythical dragon or Cyclops of legend. Behind the monster were etchings that vaguely suggested a background of Cyclopean architecture, but the images were so queerly shaped that, the harder I stared at them, the less I could comprehend their outlines.

Jacob glanced furtively at where the guard stood near the gallery's front door, leaned nearer to me and continued whispering. "Gaze on it, Nathan, penetrate it with your eyes. Try to imagine the alien monoliths and sepulchers that were fashioned in tribute to the Great Old One and named R'lyeh. Drink its madness with your eyes and let it mould your dreams. They came from the stars, as is told in the *Necronomicon*, and they brought their unholy images with them. *Ph'nglui mglw'nafh Cthulhu R'lyeh wgah'nagl fhtagn.*" The final word of his implausible chant was spoken with such emphasis that the sound of it made me dizzy; and in a state of uncanny emotion, as I stared hard at the sculpture, I saw a green-yellow mist rise from beneath it, a curling mist that easily filtered through the enclosure in which the art piece had been encased, that lifted to me and coiled through my nostrils. Overcome with vertigo, I backed away from the display, fretting that I was going to fall backward.

The security guard was at my side. "Are you all right, sir?" I quickly assured him that I was, smiling sheepishly. "We have many other interesting things on display." Gently, he took hold of my arm and guided me to another corner of the room. "Now these are fascinating. They were made by one of the more modern artists, Josephine Broers, inspired by something she had encountered in Kingsport, Massachusetts. She was a resident at Fleur-de-Lys in 1995. I don't know if she found antique bottles or, through her skill as artist, made these three look so old. I like how the inside of the glass is streaked and foggy, as if something inside had panted against the inner surface. You see the pendulums inside? If you look closely, the hanging objects take on facial form. As I said, fascinating."

Someone took hold of my other arm, and Jacob spoke in a loud voice. "Such an interesting exhibition," he sang to the guard. "I can't seem to stay away. But let's go, Nathan, I'm suddenly quite hungry, and you promised me lunch." I had promised no such thing, but I allowed my companion to guide me to the door and out onto the red brick sidewalk of Thomas Street. "It was getting warm in there. No wonder you felt a little tipsy. We can breathe again."

I looked across the street as the sun, unsheathed by clouds, illuminated the spectacular church. "I love that building. Have you ever been inside it?"

"Once, to listen to some Hindu fellow give an opening speech for some civic ceremony." Jacob was silent for some moments. "I may have something to relate about that church, another day. I've been making secret inquiries. Don't frown so, my dear, it's unbecoming. Come on, let's prowl Benefit Street. There's a charming sandwich shop that's not too far away."

The rest of my afternoon with Jacob was anti-climatic. We ate our sandwiches and drank our juices, and then we strolled along Benefit Street to a sequestered churchyard just below it, where we sat on tabletop tombs and quoted Poe. Finally my friend leaned close to kiss me, and I watched him wade through the gloaming, homeward. I rose at last and followed the path that took me to the steps that led to Benefit Street, which I crossed so as to climb the step way to College Hill and my small apartment. My room was in darkness, but I did not want to turn on any lights. Instead, I opened one of my bedroom windows, knelt before it and observed the moon. I could not see any stars, but the moon was glorious, its bright splendor surrounded by a ring of hazy white light. I looked for quite a while, until my eyelids grew heavy, and then I lowered to the floor, cradled my head inside my arms, and surrendered to slumber.

I wondered, when I floated to my feet, why the world had fallen so completely silent. The wind that had lifted me to a standing position made no moan, and the black haunted trees of the surrounding woods, though moving in that wind, were hushed. Becoming aware of a subtle pounding beneath my feet I looked downward, and it shocked me to realize that I was naked, with wet crimson streaks adorning my ebony flesh. Aware of movement, I raised my eyes to the psychotic scene before me. As if some sleeping sense awakened, I became aware of sound; but only poetry or madness could describe the din that echoed in my ears, the shrieks and yelps and snatches of diabolic chanting. I felt again the pulsing beneath my feet, and from some hidden portion of the black haunted woodland I became aware of the muffled yet steady beating of drums. Patches of flame rose here and there, and I became aware of the thing that the devils pranced around, the tall pale pillar of pockmarked stone that towered eight feet above the earth. Sitting on the pillar's flat apex was a statue of the monster I had seen depicted on the bas-relief in the art gallery. The monster's outline was crazier than ever, blurred, unsteady, expanding and diminishing. And then the sight of the pillar and its occupant was blocked as the Eskimo freak I had met in the gallery shuddered in ecstasy before me. One of her eyes was missing, replaced by a sickening slit, and she licked the bloodstained dagger that she held. Before I could protest, she pressed her wet red mouth against my own; and then her lips moved to my ear, into which she chortled "*Cthulhu fhtagn.*"

I pushed the fiend from me as, all around, a red mist rose from dark earth; and with that mist erected nightmarish monoliths that were draped with seaweed and littered with human corpses. The scene began to resemble something that Gustav Doré might have drawn to illustrate Dante. And I saw the tentacled icon expand impossibly; and the silhouette of its evil clawed hand ripped into the fabric of heaven; and from that cosmic wound a rainfall of gore plummeted upon us.

I awakened on the floor of my bedroom, reclined beside an opened window through which a heavy rainfall, driven by daemonic tempest, assailed me.

II.

Jacob Grall was a very small man; indeed, had he been any shorter he may have classified as dwarf, and his stature and effeminate mannerisms sometimes made him a target for mocking laughter. No one laughed, however, when he was with me, the very tall and muscular black man with shaved head and short fuse. I wasn't his "protector," however, because he was oblivious to the jeers and sneers of the public, especially when he performed his poetry. Those who set aside their prejudices and actually listened to Jacob's verse were almost always moved to a kind of disquieting admiration. Jacob's vision was dark and remorseless, callous toward everything that regular folk held sacred; and although one could not call his subjects supernatural, he had a way of looking at reality that filled it with a bleak and nightmarish quality. It was as if he gazed at the common world through some dark distorted glass that revealed aspects that, however warped, convinced. Jacob was especially fond of the past, and his verse often extolled the bewitching mysteries of New England history. It was the performance of his verse, spoken in his high nasal voice as his raised right hand seemed to stroke invisible inhabitants of the air, that earned him the nickname of "the mad poet." People may have mocked him behind his back, even they who pretended to be his friends, but everyone listened when he spoke his verse. Really sensitive folk often came away from his readings shaken by emotions and fears they could not comprehend, profoundly troubled by the images he had evoked.

Jacob and I shared an aesthetic link, for my paintings, depicting scenes from Shakespeare, concentrated on the bleakness of the plays, of which there was an abundance. I had learned much from my obsession with the Boston artist Richard Upton Pickman, whose morbid work I had studied incessantly when younger, who was an artist who shared the fondness for New England's murky past that so exhilarated me and Jacob. One of Jacob's finest chapbooks collected his series of sonnets that sang of Pickman's art, and it was that early book that alerted me of the mad poet's existence and inspired my move from Boston to Providence. Jacob was inspired, by our friendship, to organize a hand press edition of new poems, printed on hand-made perfumed paper, bound in delicate boards and illustrated by myself. He now rarely went anywhere without a copy of the slim volume in his small sallow hand.

Some few days passed, and then I received a late phone call from Jacob, requesting that I meet him at an all-night coffee shop on Federal Hill, requesting that I dress in black attire. He was reclining in a booth when I arrived, and I wrinkled my brow at the bulky knapsack on the seat beside him. "You don't intend to drag me onto a camping trip, I hope."

He blew air. "Don't be daft. Our adventure will be of an urban nature—at first. And then, well, wait and see. I've been investigating a moment in the city's past. You'll enjoy what I have planned for us tonight."

"You're rarely so secretive, Jacob. Why the obliqueness?"

"Artistic effect, let's say. I've been patching pieces of the past together, delving into buried records and testaments, correlating what I've snatched. It's amazing, how *alive* the past becomes when one delves into it. There are so many secrets aching to be disinterred."

"Name your discovery," I commanded.

"Go have the host call us a cab," he countered.

I rose and did so, and when I returned to our booth Jacob was pulling a black ski cap over his long blond hair. He pushed out of the booth and struggled with his knapsack. "Let me take that," I suggested, taking hold of the thing and finding that it was indeed quite weighty. "Damn, what the hell did you pack in here?"

"Relics of ritual," was his arcane reply. I followed him outside, and before long our cab pulled up in front of us. Once seated, Jacob bent to the driver and said, "75 North Main Street." I leaned back, the heavy rucksack on my lap, and after a short ride we arrived in front of the First Baptist Church. I protested, as the taxi fled from us, that the building would be locked shut at this time of evening. Ignoring me, Jacob led the way to an alley that took us to a back door of the structure. There was very little light, for the moon was curtained by clouds, and I could barely make out the small silver implement that my friend had removed from his pocket. Understanding his request that we dress in black, I watched as he slipped the contrivance into the keyhole and fiddled with it. He pushed, and the door opened.

The backpack was heavy on my shoulder as I stepped into a space that might have been a storage room, although the chamber was so dark that I couldn't make anything out clearly. I felt Jacob work at the zipper of one of the rucksack's compartments, and suddenly our way was illuminated by a flashlight's powerful beam. We walked through a wide doorway and entered the enormous Meeting House, and I followed Jacob into one of the cubicles and sat upon a pew. The flashlight's bright blue beam was switched off, and we sat in silent darkness for a little while before my friend began to speak.

"The Wilcox bas-relief that we saw in the Dodge House Gallery was fashioned on February 28, 1925, the day that the Charlevoix-Kamouraska earthquake rocked eastern Canada and portions of the northeastern United States. The young artist was living in the Fleur-de-Lys Building across the street at the time, and his recorded statement about the sculpture is curious, to say the least. He said that he had fashioned it 'in a dream,' a dream of great Cyclopean cities composed of titanic blocks of stone and towering monoliths that dripped with oceanic slime. He called what he saw a 'dream landscape,' and it's an odd coincidence that around the same time, in Paris, a fantastic artist named Ardois-Bonnot hung a profane painting of the same title in a salon. A correspondent in Holland now owns that painting, and he sent me a photograph of it. Here."

Jacob took a small photo from his jacket pocket and I heard the click of his flashlight switch. I studied the image beneath the beam. "It looks vaguely familiar," I muttered. Then it came to me: the painting was of the fantastic Cyclopean architectural background that the artist Wilcox had etched onto his bas-relief. The alien city was too uniquely fabulous to be mistaken as any other representation.

My companion began to speak again. "The pastor here in the 1920s had an adoring sister who was of a sensitive artistic nature. Inspired by her brother's calling, she became interested in the art of stained glass and found employment in a friend's small factory which specialized in manufacturing windows for religious houses. She was allowed to work on a personal project shortly following a physical and emotional collapse that she had suffered in late February of 1925, a project that inspired furtive murmurings from her fellow employees. She later presented her window, such as it was, to her brother, after which its history becomes a mystery. Come, follow me." Jacob rose and took up his backpack, and I followed as he led the way up the carpeted steps to the high place where the podium was situated. Setting down his burden, he asked me to hold the flashlight, and as I shone it on him he reached for two of the four high shuttered doors that had been built into the wall. The doors opened at his maneuvering of them, revealing an aperture of darkness into which Jacob hurled his knapsack. "Help me up there," he ordered as he retrieved the torch.

"What the hell *is* it, Jacob?"

He clucked his tongue. "It's the baptismal font, my dear. Help me inside. You'll have no problem climbing up, giant that you are." I did as asked and lifted him to the opening, and then I climbed into the chamber. I heard Jacob rummaging through his rucksack, and then a match was struck and a tall bulky candle was lit. He reached into his bag and produced another similar candle, and when it had been ignited the room's contours became discernible. The raised font was enormous. Behind it was a wall, at the center of which had been installed a stained glass window. My friend vanished for some few moments, and then I heard the sound of running water. When he returned, he flashed me a mischievous smile. "I've done my homework."

"What are we doing here?"

He began to undress as he spoke. "Some people say that the Outer Ones find us alluring because of the chemistry of our blood. Well, that may contain a modicum of truth; but the real appeal is our ability to dream, because that's the one aspect that we share with these otherwise utterly alien beings. Indeed, my little theory is that when they molded us from prehistoric mud, the Great Old Ones and their kind *instilled within us* the ability to dream, so that in our dreams we could pay homage to them. Don't look so confused. You're a student of Pickman, and he had the talent of dreaming more than most. It was in his dreams that he located many of the hidden byways that he then sought and found in wakefulness. Oh, the paths we may locate in dreaming. And I burn to find the path to that." Here he pointed at the stained glass window, but the place was too dark for me to make out what the window depicted.

Jacob was now entirely naked. The sound of running water ceased. "It's programmed, you see, to turn off once the water reaches its proper depth. You should probably kneel, Nathan, because we are about to ape religion." I did not move as he climbed the steps that led to the font's brim, and he began to sing as he flopped into the water. "Much deeper than I imagined it would be; but, of course, I am ridiculously tiny. On your knees, mortal—we are now to become fantastic!" He vanished for some moments, and I heard his playful splashing. Then his head emerged again and he began to speak the gibberish that he had enunciated in the gallery; but he spoke it in such a way, with such conviction, that the sound of it caused my bones to tremble.

The clouds that had curtained the moon must have dissipated, because beams of lunar light became to shimmer behind the stained glass window. I detected that the wall into which the window had been fastened was a false one, and that the real church wall and its wide window was beyond it. I peered at the decorative window and knew that it was the lunatic work of the former pastor's sister. It was an almost majestic representation of the pseudo-city that Henry Anthony Wilcox had etched behind the figure of his monster and it depicted the fabulous evil erections that I had beheld in my dream of blood and madness. I gazed at it, and Jacob spoke his outrageous chant once more, almost shrieking the vile words. The moonlight seemed to shudder; it brightened into beams of sickly yellow and rancid green. The large candles began to smoke profusely, and my wide eyes burned as I watched the delirious pantomime before me. I had been transported into my misty dream once more, however much I was aware of the room's solid floor beneath my heels.

Jacob sank from view as waves of water splashed from the font, onto me. He surfaced once again and gargled "*Cthulhu R'lyeh fhtagn*," and then he vanished, for such a prolonged time that I grew frantic with fear. I reached for the rim of the font and leaned over it. For a few seconds I was aware of the thing that floundered in the water, the formless white polypous with wide luminous eyes—beseeching eyes. I saw the light of life die in those eyes as the thing grew still. I sensed that the ritual required human blood, and so I smashed my forehead against the metal rim of the font and smelled my blood as it oozed into the pool. But, blood was not the life in this instance, and I cried in fury as I hurled myself over the rim, into the depths of water. I lifted the lifeless husk of the one who had been my beloved friend, and raised him out of the water, into the smoke and lunar light of dreaming. I rose, like some monster of myth, with a stained glass city of titan blocks and sky-flung monoliths behind me. I wept, because I would no longer taste the mad dreams of the acolyte in my embrace. I groaned, because I could not flex my heavy wings and rise out of the water that was not my cosmic element. And I raged, because I could not see the stars through which I had filtered in antediluvian aeons, those stars that I would terrify so that they crawled through the chaos to the baying of Nyarlathotep, those shuddering stars that would align so as to spell my appalling name.

THE LURKER IN THE SHADOWS

Nathan Carson

[HPL to SEK]

10 Barnes St.,
Providence, R.I.,
Decr. 02, 1973

Dear Mr. King:---

I greatly enjoyed receiving your letter, & find the discovery of yet another Yankee of such good taste has disturbed my traditional ennui, & indeed ignites a certain sense of wonder inspired by cosmic coincidence. As the years pass, & I delve further into my dotage, my faith in the literacy & self-education of youth culture wanes with each passing season. Well met, young scribe.

While you flatter me beyond necessity by making such declarations of the quality of my early work, as well as its apparent profundity upon your own aspirations, I must admit that you are the first ever to mention that particularly wretched paperback as anything more than poorly edited pap from an era in which the licensing of my work had truly sprawled beyond the control of an estate as modest as my own was at that time. I ask not for pity, but please believe that it was the greatest struggle to put pen to page throughout the explosive years of the 1940s as my small fictional body until that time was in a rather constant state of bastardization, plagiarism, & puzzling critical reevaluation. I'm certain that I have not seen a copy of TLITS in the last twenty years—& sincerely hope never to again!

Despite your assertions that my Mythos have [sic] in some small way led you down a dark path of your own, I must congratulate you for balancing your learned state with a love for the fantastic & horrifying. For too long, those worlds have been mutually exclusive, as well evidenced by the degradation from the once lofty written worlds of the strange, to the lurid fare projected beneath cheapened moonlight at every drive-in cinema in this nation so wretchedly obsessed with "progress" which has all but completely lost sight of its proud origins & originators.

Of course you will find no reason to extend any condolence to this octogenarian so seemingly well established & received. But bear in mind the insidiousness with which those Hollywood hucksters twisted my art into little more than scantily clad models dashing headlong into closets full of Technicolor tentacles. Fame & fortune may have been made, but the many deaths my artistic soul experienced have far exceeded anything devised in the Tower of London. Surely without the annual bloodletting throughout the 1960s of films with my name smeared in raucous red below the titles, Hammer would not be the most successful studio on the European continent.

& the recent turn toward the Grand-Guignol into which macabre cinema has spiraled seems seeped in but one colour—crimson! Why, it was but a few years prior that I encountered the severely disturbed Italian youth who directed *The Squid With the Crystal Plumage*. Pardon this old quibbler, but only certain cephalopods boast a beak, let alone quills! Exactly why that wretch was bestowed with honors at NecronomiCannes, I may never know.

May I implore—if you ever find producers urging allowance of your gruesome tales to slum their way from the sanctity of paper to gross silver celluloid, resist with all thy might, & do not ever, under any circumstances, allow yourself to be coerced into a cheap cameo. The only adaptation of my own which I can still stand to admit as having its origins in the recesses of my id is Hitchcock's *Cool Air*, & the scene in which the camera passes me & Hitch in the elevator headed toward the 13th floor makes me curse & wince to this very day.

But again, I have digressed. I myself know the sensation of reverence for an author of stature beyond my ken. In my teens, I discovered the work of one Edward John Moreton Drax Plunkett, 18th Baron of Dunsany—a lion of a man whose life experience & generosity would affect me, firstly as a literary influence, & later as a patron & provocateur. Had I not been goaded into introducing myself to keen old Drax at a reading in October 1919, I very well might have starved to death in obscurity long ago. It is no secret that my correspondence with him began immediately following, & his good will led to my liberation from the shackles of self-imposed reclusion. Not only was my work published in professional venues & the dignity of hardcover, but paunchy Plunkett went so far as to provide the funding for my first Atlantic voyage. That visit to the old country was an eye opener, to be certain. Without Dunsany, it is quite assured that I would never have pointed a pistol at a pachyderm!

Clearly you are on your own path & need far less encouragement than I did at an even more advanced age. However I would be quite honored if you would share your ms with these tired eyes, if only because us Yanks must stick together, regardless if the bond is of crusted blood & mouldering sinew.

Please give my regards to your family & "Cthulhu fhtagn" to you as well, young sir.

Most cordially & sincerely yours,
H P Lovecraft

April 08, 2016
1:00 pm EST
World Weird Con - Portland, ME
Guest of Honor Keynote

To the esteemed devotees of the World Weird Convention 2016, I thank you for your consideration here. I know that being a member of such an illustrious family makes my Featured Guest status suspect of nepotism or worse, but I do have a story to relate to you today that I believe you will find as fascinating and inexplicable as I have.

My name is Ashton Nathaniel King. Yes, *that* King. It's true that my father is widely known as one of the Big Three—King, Lovecraft, and Lockhart, (with Poe clinging to a distant but respectable 4th)—who have come to rule the literature of the fantastic, horrible, and strange.

With my father's coma so widely discussed in the last year by tabloids and social media, I believe the time for me to weigh in my opinion has come. As well, I have unearthed some documents that leave my mind reeling, and hope sincerely that by sharing them with you, I may ultimately find some peace on the matter.

Where to begin? At the time of my father's birth in 1947, Howard Phillips Lovecraft was by the far the most famous author in our field. Launched to stratospheric heights by his postwar collections and film adaptations, he had eclipsed even Poe in durability and his stories were discussed in parlors and salons.

Of course we all take for granted Walt Disney's contribution as we've lived with it our whole lives. But did you know that before Mickey's famous turn as The Outsider in *Fantasia*, Disney had considered basing this sequence on the poem "Der Zauberlehrling" by Goethe? How different might history have run for our industry then? Dancing brooms and puddle buckets? Hardly the stuff nightmares are made of.

But when that ragged cartoon mouse finally caught his own visage in the mirror, ten million children cried out in terror together, and we finally knew ourselves; for we are all outsiders. Decades later, Matt Dillon's live action turn brought the subject home for a generation of teens too jaded for the hand-painted version.

Well known is the story that my father discovered an H.P. Lovecraft collection that belonged to his father before him, stashed away in an attic space. Dowsing for black gold, he struck it, and peeled back the pages of the rare and now impossible to find *The Lurker in the Shadows*. Go no further than Wikipedia, or King's famous essay collection, *Danses in Literature of the Supernatural and Macabre* if you prefer the long version. Bottom line: Lovecraft gave him purpose from a young age, only too apparent throughout his life.

What is odd to King-ophiles, the obsessed fans that congregate on message boards and via hand-stapled magazines and at conventions such as this, is how different King's widely suppressed first novel *Carrie* (Doubleday 1974) is when considered alongside all his more famous Mythos work that followed.

Casual fans are not even aware of this earlier novel, and copies were fetching some absurd prices for a time—that is until the crudity of its language, vulgarity of subject, and overall inferiority to his later work was established by critics, eventually putting the matter to rest. Even I had not read this book until I felt compelled to quite recently by some remarkable ephemera that fell into my possession.

It is more than simple literary legend that my father visited Providence in 1974 in order to pay his respects to the dying Howard Phillips Lovecraft. But the letters I have here prove beyond doubt that the two had been in dialog for several months prior. With your permission, I will interrupt my long-winded speech by reading another sample from these missives now.

[HPL to SEK]

10 Barnes St.,
Providence, R.I.,
Decr. 07, 1973

Dear Mr. Prince (may I call you this?—It seems far more apt a sobriquet for an heir so apparent…)

I received your ms for *Carrie* & will offer what limited editorial comments this enfeebled mind may conjure. The first few pages reveal a keen intellect & superior sense of characterization with which I have struggled since the late 19th century. Still I must say that I am a bit shocked at the crude modernity you employ in regards to the scatological & even gynecological references. Perhaps that is the gentleman in me. I am sure your adolescent readership will enjoy every drop soaked into those sanguine sanitary napkins. I fear the critics, on the other hand, may find cause to laugh at you.

Impressed as I am by the fortitude of your prose & dedication to the macabre, I feel inclined to impart some of the secrets I have learned, should our relationship continue to blossom. Words can contain a certain magic, some more potent than you perhaps imagine. I find myself wondering about your age & strength & susceptibility to illness...

I am very sorry to hear about your mother's health. If it may provide even the slightest condolence, my own family is long passed, aside from nearly nameless extended cousins, & my own fair Mia F.L., though I fear daily that she will discover that our age discrepancy is beyond her patience & tolerance.

Did you know that before she & I ever met, I received a letter from one C. Manson? Of course I never responded to it, & thought nothing of it at all until the news of 1969. For some unfathomable reason, every time something remotely linked to the occult fans the flames of media hysteria, my publicist is contacted for quotes.

You will not be surprised at my utter disgust that a group so mad & unkempt as Manson's should be in any way linked to my own explorations of cosmic doom. Yet alongside his bacchanal Beatles & Beach Boys albums & other cacophonous aural detritus was a stack of my more recent tomes. Helter Skelter, indeed!

Your concern expressed in regards to my rather conservative views on certain politically sensitive matters is well intended, & timely. It is true that for much of my life I harbored rather irrational perceptions of genetic superiority underscored by my antiquarian preferences. For decades I clung to these unfashionable bigotries, only to have the moldiest shingles of my gambrel-roofed mind slowly peeled back over the course of the Swinging Sixties & their associated civilities. I hope it will assuage your concerns to know that it was none other than Sammy Davis who finally enlightened me on the subject. When witchy young Karla LaVey cleverly inducted the two of us as Honorary Warlocks at the same ceremony, I was initially taken aback. But that wicked black Cyclops charmed me like the Candy Man that he is, & I have continued to revise my views ever since. It is through him that I met Mia, & for that will ever be grateful. He truly is a credit to his tribe.

If you will allow the digression, I cannot help but recall a particularly festive gathering that began with a swirling crystalline midnight punchbowl, & ended with Sammy & myself staggering & laughing like utter fools on the hillock below the kaleidoscopically fracturing Hollywood sign as glorious sunrays broke on the horizon. It was at that moment of madness & lucidity that I pledged to re-grow my hair in the style of my earliest youth—the flowing locks you have likely smirked at by now, as immortalized on my more recent dust jackets.

As you will have undoubtedly realized before setting paperknife to thread, I have attached this missive to a signed copy of my latest hardback, 1972's *Hastur La Vista*—a continuation of my latter day Latin American Mythos saga that steeps itself in Mayan history & storms to the present with Congressional cultists trading high tech weaponry for hieroglyphic scrolls & tools made of metals that seem somehow…unearthly. I sincerely hope that you will find it a fraction as enjoyable to read as I did to write.

Well the winter wind doth blow, & the ink in this pen grows leaden as I rest my aching elbows on this ancient escritoire. Out my window is the white blanket over Providence at Yule. Your own Cumberland County can only be nether side of still deeper drifts. Perhaps when the thaw comes next Spring, I can muster the energy to visit you, & share a few of the things I have learned. The salt marshes of Scarborough have a certain allure, & I have long read of the bonfires once lit atop Scottow Hill, which looms over Saco Bay. Those are sights I would drink in deeply with the company of a young aspirant as enlightened as thee.

Most cordially & sincerely yours,
H P Lovecraft

April 08, 2016
1:06 pm EST
World Weird Con - Portland, ME
Guest of Honor Keynote

I thought that might whet your appetite. Now, if you'll bear with my own part in this, I promise to read the rest before the day is through. My mind has been dancing in circles since the moment I discovered this invaluable and long lost correspondence.

Lovecraft loomed large over our household when I was growing up. I recall simple games of "Ring a Ring o'Roses" with my siblings being violently disallowed until one of us was clever enough to replace the phrase with, "That Is Not Dead, Which Can Eternal Lie…" Then my father would give us a calm smile and resume sipping his coffee and petting one of his many cats, all the while poring over some moldering gothic novel or another.

Certainly dear old dad kept an obscenely complete library of Lovecraft's work, relaxing only when his own legacy seemed to have indeed matched that of his stylistic hero. And then there is the aforementioned bit that you all know well: that in 1974, less than a year before my birth, King visited Lovecraft in Providence on the latter's deathbed. The two met in person that one and only time. To think of the conversation those two men had…it defies comprehension and has been shrouded in mystery and imagination, until…

But I'm getting ahead of myself again. God, my hands are sweating. Are there towels? I was promised clean white towels. Ah yes, thank you. Continuing on…

Though he was dead before I arrived in this world, Lovecraft and I shared something: Both our mothers were institutionalized when we were very young. It's not something I've ever enjoyed talking about. I've only ever been pressured to speak of her by therapists and girlfriends—but poor old Tabby was locked up during the first trimester of pregnancy. I was the only bit of her to make it beyond those padded walls in the Cumberland County Asylum.

I've been estranged from my father for a long time, and I am his fourth and youngest child by Tabitha. Yet our family attorney recently produced a will that named me his sole heir, for which I am both stunned and awkwardly grateful. Certainly there was no love between us, and his craft as an author will always outshine my own pitiful attempts. Yet here I stand before you, a millionaire at forty-two, with one parent in the grave, and another raving upstate with wide eyes and fingernails torn off at the cuticle.

It's difficult to come to terms with death when machines keep the heart beating. Our distance was great, and my first warning was a series of bizarre phone calls from a buzzing voice that never seemed to construct logical sentences, yet somehow rang in from my father's number. As it turned out, all of these tasteless pranks were conducted after he'd already been hospitalized as a breathing vegetable. But someone as famous as him, despite wealth and resources, was not likely to go unrecognized, and soon the tabloids had their field day. Headlines read, "The King is Dead"—weeks before we'd even begun to consider pulling the plug.

Even if my father had wanted to descend into solitude at his advanced age, it would have been nearly impossible after displaying his face on postage stamps, talk shows, and hundreds of millions of dust jackets. The police, the attorneys, and the medical team were convinced that he would never awaken, and that his soul had passed on. I hope he will find the peace in death that his days on Earth seemed never to provide.

In grave preparation, I visited Tabitha at the asylum. Throughout my life, we've had few conversations that ever amounted to much more than tears and sorrow. In fact, during my first voluntary visit as an adult, she rambled that my father had once been a good man, and had given her *three* beautiful children. That statement alone was enough for me to halt all visitations and cancel the fruit baskets for a decade.

But with SEK for all purposes deceased, it seemed one last attempt to communicate was the thing to do in good conscience, especially since all my older siblings had died young. They say there is nothing worse for a parent than to outlive her children. If Tabby wasn't already nuts by the time I was born, she certainly lost the rest of her marbles as her darlings passed. Car accident, overdose, illness… Each unrelated and emotionally devastating. Of course I feared for my own life after Joe was the last to go. But as you can see, I stand before you with my health, my father's wealth, and the ears of the horror elite.

Where is this all going, you may ask? At that final visit to the asylum, I told Mother that she was soon to be a widow. Her mixture of grief and glee only underscored her unalterable madness. But behind her bloodshot eyes and beneath that shock of white hair came a memory. She urged me to return to the attic of our old family home. It seemed pointless, but her insistence revealed the only brief clarity of conception that I could recall her offering during my entire adult life.

It was a two-hour drive from Bangor down to Stratford, and I questioned my own sanity the whole time. Here I was, the only living member of my immediate family, save my own mother who was institutionalized. Sure, I have many half-siblings younger than myself, but most of us have never spoken, save for the few that came sniffing for funds after the will was read, in order to augment their pitiful, dilettante lifestyles.

As I twisted the key in the rusting lock to the apartment where my father lived as a boy, I couldn't help but note how much the setting seemed to spring from a gothic novel; the clinging weeds and clouded windows were thick with dust and cobwebs. But this is real life and a flashlight can do wonders to banish dark spirits.

Though choked with old air, and what I presume was bat guano, the crawl space was accessible, if quite cramped for one of adult stature. There were many teetering stacks of boxes, which yielded books, maps, and old documents in various states of decomposition. I was frustrated at driving so far, for nothing particularly unusual had turned up on casual investigation.

Then I recalled one of the earliest interviews my father had given as a published author, in which he cited my great-uncle's use of an apple branch to dowse for water. SEK had been inspired to try something similar when he had discovered the Lovecraft book in this same attic, over a decade before my birth. This is also in the Wikipedia article. I have double and triple checked. And shuddered.

Feeling a bit sheepish, I scavenged an old coat hanger, bending it for my needs, and clipping it into shape with the multi-tool I carried. You know the ones they make in the other Portland? Anyway, with the divining rod in one hand and my keychain Maglite in the other, I followed the swaying.

If such things as ley lines do exist, I was standing atop one that day. Mere seconds passed before the dowser snapped to my right, and led me to an obscure attic shelf with a board nailed diagonally across its backing. I swept cluttered junk off the shallow ledge and prised away at the wood, which tore more easily than the hand-hammered nails that had held it secure for so many years.

Behind the wall was a small recess with a brown folder that bore my father's initials. Inside was a bundle of letters that I have brought with me today.

It is unfortunate that only Lovecraft's side of the correspondence is extant. It is most strange since scholars have discovered that he kept so many others that he received throughout his long life. Perhaps these missives from a young author to his hero were inconsequential to a man so long in the tooth and revered the world over. Perhaps… Still, much can be inferred from the surviving posts. I simply cannot help but wonder what became of my father's letters, or why they might have been suppressed or destroyed. What I read to you now makes loss or accident seem ominously unlikely…

[HPL to SEK]

10 Barnes St.,
Providence, R.I.,
Jan. 12, 1974

Dear Mr. Prince,

Please accept my deepest regrets on the passing of the late Ms Pillsbury. I can only imagine grief over the death of a parent who actually contributed to the development of your life in a direct manner. The closest I can come to such emotion is in regards to my auntie, now many years gone. R.I.P.

It seems an insensitive time to delve into criticism of your novel, but I will admit that there is a great promise in your work, along with vistas of potential after certain growth & maturation is reached. Let us set that conversation aside for now, perhaps to resume upon our meeting this Spring. Indeed, I am delighted to read your enthusiastic response at such a prospect. Believe me, there are few minds in this world sensitive to the themes we enjoy, & all too many of them disregard the basic concepts. While Bradbury & Bloch handled my milieu with respect, fools like Derleth attempted to insert Good & Evil into the equation. Thankfully a Cease & Desist from my attorney brought that matter to a rather Neutral & Objective conclusion!

Perhaps it will give you some small pleasure to know that I recently combed my archives & discovered that I possess a certain issue of *Startling Mystery Stories* from 1967 that bears the byline of one SEK. Yes, I knew that your name rang one of the cracked bells in the labyrinthine towers of memory. More than anything, your rapid development over the last few years is staggering, & the hints you have dropped thus far of the progress on your *Jerusalem's Lot* bears all the evidence of that crucial first masterpiece.

But the cosmic coincidence runs deeper. As I sift the cobwebbed strata of remembrance, the image of a merchant seaman comes to mind. Some thirty years prior, I was forced by my publisher to promote a certain paperback with which you are familiar—*The Lurker in the Shadows*. It was in a seaside bookshop on the coast of Maine that this seaman purchased one. I only now recall signing a copy for him. His name was King. I wonder if your ancestral library still contains this memento from a lost age…

I know that I once dismissed this wicked little tome in my initial correspondence, but our deepening confidence inspires me to reveal the grave rarity & potency of its words. It is true that I have allowed "The Whisperer in Darkness" to be reprinted, & the story of Mr. Curwen's unfortunate inhabitation by interplanetary beings spirited throughout the cosmos in consciousness-binding cylinders to be enjoyed as a bone-chilling yarn in myriad collections. But the remaining story cycle has never reared its many blasphemous heads since that single abominable printing. & for good reason.

More than once I have implored you not to postpone your imminent visit, that we may discuss matters that only scribes such as ourselves can fathom. In the interest of piquing your curiosity a touch further, I have included a magnetic audio reel capturing my own voice reading a bit of verse you may recall from the titular tale in TLITS. Do listen at once, my good man. I am certain you will find it efficacious.

Best wishes to you & Tabitha & the children. Stay warm & keep your pen to page. Do not let misery overtake you, or rather, use it to the advantage of your dark fantasy.

With utmost concern & regret,
H P Lovecraft

[HPL to SEK]

10 Barnes St.,
Providence, R.I.,
June 23, 1974

Dear Mr. King,

Please accept my apologies for not writing over these past few months. I have received all your letters, but declining health has brought my correspondence to a veritable halt. Mia has left, & once again I am truly alone. There are factors at work that are vastly beyond my powers, & aversion of the inevitable seems but a childhood dream. I have no belief in the afterlife, & well fear that if we do not meet soon, it will be a regret that you will live with while I inhabit the infinity of oblivion.

It was once my wish to travel to you, & explore the mystic side of Maine with a guide born & bred. Instead I must implore you to come to Providence, & soon. Enclosed here is a date & location. If you will indulge an old gentleman, tell no one any details of this trip. For there are things I would reveal to you that I have not shown another.

You once whispered a dark fondness for my depiction of the cylinders... I know you will attribute this to careless jest, or perhaps the lunacy brought on by my entropic state of being, but I would *show one to you.* Come see for yourself from whence my dreams have sprung. Let us read together from the last crumbling copy of *The Lurker*...

Agh this gnawing in my gut has returned with the vengeance of forty damnable years.

Do come,
& graciously allow your host this one final request?
H P Lovecraft

April 08, 2016
1:23 pm
WWC event Portland, ME

This was the last letter of the bunch. And its implications leave my mind reeling. My nerves these last few weeks have caused me to feel a bit of Tabitha's blood coursing through my veins for the first time in my life. Someone please bring me a refill? My hands are shaking.

My father did make that fateful visit. And shortly after their meeting, Lovecraft's body was buried, forever honored by the famed statue and elegant crypt erected in his honor. Whatever spirit was locked in that mausoleum remains an influential, indeed stifling, cloak upon my family.

The night he returned from Providence is the night I was conceived. Of this there can be no doubt, for my mother's sanity fled within days. Medical reports document that she had convinced herself that the good man she'd married was no more. Her mongrel mutterings of whispers and cylinders and Pluto were more than adequate to institutionalize her for the rest of her days.

Added to this was the literary influence of HPL on my father. "More Lovecraft than Lovecraft," read the blurb on the dust jacket of every subsequent novel he wrote, from *Arkham's Lot* to his latest and yet unpublished final masterpiece of misery, *Betwixt the Mountains of Sadness*. Scholarly analysis has proven that *Carrie* was not only suppressed, but the style that my father had formed up to that point was completely abandoned, irretrievably it seems, from the time of that road trip to Rhode Island.

Until this moment, standing here before you, I have not let my mind connect these dots so fully. May God help me, for letters were not all that I found in that crawl space. There were cylinders of wood and brass that seemed to have been crafted by hands not human. And the machines… And the stained and yellowed fragments of pages from an old pulp paperback…

I am living a cruel nightmare and feel my wits have finally left me. I fear that…does anyone here feel a vibration? Forgive me… what is…? Who would call me in the middle of my speech? This can't be! My father's number?

Excuse me while I take this call. Hello? Yes. I'm listening. Who is... Uhhh...

Uhhhhhggggnnnnn...

...

...

Where am? Ah, it is done. And I feel so...yes.

Pardon me. I must excuse myself. Someone kindly show me to the exit at once.

April 7, 2018
World Weird Con — Houston, TX
8:00pm
Best New Author Award Acceptance

Well I must say this is truly awkward and humbling, to be welcomed back to WWC after such an inauspicious exit those two years back. I have listened to the transcripts and cringed like a nightgaunt whose prey, once released from so lofty a height, missed the chasm entirely. But let us now turn our gaze to the event at hand.

Thank you, my colleagues of the cacodaemoniacal and spinners of the strange. I attest that writing a book of this depth should have taken much more time, yet perhaps genetic instinct surfaced from creative pools so deep and black they were warmed only by vents of vulcanism at my very core.

Indeed, I found a dark delight in crafting my latest, er rather my debut tome, *Cthreelhu*, the first hardbound to bear the byline of Ashton N. King. It seemed no stretch to set Johannesburg as the site of recursive rites and pale pageantry. I speak of course of the backward South African minority that cannot accept the true nature of man. It was on a humanitarian visit and honeymoon that I came to know the place and its shamefully white-hooded dark side. All proceeds from the book will be donated to benevolent charities in the region chosen by my fiercest of brides, and today's award will only bring more attention to our mission.

I look now to the front row and see love and tears in the eyes of my forever one. Oh how I find myself dangerously in love with my mononymous paramour, my child of destiny, Beyoncé. Though I found fortune long ago, a love so true has long eluded me. It seems lifetimes that I have waited for such an angelic being to touch my jaded heart and bring new purpose and hope. Misanthropy be damned! So many years, wasted in bitterness and fear of the unknown.

Together, our combined wealth and notoriety can do wonders for this ailing globe. But I fear it may be too little too late. Feed the poor, we may. Still, there are things I *know*. Things I've *seen*. Call it dwarf or planetoid, Pluto or Yuggoth. It matters not. *They are coming*. Our world is not ready. Please do not misread my words as jest or performance. We must prepare. My next book arrives in the Fall of '19. It shall be no mere flight of fancy—but a survival guide for our species. You must believe me. I have done many wrongs and am all but damned myself. But I have learned to love my fellow man, and would save you all if I can. Thank you, and may your dreams lurk in lands less shadowed than my own.

THE INSECTIVORE

Orrin Grey

There was an old man on our street who ate bugs. Beetles, pill bugs, those things that my mom called locusts but that were actually cicadas. Anything with a crunchy exoskeleton, pretty much.

We'd see him sometimes, picking cicadas off the trees, hanging out under the streetlights at night, scooping up June bugs. On the porch of his house were a dozen of those bug zappers, with their eerie purple-blue glow and their low-key buzzing. They were a buffet line to him. Us kids would stand on the other side of the street and watch as he walked from one to the next, picking out the beetles between two fingers and popping them into his mouth—a delicacy!

His name was Mr. Petrie, and he lived all alone in an old two-story house that had once been white but was now fading to gray. Its windows always looked dark, and the porch was screened with trellises, though nothing grew on them but the occasional brown vine. As kids, he was a figure of equal parts fascination and terror to us, and we'd sometimes dare each other to go up and peer in those darkened windows, but we rarely saw much when we did. Old furniture, dirty dishes. Desks and sideboards stacked deep with books and papers and objects that were indiscernible in the gloom.

Of the old man himself we saw plenty. Though he wasn't exactly social, he came out of his house all the time to wander the streets looking for bugs to eat. He seemed pretty unassuming, old and bald with papery skin over his skull, always wearing old-fashioned brown suits that I imagined smelled like mothballs, though when I was little I never got close enough to find out. I was born early enough and our town was small enough that the paranoia concerning the safety of young children that seems to define our age hadn't yet taken hold, and the parents on our street considered him harmless, "just a crazy old man."

He lived off Social Security or a pension or something, so he didn't have to go to work. He just walked around the streets talking to himself and eating bugs. Sometimes I'd see him hanging around in front of the library or the post office. Sometimes I saw him coming home carrying armfuls of books. He got groceries delivered to him from the Golden Apple Grocery—an older boy with shaggy blonde hair pulled up in a hatchback car and unloaded brown paper bags up to the front door of that old, dark house.

When I was a little older, I was that boy. I had a job behind the video counter at the Golden Apple, and because I had my dad's old Subaru and a driver's license, I got the task of doing the deliveries, hauling bags of groceries to old ladies and the guy who'd lost his leg in Vietnam and other people who couldn't come get them on their own. How exactly Mr. Petrie made that list I couldn't say, since he seemed to still be able to get around just fine, but maybe mental stability was factored in. Anyway, that's how I got to get closer to Mr. Petrie's house—and Mr. Petrie himself—than any of us ever had as kids, and why I got a ringside seat to what ultimately became of him.

***

The first time I delivered groceries to Mr. Petrie, I was still pretty scared of him. The house seemed a little smaller now that I was in high school, but it was no less dark, the faded paint no less peeling, the whole edifice no less grim. The first time I walked up his creaking front steps and pushed the button on the doorbell, my skin crawled.

On the other side of the door I heard a sound, a rustling, like something big moving under a bunch of newspaper. I imagined a giant cockroach, scuttling out from under the refuse that cluttered the house and creeping toward the door. I imagined the door opening inward onto darkness, and rough, segmented legs reaching out to draw me in. I wanted to run, but I knew that Mr. Jorgen at the Golden Apple was expecting me to come back with payment, so I couldn't.

I don't know why I pictured Mr. Petrie as a giant cockroach—I hadn't yet read "The Metamorphosis," and wouldn't until college. You are what you eat, maybe? That's what my mind's eye conjured, anyway, and when I heard something on the other side of the door, and then saw the door begin to fall open, the bags slipped out of my hands and split on the porch, spilling onions and a single orange to go rolling across the uneven boards.

That distracted me, and when I looked back up, there was Mr. Petrie, looking as he had when I was a little kid. Not a monstrous insect, just an old man in a rumpled brown suit. He blinked at me, and at the groceries that lay scattered on the porch, and I began stammering an apology, and offering to help him gather them up, to carry them inside. And that's how I wound up stepping into Mr. Petrie's house for the first time.

Given his dietary predilections, imagining Mr. Petrie as a giant spider, rather than a cockroach, would probably have been more apt, but it didn't occur to me until I was already stepping across his threshold. At that moment, the whole "welcome to my parlor" thing popped into my head, and I called up images of Mr. Petrie standing behind me, his shadow crawling up the wall, sprouting too many arms. But still, as I glanced back, he was just an unassuming, sad-looking old man. Nothing terribly sinister.

His house was dark inside, even in daylight. When I went back out to my car and looked back up at the house, I realized it was because all the windows were strangely recessed, sinking them in wells of shadow. From inside the house, it just looked like the sun was always shining the wrong way, always turning a corner to avoid coming inside.

It wasn't as dark in the house as I'd always imagined when I was a kid, though. There were lamps with dusty shades standing here and there, casting little spheres of light that I'd struggle to call golden but also wouldn't quite just call yellow. From inside, the whole house looked like an antique store or a museum that someone had long since abandoned to neglect. Cobwebs were everywhere except in the main thoroughfares, and all the furniture seemed to be piled with discarded papers and other bric-a-brac.

Then there were the bugs. Wherever I looked there were glass cases filled with insects pinned to boards. Not just beetles, either. The walls were hung with butterflies and moths preserved behind two sheets of glass, their wings still iridescent even in the dull light. Insect collections like the ones you see in the 4H building at the state fair lay on desks and chairs, some of them completely enclosed in glass cases and bearing careful hand-lettered labels, others open to the air in various stages of dissolution or deconstruction. There were bell jars and mason jars, and just about everything made of glass in the place seemed to hold at least one dead bug.

I saw everything out of the corner of my eye—just jumbled impressions of the mosaicked shadow-space that was the interior of Mr. Petrie's house—as I carried groceries in handfuls into the kitchen at the back. I don't really know what I expected to find there—ice cube trays piled full of pill bugs, meals left out to rot—but aside from the same signs of neglect that were everywhere in the house, the kitchen looked no different than any other kitchen I had ever seen.

As Mr. Petrie was walking me back to the front door and pressing some crumpled bills into my hand in payment for the groceries, it struck me for the first time in all my then-seventeen years that Mr. Petrie must have once had a family. As kids we'd sometimes seen an adult son come to visit, parking a silver car along the side of the road and going up to ring the bell on the front door. He didn't come often, and never stayed long, and if Mr. Petrie had any grandchildren, he never brought them by. But once Mr. Petrie must have had a wife, and she and the son must have lived in this house with him, and I realized as I walked back to my car that the house was less the home of a madman than an archaeological relic, the ruins of a life that had crumbled under some unguessed weight.

***

After that, I brought all of Mr. Petrie's groceries through to the kitchen, though I gathered that I was the first delivery boy to ever do so. Soon, I wasn't even coming up to the front door at all, but walking around the house to the screened-in back porch where Mr. Petrie often sat. Over time, he came to tolerate me pretty well, if not exactly *like* me, or maybe he was just lonely. Whatever the case, he began to open up to me, and so I learned his odd story, or some of it.

Mr. Petrie had been a psychic. Not just casually, he did it for a living. He didn't start out that way. First he was an 8th grade social studies teacher, but he started doing psychic readings on the side, and eventually it became his career. He toured the country, gave lectures, went on the radio and the TV, wrote two books. That last part, at least, was true, because I saw them.

So what happened? "I was a fraud," he told me. "Oh, not on purpose. I really believed in what I was doing. But at best I was squandering my gift, using it for frivolous things. 'Is my husband seeing another woman, where did Aunt Ida leave her jewelry?' There wasn't much call for finding bodies or tracking down killers, like you see on TV. It turns out that psychics go over badly in the courtroom. But I had no complaints, until I experienced a *real* vision."

Apparently, this real psychic vision didn't happen all at once. It came to him piecemeal, a bit at a time, over the course of months. When it did finally come together, though, it ruined him, destroyed his life. It concerned the fate of the world after humanity had died out, and the race of coleopterid people who would ultimately take our place. Not kill us off, he was unclear about what did that, just rise to fill our niche. I had to ask him what "coleopterid" meant, and he replied, "Beetles, son. We're going to be replaced by beetles."

So there was the root of his odd mania, anyway, at least according to him. At first, he'd gone about it in different ways. He'd tried to warn people, to take the audience that his psychic abilities had gained him and tell them about what was coming, maybe try to prevent it. To change the course of humanity so that we would never die out, so that *they* would never evolve. Since he didn't know what destroyed us, he focused on what he *did* know: the identity of our successors. He'd gone to the civil authorities, tried to go on TV, but no one listened. "People don't want a genuine psychic revelation," he said. "They want comforting parlor games, the sense that there are invisible threads that hold the world together. They don't want to know that the world is vast and grim and hungry. They know that already."

As he became increasingly obsessed with this glimpse of the future, it gradually destroyed his marriage and his relationship with his children—I learned that, in addition to the son, he also had a grown daughter, who never spoke to him at all anymore—just as it destroyed his credibility and his career. "Ironic," he said, "the one time I can be really sure I saw something was the one time no one would listen."

None of this fully explained his odd dietary habits, however, and it took months of talking with him, bringing him his groceries and sitting with him on the screened-in back porch where June bugs sometimes caught their hooked feet in the wire, before he finally explained it in any way that made even a little sense.

"There's a story by Ray Bradbury, maybe you read it in school—"

"We read *Fahrenheit 451*."

He ignored me. "It's about these people who arrange time travel safaris—to hunt dinosaurs and things, you know? Anyway, they're very careful. They have these floating paths they walk on, and they only kill things that are about to die anyway, so that they don't do anything to change the future. But one time a guy falls off the path, and he kills a butterfly, I think. And then when he goes back to the future, he finds that the world is a completely different place, just because he killed that one butterfly. Do you understand?"

I told him I didn't, but he didn't really seem to hear me. "The thing is," he said, "I think they know that I know. The beetle people. I mean, they must have history books, right, something that tells them about what came before? Beetle archaeologists digging up fossils of man's reign on earth, just as we dig up the dinosaurs. I think they know that I'm onto them, and I think that one of these days one of them will come back in time to kill me, to put a stop to me before I can put a stop to them. I tried warning people, tried stopping them through organized force, but maybe I don't have to. Maybe if I just find that one right butterfly..."

***

I continued taking Mr. Petrie his groceries until I left for college. The summer after my freshman year, I came back home and moved back into my upstairs room, which remained unchanged from how I'd left it, except that my mom had moved her sewing machine in there to get more light. I got another job at the Golden Apple Grocery, though someone new was standing behind the video counter looking bored and helping old ladies reach movies off the top shelf, so I ended up unloading trucks as they came in.

There was a new kid doing the deliveries—he drove a pickup, and had hair that fell down over his eyes. I asked the manager about Mr. Petrie, and he said that after I left the old man stopped taking his deliveries the old way. He still phoned in the orders every week, but now he mailed a check, and the delivery kid just left his bags on the front porch.

After I'd been back home for three weeks, I tried going to see Mr. Petrie. For old time's sake, I guess, or maybe because I was curious, or because I felt sorry for him. Distance from my childhood and from the town had taught me that Mr. Petrie was probably schizophrenic or something, probably in need of better care than he had ever gotten.

When I approached the house, it was as dark as ever, the paint now completely faded to gray and flaking off in swaths. The lawn needed mowing. Back when I was a kid Mr. Petrie had always mowed it with an ancient push-mower, and once I started taking his groceries to him I would bring our newer mower up and cut the grass once every couple of weeks. It didn't look like anyone had gotten to it since I'd been gone, and I felt a stab of guilt at going away without giving the old man a second thought. There were dandelions sprouting everywhere, growing almost obscenely long, their heads weighted down with seeds. Other than that the house looked just as I remembered it, except that the bug zappers were gone from the porch.

I rang the bell and peered in, but could see nothing through the gloom inside. There didn't appear to be any lights on beyond the windows that I could see, and while I occasionally thought I detected movement in the dimness, I could never be sure.

I walked around to the screened-in back porch. The back yard was in even worse repair than the front. Grass grew up past my knees, and an old birdbath just barely poked above the verge, with only a bit of brown water standing in the center of it. The porch was empty, the metal chairs on which Mr. Petrie normally sat just crouching there in the gloom. The back door was locked, which I knew could only be accomplished with a hook-and-eye on the inside. So if Mr. Petrie wasn't home, he must have gone out the front.

I went by a couple more times over the next few weeks, and the thought occurred to me that maybe Mr. Petrie had died while I was away—he must have been getting on in years, since he had been an old man in my memory for as long as I had been alive. I wondered how I would know if he had. Who would I ask? Aside from me, who in town really knew him? I asked

Mr. Jorgen at the Golden Apple and he told me that the phone calls still came in every week, regular as clockwork, but when I asked my mom when the last time she'd seen Mr. Petrie was, she couldn't recall.

If not for that mystery, I might not have been paying close enough attention to see what happened next. I had my own life now, after all, my own concerns. I'd met a girl in my freshman ethics class—with straight brown hair down her back, and cute freckles across her shoulders and cheeks—and I spent a lot of time on the phone with her that summer, since she'd gone back home too, a couple of states away. But Mr. Petrie's absence made me wonder, and wondering made me watchful. I could see just a corner of his house out of my bedroom window, and at night, when I was waiting to go to sleep, my arms sore from unloading boxes, I would look out that window at the dark shape of his house past the streetlights.

That's why I saw it, a flash of purple-blue light, like one of Mr. Petrie's bug zappers going off. But they were gone, all of them missing from their hooks on the porch, and the flash had seemed too bright for that anyway. It was enough to drag me out of my bed—where sleep was hard in coming, the summer night sticky, my parents, as always, too cheap to run the window units after dark. I pulled on my shoes and crept downstairs, not turning on any lights, not waking anyone, and out the door and onto the street. I passed under the streetlights and beneath the trees where as a kid I had seen Mr. Petrie eating bugs. I went up the front steps of his darkened house, but not onto the porch.

I don't know what made me hesitate. Why I didn't just ring the doorbell—besides that it was two in the morning—and instead slipped around the side of the house. I felt like a kid again, that thrill up your spine that comes with trespassing, with transgressing. I felt like I was on a dare, creeping up to peer into Mr. Petrie's darkened windows.

There was a glow coming from the back of the house, and my first thought was that Mr. Petrie had moved all his bug zappers to the screened-in back porch, though what good they were going to do back there I couldn't say. But no, the glow wasn't coming from bug zappers. It was brighter, and it emanated from a single source.

In that unearthly light, I saw Mr. Petrie. He knelt on the all-weather carpet next to his favorite chair, his hands held up in some kind of supplication, his mouth moving constantly, though I couldn't hear any words coming out. He looked like he'd aged ten years in the few months it had been since I saw him last, the strange violet light mottling his complexion, making his already papery skin look almost translucent.

Before him stood what I initially took to be a man in a suit of armor, but there was something wrong about that. The shape was a little off, the plates too shiny. The glow was coming from this figure, somehow. Radiating from it like a cave fungus, oozing out from beneath the plates of its armor, from the gap between the horns that sprouted from its head. Below the arms, two smaller, supplementary arms jutted, and between them they held a ball of squirming purple-blue light. We'd learned about plasma in my freshman science class—the boiling, liquid energy of which the sun is made—and aside from the color this was exactly how I'd pictured it.

It was the arms that made the figure make sense—the horns sprouting from the helmet not horns at all but mandibles, working gently back and forth, the glowing orifice below a nest of moving mouth-parts, the armor a carapace from which lace-delicate wings might unfurl.

In that final moment, I think Mr. Petrie saw me. He looked over, his eyes black in the strange light, and he seemed like he was about to speak to me, but then the ball of energy that the armored figure held leapt from its hands, arced through the space of the porch and touched Mr. Petrie. For a moment he was made translucent by the light, his skeleton visible through his parchment flesh, and then the whole scene exploded in a flash that left miniature purple suns dancing in my vision.

Neighbors reported seeing a bright light in the back of Mr. Petrie's house, and when the sheriff broke in they found nothing of Mr. Petrie or the thing that had killed him except a singed spot on the carpet and a pile of black ash. Chalk another one up to those reports of unexplainable spontaneous human combustion. I looked it up later, and found that there have been over 200 unverified reports over the years. That's something to think about, late at night.

I was gone before the sheriff arrived, and no one ever reported seeing me near the house. No one asked me about what had happened, and I never told. Mr. Petrie's own life lessons had taught me the reward that came with sharing that kind of revelation.

Here's what I wonder, though: If old Mr. Petrie really was some kind of real-deal psychic, could he have conjured up the specter of his own demise from nothing more than his own fear? Would he have had the power to create the thing that he believed was one day going to kill him, a kind of psychic suicide? And do I find that thought more or less distressing than a beetle assassin come back from the future to slay him with a lightning bolt?

THE BODY SHOP

Richard Lee Byers

One man is black, good-looking, and lanky, the other, white, homely, and squat like a bulldog. Yet in the ways that matter, they look alike, both dressed in urban camouflage, both carrying M4 rifles they may have scavenged from the corpses of Army Rangers, and both still holding on to anger. I see that last in the way they carry themselves.

In other words, not my typical customers, who tend to be ragged, hungry, and desperate. Some are downright twitchy.

So right away, I wonder. But I have a successful business and the comforts it provides in a time when most people live like savages or rats, and I keep it going by trying to accommodate anybody who walks in the door. So I pull the buds out of my ears—I give good value for iPods and such if they have plenty of New Country on them—smile, and stand up to greet the newcomers.

"Clark Davis," I say, extending my hand.

The black man takes it in a strong grip. "Bill Pryce. My friend is Paulie Larocca."

Larocca looks around the front of the store. It was a tattoo and piercing parlor before the aliens came, and the outer area still is, give or take. "You've got electricity," he says, envy in his voice.

"I have a generator," I reply, "and I accept gasoline as payment. So that's one way we might be able to do business. If you want to tell me how I can help you?"

"I'm not sure," says Pryce. "I mean, obviously, we've heard *something* about what you do, or we wouldn't be here. But I don't know if what we've heard is exaggerated or..." He shrugs.

"And you don't want to put yourself in my hands until you do know," I say. "I'd feel the same way. I'll tell you what. Why don't I give you the tour? That way, you'll see the full range of services I have to offer."

Pryce nods. "That sounds all right."

"Then we can start right here." I wave my hand at the walls. Before the invasion, they were hung with flash and photos of work I'd done on customers. They still are. But not the same flash or the same photos.

"I guess you understand the basics," I continue as they move in for a closer look. "Since the invasion, some people have changed. Sometimes the monsters take them and experiment on them. Other times, the changes just happen. It could be poison in the air or water. Or maybe the king alien, the god that's moved into—"

"It's not a god!" Larocca snaps.

It's possible he hasn't yet glimpsed it in his dreams. Anyway, why argue? "Sorry. Or maybe the thing living in the Macmillan Center affects the city just by being here. No matter why it happens, the fact is, once a person is altered, the aliens are less likely to attack him."

Pryce grunts. "Less likely."

"There are no guarantees," I answer. "But if somebody wants to play the odds, that's where I come in. Maybe you've heard about the dead rising or seen some of them yourself? Then take a look at this."

The imitation zombie in the photo has a gray cast to her skin, shadowing under her eyes and cheekbones, and what look like little rotten patches spotting her face like acne. The customer heightened the illusion with a slack mouth and empty stare.

"Yuck," Larocca says.

I smile. "I'll take that as a compliment. But really, this is only the most basic kind of disguise. If the customer is willing to take the next step, we can do something like this." I point to a different photo.

Larocca winces. "Her nose!"

"And her left ear, part of her upper lip, and the last digit of her left pinkie. Obviously, I don't take anything the person can't manage without, but short of that, the more the customer is willing to part with, the more convincing the results."

It's Pryce's turn to point. "But these are better still?"

He's indicating the picture of a shirtless middle-aged man. I inked the suggestion of blue scales into his skin, cut a long horizontal scar onto his chin, and melon-balled pieces of flesh out of his chest so the hollows march down from shoulders to waist like a double row of buttons. He looks like his body was trying to develop the second mouth and extra eyes of a Subway Howler, but the change didn't take.

"Yes," I say. "The aliens are less likely to bother a zombie than they are a living person, but less likely still to mess with a person who looks like his body is trying to mutate into one of their own kind. I have to warn you, though, there's no way to get to any version of this without a fair amount of cutting and shaping."

"But afterward," says Pryce, "it's at least near-perfect protection?"

"Sure," I say, "from a block away. Closer than that, though, and all these options start to run up against the same limitations. The creature may recognize the tattooing or scarification for what it is. Or maybe its sense of smell comes into play. Who knows? But if you stick to the parts of the city where there aren't as many of them—which is what smart people do anyway, right?—it will definitely improve your chances."

"But what if you have no choice but to get up close?" asks Pryce. "Is there anything more?"

I eye him for a moment but don't pick up on any clues to what he's got in mind. I tell myself it's none of my business anyway.

"There's more," I say. "Follow me."

We push through the beaded curtain that separates the front room from the next one. I flip on the fluorescent lights, and Larocca mutters, "Shit!" He isn't the first. It's a pretty good collection if I do say so myself.

Writhing slowly, a severed tentacle floats in an aquarium. Across from it, the head of a Laughing Cyclops grins from its own jar of alcohol. I've opened the torso of a Black Kid and sawed away the tangled ribs to expose the glistening organs that crowd the chest cavity.

The specimens are impressive, but their only purpose is to convince people I really can deliver the goods. This is all material that I suspect—it's hard to tell for sure—has passed its Sell By date. The real merchandise is in the freezers.

"This is the next level," I say. "Instead of giving you fake monster parts, I give you real ones. Real spurs on the backs of your legs. Real Cold Moth wings attached to your shoulder blades. A real set of Blind Dog feelers on your face. The face is always the best if you can stand it. Take a look at these." I gesture to the photos on the wall.

I think the work on display in the front room is pretty darn convincing. But when a person lays eyes on what I can do with real parts, he sees the difference. And occasionally throws up in his mouth a little.

Or resists believing the pictures of the human form blended with things from beyond can possibly be real. "These are fakes, too," Larocca says. "Just better fakes. A real doctor couldn't graft alien body parts onto a human. The human's system would reject them. And this guy—"

"Is only a tattoo artist," I finish for him. "Except, not anymore. Would you believe, the aliens themselves taught me how to do this."

"Convince us," says Pryce.

"Okay. Do you know that during the first hours of the invasion, the Burning Flyers snatched up a lot of people and carried them away?"

Pryce nods. "They nearly got me."

"Well, they did get me and took me to one of those domes that popped up all over downtown like mushrooms. Inside was a kind of creature most people still haven't seen. Like a lot of the invaders, they're hard to describe. But if you imagine smoke crossed with a pile of maggots, that's in the ballpark."

"Why did they take you?" asks Pryce.

"They wanted information," I say. "Not that I knew anything that mattered. But like you saw, they were grabbing people at random. Anyway, the important thing is that when they look into your head, it's a two-way street. You see what's in their minds, too."

Larocca sneers. "Bullshit. They wouldn't let a human know their secrets."

"It's not a problem," I reply, "if they kill the human when they're done. And as far as I know, I'm the only person who ever went through it and got away afterward."

"How?" asks Pryce.

"Since it was the first night, America still had a military. Bombs fell on the base and blew it apart. The explosions killed the monsters and all the other prisoners, too, but I got lucky and survived."

"And came away with the knowledge to do what you do?"

"At first I didn't know I had it. I couldn't understand most of what I'd taken in and didn't want to try. I was pretty sure that if I didn't forget it, it would drive me nuts. But over time, the medical knowhow started making sense. Maybe it piggybacked on the skills I already had."

"Right," drawls Larocca, "because really, what's the difference between a tattoo artist and a doctor?"

Pryce gives his friend a look that tells him to zip it, then turns his attention back on me. "And after that you started disguising people?"

"Well, not for a while. It took me about a month to accept that the monsters really had won and we lost. Then the idea had to come to me. Then I needed tools, medicine, and parts. I was able to dig the tools and drugs out of the same bombed-out base where I'd been a prisoner. As for the organs, you've probably noticed that these days, the aliens sometimes fight each other. And luckily, don't always bother to haul the bodies away afterward."

"All right," says Pryce, "I believe you. Just how effective is this?"

"I already said there are no guarantees. But one customer told me he turned a corner, came face to face with a Cyclops, and it ignored him. Another was sneaking along in the dark, stepped in a patch of Leopard Mold, and it didn't poof out any spores. You wouldn't think that stuff is even aware, but apparently it is."

Pryce smiles. It's a cold smile. "Then this is what I need."

"Believe me," I reply, "if we can make a deal, I'll be happy to sell it to you. But first I have to warn you about the downside."

He shakes his head. "That isn't necessary."

"Yeah, it is. Early on, I had a couple dissatisfied customers come back here screaming that they hadn't understood what could happen. I don't need that. These days, I spell everything out."

Pryce shrugs. "If it will make you feel better."

"First off, you'll almost certainly get to where you can't stand looking in a mirror."

"I don't do a lot of that anyway."

"Fair enough, but other people may not be able to tolerate looking at you, either. Even if they care about you. Even if you keep the deformity covered up most of the time. Even if they're carrying similar grafts themselves. I transplanted pieces of Window Crab shell onto the faces of a father, mother, and their little son and daughter. You never saw a family that loved each other more. But when I ran into the dad later, he told me they'd all gone their separate ways. They just couldn't bear to be around one another anymore."

"Still not a problem."

"Okay. But this could be. Maybe you know that after the monsters change the outside of a person, he sometimes changes on the inside, too, until he basically stops being a person. Well, what I do is more or less what they do. For a different reason, and without any deliberate fooling with the customer's brain, but still, once or twice my work has pushed people down the same slide."

"You mean once or twice that you know of," Larocca says. "In the long run, maybe it happens to everybody."

"Could be," I say. "But you know the saying: 'In the long run, we're all dead.' And when has that ever been truer than now?"

"He's got you there," says Pryce. "And I know you don't like any part of this, but I believe what Mr. Davis is telling us. So let's move ahead." His eyes shift back to me. "Have you read me the entire warning label?"

"Pretty much," I say, "and if it didn't scare you away, we can start negotiating. What do you have to offer?"

"Freedom," Pryce replies.

I blink. "What, now?"

"You're wrong about the Army," he says. "There's some of it left outside the cities, and it coordinates with the resisters inside."

I hold up my hand. "Stop. I don't need to know about this. I don't want to know it. I do what I do to take care of myself, and that's that. Tell me if you've got something real to trade."

"Don't you want the human race to rise up and defeat the invaders?"

"That sounds like a no." I sigh. "Look, let's say that whatever your little scheme is, thanks to the disguise, it works, and you kill a hundred aliens. Hooray for you. Naturally, everybody would be happy to see it. But it wouldn't change a thing. There are just too many of them."

"But we're not after them," says Pryce. "The Army gave me a canister of what's supposed to be the deadliest nerve gas ever invented. I mean to carry it into the Macmillan Center and turn it loose on the king alien. There are scientists who think that if you kill it, its servant creatures will die, too. Or at least their social organization will fall apart."

Larocca gives me a leer. "That should make sense to you. You're the one who thinks it's a god."

"You're out of your minds," I say. "The military already tried to kill the king aliens. They tried with everything they had."

Pryce shakes his head. "Not this gas. Not from up close when the alien's not ready for it. Or so my contact tells me."

"Then your contact's full of shit. And just to be clear, I don't care if you come back here with every luxury item left in the world. I am not going to do anything that might draw the king's attention." I imagine the huge eye from my dreams rolling toward me, the double pupils dilating. I shudder.

"Whatever else the gas does," Pryce tells me, his tone gentle, "it will kill me instantly. So there won't be any way for the creature to know you were involved."

"Really?" I say. "What if it already knows who disguises people as monsters, but up until now, it hasn't cared? What if you being dead doesn't stop it from pulling information out of your brain? What if it can see through time like you and I see across space and it backtracks you to my shop?"

Larocca makes a spitting noise. "You're letting your imagination go crazy."

"It's dangerous to assume that these things have human limitations," I reply. "If the last year hasn't taught you that, then you're the one who's crazy."

With one sure, sudden motion, he points his M4 at me. I freeze.

"Let's cut through the crap," he says. "Bill's right. I don't like any part of this. But if he says this is the plan, then I guess it is. Meaning, if you don't operate on him, I'll shoot you. Simple as that."

I look to Pryce. "Is it?" I ask. "As simple as that?"

He looks regretful but not enough to matter. "I didn't want it to go down this way. I hoped you would want to help. But yes, if we have to do it like this, we will."

"If you kill me, that's the end of your stupid plan. Nobody else can perform the surgery."

"But if you refuse, what's the difference?"

"None to you, maybe. But other people will come here. Not with some insane plot but because they need my help to survive for a little while longer. Are you going to take that away from them?"

Larocca laughs. "A minute ago, it was all about what's good for him. Now all of a sudden he's a saint."

Pryce ignores that to stay focused on me. "I am willing to let those few people suffer," he says, "just like I'm willing for you to die if you won't cooperate. It's not right or fair, but Paulie and I are fighting for the future of the whole human race. Once we win here—"

"But you won't!" I explode. "Hell, forget the god itself. Have you seen the Macmillan Center? It's covered in barnacles, and it's got monsters wandering in and out of it all the time. If just one of them gets suspicious, you're toast."

Pryce smiles. "That sounds like a reason for you to do your best work. Because the way you live through this is if you get me to the target and then the gas turns out to be everything it's cracked up to be."

"Shit," I say.

Pryce claps me on the shoulder. "You'll see, you're doing the right thing. And afterward, nobody has to know we twisted your arm. You'll go down in history as a hero."

"Let's just get it over with," I answer.

The preparations are pretty straightforward. I take the parts I'm going to use out of the freezer to thaw. When they're nearly ready, I have Pryce strip, and then we both wash at the bathroom sink. It probably doesn't get us perfectly clean, but the aliens' sterilizing spray kills whatever germs the soap and water miss. I park Larocca in the corner, and he hunkers down to glower and point his rifle in my general direction.

He keeps it pointed, too, through the administration of the anesthesia and the hours of cutting, grafting, and laser-splicing—I call the beam a laser but it may be something else—that follow. The gun makes it that much harder to keep my hands steady.

I manage, though, and when the job is done, I give Pryce the shot that will wake him up, pull down my surgical mask, and peel off my latex gloves. My hands tingle and ache. I go back into the bathroom, bend down to the faucet, and gulp my thirst away.

Behind me, Larocca yells, "Hey! Hey! Talk to me, Davis! Tell me how it went!"

I wipe my mouth with the back of my hand. "Look for yourself. And ask him. He'll wake up in a second."

Larocca moves to the surgical table. Then his mouth pulls into a grimace. He already had some idea of what I was doing. But watching from across the room isn't the same as seeing the results up close.

Pryce's human eyes flutter open. Larocca tries to hide his revulsion but isn't fast enough.

"I guess our friend did a good job," Pryce croaks.

I bring him some water and hold the glass while he sips through a straw. "How do you feel?" I ask.

"Not too bad."

"The anesthesia's still wearing off. There'll be more pain later. But I can give you pills."

"Thanks." He tries to sit up, and I help him. "Let me see what's got Paulie's so shaken up that he can't look at me straight on."

"You should brace yourself." I bring him a hand mirror.

Give him credit. Unlike Larocca, he doesn't flinch even though it's his own face he's looking at and even though I've given him what he asked for: my best work ever.

Mottled black and yellow like a bruise, oily hide covers his head and neck completely, and, together with the lack of external ears, the three extra eyes bulging from the forehead, and the serrated mandibles framing his mouth, nearly erases any trace of humanity. Thanks to the implants, even the shape of the skull is different.

The same slimy new skin covers his shoulders, from which flop the flabby tubes a Barnacle Man uses to connect itself to the inside of its shell. From there, the hide runs downward to make sleeves for his arms and mittens for the hands that now resemble flippers with thumbs.

"It's perfect," says Pryce. His voice is almost steady. "How could the monsters not believe I've turned into one of them, physically and mentally both."

"Glad you like it," I say. Waiting, hoping the resistance fighters can't tell that I am, I move to the instrument stand and start cleaning up.

Meanwhile, Pryce looks to Larocca. "Can you grab my clothes? Davis, leave that. Just pack a bag. We're moving out as soon as I feel up to it."

"What?" I say.

"You're coming with us," he tells me.

"That wasn't the deal!"

"I know, and I'm sorry. But you said it yourself. Nobody else in the world knows how to do what you do, and the human race needs you to do it over and over again until all the aliens are dead."

"Then the human race is out of luck."

Larocca hands Pryce a ball of tangled clothing, then aims his M4 at me. "I don't believe you," he says. "Bill's about to give his life for the cause. You just need to work for it while the rest of us do everything we can to keep your safe. So get with the program, you cowardly son of a bitch!"

For another moment, I wonder if I really will have to. Then Pryce jerks, sways, and makes a retching sound.

Larocca turns back toward his friend. "What's wrong?" he asks.

Pryce's mouth moves, but nothing comes out except drool.

Larocca looks back at me. "What's happening?"

I could tell him. It gets back to what I said before, about how you shouldn't make assumptions about an alien, even one of the lesser monsters, based on what's true for human beings.

A Barnacle Creature doesn't have a brain. But it has strings of nervous tissue running through its skin that serve the same purpose.

Normally, I lobotomize the brain web when grafting Barnacle-Man hide, and lobotomized or not, I don't connect it to a customer's own nervous system. But Pryce isn't really a customer.

Of course, I don't want to tell Larocca any of this, and Pryce—or the thing that used to be Pryce—saves me the trouble of lying. By throwing its arms around Larocca and pulling him in close.

Larocca shrieks and tries to get his rifle pointed at the Pryce-thing. But before he can, the hybrid's scissoring mandibles find his neck and puncture the left carotid artery. Blood spurts in an arc.

By then, I'm scrambling for the other M4, the one Pryce carried into the operating room. The creature either recognizes the danger or just wants to make sure I don't escape. Anyway, it shoves Larocca away, jumps up, and lunges after me.

I snatch up the rifle and lurch around. The Pryce-thing is nearly on top of me, but not quite. I fire and fire until it falls down, then shoot it three times more.

Afterward, my ears ringing, gasping like I've run a mile, I realize my half-assed plan worked better than I had any right to expect. Yet what I mainly feel is ashamed.

That's stupid, though. Because while there may be a tomorrow, there won't be a day after tomorrow. And if you let the fools who think there can be call the shots, they'll rob you of the last little piece of life that you have left.

ON A KANSAS PLAIN

Michael J. Martinez

I've never been to Kansas.

In fact, this is the last place I thought I'd end up visiting. Yet here I am, heading north on a two-lane highway out of what passed for "town," surrounded by fallow fields and cold blue skies and a whole lot of nothing.

But this is where the trail led. If I'm right, I finally found Jim.

Once upon a time, James Williamson was probably one of the best equity traders out there. He had an almost preternatural sense of the market. His ability to spot trends and put two and two together made him a legend, and a rich one at that. And he leveraged it well. He married our mutual college friend, Jane Esperance, an old-money New Englander. They lived large on the Upper East Side. They gave to the right charities, went to the right parties.

I don't run in the same circles, of course; reporters rarely do, even if they work for the big papers like me. We get all the political pull with, like, 1% of the income.

Anyway, Jim wanted to have kids, but a decade into the marriage, it just didn't seem to be happening. When we got together for drinks—something that happened less frequently as time went on—I didn't pry, but I could see there was stuff weighing on him. The last time I saw him, right before the incident, he confided that his marriage was on the rocks.

Then the incident happened. Jim was caught on the wrong end of a huge trade, and all his hedges blew up too. It was a one-in-a-million thing, apparently, but the odds weren't with him. By the time it was done, he'd lost $3 billion of the company's money, and a decent chunk of his own, too.

He disappeared that night. Nobody's seen him in three years.

Four months ago, Jane asked me to take leave from the paper and try to find him, something I'd already been doing in my limited down-time; the stipend she offered made it easy to say yes. Jane handed over all his papers and his computer, all left behind the night he took off. It took some digging, but it turned out he set up a tiny little shell company in Bermuda—you can do that without actually going there—and bought a scrap of land out in Kansas about four months before the incident. It was the only thing he had left besides about $50,000 in cash, withdrawn the day after the incident.

With nothing else to go on, I booked a flight, rented a car…and here I am, turning off the highway onto a little dirt road, past no more than four "NO TRESPASSING" signs, going up to a rickety old trailer that looks as though a stiff breeze could send it tumbling. The pickup next to it—imagine Jim in a pickup!—looks just as decrepit.

I park the rental about ten yards from the place, where the road ends and wild grasses take over. I can see where the grass flattened out into scrub, but it feels like I'd be driving on someone's lawn, if you can call that straw patch of crap a lawn.

"Don't move."

I nearly jump out of my skin at the voice behind me, which is followed by a metallic click. You know the click, the one you hear in the movies when someone cocks a gun. And what do you know, it sounds exactly like the movies.

"It's me, Jim. It's Steve," I say, reflexively raising my hands. I don't turn around yet. I don't know if I should.

"Maybe, maybe not," Jim says. "You *look* like Steve. How do I know it's you?"

This is the point where I start getting nervous. Is this what the deep end looks like? "Jim, we went to school together. You majored in econ, I majored in English. We pledged Alpha Xi together. Roomed for a year in

Jenkins Hall. You had the top bunk."

"Asshole," he says. It's not an epithet, more like a leading statement.

"Twenty-eight consecutive turns," I say, remembering that one epic drinking game we had. "That night our freshman year. I was sick for four days."

I can practically hear him relax behind me. "All right. Get inside. It's cold out here."

With that he trudges right past me toward the trailer. I can't see his face, but I can see the rest of him has totally gone to seed. No more Brooks Brothers here. His hair's a long, matted mess, and he looks like he's got a good bushy beard now. His clothes are pure hick, faded Wal-Mart jeans and flannel. The boots look sturdy, though.

The rifle—the one now on his shoulder—looks pristine.

"Where'd you come from?" I venture as we approach the door. It's got six locks on it. His keys jangle as he methodically unlocks each one, top to bottom. I can see his windows are barred from the inside, too.

"Brush," he says. "Saw your car make the turn off the main road. Good sightlines here."

Sightlines? I'm not sure exactly when Jim turned into a survivalist nutcase, but seems like the transformation is pretty far along. I slip my hand into my jacket and feel the cold lump there—my backup, just in case. Given that my worries thus far have been spot on...well, I don't want to think about it.

The smell of rot and mildew hits me as the door opens. I knew from past history that Jim could be a bit of a slob, but it seemed Jane cured him of that, once upon a time. Not so much, now. I follow Jim in and find my worst fears keep getting confirmed.

The living room is some kind of office now. There's a desk—a old door held up by cinder blocks—and it's covered in papers and books and drawings. There's a computer there, too. The walls are covered in maps and charts—maps of New York and New England, and oceanic maps as well. Lines and notes are scribbled here and there, and I can't even read the scrawl. The sofa's ratty as hell, and so is the desk chair. The alleged coffee table is some two-by-fours and more cinderblocks. Everything is covered in more books, more paper, more scribbling.

"It ain't much, but it's home," Jim says dully. I hear the click of the locks being applied again and try not to feel like a caged animal. "You want something to drink?"

"No, thanks," I say. Honestly, I wouldn't trust anything in this pit to be healthy. "So...wow. Been a while."

I turn to him and finally catch his face. He's lost weight—it was hard to tell under his mountain man clothes, but his face is drawn and gaunt, hollowed at the cheeks, dark rings under the eyes. The beard is just as unkempt as his hair. But his eyes...they shine. He's in there somewhere. Or...well, is that something else I'm seeing? Fear? Predation? Both?

"Didn't think anybody'd find me," he says, propping the rifle up by the door. He shucks his flannel jacket and I see he's got a pistol in one of those shoulder rigs. Christ. He goes off to the kitchen and I hear him grab something out of the fridge, followed by the familiar hiss-pop of a can. "Thought I squared everything before I left."

He waves me to the one open spot on the couch and I gingerly sit on the edge, trying to avoid a particularly nasty stain. "Pretty close," I allow, taking the conversation just as gingerly. "The Bermuda company registry."

Jim plops into the desk chair and smiles a particularly feral smile. "Aw, shit. I thought I took care of that. Well, hell. When you're on the run, you're bound to forget something."

"On the run?" I ask. "From the Feds? For that trade that blew up?"

He barks out a short, bitter laugh. "You know in the movies where they say, 'You wouldn't believe me if I told you?'" he says, followed by a swig of beer. "It's like that."

Maybe he's right; I can already see there's a pattern to the paper detritus strewn around this crappy little trailer, and it's making me even more nervous. "So what is it, then? You skim money off the firm or something? You kill somebody?" I kind of regret that last bit. I'd hate for him to get ideas. Then it occurs to me that I'm thinking this way about one of my oldest friends.

Naturally, I've managed to piss him off. "Of course not! And I didn't do a damn thing to the firm!" he snaps, pointing the can at me for emphasis. "That whole trade was pristine. I said it then, and I'll say it now. That was a goddamn setup."

"Hey, I'm no finance whiz, but isn't it a bit over the top to stick a Wall Street bank with a $3 billion loss just to screw someone over?" I ask, as gently as possible. "I mean, there's compliance systems. Tracking. Someone would be able to trace it back."

Jim just smiles and shakes his head sadly. "You'd think. But they made it happen."

"Who?"

Jim stares off into space for several moments. The light in his eyes dies out as his mind retreats. Then he snaps back and looks me over. Weighing me. It's disconcerting as hell. "You want to know what really happened?" He doesn't even let me say yes. "Fine. Now that you found me, I'm gonna have to move on anyway, so might as well get it off my chest. Besides, I got most of it figured out anyway."

Oh, boy. This is going to be some kind of inspired conspiracy schtick. Jim doesn't disappoint.

"You ever hear of the Church of the Returning King?" he asks.

I nod slowly. "Yeah, I think so. Kind of a small little religious thing. Fair number of rich guys and socialites in the city. Lots of philanthropy. There was kind of stink a few years back about something, though. Can't quite remember what."

Jim reaches back and pulls out a couple of printouts from a random stack on his desk and hands them to me. The headline on the first one reads: "Church hit with ritual allegations." The next: "The Church of Kink?" The third: "Former CRK member recounts abuse."

"So the CRK was big on the Upper East Side, you know? Jane's family had been members a long time, and I figured, okay, that's nice. I figured it was a little like Scientology, though. Kind of weird but basically harmless," Jim says. "I went to some of their services, the ones open to the public. Talked about devotion to the Returning King, how he'd come again to rule the world and remake it in his image. Honestly, sounded like an amped-up version of the Protestants. Hell, most of the folks at the services *looked* like Protestants."

Jim laughs at his own joke as I set the papers down gently. "And?" I ask.

He takes another swig of beer. "Well, it ain't like that," he says. "I mean, I didn't even know Jane was one of the Church leaders until I got engaged, and I had known her for years. Really took me by surprise. She was never one to keep secrets, or so I thought. But here she is, talking about the Returning King in services."

He pauses a moment and gets a little lost in his head again. I wait until he winds back up. "Anyway, she says it'd mean a lot to her if I got involved, so I did. There was some one-on-one counseling, some reading. Pretty innocuous. I mean, they were rigorous and all about services and stuff, but I figured that's where Jane got her discipline from, you know? She was always so focused…."

His voice trails off. I can tell I'm losing him again. Already. "Okay, so were the stories true, then? Kink? Abuse?"

He downs the rest of his beer and crumples the can in his hands in a swift motion that makes me jump again. "Worse," he growls. "They got this philanthropy going, they do all these good works, they come off as just some kind of Protestant sect, like a weird cross between Hollywood liberals and neocon religious freaks. But, you know, I'm supporting Jane, so I go and do the study and a couple years after we get married, I get baptized. In blood."

And this is where we start to head off the rails. "Blood?" I ask.

"Yes, blood. Real human blood," he says. "The priest there, he cuts himself and just smears some kind of sign on my forehead. Wasn't a cross, I can tell you that much, but it smeared pretty bad so I couldn't see what it was. I have some ideas, though." He reaches forward and pulls another sheet of paper from a stack on the coffee table. It's a picture of a star with what looks like an eye inside. "I think it was that."

I stare at the image, dumbfounded. I mean, what do you say to that? "What is it?"

"Can't even speak the words, man," Jim says quietly. "It's bad, though. See, I thought this whole Returning King thing was Jesus Christ, you know? I mean, they never actually said the name, but they had the death and resurrection, the second coming, all of it. Judgment. The chosen ones. Getting humanity ready for the Return."

"But it wasn't Christ?"

"Nope," Jim says, and I swear there's a hint of satisfaction in his voice, like this is the result of all his hard work since losing his marbles. "It's something worse. Far worse."

"Well, this does look a little like a pentagram," I allow. I really kind of want to wrap this up at this point and just get out of here. "So they were Satanists?

Jim barks out a laugh. "You're kidding me, right? Please. Satanists are Saturday morning cartoons compared to these guys!!" He calms down, leans forward and stares me right in the eye. It's creepy as hell. "This shit's older than Satan. Older than Christ. Older than the planet. And it's coming back."

I open my mouth to speak, but the words just aren't coming. He leans back and smiles at me again.

"Steve, Steve, Steve...I knew you wouldn't get it," he says. It sounds menacing, but honestly, I'm pretty well freaked out by now, so who's to say? "There's stuff in the world that you just don't hear about. The Church, the other groups that are out there, they make sure you don't hear about it." He gestures around the room. "It's taken me years and years to collect all this. They're in government. Business. Entertainment. They're making us good and fat and happy and clueless every day goes by. We're lambs to the slaughter, Steve."

I look around again. Years and years of work. He's been doing this conspiracy thing since before his life went to crap. "So what happens, then?" I ask. I try not to make it sound like a challenge, but it comes out that way. "Who's coming back? Space aliens?"

I thought this might make him laugh, but his eyes widen and he grows really disturbingly intense about it. "Steve, it's already here. On Earth. The Church, they know where it is. They sacrifice to it." He must've caught a look on my face, because his eyes flash and he frowns hard. "Yes, dammit, sacrifice! I've seen it, Steve! My God, I've seen it! Jane...she...."

And he loses it. He tries to spit out the words, but the tears come instead, and soon he's wracked with choking sobs. The only two words I can hear clearly are, "Our baby."

I don't know what to do. I let him cry it out. It takes about five minutes before he swipes a grimy hand across his face to stifle the sniffling. "Sorry, man," he says.

"It's okay," I say, trying hard to stay calm and rational. "You say you saw this yourself?"

He nods, still trembling. "I wasn't supposed to be there. I wasn't high up enough yet to be there. But...I had some great news at work, and I wanted to tell Jane. She'd been up at her folks' house in Massachusetts for the whole summer while I worked, but she texted to say she'd be back at the Church meeting house and then come home right after. So I went to the house. I'd had my doubts about the Church for months, and I wanted to see about this rite they were supposed to be doing. But really, I just wanted to see her."

Jim puts his hands on his knees and straightens his back, looking down at the coffee table. The words come out in a rush. "I saw them there. In a circle. Inside, on the altar, was a baby. I thought it was like a baptism, but the baby seemed, you know…really fresh. Just born. And they were chanting. I could hear it. I remember it word for word." He closes his eyes and recites: "*Ph'nglui mglw'nafh Cthulhu R'lyeh wgah'nagl fhtagn.*"

He grips his knees hard and rocks back and forth. "And then…and then…." He can't finish it.

"I get the idea," I say gently, reaching out to touch his hand. "And they saw you there after, didn't they."

Jim nods. "It was all downhill after that," he says. "Jane never came home. I didn't know what to do. I mean…." He shakes his head violently as if to clear it. I know it won't come clear, though. Not with that look on his face. "So I go to work the next day. I mean, I'm in shock, right? Do I call the cops? I have no clue. So I go to work. And that's when the trade went south."

Of course. "And then you left town," I say.

"I had to!" Jim says, that intense look back on his face. "They knew everything about me! I worked right next to two Church members! Jane's family…the police…the guys in the attorney general's office…all members of the Church. I had to go."

I take my hand off Jim's and place it in my jacket pocket again. "And here you are."

Jim nods and slumps back in his chair, staring off into space again. "And here I am."

I sit in silence for a few moments, weighing my options. I know now he'll never come back on his own, and forcing him to come with me is going to be…difficult. Probably too difficult.

"Jim, I want you to look at me," I say finally, deciding to give him one last chance. He turns his head and I can see the dull ache in his eyes. The despair is palpable. "This isn't your fault. You can still go back. You can get help. You can—"

Jim laughs again, bordering on maniacal. "Haven't you heard a *word* I've been telling you?" he says. "There's no way I'm going back! Soon as you clear out of here, I'm packing up and leaving. This is the last time you're going to see me, Steve."

I nod, sadly, and pull my backup out of my pocket, my fist enclosed around it. "I guess you're right, Jim," I say. "This is it."

He looks at me quizzically. "Just like that?"

"Just like that," I say, standing up from off that godawful couch. "You've got a rifle and a gun, so calling the cops or mental health services would probably be a waste of time." I walk over to the door and start undoing the locks, one by one. "You believe your story wholeheartedly. I can tell there's no talking you out of it."

I hear him stand up behind me. "That's it?" he demands. "I tell you all this and that's all you're going to say?"

I turn around and see him, arms spread wide, looking even more distraught. I think he expected more arguing from me.

"Pretty much," I say. "You've been through a lot. You lost your job, your wife, your money. Even your baby, if that's what you think you saw. So yeah, what do I say to that?"

I open my hand. The flat stone, carved with the Elder Sign, begins to glow.

"In fact, I think you should probably just shoot yourself in the head and be done with it," I say.

The shot rings out a moment later. Thankfully, he didn't turn his head in my direction. Instead, it spatters onto the wall in a shower of black and crimson.

I ponder calling 911 to report Jim's suicide, but I'm tired of play-acting and I doubt I'd nail the terror and horror of it all. I've seen too much to fake it well enough. I think about just setting the place on fire, but why bother? With winter just around the corner, nobody would be coming up here for months.

Instead, I go through all his evidence and gather up the most incriminating bits, leaving behind just enough red herrings to put overly ambitious investigators off track. I use the stone to lock the doors behind me, with the keys still in Jim's pocket inside.

I go back to the rental car, fire it up and head back down the dirt road. When I'm a good fifteen miles from Jim's place, I pull out my cell phone and make the call, but I get voicemail. "Jane, it's Steve. It's done. He's gone. Details later."

Jane won't be happy. She wanted me to bring him back so she could really go to work on him. He was going to be the next one in the circle. He would've suffered for days, his horror and agony fueling the rise of the Returning King from R'lyeh.

Instead, I gave him the easy out. I guess I'm still capable of compassion.

I'm sure that won't last long.

THE PRINCE OF LYGHES

Anya Martin

Jenny didn't go looking for it. Todd didn't mean for her to find it.

She felt an odd sensation after dusting a book or maybe wiping a shelf, like a spider slipping onto her arm, scuttering rapidly up her sleeve and wriggling into her ear. She slapped her hand up quickly, wondering if perhaps a mosquito had bitten her or maybe the itchy burn of built-up wax. Then she sensed something squishy behind her eyes for just a moment. Perhaps a speck of dust that could be washed away with a stray tear? Finally a squeeze around the nape of her spine like something grabbing hold with tiny pin-like claws.

Later a vague pain developed that a pair of aspirin did nothing to relieve. That evening she planned to go to bed early, thinking that sleep would cure her headache, but somehow she stayed up late washing the dishes and then the laundry while Todd locked himself up again in his office.

Business, he said. Always business: emails to Hollywood executives about the latest potential deal that never happened, self-consciously clever social networking updates that generated fawning responses from a few of his four thousand acquaintances, messaging sessions so crucial that dinner had to be postponed for an hour or two, and then he would complain about it being cold or overcooked or just plain shit. Everything was shit when the side dish was Scotch or 1.5-liter bottles of cheap white wine. Not that she ever saw the bottle until the dead soldiers lined up behind a door. Nor did he ever admit he was drinking.

As Jenny headed downstairs to unload the clothes from the dryer, she noticed the door to Todd's office was now ajar. Through the crack, she could see his body collapsed and akimbo over the cluttered paperwork on the forest-green carpet. A snort from his nose trumpeted, made her head twinge again. Or maybe it was a light pressure as if something behind her temples were expanding?

Basket full in hands, she headed back up to their bedroom, emptied its contents into the dresser drawers and changed into pajamas. For most of the twelve years of their marriage, Todd had come to bed and held her, at least for part of the night. She'd taken those embraces—hugs that joined the two into a comma—as proof of his love for her even when they'd had arguments the day before. But now he rarely came to bed, and if he did, he barely held her at all.

When Jenny woke alone the next morning, cigarette smoke wafted in through the heating vent. The heavy aroma of tobacco intensified her headache, and a slight pain now welled in her mid-back and curved around to her stomach. This time, she took three aspirin. Maybe later she'd try four ibuprofen.

Was her heartbeat a bit quicker, too? Surely that was just because she was so angry at Todd not only for starting to smoke again after seven years of kicking the habit but also for breaking the inside house no-smoking rule. She thought about confronting him, but didn't want to hear his derisive denial again, or worse, risk him striking her. So she lay in bed and fumed quietly, waiting for the pain in her head to ebb enough for her to crawl downstairs and start a pot of coffee.

***

Jenny could usually concentrate herself into a machine and grind through even the most mundane and boring of design assignments. But today, even after two cups of coffee, the odd tactile aches and sensitivities made it difficult for her to focus. She had to email one of her clients for a deadline extension—something she hated to do in this unstable economy. She met Todd briefly in the kitchen, making himself bacon and eggs and baked beans. All she could stomach was one slice of toast with honey. They exchanged a few vague words about weekend plans and who might go grocery shopping, though she doubted he'd be sober enough to drive to the store. If he insisted, she'd have to choose between letting him and risking one more DUI or triggering another fight, another blow to her head. She watched him carry the plate downstairs, suspecting he'd eat no more than a few bites. She wondered if he'd remember to return the dish or abandon it on his desk until the leftovers attracted roaches.

Jenny's only other contact with Todd today was when a deliveryman rang the doorbell with another box. As always, she noted the same return address—Kolonia, Pohnpei, FM. When she looked it up, she found the abbreviation stood for Federated Micronesia, until 1986 a U.S. territory and still closely tied. She carried it downstairs to his office and knocked gently on the door.

"Todd, you've got another package."

Todd cracked open the door, eyes glazed, thinning hair disheveled, chin peppered with brown and gray stubble, wearing a faded black Led Zeppelin T-shirt and sweat pants so gnarly with holes that they belonged nowhere but the trash.

The customs labels always simply read "books," and Jenny assumed they contained books. After all, Todd was a writer and owned lots of books, so why shouldn't they be books? She sometimes asked him what books they were, worrying about the high cost of ordering books from so far away. They'd already taken out an equity line to reduce the interest rate on his credit card debts. He told her that books in English weren't popular in Asia and the cost of living was cheap, so Micronesian book dealers were willing to sell whatever was left from the libraries of Americans from territorial days, which often could be extensive, for surprisingly inexpensive prices. And the sellers gave good deals on shipping, too.

If Jenny pushed Todd a little further, he'd get increasingly edgy. He'd say that he was researching entomology or otolaryngology or the archaeology of some ancient city—what was it called? Yes, Nan Madol—or some other obscure topic that she would have no interest in, and remind her he didn't ask questions about her packages. Not that she received many, for she was very frugal with her meager earnings which barely supported both of them. Todd rarely made much money any more and seemed to spend all of it paying off an unknown amount of credit card debt, which Jenny assumed was spent mostly on booze, cigarettes, and the contents of the packages. She knew she ought to demand that he tell her his card balances, but he'd get so angry when she asked. One time when she suggested he take out a new card with a 0% balance transfer offer, he punched her so hard that he broke one of her ribs.

Jenny preferred to hunt for her bargains in person at thrift shops or discount stores—"treasure-hunting," she called it. She excelled at finding that unique vintage dress or perfect-fitting pair of tight jeans at a great price. Today she was wearing a Bettie Page-label pencil skirt and a tight-fitting red shirt with white polka-dots and ball sleeves.

But Todd didn't notice how cute she looked in her pin-up ensemble when she told him she was lunching with a friend. His eyelids fluttered as if he could barely focus. He just coughed and spit a gelatinous ball of brown tobacco phlegm on the rug. Then he took the package from her hands and closed the door. She could hear him shuffle his feet over the papers on the floor, the loud rustling of unpacking, then what sounded like a tiny chirp. She turned away and headed back upstairs to fetch a paper towel and carpet cleaner before the gooey stain set in the fabric.

Halfway up, a pang of nausea assaulted her, and she grasped her stomach. But the pain passed swiftly, and after the clean-up, she stumbled back to her computer screen. An hour later she had canceled lunch and curled up in a ball on the bed, trying to nap away throbbing pain that began between her temples and descended deep into her abdomen.

***

By the second morning, the disconcerting sensation had spread to Jenny's arms and legs, making them mysteriously tingly. The last few times this happened, Todd hadn't been as drunk and stirred up an antidote, which he said included Alka-Seltzer, pickle juice, ginger beer, and a secret ingredient he wouldn't divulge. The concoction tasted terrible but it always did the trick. She'd throw up about ten minutes later and then feel rejuvenated, normal. In those times, he'd tell her he'd given up drinking and collecting. She'd believe him, her being an optimist—both a blessing and a curse. They'd go out to movies, watch TV together snuggling close on the couch in the den, and he'd fix her a few lovely dinners—lamb with mint sauce and roast potatoes or chicken Tikka Masala. These idyllic "staycations" sometimes lasted just a couple of days but occasionally endured for weeks or even months, further filling her with an inexplicable and reckless sensation of hope.

But this time Todd was spending more and more hours locked in his office, so many that he didn't notice that Jenny was sicker than on the other occasions. When she made even the slightest pain complaint, he told her to "shut the fuck up" because he didn't have time to listen to her whining. She was "interfering," trying to "control" him, and he needed to get back to work. Every time he spoke cruelly to her, she felt a slight heave inside her head or her stomach or her arm as if whichever body part was expanding. But that was ridiculous. Perhaps she had the flu.

The cramps resonated so severely the next morning that Jenny stayed in bed. She was drifting back to sleep when she heard a high-pitched wail rise up through the vent—the cry faint at first and then growing steadily in volume until she almost had to clamp her ears. It stopped as suddenly as it started, and then silence for about five minutes. The next screech grated against her ears so violently that she pulled a pillow over her head. As it dissipated, she unburied her face, and a chorus of chitters followed, like an army of cicadas accompanied by metal spoons banging against pans.

Jenny crawled out of bed and crept into the hallway, alternately massaging her temples and holding her stomach, her aches almost overwhelming her with each step. Leaning over the landing, she could see that Todd's office door again was half-open, the cacophonous sounds drifting out from behind it and now including the frenzied chatter of what sounded like mewling cats, croaking frogs, and other animal noises she couldn't identify. Her head throbbed even more urgently at the sharp sounds that spiked again in volume as she slowly descended the two short flights of stairs. Once she reached the door, she paused to listen in case Todd might be shuffling behind it or rummaging in the closet. With all the paper scattered on the messy floor, he couldn't move around without making noise, though she couldn't be sure with all the other ruckus.

Peeking inside, Jenny saw no sign of Todd. Maybe he was smoking outside, or more likely he'd slipped out the patio door to sneak to the neighborhood liquor store or make a cell phone call. He always insisted the signal wasn't good in the house, though she never had any trouble with her own phone.

Still, not knowing if he could return at any moment, she entered carefully, tiptoeing through the paperwork. To the right, the cabinet doors in his bookcases vibrated in and out, the source of the animal chatter behind them.

Unexpectedly, she thought she heard Todd's voice, making her spin around to see just the empty hallway.

"I love you. The one thing I fear most in the world is you leaving me," the voice repeated three times like a broken record.

Then other words…accusatory words…

"Why is it you just lie there? Why is it you shrug me off when I touch you in the middle of the night?"

"That's because I'm asleep. I don't remember…," her own voice protested.

"You should be ready to make love whenever I'm ready to make love to you.

"You just want to control me.

"You don't know what love is.

"Rancid cunt."

Now the cabinet doors rattled like a rapid heartbeat. The palpitations frightened her but also beckoned Jenny's curiosity until she could do nothing else but fling them open. The action felt strangely freeing, even electrifying. She was finally going to see the books that came in the packages. But inside were no books—just cages and terrariums of various sizes filled with strange creatures.

Some beasts twitched their clusters of long gelatinous appendages, beating them like thumping cats' tails. Others leered with gaping eyes over-sized for their bodies and their vaguely amphibian heads. Some spread razor-blade teeth and sashayed left to right on scaly chicken-like legs that weren't quite in the right places. But most didn't resemble anything she had ever seen—lacerated red flesh with spider webs of purple veins on translucent pale skin interspersed with dreadlocked fur and bulbous sacs that looked stretched almost to bursting with yellow pus. Things with too many ears, too many eyes, ears but no eyes, eyes but no ears, lips with teeth on the outside, others that puckered and occasionally extended long blue and green cyst-covered tongues.

Then their voices lowered and those that had appendages lifted them up and beckoned as if welcoming her, inviting her closer and still chittering, chittering, chittering.

Jenny's head pounded with every scratch-on-a-chalkboard sound the creatures emitted. Her back stiffened as if the slightest movement would break it in two, her stomach churning painfully and melting into oscillating gelatin. The creatures' chattering escalated, flesh glowing effervescently like cameras flashing, photographing not just her most intimate parts but x-raying beneath her skin to her brain and internal organs.

Then the shimmer faded like lights dimming in the cinema, replaced by fuzzy images that gradually cleared until she could see Todd in every one—a wall of TV sets, each broadcasting him having sex with another woman. At first, the sex was just sex, warm and sweaty. A black woman in missionary position. A tiny Asian body with long dark hair writhing in 69—perfect toned buttocks pointed in her direction. A redhead doggy-style.

Those images dissolved and were replaced with more deviant ones. A threesome with two women, one sucking his penis, another perched over Todd's face, his tongue eagerly licking. Him rolling a nerve wheel over the nipples of a laughing brunette. Todd in black leather furiously beating another Asian girl with a riding crop as he roughly penetrates her ass, his partner screaming in delight.

The pictures then dissolved into multiple views of one petite woman with long straight blonde hair. Todd spooned against her like he used to do with Jenny, fondling a nipple, kissing her neck. She giggles. He whispers in her ear, "I love you. I love you unconditionally."

The blonde turns, fixes her icy blue eyes on Jenny, and hisses, the "s" holding long and snakelike on her tongue.

"What are you doing in my office, cunt?!" Todd's real voice shattered the spectral woman's venomous face into broken shards of glass. The vision readjusted back to the creatures, now shaking furiously in their enclosures.

"This is my office and you don't belong in here."

Jenny's head jerked towards the doorway and took in his angry visage and arms wrapped around a big brown paper bag. He chugged a hefty swig from the value-sized wine bottle wrapped within and placed it on top of a filing cabinet. And before she could even process her lack of an escape route, his fist pounded down on the top of her head.

Jenny crumpled to the floor, and Todd's fist descended again. Her skull rang with its impact, her head immediately heavier, swelling, and the beak of his sharp silver raven's head ring cut into her skin. The third time, his fist fell on the side of her temple, and as the pain registered, she also sensed scratching inside, as if something was moving, repositioning. Jenny heard herself screaming, "Help!" Or was it the victim of some other crime far away in the distance?

Jenny wanted to fight back, but Todd had her pinned so she couldn't move. Again and again, his fist throttled her head. Then the pointed toe of his cowboy boot kicked her side, triggering a loud crack and a sudden burning pain. Had he broken another rib? She tried to curl up into a ball on the floor so he couldn't reach her stomach or her breasts, and she felt the next impact beat into her lower back. She was just screaming now. At the top of her lungs, surprised at how loud she could scream, her head expanding from the inside—big and airy and burning.

This was how it felt to die, the part of Jenny's brain that wasn't in full shock thought as she continued to scream, the windows shut so no one was likely to hear, call the police. Was there even time for her to be rescued? The blows came down again and again. Todd twisted her arm, pushed her face to the floor to better position his fist to target the rear of her head. Her insides churned and bile rushed up into her throat, the first spasm of vomit. But as orange chunks exited her mouth, something else did as well. The pressure stretched her esophagus, neck and head, excruciating as each expanded to its limit, and Jenny felt like she was choking, hemorrhaging, coming to an end.

Then a rush of fresh air flushed through her lungs as something inside shot from her open lips onto the floor. The chittering around her mounted, became deafening. Stringy appendages draped across the carpet, a mass of discoid flesh using them to pivot and leap across her head.

Todd's blows stopped as suddenly as they had begun. Glass shattered, bars broke, a thousand scurrying, scampering, slithering sounds. Then Todd began to scream, a prolonged screech of agony. Aching, throbbing tension overwhelmed Jenny's head as she forced herself to roll over onto her back and see what was happening.

Through blurred vision, she barely made out Todd's body covered in the creatures, nibbling, gnawing, sucking, bits of his flesh crunching in the mouths of those that had mouths, bright red blood showering them en masse, dyeing their amorphous shapes in his gore. The protruding appendages of the thing that had been inside her stuffed Todd's mouth, as if he'd swallowed something much too big to chew and the rest was trying to force its way in, pushing, curling back and pushing again. He could no longer scream, barely groan, his cheeks bulging. His eyes expanded out of their sockets. His nose exploded in a giant sneeze, blowing off his face into myriad tiny pieces.

Todd's blood and snot soaked her, but other than clamping her own mouth shut, her hands and arms were too injured to reach up and wipe her face. Though basted in slime, she found herself silently smiling. Each bite or suction served as a release to her, a sign that he was feeling the physical manifestation of the beatings and emotional pain she had lived with for so many years. The old Todd that she had loved so deeply had dissolved into a distant memory, and this stranger who drank, smoked, and fucked everyone but her—that one blonde woman especially—held no resemblance.

His suit of skin was completely ripped off now, remnants of tattered red muscles all that lingered. As the creatures parted slightly, she could see Todd's heart still pulsating—purpling with the pressure of pumping blood through severed veins. She looked up into his eyes to search for any sorrow or regret, but she could not identify either emotion. And then Todd's eyes were gone, bursting from their sockets, shooting past her face like soft torpedoes and squishing into the wall behind her.

Todd's heart was slowing now, the red meat almost completely devoured, inner organs bitten through, bones sparkling pearly white thanks to licking tongues and fleshy, suctioning pressure. The monster that had been inside her was visible again, a pale amoeboid entity fluctuating between solid and transparent, widening and narrowing as it navigated organs, thinning as it slipped inside Todd's esophagus, expanding into a hammer shape as it battered against his stomach. Its spidery tendrils had fully looped themselves inside his skull mouth, curling into what was left of his arms and twisting around his spine like nerves in an anatomy model. The thing had completely avoided his brain, however, concentrating first on the destruction of the rest of his body. If the loss of blood had not been enough to make him comatose, might his mind not still be functioning, feeling every bite, every thrust, every squeeze?

The monster's head penetrated Todd's stomach with a loud splat, undigested food and fluids suddenly flying outward. But it didn't linger long, its appendages pushing down to grasp his intestines, unfurling them like jump-ropes, ripping into his colon and pushing out of his buttocks like a cat of nine tails.

Jenny felt sad that Todd's heart finally stopped before the monster reached his penis, inhaling it in a motion so quick that she could not tell if it was a gulp or simply an absorption. The devouring process was satisfying to watch but far too fast. She had suffered the bites Todd had taken verbally from her self-esteem, her creativity, her dignity, and the more overt pushes and punches for years, and especially the lies that twisted into her like slow-growing cancers. The denials of his drinking had been impossible to hide thanks to the sometimes subtle, sometimes blatant changes in his personality from kind to cruel. And worse, the secret liaisons. She'd realized neither that he had committed so many transgressions nor the extent of their deviance and the relish with which he enjoyed inflicting pain on other women, women who enjoyed it. And worst of all, that he'd given his heart to another. At one time Jenny'd even had the naive thought he'd never cheat on her, that her battle was only with the sweet lure of alcohol. If she was safe from anything, for so long she had been so sure it was from him fucking another woman. Then she found out about one—maybe the blonde; she never saw a picture—and he begged her back, promised to cut it off right away, even quit drinking for a while, made her believe. And she did, even though she was a smart, educated woman. He was sober for six months, and then the packages began to arrive again.

A sharp crack woke Jenny out of her reverie. The beasts were now down to consuming Todd's skeleton, a chorus of sharp crunches, chewing and squishy ingestion. The big thing hadn't forgotten his brain, just saved it for last, tendrils and fleshy mass cracking the skull like a nutcracker, then allowing the little ones to slide in and slurp on it like a fine delicacy. The last body parts to disappear were his feet, ironic perhaps because Jenny had thought so many times that if he'd broken a foot or leg, Todd wouldn't have been able to walk to the liquor store, push the gas pedal on the car, or make it across the room to hit her.

Finished with their meal, the creatures fell into a deep hum. Was it a song of satisfaction, satiation? They spread all around her on the floor. The larger monster, the one that had gestated inside Jenny, was now fully revealed—a bulbous thing with no discernable shape, fluctuating from spherical as a fat spider, then stretching long and flat with hunched sores and bubbles. At first, its many eyes seemed glazed and unfocused, but as if becoming conscious of the intensity with which she was watching it, they shot open wide and engaged her. And in that moment, all the creatures that had eyes did the same, turning in her direction in one sudden wave.

Jenny felt her terror return. Their food source fully devoured with Todd, would they now eat her for dessert? Those creatures that had nostrils seemed to be sniffing the air, considering.

The beasts crawled slightly in her direction in one great oozing wave, but then they turned towards the outer wall, climbing or slithering or simply spreading up the legs of Todd's desk and onto its surface. Shattered glass and a few quick gnaws—or was that a burst of acidic spit shot from one thing's mouth?—and the window and screen now bore a large hole. Tiny behinds, gelatinous masses and jittering tails disappeared into the darkness of the night. Were they looking for more people with damaged souls to feed on their twisted dreams, their desire to inflict pain? Or were they simply returning to the soil until someone else placed the next order in the mail?

Soon Jenny's only companion in the blood-splattered office was the monster that had gestated inside her. Was it the queen bee, the mother alien? Or was it just the catalyst, the leader, the top chef that the others needed when the time came for the final devouring, when the human being was fully prepared, seasoned with negative thoughts and marinated with pain inflicted on others?

Jenny waited and it waited. Then it lifted one of its tendrils and gestured in a wavelike motion, slowly, gracefully easing towards her—not a threatening movement, more a question. Its body didn't move, just this armlike appendage, until it stopped right in front of her face, still undulating as if it wanted to touch her forehead but wasn't sure if she would recoil or slap it back.

She knew she should be scared. Shouldn't she? She should pull back and not risk that it would change its mind, hurt her. But the creature had been inside her and had not killed her, and she had already faced death tonight from her husband. What did she have to be afraid of? Instead she felt a mutual curiosity. What did it want from her?

Jenny leaned in, let the tendril touch her brow. A tingling surged through her head and into her arms, down her spine and legs and toes. Not an unpleasant feeling, almost healing though her rib bone was not re-aligning nor did the dull ache in her head from the repeated pounding dissipate. She felt an activity in her mind, and realization came to her. It wanted to understand. What exactly she wasn't sure—probably why she had stayed with Todd so long and put up with all the pain he unleashed on her. That made sense, didn't it? But she didn't understand it herself. She wondered if she ever would.

After what seemed a long time but was probably less than five minutes, it pulled back its limb, stared at her for one more long moment. And then it, too, climbed onto Todd's desk and out the window.

Once it had fully disappeared into the night, Jenny crawled to the desk herself, pulled down the cordless phone and dialed 911.

THE CURIOUS DEATH OF SIR ARTHUR TURNBRIDGE

G. D. Falksen

Now that the tragic death of Sir Arthur Turnbridge has largely subsided from the press, I feel it my duty to put right certain details of the case that have until now been kept from the public. I realize that my words will cause no small amount of resentment from the police, who, it will be remembered, were quite confident in their conclusions, but I feel I must put the record straight, especially given the role played by my friend Hieronymus Vos, the great Flemish detective. And let me be very clear on one salient point: everything that I am about to relate was witnessed by my own eyes.

It was 1922, only a short while after my retirement from the Army and following close upon the heels of Meester Vos's great international fame following the Case of the Parisian Eviscerations of the previous year. While summering along the English Riviera with Vos, I chanced to encounter an old friend of mine from the Great War, Captain James Turnbridge, with whom I served at Ypres.

"Jamie," I said, as we sat down in the hotel saloon with our drinks, "what ever are you doing in Torquay? I thought you resided in London now. Whitehall appointment or something."

"War Office," he agreed. "But Hazel and I are down visiting Pater for a few weeks and we thought we'd take a turn of the resort while we were here."

"How is your father?" I asked.

"Remarried, actually," James said.

"No!" I exclaimed. "I don't believe a word of it!"

Old Sir Arthur was a notorious recluse. He hadn't married his first wife until he was more than forty, and after her unfortunate death it had seemed unlikely he'd ever bother himself with the institution again.

"The Lord's honest truth," James told me. "Mind you, he did his damnedest to hush the whole thing up. Had the ceremony while Hazel and I were in India last year. I only heard about it because Susan wrote me after it was all finished with."

"Isn't that a bit odd, Jamie?" I asked, mulling over my whiskey and soda. "Not having the family at the ceremony, I mean."

From James's countenance I could tell that he was bothered by it too, but he replied cheerfully:

"Well, it was a quiet country affair. Nothing ostentatious. I expect Pater didn't want any fuss. Gwen was in New York, so she only heard of it when I did. At least Susan was there."

"Good of her," I said cheerfully, though the fact wasn't terribly surprising: the last I'd heard, the elder daughter Susan still lived under her father's roof, having lost her fiancé in the War.

"How is Susan?" I asked.

"Unmarried," James replied sadly.

"Oh, what a shame."

"She's corresponded a few times with a chap from Anchester name of Norrys, but I doubt anything will come of it. Royal Flying Corps during the War. You might remember him."

"What, 'Piggy' Norrys?" I exclaimed. Norrys and I had known each other at Eton and Oxford.

"That's the one. Capital fellow."

"He really is," I agreed. "Don't let him slip through Susan's fingers, that's what I say."

James shrugged.

"Trouble is putting them into a room together," he said. "Getting Susan out of the house is rather like crossing no-man's-land. Hazel and I invited her to join us in touring India and she simply wouldn't have it."

"Well my dear fellow," I said, "simply have Norrys come to her. Invite him down for a country weekend. I can't imagine he'd refuse, especially at the request of an old war friend. Say it's to celebrate Pater's nuptials or something."

James flagged down a waiter to have our drinks refilled and scratched his chin.

"Not a bad idea, Stamford," he said. "Come to think of it, you ought to come as well. It'll be a treat having an old friend to cheer the place up. Maybe give that Norrys chap some nerve while you're at it."

"Oh, well, I—"

"Gwen's there as well," James added. "Came back from America for the occasion. And I know she'd be happy to see you."

"Oh, well, I…" I repeated. My heart skipped a beat at the mention of James's younger sister, who I'd always regarded as something of a dish. "Unfortunately, you see, I've got this friend staying with me for the summer. I'd feel dashed awful abandoning him."

"Bring him along!" James exclaimed.

"Are you sure it would be alright?" I asked. "He's foreign, you see."

James frowned. "Not German, is he?"

"No, Belgian."

"Oh, well that's fine then."

"In fact—"

As we spoke, I saw my friend enter the saloon and look around. If you paid any attention to the press coverage of the Paris murders of '21, then you have some knowledge of Hieronymus Vos's appearance. He is very short, I suppose only a little taller than five feet, but he carries himself with great dignity. His skin is pale like a white sheet, except for his rosy cheeks and the tip of his pointy nose, which is almost pink. This, coupled with his blond hair, gives his head a peculiar appearance like a bare skull, which I have often found to be his second most striking feature—the first, of course, being his curiously curling upturned moustache that always puts one in mind of an octopus about to devour some hapless ship.

To my surprise, I saw that Vos was in the company of James's wife, Hazel Turnbridge, a rather sporty woman of about twenty-five whose hair and eyes quite suited her name. Hazel walked on Vos's arm, guiding him toward our table, and James, misunderstanding Vos's intentions, turned bright red and looked about ready to punch my friend on the nose.

"Look," I said, quickly putting things right, "here he comes. It seems he's met Hazel already."

"Oh," James said, huffing a little.

He and I stood as Hazel reached us, just finishing some words with Vos.

"James, you'll never believe who I met!" Hazel exclaimed. She pointed toward my friend and said, "Monsieur Vos, the Belgian detective!"

"I—" James stammered.

"You remember," Hazel insisted. "The one who solved those witch murders in Paris last year."

"Ah," Vos interrupted, raising a finger. "Meester Vos."

"Oh gosh, did I say it wrong?" Hazel asked. "I'm dreadfully sorry, I thought you Belgians all spoke French."

"Vos is Flemish, actually," I quickly explained. "They speak Dutch. And he's been to University for…something."

"Antiquities," Vos clarified.

Hazel turned to me and smiled brightly.

"Hello, John!" she exclaimed, giving me a tight sisterly hug, which I fear nearly dislocated my shoulder. When I say that Hazel's a sporty sort of girl, I don't use the word lightly. "What ever are you doing in Devon?"

"Well, I—" I replied, rubbing my arm where it hurt the most.

My friend Vos came to the rescue:

"Stamford has kindly offered to show me his 'English Riviera'. And I find it quite illuminating."

He did not elaborate on just what he meant by this, but merely smiled in his warm and unassuming way.

"James, we simply *must* invite them to the house this weekend," Hazel insisted. "It'll make a nice change from your father's present company. We're practically inundated with academics," she explained.

"But I am—" Vos began.

James sighed. "Hazel dear, one antiquarian and a local folklorist do not make an inundation."

"He's a very loud antiquarian," Hazel replied.

Vos tried again: "*Ja*, but you see I also am—"

"Always arguing with your father about 'Schacabac' and 'Iram' and 'Al-Hazred' in the middle of the night," Hazel continued. "It's very tiring."

James laughed awkwardly and hushed his wife:

"Come now, Hazel, I'm sure John and Mister Vos aren't the least bit interested..."

"*Nee, nee*," Vos said quickly, his attitude suddenly changed to one of great interest. "Stamford and I would be most delighted to accept your invitation. Is that not so, Stamford?"

"Oh, well," I said. "Right."

Hazel looked pleased as punch and even James seemed relieved at our acceptance.

"That's just splendid!" Hazel cried. "Isn't it, James?"

"Capital," James agreed. "But John, you must promise to help with Norrys. I don't want that man leaving without at least one proposal of marriage to my sister."

"Rather," I agreed.

Vos looked puzzled and said, "What is the Norrys and why is it proposing?"

I quickly outlined the situation to Vos, who then smiled and bobbed his head.

"Have no fear, *mijn vriend*," he said. "I am very good at getting people to do things."

***

So it was that the following weekend, Vos and I drove up to the little seaside village of Walbury, which rests just on the border of Cornwall. It was a lovely day for motoring, but poor Vos seemed quite put out by the ordeal, covering his nose with a handkerchief to ward off the dust and clutching his bowler hat tightly on his head, lest it blow away in the wind.

"I say, Vos," I shouted, "you don't look at all well."

"I am not well, Stamford!" Vos replied. "*Mijn God!* This motorcar will be the death of me! They shall say: 'It was the Rolls-Royce that killed him!' You will see!"

"Steady on, Vos," I said, laughing.

The village of Walbury was a quiet place nestled in between two sets of stony cliffs. I had seen it a few times before when visiting James after the War, and though it might seem rude of me, I quickly sped past the ramshackle assortment of wharves and decaying wooden houses that occupied that little hollow by the sea.

I say 'quiet', but really 'sullen' would be a better term. The fishermen of Walbury had always been a different breed, if you take my meaning, not at all like the hardy country folk of Essex I knew so well. I kept to the high road and steered clear of the town, nearly running over a couple of Walbury men in my haste as I did so. As we passed them, Vos turned in his seat with unusual interest, and studied them until we drove out of sight.

"Ghastly looking fellows, aren't they, Vos?" I asked.

"*Ja*," Vos replied. "Very interesting indeed is their look."

About two miles further down the road, I rounded a corner just as a man on a bicycle darted across my path. We swerved to avoid one another and the poor fellow careened off the road and into a ditch.

"Oh dear!" I cried, pulling on the brake to stop the car.

"Oh dear, indeed, *mijn vriend*," Vos said. "I do believe you may have killed that man, Stamford."

"Don't be horrible, Vos!"

"*Nee, nee*, Stamford," Vos replied, as we alighted and hurried across the road. "I merely state what is a most likely outcome."

But thankfully it was not the case. As we reached the ditch, the young man appeared over the edge and began to climb out, laughing as he did. At first I thought he would be angry with me, but instead he raised his cap in greeting and began to brush dirt from his tweeds.

"Good Lord, you appeared from nowhere!" he exclaimed.

"Yes, I'm awfully sorry—" I began.

"Entirely my own fault," he said. "Not a car on the road all morning, but still I shouldn't have been so careless." He quickly offered me his hand. "Charles Newbury."

"John Stamford," I said, shaking his hand. "And this is my friend, Hieronymus Vos."

"*Goedendag*," Vos said, touching the brim of his hat rather than shaking Newbury's dirt-covered hand.

Newbury brushed his palm off on his sleeve, which only made Vos shudder at the sight. I have long known my friend Vos to be of an especially fastidious nature. I daresay he would fear the touch of a mud puddle more than a bullet.

"Bound for Brympton?" Newbury asked.

"Why, yes," I exclaimed. "How ever did you know that?"

"Mister Newbury knows because he is a guest there also," Vos replied. "Is that not right?"

"I am!" Newbury replied, sounding surprised but also amused.

"How else would a young man of obvious means, dressed in tweeds like a gentleman, wearing expensive spectacles, come to be bicycling along the road so close to the Brympton House, Stamford?" Vos said.

"Well, I suppose when you put it like that…" I said.

"And as Mister Newbury is obviously not the Captain Norrys," Vos continued, "he is either the learned antiquarian or the local folklorist."

"Folklorist," Newbury answered with a grin. "Though hardly local. My family hasn't lived in these parts for almost a hundred years."

"But your family, it is from Walbury originally, is this not so?" Vos asked.

Again Newbury looked delighted.

"Dashed clever of you, Mister Vos! My great-grandfather was a ship's captain in Walbury. He made a fortune in the Spice Isles and moved the whole family to Oxfordshire."

"And that is what has brought you back to this country?" Vos asked.

"Oh, hardly," said Newbury. "I'm conducting a study of old Celtic folktales from around these parts. Stories about little people beneath the earth and haunted barrows, that sort of thing."

"Most interesting," Vos replied. "You must tell me some of these stories when we meet again, Mister Newbury, but for now, we must be on our way."

"Yes, of course." Newbury adjusted his spectacles and then climbed back onto his bicycle. "Good day to you."

As Vos and I returned to the car, I asked him:

"What do you make of that?"

"I make of that a young scholar must enthusiastic," Vos replied.

"A fine job I didn't hit him, you know."

"*Ja*," Vos agreed. "But it was not your fault, Stamford."

"Thanks for that, old boy," I said.

"*Nee*, truly Stamford," Vos insisted. "Young Mister Newbury was reading a book across the handlebars when we encountered him."

"Gosh, I hadn't realized."

"Mmm," Vos mused. "And what was in the book, I wonder."

***

Brympton House, the Turnbridge family home, was about a mile on after our encounter with Newbury. Brympton was a charming if rather small manor built in the Palladian style. I had spent some very pleasant weeks there while on leave during the War, but the house was more weathered than I remembered, definitely in need of some fresh paint, and the lush gardens I had once strolled through were beginning to go to seed. But I saw a familiar face toiling in the soil by the hydrangeas.

"Susan!" I called to her.

Susan, James's elder sister, stood and waved to me.

"Major Stamford! We didn't expect you until dinner."

"Too lovely a day not to come early, don't you know," I said, climbing out of the car. I motioned to Vos. "Susan, may I introduce you to my friend, Hieronymus Vos?"

"Hello, Mister Vos," Susan said excitedly.

She offered Vos her hand, but Vos simply smiled and touched the brim of his hat.

"*Goedendag*, Miss Turnbridge," he said. "Such beautiful flowers you have."

"Oh!" Susan exclaimed, perhaps surprised. "Thank you."

"You clearly have the…what is the word…? The green thumb, *ja?*" said Vos. "Are these your favorites?"

Susan looked very happy at the question. "Oh yes, I simply adore hydrangeas."

"And am I right to think that the Captain Norrys has not yet arrived?"

"Well, yes," Susan replied, looking very surprised. "His train won't arrive until evening."

Vos smiled warmly. "Of course."

Susan turned to me and said, "James, Hazel, Gwen, and Bella are at the tennis lawn out back."

"Bella?" I asked.

"Stepmother," Susan explained.

"Oh, right."

"Follow me, I'll take you through."

We followed Susan into the house, which was in no better repair on the inside. The wallpaper was peeling in places and the carpets were very worn. I was more than a little shocked to see it, I don't mind telling you. The Turnbridges had always been a respectable family since I'd known them, but recently it seemed Sir Arthur had practically given up on it all. No wonder he'd remarried: someone had to keep the servants in line.

As we went, I whispered to Vos, "Funny you guessing right about Norrys."

"Oh, it was no guess," Vos replied. "Simple deduction. The house is in disrepair, so I surmise that the senior Turnbridge does not bother to have it maintained. But the flower garden in front is in perfect condition. *Ergo*, the young Miss Turnbridge cares for the flowers, so she does the work that clearly the gardener is not doing."

"Yes, but what about Norrys?" I asked.

"Think, Stamford. Miss Turnbridge is in the garden tending to the flowers while her dear brother and sister and sister-in-law are playing the tennis? She is making the house appear as presentable as she is able before her young man arrives. Were the Captain Norrys here already, the two of them would be in each other's vicinity, circling and eyeing each other like the stray cats."

"Oh," I said, a little confused. "Right. But what about—"

Before I could say more, I was interrupted by shouting on the upstairs landing. I recognized one voice as belonging to Sir Arthur. Susan looked terribly embarrassed, while Vos seemed intrigued.

"I tell you, Howard, it's a shambles!" Sir Arthur shouted. "A shambles! Where am I to find someone who reads ancient Sogdian, Howard, tell me that?"

"Sir Arthur, please—" protested a second voice.

"A damn good thing I know it's authentic, or I'd assume you were swindling me with this piece of rubbish! Two thousand pounds for a grimoire I can't even read! It might be a Tang Dynasty cookbook for all I know!"

At that moment, Sir Arthur and his companion appeared on the landing above us. Sir Arthur was as I remembered him: gray-haired and disheveled, and his dour mood had only worsened in the past few years. His companion was another man of about the same age—somewhere in his sixties—who looked rather like the sort of fellow one found cluttering up a university library.

"Daddy!" Susan called to him, interrupting her father so that he might save face in front of guests.

"Susan? What is it?" Sir Arthur turned toward us and, after a moment of shock, he descended the stairs and held out his hand to me. "Well, well, Major Stamford! We weren't expecting you until dinner."

"Wonderful to see you again, Sir Arthur," I said, shaking hands. "I understand congratulations are in order."

"What?" Sir Arthur asked. It took him a moment to catch my meaning. "Oh, yes, Bella. She's outside, I expect. I suppose you'd better meet her."

I was taken aback by Sir Arthur's dismissal of his own marriage, and I didn't rightly know what to say. So instead, I simply stammered, "Oh, right," and then motioned to Vos.

"Uh, Sir Arthur," I said, "may I introduce my friend, Hieronymus Vos?"

"What?" Sir Arthur harrumphed. "Oh, yes, the detective fellow. Hazel said you were bringing a foreigner along."

I expected Vos to be offended, but he smiled and said, "*Ja*, that is I. It is very nice to meet you, Sir Arthur." He turned to the other man. "And you also, Professor Howard."

Howard seemed surprised at being recognized, but he grinned as he shook hands with Vos.

"Very nice to be noticed, sir," Howard said.

"Howard, you mean to say you know this man?" Sir Arthur demanded.

"*Nee, nee*," Vos interjected. "We have never met, but how could I fail to recognize Professor William Howard of Oxford, the noted archaeologist?" He smiled at Howard and said, "I read with great interest about your excavations in Arabia two years ago."

"Oh," Howard said. He suddenly seemed a bit put-off, though I couldn't imagine why.

"It is a great honor to meet two such distinguished intellectuals," Vos continued, bobbing his head to Sir Arthur and Professor Howard. "Though I am only an amateur...." He paused and raised a finger, an idea coming to him. "Forgive me, but did I hear mention of Sogdian?"

Sir Arthur exchanged a look with Howard.

"Yes," he said hesitantly. "Why?"

"It so happens that I have a very passing familiarity with the language," Vos explained. "I do not wish to impose, but if I might be of some service to the friend of my friend Stamford...."

Sir Arthur looked at Howard. "You put him up to this, didn't you?"

"No, I—" Howard stammered. "I've never met this man before in my life."

"*Nee*," Vos said, "it is simply a felicitous coincidence, and one I thought I might use to be of service. Oh, but if it is of no interest to you, Sir Arthur, I must beg forgiveness for my presumption and withdraw the offer."

Sir Arthur narrowed his eyes and studied Vos silently. After a moment, his expression became rather hopeful and he said:

"Well, if it is just coincidence, it is a fortunate one. Let's speak more about this after dinner, Mister...Vos, was it?"

"*Ja*," Vos replied, bobbing his head.

"Hmm," Sir Arthur answered. Then, without another word to us, he turned and continued on his way, vanishing into the depths of the decaying house with Howard hurrying along behind him.

Susan looked a little embarrassed at her father's behavior.

"Do forgive Daddy," she said. "I fear he's become rather reclusive in his old age."

"Not to worry," I told her. I turned to Vos. "Still, dashed good luck you knowing about that Soggy-Dinny thing."

Vos looked pained for a moment.

"*Mijn vriend*, the Sogdian language was practically the *lingua franca* of the Silk Road during the Tang Dynasty. How could I not have studied it?"

"Oh, right," I said, trying to hide my confusion.

***

Susan led us to a little patio in the back, which lay at the edge of the dense Brympton forest. The lawn was in rather a bad shape, overgrown with weeds in places and not at all well tended, but I did see James and Hazel on the tennis lawn making a go of things. There were two women sitting in chairs on the patio, sipping lemonade while they watched.

"Everyone!" Susan called. "Look who's arrived!"

James paused and waved to me with his racquet. "Hello, Stamford! Glad you could make it!" He was then narrowly missed by Hazel's next serve, and the two began playing again amid shouts of "Unfair!" and "Buck up!" and "I'll hit you in the head properly next time!"

"Ah, life as usual," I mused happily. Despite the poor state of the grounds, I was suddenly put in mind of idyllic summers past.

"*Ja*," Vos said dubiously.

"Is that John Stamford I hear?"

I recognized the voice as belonging to Gwen, James's younger sister. She bounded out of her chair, lemonade in hand, and gave me a long look.

"Well, well," she said, gazing at me like a cat that has taken a sudden interest in a mouse.

"Hello, Gwen."

She was as I remembered her: rather attractive and with a devious look in her eyes. She looked thoroughly American now, with her dark hair cut into a short, sharp bob. I caught myself staring and quickly introduced Vos:

"Uh, Gwen, this is my friend Hieronymus Vos. He's Flemish."

"Oh, how deliciously continental," Gwen said.

"He investigates murders!" Hazel called from the tennis lawn. "Grisly ones!"

"Continental *and* grisly." Gwen grinned. "How delightful."

"A pleasure to meet you, Miss Turnbridge," Vos said, gently shaking her hand. He turned toward the last member of the party, who had just begun to rise from her chair. "And finally…?"

Susan rushed to make introductions:

"And this is our stepmother, Bella Turnbridge."

Now I don't want you to think I'm a brute or anything, but I must confess that when I first laid eyes on Bella Turnbridge it gave me a shock. She wasn't exactly ugly, but neither was she any towering beauty. Her eyes were large and milky, though she was able to hide some portion of this behind a pair of thick glasses. They were also spaced a bit too far apart for comfort, and her mouth, as she smiled, was thin-lipped and far too wide. Against my own intentions, I recoiled slightly at the sight.

"A…pleasure, Mrs. Turnbridge," I stammered.

Vos seemed to have no trouble with Bella's queer look, and he simply smiled and tapped his hat politely.

"*Ja*, it is very nice to meet you, Madam Turnbridge. Forgive me, but you are a local of the village, are you not?"

Bella smiled again and said, "Yes, I am. How did you know?"

"A fortunate guess," Vos replied.

"Is it true you're a detective?" Bella asked.

"*Ja*," Vos said, "among other things."

"I do so love detective stories," Bella said. I glanced at the book she had been reading, and sure enough it was some tawdry thing about murder and whatnot.

"Well, I…." Vos motioned to Gwen's empty chair. "May I sit?"

"I'm not using it," Gwen said, still looking at me.

"Oh, please do," Bella told Vos. "It's nice to have someone to talk to. I don't understand all of these sports and things."

Vos chuckled. "Me also, I do not understand them. But I do understand murder. Would you like me to tell you about some of my cases?"

"Goodness, yes!" Bella exclaimed.

As they spoke, Gwen nudged me in the arm and motioned toward the woods with her head.

"Care to take me for a walk, John?" she asked coyly.

"Oh, gosh, yes," I replied, rather more enthusiastically than intended.

***

Our stroll took us through the woods on the far side of the grounds, where they ran along the cliffs above the sea. Gwen and I had gone for walks together during the War, including one particularly poignant time shortly before Passchendaele when I asked her to marry me. After the War we both saw sense and abandoned the engagement, but I still carry happy memories for it.

As we walked, Gwen told me about her new life in America, as an actress in New York. It all sounded very glamorous, and I assumed it was a rather profitable occupation at that, for the parties she told me about sounded dashed expensive. I told her about my travels with Vos, including that rather unfortunate incident in Cairo in '21 when I was very nearly buried alive. We both had a grand laugh about things, and then suddenly Gwen stopped short and looked around. Her face grew pale. We stood at the edge of a low hill that rose to about eye level and then dropped away very suddenly toward the seashore. The trees there were especially tangled and overawing, and the shadows they cast put me in mind of some rather silly words, like "eldritch" and "Brythonic".

"Goodness," Gwen said. "I hadn't realized we were going this way." She paused before she explained, "This is where Mother died."

"What, here?" I asked. I quickly checked under my feet to be sure I hadn't trodden on a gravestone or anything.

"Well, here's where she caught the pneumonia," Gwen said. "Out in the middle of a thunderstorm looking for fairies living under the hill. Damned stupid of her." Gwen sighed. "Sorry, I shouldn't have said that."

"No, no, not at all," I assured her.

"And now that idiot Newbury's running about the place doing the same thing."

"Is that what he's doing here?" I asked. "You know, I nearly ran him over in my car coming down."

Gwen laughed. "Serves him right. Dashing here and there on that bicycle of his looking for trods and fairy rings and goodness knows what else. He'll get himself into mischief, mark my words."

"And what about that Howard chap?" I asked. "Is he looking for fairies and whatnot as well?"

"Oh, Lord, no," Gwen replied. "No, he works for Daddy. Helps him buy and authenticate antiquities for his collection."

"Does he have the money for that?"

"What?" Gwen asked in surprise.

"Well...." I suddenly felt rather awkward. "I thought he might have fallen on hard times, state of the house and all."

"Oh, that," Gwen said. "No, Daddy's still rich as Croesus, he just spends all his money on statues and old manuscripts."

"But the servants?" I asked, in reference to there seeming to be none at all.

"Let most of them go," Gwen answered. "Didn't trust them around his collection. He's only got our old butler, the cook, and Susan's maid left. Poor thing does for both her and Bella now. Father doesn't even talk to them anymore. He just shouts orders apparently. Lets Susan and Bella manage everything else. Probably the only reason he remarried."

"I suppose there are worse reasons for mar—" I began.

We were strolling along the edge of the hill, and at that moment I put my foot wrong on a loose stone and suddenly lost my balance. With a cry of alarm, I tumbled down the slope, my coat catching against every bush and bramble I passed. I grabbed for some sort of handhold to stop myself, but there was nothing I could do until I finally came to a halt at the bottom.

"Oh Lord!" Gwen called to me. "John, are you alive?"

I stood and brushed myself off. I'd been bruised, but everything was more or less intact.

"Alive and well!" I called. "Just…um…. Just a moment and I'll find a way back up."

"No, you stay there!" Gwen shouted. "I'll come down and we can walk back along the shore. There's a path around here somewhere."

Before I could protest, Gwen had vanished from sight and I was left in the arboreal twilight of the overhanging trees. I waited there for a little while, when I heard the sound of someone moving through the brush a little further along the hill.

"Gwen?" I called.

There was no answer and the noise stopped, but soon I heard it again, now moving in my direction. Being of an adventurous nature, I crept forward, peering through the brush to get sight of the stranger. I suddenly began to suspect that it wasn't Gwen at all.

Then I passed through a tangle of brush and into a sort of overgrown hollow at the base of the hill. It was very dark, like the rest of the wood, but I managed to see that there was *something* crouched in the mottled darkness beside a tumble of stones. I did not see it clearly, but I made out a curious bipedal form covered in some manner of rubbery flesh. It slowly raised its elongated head and fixed me with a pair of baleful eyes that glinted in the shadows. At the time, I saw little of it clearly, and for that small mercy I am grateful.

Slowly, the thing raised one skeletal arm and extended a bony finger at me like Death itself. I consider myself to be a man of instinct, and as my first instinct was to flee, I fled. I scrambled through the undergrowth in the opposite direction, desperate to be away from the thing that I had scarcely seen and could not clearly remember. The vagueness of it made my fear all the more real, as is so often the case.

And so, I ran: I ran and ran and ran, until suddenly I broke from the trees and very nearly collided with Gwen.

"Good heavens!" Gwen exclaimed as I stumbled to a stop and she reached out to steady me. "John, what is it?"

"I…I…."

"You look as if you've seen a ghost!"

I leaned against a tree and took a few deep breaths.

"I think perhaps I did," I finally replied.

There was a pause and then Gwen began laughing. At first I was a bit angry at this—imagine, laughing at my evident distress!—but soon I was laughing with her. The memory of what I had seen was now little more than a fog and it was very easy to dismiss my moment of panic as the work of shadows and nerves.

"You're not serious, John," Gwen said.

"Not at all," I replied, trying to look my most unruffled. "I think I saw an animal and it gave me a fright."

"Oh, John, you are an old silly sometimes." Gwen shook her head and laughed again. "Come along, it'll be time for dinner soon."

We went back along the shore, enjoying the cool breeze blowing off the sea. As we left the woods behind us, I convinced myself that the entire thing had been the product of a wild imagination. Ghosts and goblins weren't real, and no cool-headed Englishman should entertain such fantasies.

As we went along, we saw Newbury bicycling along the edge of the forest nearby. Sighting us, he gave a wave and we three converged and exchanged greetings.

"Evening all!" Newbury exclaimed. He pointed at me and grinned. "I say! You're the fellow who nearly ran me over, aren't you?"

"Well, I—"

"Jolly good laugh," Newbury continued.

"Quite," I agreed halfheartedly.

Gwen quickly changed the subject:

"And how have your studies been progressing, Mister Newbury? Find any interesting fairy circles today?"

"Well, no," Newbury replied, "but I believe I may have found your mother's cave."

"Cave?" Gwen sounded bewildered.

Newbury pulled a small notebook out of his satchel and held it up for inspection.

"In her notebook, your mother talks about a cave beneath the big hill," he explained, waving in the general direction of the woods. "She was searching for it the night that she—" He quickly caught himself. "Apparently she believed it was part of the old Celtic legends about the area. The Fair Folk hiding beneath the hills and all that. And I do believe I've found it."

"Who gave you Mother's notebook?" Gwen asked, sounding a little angry.

"Oh, Miss Susan," Newbury said quickly. "When she found out that I was interested in carrying on your mother's work, she insisted I take it."

"Very generous of her," Gwen mused. "Is there anything interesting in it?"

"Absolutely!" Newbury replied. "All manner of exciting things. Recounting of local legends, records of her own observations and sightings, even some stories about 'dog-men' and the ancient Wild Hunt. Very thrilling."

"If you say so," Gwen said.

The mention of 'dog-men' gave me a queer turn, but at that moment I could not remember why. Still, the unease it caused me made me fall silent, and so I remained for the rest of the walk, every so often glancing back over my shoulder at the woods and the mournful hill.

***

My nervousness had all but vanished by the time Vos and I joined the others in the sitting room to await the gong for dinner. Newbury was playing the piano, to the delight of Susan and Bella. I saw Gwen seated by the windows with Hazel and John, but before I could go to join them, Vos and I were accosted by Sir Arthur, who seemed much more amiable than when we had first arrived.

"Good evening Major, Mister Vos," he said. "Settling in well, I trust."

"Oh, rather," I replied. "Always a treat to be visit—"

Sir Arthur rather ignored me and focused his attention on Vos.

"And you, Mister Vos?" he asked. "Will we be enjoying your company for a few days?"

Vos considered the question and said, "*Ja, ja*, that is the plan, I believe."

"Good, good," Sir Arthur said. "And you say you can read Sogdian?"

"*Ja*, well enough."

"Good," Sir Arthur repeated. Then, without another word, he turned and walked away from us, like we were no longer there.

After an appropriate pause, I turned to Vos and asked, "What do you make of that?"

"I make of that a man who knows just what he wants and who has little interest in anything else, *mijn vriend*," Vos answered. "And what is desired most by Sir Arthur Turnbridge at this moment is a translator."

"But why?" I asked.

Vos chuckled. "I do not know, but rest assured that it shall be revealed to me soon enough." He glanced toward the door, where the butler had just appeared. "Ah, and now I think this must be your old friend."

"How…?" I began.

"Do not play the fool, Stamford," Vos chided. "He is the only one among the guests who has yet to arrive."

The butler cleared his throat and announced:

"Captain Norrys, sir."

He stepped aside as my old friend Norrys entered, tugging on his dinner jacket to make sure it was in place. He had clearly rushed to change in time for dinner as soon as he had arrived at the house.

"Piggy!" I exclaimed, hurrying to meet him.

"Bridgy!" Norrys answered, shaking my hand warmly.

Norrys was a plump and amiable fellow, which had been the source of his unfortunate nickname back at school. I realize now that it had been rather cruel of us, but Norrys had shouldered it all the same. Of course, he and I could never pass words without him at least once referring to me as "Stamford Bridge", so I suppose it rather evened out.

"How are you, old boy?" I asked. "Still up in Anchester?"

"No better place in the world," Norrys replied.

"What are you doing these days?"

"Funny story," Norrys said. "You remember that friend of mine from the RFC? Delapore?"

"Alfie Delapore? Rather!" I exclaimed. "How is he?"

Norrys frowned for a moment. "Bought it, I'm afraid."

"Oh, what rotten luck," I said. "Was it the…?" I motioned vaguely in the area of my head to indicate the late Delapore's war wound.

"Afraid so." After another moment, Norrys brightened again. "Anyway, seems his father's decided to move back into the old family seat at Exham Priory. Bought it from my uncle and everything."

"Good show," I told him.

"So I'm helping the chap with renovations and whatnot," Norrys said. A thought came to him. "I say, you'll have to come up and visit once it's all done. I'll introduce you."

"Jolly good of you, Piggy," I said.

Vos cleared his throat softly.

"Oh, right. Piggy, this is my friend Hieronymus Vos." I motioned from one to the other. "Vos, this is my old chum, Captain Norrys."

"*Goedenavond*," Vos said, bowing his head to Norrys.

"Oh, hello," Norrys replied, looking a bit baffled.

"He's a detective," I explained.

"An antiquarian," Vos corrected. "Detecting is merely a.... What is the word?" He thought a bit and then smiled. "Ah yes. A hobby."

Again Norrys looked somewhat baffled by Vos and simply said, "Good show."

I cleared my throat and looked across the room toward Susan. She was gazing in our direction, so I nudged Norrys to get his attention.

"You know, Susan's here," I said.

"Well, yes," Norrys said, a little breathlessly.

"You should go talk to her."

Norrys looked at Susan, but Susan, realizing she had been observed, quickly looked away. Norrys's face fell.

"I couldn't," he said.

"Go on, old boy," I insisted. "It's the whole reason for the evening, you know."

"Really?" Norrys suddenly looked guilty. "I hadn't realized...."

"Yes, now *go on*," I repeated. "The stars are right, Piggy, now go over there and talk to her."

Norrys nodded and smiled nervously. "Wish me luck."

He quickly squared his shoulders, held his head high, and went to talk to Susan like a man going over the top. I watched with growing distress as the two of them began speaking in awkward, hesitant half sentences.

I sighed. "Well, we tried."

"As I told to you, *mijn vriend*," Vos said, "they are like the two cats circling one another. Such are the timid in love."

"Better to be confident, I suppose."

"*Nee*," Vos replied. "Then they are like two bulls colliding, until they dash themselves to pieces."

"What a gruesome thing to say!" It was Hazel who spoke, having joined us along with James. "Are you always so morbid, Mister Vos?" The way she asked, it sounded like a compliment.

Vos shrugged a little and smiled.

"Who can say?" he mused. "I enjoy the company of old books and dead things. If that is morbid—"

"It is," James interjected.

"—then morbid I must be," Vos finished. He raised one finger and gently brushed his moustache. "But let us rejoice. The night's work is accomplished. The Miss Turnbridge and the Captain Norrys are in a room together making the awkward conversation. It is the blossoming of romance."

"I don't think that's quite the same thing, Vos," I said.

"Perhaps not," Vos replied, "but we must wait and see the result."

He might have said more, but he was interrupted by a low, mournful howl that drifted in through one of the open windows. It was more peculiar than frightening, though in light of my earlier experience it did give me a bit of a turn.

"Goodness, what was that?" I exclaimed.

"Sounded like a hound," James said.

"Oh yes!" Hazel exclaimed. "A hound howling upon the moor like something out of Sherlock Holmes! How delightfully sinister!"

"Darling," James said, "the nearest moorland's twenty miles away. I hardly think it's that."

"That only makes it all the more peculiar," I added.

Vos looked thoughtful and said softly, "*Ja*, peculiar. It is the question most interesting."

"The question of why a dog is howling?" James asked. "Hardly needs a reason, does it?"

"On the contrary, Mister Turnbridge," Vos replied, "unlike man, a dog always does things for a reason."

The howl sounded again, closer this time. I suddenly felt unease brimming up inside me, which made me quite angry.

"Well, whatever it is, it'll spoil the evening," I said.

I marched straight across to the window in question and looked outside. I confess, I had actually expected to see some monstrous phosphorous-mouthed beast lumbering across the lawn toward us, but to my relief there was nothing to be seen. I pushed the window shut and latched it firmly.

Then, as I prepared to turn away, I half fancied that I saw a shape flit across the grounds just at the edge of the woods. It looked vaguely man-like, though it scurried along on all fours, so it was hardly that. And it was gone in an instant. If not for my encounter in the wood, I'd have thought little of it. I waited a moment longer, but I saw nothing.

Instead, I heard Gwen and Sir Arthur speaking softly nearby. I looked and saw that they had retired to one of the corners, where they might avoid being overheard, but in going to the window I had moved just into earshot.

"Daddy, please!" Gwen insisted, her tone desperate.

"Not a penny more," Sir Arthur replied.

"But Daddy, New York is expensive. Plays are expensive!"

"Yes, and parties with your degenerate friends are also expensive," came the reply. Sir Arthur frowned at her, looking very annoyed. "You have your allowance. Be grateful I don't cut you off entirely."

"You wouldn't—"

"Oh, wouldn't I?" Sir Arthur scowled at her. "You're nearly twenty-four, Gwendolen. You should be married by now. Perhaps I should cut you off until you find yourself a husband!"

Gwen's eyes flashed with anger and she seemed about ready to shout something. Then she thought better of it and walked out of the room without another word.

I quickly turned away before Sir Arthur could notice me listening. I looked out the window and in the growing darkness I saw the shape again. It had drawn closer now, and it stood just at the edge of the flower beds. I could discern little beyond its hideously elongated appearance, but its eyes shone in the dying sunlight, glinting like a cat's. I tried desperately to close my eyes, to blot out that creeping thing as it slowly neared, step-by-step, but I couldn't.

And then, mercifully, the gong rang for dinner, and I almost jumped in fright. I looked away from the window and then back again. The creature was gone. Or rather, it had never been there, I told myself; and that lie comforted me until the events of the night.

***

Dinner was pleasant, enough so that it allowed me to push the strange sights of the day from my mind. Norrys and Susan were beginning to converse more freely, which I counted as a success for the evening. Hazel pestered Vos about his cases, while Professor Howard did likewise about his knowledge of archaeology. Vos seemed to enjoy both conversations at once, and every so often found cause to draw the one into the other. James and I chatted about his work in London, and Newbury eagerly told me more about his peculiar research regarding fairies living under the ground.

Everyone seemed to be having a good time other than Sir Arthur and Gwen, who sullenly watched one another from across the table, even in the midst of other conversations. Recalling their words in the sitting room, I wasn't at all surprised.

As everyone made ready to retire after dinner, Sir Arthur approached me and Vos.

"Mister Vos," he said, "I wonder if I might drag you away for your opinion about my latest acquisition…."

"The Sogdian text?" Vos asked. "*Ja*, I would be delighted. May Major Stamford join us? I should like to broaden his horizons."

"Steady on," I protested.

"Yes, why not?" Sir Arthur replied. "No harm to be done. Just keep your hands to yourself, Major."

"Look, I say—"

But they had both stopped listening, so I gave up talking. Sir Arthur led us to his study, which was large and furnished with more attention to modernity than I would have expected. Perhaps it was simply Sir Arthur's way of combating the creeping hand of age, by surrounding himself with things that were new and young, like his second wife.

Sir Arthur unlocked a wall safe and removed a bundle of old papers and bits of parchment held together in a sheaf. He set the bundle down on his desk and began gently sorting through the manuscripts until he came to the one in question. Vos peered over his shoulder, studying the other papers as they were sorted.

"Goodness me," he said. "Is this Philetas's translation of the *Kitab al-Azif*?"

Sir Arthur looked up with great surprise and asked, "You're familiar with the *Al-Azif*, Mister Vos? You are full of surprises."

Vos made a great show of modesty and smiled.

"Only by reputation, I assure you," he said. "But I am intrigued to see a copy in person. May I…?" He motioned to one of the pages. "With the utmost care, of course."

"Look but do not touch," Sir Arthur said. He grumbled a little. "It's not even a copy, I fear. A transcription of a copy, and not a complete one at that."

"Still, such a marvelous acquisition for a scholar of ancient things, *ja?*" Vos mused.

I glanced at the manuscript in question, but I could make neither heads nor tails of it.

"It's all Greek to me," I joked.

Vos looked at me sternly, but it was Sir Arthur who replied:

"It *is* Greek."

"Oh, right," I said.

Presently, Sir Arthur found the document he wanted and showed it to Vos. It was a large rectangle of vellum marked with both pictures and script. I took a look too, but I couldn't understand any of the writing. Only a few associated images had any sort of meaning to me, and one particular depiction of a queer sort of dog-thing gave me a turn, so I quickly turned away and found something else in the study to occupy myself with.

"*Ja*," Vos said softly, studying the document through his gilded *pince-nez*. "*Ja*, Sogdian indeed."

"What is it?" Sir Arthur asked, his tone betraying a hint of excitement. "Can you translate it?"

"Well… *ja*," Vos told him, "but it will take some time. Perhaps tomorrow I could examine it properly."

"But you must have some idea of what it says!" Sir Arthur insisted.

"Of course, of course," Vos reassured him. "It is… let me see.…Some manner of alchemical formula, I believe. There is something about a *ghûl* and long life, but...." He sighed. "Alas, it is late and my eyes, they are tired. Tomorrow, as I say, I shall give it my utmost attention."

As they spoke, I had occasion to pass the open safe. It held the usual contents one would expect—some money, important documents, and the like—but in addition, it was filled with scrolls and papers and some assorted trinkets of no apparent value. Most intriguing, I saw, sitting atop the pile, a little amulet made of green jade and carved in the shape of a sphinx, or something near to it; though in truth, it was rather more hound-like than feline in its appearance.

"I say," I said, "what an odd little thing—"

"Don't touch that!" Sir Arthur shouted, making me jump back in alarm.

"I...I didn't—" I began.

Sir Arthur hurried to the safe and pushed it shut. Looking at me angrily, he said, "Gads, man, you're as bad as Howard, poking and prodding in my private things!"

"Look here," I protested, "I'd no idea—"

"I think perhaps you'd better go for the evening, Major," Sir Arthur told me, taking a deep breath to calm down. "I'm certain James would like to see you for billiards or something."

I frowned a bit, embarrassed at having offended my host without meaning to, but I nodded my agreement.

"Yes, alright," I said.

"I also shall retire," Vos said brightly. "But tomorrow I shall assist with the translation, *ja?*"

"Yes, good," Sir Arthur said. "Good night."

As we left the study, I saw him open the safe again and reassure himself that I hadn't damaged any of the contents—the idea! In the hallway, we passed Professor Howard, who exchanged a friendly nod on his way, before he vanished into the study.

"Most interesting," Vos mused.

"What is?" I asked.

"Did you notice anything peculiar about the amulet in the safe? The one that Sir Arthur was so insistent you not touch?"

"Well, yes," I said. "Come to think of it, it looked rather like one of the pictures on that Soggy-Dinny manuscript."

Vos winced slightly as I spoke this last bit, but he nodded and said, "I do believe that Sir Arthur Turnbridge is playing a great trick on all of us. He clearly believes that I do not understand what he has laid before me…or perhaps he is desperate enough that he does not care. It is most interesting."

"What are you talking about, Vos? What trick?"

"Why, *mijn vriend*," Vos answered, "the greatest trick of all. The trick of eternity."

***

Vos retired for the night without explaining any more of his cryptic statement to me. I won't bore you with the details of the rest of my evening. Suffice to say that James, Norrys, Newbury, and I spent a couple of hours smoking and playing billiards. Newbury was the first to retire, then Norrys, and finally James and myself went our separate ways.

As I went along the upstairs passage toward my room, I happened to pass by Newbury's door. I saw that his light was on, which surprised me enough to stop, and then I heard voices speaking. One was Newbury's, while the other one was soft and raspy, and I could not place it.

"Tonight?" Newbury asked. "I can't! I need more time!"

"No time," said his companion. "Tonight or never."

I wondered if it was Newbury talking to himself, perhaps pantomiming from a story or something. I raised my hand to knock, to see what was going on, but something stopped me. Instead, I resolved to ask him about it in the morning.

And I think it was well that I did so, for my own sake if not for Sir Arthur's.

***

I awoke in darkness for a reason I could not remember. I had vague recollections of some infernal howling, and of the misshapen things that I had seen on the grounds, but any memory of my dreams vanished in the time it took to turn on my lamp. But as I sat there, I heard the faint sound of breaking glass. Alarmed, I jumped to my feet. I found an electric torch in the bedside drawer and, switching it on, I hurried into the hallway to investigate.

The noise had come from downstairs, so that was where I went. Just above the stairs, I almost collided with Norrys as he hurried out of his room.

"Good Lord, man!" I cried softly. "You gave me a dreadful fright!"

"*I* gave *you* a fright?" Norrys answered, putting a hand to his chest. "Did you hear it as well?"

I nodded. "Sounded like glass. Could be a window."

"Robbers, do you think?" Norrys asked, as we descended the stairs.

"Could be," I said. "Someone else might have heard it too, but we should investigate before we rouse the whole house."

"Agreed," said Norrys, as we reached the foyer. He pointed down one hallway. "I'll go this way, you go that way, and we'll meet at the back?"

"Sensible enough," I replied.

Having parted company from Norrys, I suddenly was given cause to regret it. As I crept along the main corridor, I felt my hair standing on end with anticipation. The very thought of burglars in such remote country was far-fetched, but what troubled me the most were the vague and insubstantial memories of my recent dreams.

Then I turned a corner and what I saw made me freeze in place with fear.

I cannot quite explain how dreadful it is to see such a thing clearly in the light. Ghosts are always the most frightening when they are vague and unseen, but material horrors only grow with clarity. In that instant I knew that the things I had seen in the forest and on the grounds were not tricks of the light or phantoms of the imagination.

The thing in the corridor was hideous and elongated, bony, as if its rubbery skin had been pulled too tightly over its half-human form. Indeed, *half-human* was the only way to describe it, for while the form was in essence that of a man, it was hunched over and contorted in ways that even an ape might balk at. And worse, its head, its hideous, twisted head, was more dog than man, yet it still carried with it some semblance of lingering humanity that distorted its canine visage into a parody of Nature.

Mercifully, many of the details still elude me, blocked from my mind by some instinct of self-preservation. But I remember the eyes, those glowing, bestial, human eyes; and the blood that dripped from its gore-covered hands.

The torch dropped from my numb fingers and flickered into darkness on the floor. But while the darkness freed my eyes from seeing that which they could not understand, still I sensed the creature lurking in the passage, regarding me just as it had done in the forest. I almost imagined its hand, its blood-encrusted hand, outstretched toward me, and I still shudder to think that I very nearly extended my own in reply.

Suddenly I heard Norrys shouting for help. This brought me back to my senses just in time to see the shape before me lope away into the sitting room. I grabbed my torch and hit it a few times to turn it on. When the light shone again, the corridor was empty save for the trail of blood. I ran to the sitting room and looked inside. There I saw the broken window and more blood, but no creature and nothing else.

I ran to find Norrys, which coincided exactly with the trail of blood. I found my old chum standing in the doorway of Sir Arthur's study, holding himself upright with one hand as he swayed on his feet. As I pushed past him, I saw what had so overpowered him, and suddenly I was nearly faint myself.

Sir Arthur's body sat slumped in his chair, almost unrecognizable. It had been torn asunder, spraying the poor man's blood all over one corner of the room, and leaving the desk and part of the floor drenched.

"Oh, dear God," I said.

"Who could have done such a thing?" Norrys cried.

I heard footsteps from down the corridor, and more on the floor above us. It seemed that Norrys's cry had raised the whole house.

Professor Howard was the first to arrive. He clapped his hands over his mouth and slowly walked into the room as if in a daze.

"No, no, no," he mumbled. "Sir Arthur…."

I quickly grabbed him by the arm.

"Look, um, everyone stay back," I said, doing my best to keep a cool head. Strangely, the shock of the moment made it all the easier for me to forget what I had seen in the corridor. As the others began to arrive, I repeated myself: "Everyone, stay back. Don't disturb the room."

Presently, Vos arrived as well, looking rather sleepy. He had a hairnet on, and another for his moustache, which would have been comical under any other circumstances.

Vos yawned a little and said softly, "What has happened, Stamford?"

"It's Sir Arthur, Vos. He's been murdered."

There were cries from the others. Bella put a hand over her mouth to keep from crying out and Susan sobbed into James's shoulder. Her brother was pale at the news, but he kept his composure like a proper soldier, as did Hazel and Gwen, though I saw the anguish on the faces of all three of them.

Meanwhile, Vos was busy counting the heads in the hallway.

"I see that we are all here," he said. "All here but young Newbury. Would someone kindly go and rouse him."

"I'll do it," said Norrys.

"*Goed*," said Vos. When Norrys had gone, he confided to me, "I do not think that he will find anyone there, but all the same...."

Vos rubbed his hands together and went into the study, carefully avoiding the blood. He first examined the desk and its contents, notably the papers and the dead man's glass of brandy. Then he went to the safe, which I saw was left open. After a moment's scrutiny, he motioned for me to join him.

"Tell me, Stamford," he said, "what is wrong with the picture we see here?"

To my surprise, I saw that the safe's money and valuables were all still there. In fact, there was only one thing missing at all.

"My God, Vos!" I cried. "The jade amulet! It's gone!"

***

The police were summoned, of course, and I don't think I need dwell on the details of their investigation, which was reported on by the press and which was concluded very quickly anyway. I imagine you already know the official verdict: for reasons that are largely unknown, young Charles Newbury murdered poor Sir Arthur at his desk, broke into the safe, and stole a few select *objets d'art.* As Newbury has yet to be apprehended, the reason for the murder remains unknown, but the police suspect an argument that may have become too heated and grown out of control.

But let us ignore that conclusion, for I fear that the police are wrong. Their manhunt for Charles Newbury must inevitably come to nothing. They will never find Newbury, nor would it matter if they did, as I shall explain.

***

Thanks to Vos's careful managing of the police, the investigation of the house was largely concluded that day. The local Chief Inspector hit upon the notion of Newbury's guilt quite quickly, and by the following evening, the rest of us were left undisturbed at Brympton House. There had been some attempt to scour the grounds with dogs, but these had become quite unmanageable within a few minutes of setting foot on the property, and the search had been abandoned. Now the only police on hand were a pair of constables left to wait outside the front door in case Newbury showed his face again.

At Vos's insistence, the rest of us gathered in the sitting room. The broken window had been covered up, the glass thrown away, and the blood concealed by a fresh rug; but still everyone looked uneasy. Vos was very cheerful despite all this. He had tea brought for everyone and served it up himself, bringing each guest their cup and saucer by his own hand.

"Look here, Mister Vos," James said, "as you're John's friend, I'm willing to indulge this meeting of yours, but would you please explain what all this is about?"

"It's horrid, simply horrid," Susan murmured, sniffling into a handkerchief and leaning on Bella for support.

"*Ja*, this I know," Vos said, "and I assure you that it will all be over soon. But surely you wish to know the truth about your father's death."

"The truth?" Gwen demanded. "That beast Newbury killed him!"

"And to think, he seemed like such a nice young man," Bella said, looking down sadly.

Vos smiled. "Of course, this we all know: Newbury, for no reason at all, rises in the middle of the night, takes a knife that has not yet been found, stabs Sir Arthur to death, and then flees into the wilderness." Vos held up a finger. "But...what if, for the moment, we entertain another possibility, a more fantastical possibility."

"What are you talking about, Vos?" I demanded.

"Before I begin, would you be so kind as to rouse the Captain Norrys, Stamford?" Vos asked.

I glanced toward Norrys, who sat on the sofa beside me. The poor chap seemed to have dozed off, though it was quite unlike him. I gave him a gentle shake; then, as he did not respond, I shook him harder.

"Good God!" I cried, my alarm echoed by the others.

"Is he asleep or is he dead, Stamford?" Vos asked.

"Asleep," I answered, "but he's just dropped off!"

Vos crossed to Norrys and took the teacup from his slumbering hand before it could tumble onto the floor.

James leaped to his feet and shouted, "What have you done, Mister Vos?"

Vos did not seem to mind James's angry tone, and replied with a gentle voice:

"Ladies and gentlemen, I have given Captain Norrys what I believe to be a sleeping draught. I took the liberty of removing it from the late Sir Arthur's glass on the night of the murder. This confirms what I suspected: that Sir Arthur Turnbridge was dead asleep in the moments before he died. For this reason there was no cry, no struggle. Had there been a fight, as the police believe, there would have been signs. The upturned chair, the broken accouterments, the body upon the floor. But there were none of these things."

"My God!" James shouted. "You *drugged* Norrys?"

Now Vos began to look irritated.

"*Ja*, Mister Turnbridge," he said. "Now if you please, be quiet and sit down while Vos speaks."

"I…" James began, but he slowly sat all the same.

"The question then becomes, who drugged Sir Arthur?" Vos continued.

"You mean who killed him?" I ventured.

"*Nee*," Vos corrected. "Who drugged. You see the killer is already known to Vos—"

"*What?*" Now it was Gwen who cried out and sprang to her feet. "You do?"

"—but we shall attend to that shortly." Vos smiled and brushed his moustache with one fingertip. "For you see, the person who drugged Sir Arthur is the very same person who robbed him."

"Yes, but who would want to rob him?" I asked.

The room fell silent and suddenly everyone more or less looked in Gwen's direction.

"Oh, thanks!" Gwen protested, slowly sinking back into her chair. "You all think I did it, do you?"

"Well…you are a bit hard up most of the time—" James began. Then Hazel slapped his arm for rudeness. "Ouch!"

"What James means is—" Hazel said.

"What he means is that I'm an actress in New York and I go to parties and

I want to produce plays," Gwen snapped. She glared at the others. "Don't pretend you aren't thinking it. You've always thought I was a wastrel, haven't you?"

There was a long silence and then Susan shouted, "Well yes! Dash it all, yes, Gwen, you're a wastrel! I devote my life to taking care of our father and you go flouncing off to America!"

"Um," I said, clearing my throat, "I think this is getting a bit off the mark."

"At least I can say 'hello' to a chap when I fancy him," Gwen retorted. "You can't even do it when he's out cold!"

"Just please, stop fighting!" Bella shouted, her voice croaking with the emotion of it. More softly she said, "Please stop. My husband is dead and I would prefer for his surviving family...my surviving family...not to bicker like dogs!"

The siblings were suddenly quiet again, looking down at their hands.

"Sorry," they all mumbled, more or less at the same time.

"Besides," I said, "there wasn't any money taken. We all saw the contents of the safe. Almost everything was there."

"Ah, but it was not the money that was taken, was it, Stamford?" asked Vos.

I was confused for a moment, but then I gasped with realization. "Oh, right! That jade thingy! That was missing!"

Vos shook his head. "Stamford, you are truly a lighthouse of elucidation in a fog of confusion. *Ja*, the...how you say...'jade thingy'. It was stolen, along with the Sogdian manuscript that I had only that evening offered to translate for Sir Arthur."

Vos folded his hands and continued:

"And so, let me tell you a story. It is a story about an old man who, as he moves onward into the twilight of his life begins to feel the weight of age. Everything makes him feel old. His body? Withering. His house? Decaying. His children? Young enough, almost, to be his grandchildren. And so he surrounds himself with that which is new, that which is young. The modern furniture, the young wife, the even younger second wife.... But it is not enough. Ah, but this man, he is a scholar of that which is arcane, and so in the course of his studies, he discovers his solution.

"He turns to forgotten legends and secret, forbidden texts. He obtains and reads portions of the *Kitab al-Azif*, that which in Greek is called the *Necronomicon*. And in these fragments he learns a great many things, things that man was not meant to know, but which *man will always strive to know!* And he reads that most significant of passages: 'That is not dead which can eternal lie. And with strange aeons even death may die.' And so Sir Arthur comes to believe that he too can escape death!"

Vos began to pace, becoming so animated that the tips of his moustache seemed to quiver like a thing possessed of life.

"And over the course of his studies, Sir Arthur learns of a profane and secretive corpse-eating cannibal cult that so terrorized Central Asia in the seventh century. He discovers that through strange and occult practices, these *ghûls*, as they were called in Arabia, possessed the secret of immortality. And he must have that power."

"But this is all nonsense!" protested James.

"Ah, *nee*, *nee*, I fear it is all too true," Vos answered. "I merely tell you a story of the facts as I have observed and deduced them. You are free to deny the truth if you so choose. Such voluntary blindness has served mankind well for our short time upon the Earth. But what you cannot deny are the actions of your father. Sir Arthur obtained these texts and artifacts at great personal expense, even to the abandonment of his children and the disintegration of his house...did he not, Professor Howard?"

Howard looked startled at being addressed, and for a few moments he merely stammered. Finally he managed to reply, "How should I know?"

"You know, Professor, because you obtained them for him!" Vos shouted. "You, Professor Howard, who were ejected from Arabia two years ago for *grave robbing!* Just as you had done before the War! Sir Arthur knew about your criminal activities, did he not?"

"No, I—"

"He knew, and in exchange for helping you conceal them, Sir Arthur put you to work as his errand boy, scouring the world for his accursed artifacts and books of forbidden knowledge! He held your black market dealings like a sword above your head, all the while forcing you to call upon them to obtain his collection!"

"I...I..." Howard stammered. He looked at the others, his face pale, nervous sweat upon his brow.

"And what cruel irony for you, Professor," Vos continued, "that it was only by your work, your digs, your contacts, your risk that Sir Arthur could obtain his ghoul amulet and the Sogdian text and the other countless keys to immortality he had assembled! You, who were as old as he, who were as terrified of old age and death as he!"

"It…I…."

"With the Sogdian text, you finally had the last piece to your puzzle," said Vos. "But how to obtain them? You yourself know Sogdian. How else could you have known the validity of the manuscript? But to complete the ritual, you need also the amulet, and that was always kept either under Sir Arthur's watchful eye or in his safe. You had all the time in the world to wait and plan and find an opening to steal them…until last night.

"Last night, when Vos came to visit with his friend Major Stamford, to visit the friends of a friend for the sake of a friend. The most unlikely of chances. And to your horror, you learn that Vos, he knows Sogdian. Vos, he can translate the manuscript for Sir Arthur, and then Sir Arthur will have his immortality and you will have nothing. Perhaps even he will kill you, so that you cannot reveal what you know, for what crimes and betrayal would a man not commit for eternal life?"

"But this is balderdash!" protested James.

"Steady on, Jamie," I said. "I think Meester Vos is onto something."

Gwen looked at me, astonished and horrified.

"You can't mean that, John! Your friend is clearly insane!"

Normally I would have agreed, but I have never known Vos to be wrong about such things, no matter how impossible they sound. And what was more, as I watched, I saw Howard sink back into his chair, growing more and more distressed with each word that Vos spoke:

"And so, Professor, you resolved to take the amulet and the manuscript that night, before Vos could provide the translation and undo your years of patient waiting! You took a portion of sleeping powder, which any sensible household has on hand, and with it you lace the drink of Sir Arthur so that he will fall asleep at his desk, while his safe is still open. When this is done, you sneak in and steal what you believe to be rightfully yours."

Howard twitched rather vulgarly, perhaps weighing his options and finding none of them agreeable.

"Yes, yes, alright!" he cried. "I drugged him! I stole it! But I did not kill him! I swear it!"

"You filthy dog!" shouted Hazel as she bounded to her feet. "I should give you a damn thrashing for what you've done to this family!"

"I didn't kill him!" Howard repeated, his voice desperate and fearful.

"Liar!" snapped Bella.

Vos quickly raised his hands to silence the others. "*Nee*, *nee*, I believe that Professor Howard speaks the truth. Having obtained the amulet and the manuscript, what reason would he have to kill Sir Arthur?" Vos paused for effect and then answered his own question: "None at all. And better still to be on the run as a thief rather than a murderer. *Nee*, in fact it was the murder of Sir Arthur that *prevented* Professor Howard from fleeing. Once the body was discovered, he had no choice but to remain and trust that the police would lay blame for the theft at the feet of the murderer. And so, Professor Howard, he hides the amulet and the manuscript about his person and waits for the opportunity to leave."

Howard nervously touched the front of his shirt.

"My God! He's wearing it!" Susan exclaimed.

"Ah, ah," Vos said, "let us leave that for now. And let us address the identity of the murderer."

"It must be Newbury," I said. "He's the only one not here. And I overheard him talking to someone about that night being 'the night'." I paused. "Oh, wait a minute.... If he's the murderer, who was he talking to?"

"You are learning well, Stamford," Vos exclaimed, clapping his hands. "Who indeed? And I tell you truly, it was not Newbury."

"One of us, then?" asked Gwen.

"*Nee*, not one of you either. No one in this room was responsible."

"I don't follow," said James.

"Allow me to tell you another story," replied Vos. "A story about this same cannibal cult of ghouls. They were not confined to Central Asia nor to Arabia, but rather spread out across all the world, scurrying to the furthest reaches of the Earth with bloody claws and plague-ridden hooves. Some of them even traveled to this 'sceptered isle' where they lurked in hidden places in days before even the Celts took possession here. And in time, in their mysterious comings and goings, plundering and haunting, they were forgotten, remembered only as 'Fair Folk beneath the hills'.

"Then one day a young man named Newbury comes to study the legends they have become, and he discovers them and they discover him, and so one night they take him down into their stygian charnel houses, to a fate that even the wise can only imagine.

"For you see, on that same night, these ghouls arose from their pits and came to reclaim that which was stolen from them: an amulet carved from jade in the manner of their kin, adorned with wings for a reason known only to them. It is my conclusion that Sir Arthur Turnbridge was brutally murdered while he slept by a ghoul from beneath the hill, perhaps even the same ghoul that enticed Newbury to join them in their rotting Tartarus."

Silence again fell over the room as the others exchanged looks. After what I had seen in the woods and on the grounds, and given what little I remembered of the vision in the house, I grew uneasy, perhaps accepting Vos's words more readily than the rest. But Howard's reaction was the most remarkable. He sank back in his chair, clutching at his chest in fear.

"Oh God, no…" he murmured.

"You don't expect us to believe this, do you?" demanded Gwen.

"Whether you believe it or not is of no consequence to me," answered Vos, smiling a triumphant smile. "All that matters is what is true." He turned his eyes toward Howard. "As for you, Professor, I would advise you to return your trophy to wherever it came from, and with all speed. These creatures will follow you to the ends of the Earth to have it back, and if they find you first…." Vos sighed. "I suppose you gave Sir Arthur a certain mercy by drugging him before the ghoul found him. But unless you spend every moment addled with opium, you have no such fortune."

Now shaking visibly, Howard bolted from his chair. He staggered toward the doorway, still clutching at his chest and what I assumed to be the amulet hidden beneath his shirt.

"I…I must go…" he stammered.

James looked astonished. "You can't expect us to let you just leave! You're a thief!" He looked to the others for agreement. "He's a thief!"

Bella's wide mouth contorted into a horrible frown of sorrow and resignation.

"Let him go," she said. "Let him take his horrible prize and be gone!"

"You can't be serious!" James protested. "After he stole from Pater!"

"Please, James," Bella said. "I just want him out of my house and out of our lives."

James scowled openly, but he nodded.

"Get out," he snarled at Professor Howard.

Still pale and sweating with fear, Howard ran for the door. I could hear him flee out of the house and into the night.

There was a pause and then suddenly Norrys let out a tremendous yawn and stretched his arms above his head. Blinking sleepily, he looked around at the rest of us and said:

"Oh gosh, dreadfully sorry. Must've dozed off. Did I miss anything?"

***

That night, when sleep would not come to me and my dreams were troubled by what had been seen and been said, I went to Vos's room. I knocked softly, expecting him to be abed, but instead I heard my friend call:

"*Ja*, what is it?"

"Vos, may I come in for a word?" I asked. "About…about today."

"*Ja, ja*," Vos answered. "Come in, the door, it is open."

I opened the door and stepped inside. To my surprise, Vos was neither in bed nor in one of the chairs reading, but rather he knelt upon the floor, prostrating himself before what I could only imagine was some manner of shrine. It was a little box made of ebony wood, but it was tilted away from me so that I could not see what lay inside.

Vos slowly stood and smiled at me.

"What troubles you, *mijn vriend?*" he asked. "Would you care, perhaps, for the cup of gin?"

"No, no, thank you," I said.

Vos smiled again and motioned to a pair of chairs. When I had seated myself, he sat in the one across from me.

"You see, Vos," I said, "I'm not really sure what to make of all this. These *things* you talked about. Are they real? Or was it just a story?" Vos opened his mouth to speak, but I kept talking. "And if it isn't just a story, how can it be true? It's impossible!"

"*Nee, mijn vriend*," Vos answered. "What is it your great poet says, Stamford? 'There are more things in heaven and earth…than are dreamt of in your philosophy', *ja?* And I tell you Stamford, it is true."

I closed my eyes, trying not to think about the things that I had seen; about how such things could not be and yet they were too real to be dismissed save by a delusion of ignorance.

"How do you manage it, Vos?" I asked. "How do such things not terrify you? How can you know such things and still go on? How can they not drive you mad?"

Vos chuckled a little and brushed his moustache with his fingertip.

"Oh, Stamford, how little you know," he said, sympathetically. "I once was like you, sheltered and confused. But all that is changed. Perhaps one day I shall tell you the tale of those three hellish nights I spent in the secret fane of the Dark Pharaoh, Nephren-ka. But not tonight."

"How are you not terrified of every waking moment, Vos?"

"It is simple," Vos answered. "For you see, I need fear nothing, for I belong to my Lord and Master, Nyarlathotep, the Crawling Chaos. I fear nothing, Stamford, because I have faith. I have faith that when my time has come, my master will arrive and devour me body and soul. And until such time as that, I am free to walk to Earth unafraid, and to work His will."

"What…?" I gasped, not quite able to speak nor quite able to understand. "The who? The what?"

Vos smiled in his usual disarming way, placed a finger to his lips, and motioned toward the box shrine that stood open on the floor nearby. I turned to look at it, and whatever I saw inside made me scream and scream until I remembered nothing else.

***

I do not recall what was in that box save in fleeting, haunting moments. It is like the dog-things at Brympton, and the fish men in Innsmouth, and the secrets buried beneath that accursed Exham Priory. What I remember I must recount, and what I do not remember *I must not and cannot recall!* I am at the end of my tether. After all these years, there is nothing left for me.

I have resolved to write these things down that someone may do something useful with the scraps of my miserable life.

Once I am done, I have a bottle of whiskey and my old service revolver lying next to one another on my desk, and I pray to God that the one will give me the courage to use the other.

AERKHEIM'S HORROR

Christine Morgan

Thor's hammer shattered the skies, splitting them jagged with white-hot lightning-strokes. The great noise crashed. The sea heaved. The wind howled a cold death's breath from a fimbul-wolf's throat.

Sails furled and oars stowed, at the storm's mercy, the ship tossed upon the waves. The timbers groaned with the agonies of a living beast. In that beast's belly, bodies huddled under cloaks and limewood shields for shelter, amid close-packed chests, crates and barrels laden with provisions and possessions. In the livestock pens, goats bleated and pigs grunted, protesting the conditions of their confinement.

Mjiska clung to the prow, its post bereft now of a carved dragon's head because they were on no errand of war but in hope and search of settlement. The rain dashed her face and the salt spray stung her eyes as she squinted into the turbulent darkness, waiting for the next bright crack of the thunderer's mighty weapon.

A thick blonde braid swung against her back, slapping like a length of wet rope. Drenched garments of linen, wool and leather plastered her frame. An axe hung at her belt. She was tall for a woman, broad through shoulder and waist and hip, broad of brow and nose and chin.

In looks as well as manner, she was very much her father's daughter… just as Aerk, her brother, was in looks and manner very much their mother's son, black-haired and slender, with fine features of which he was notably vain.

God-fire struck again, dazzling in its brilliance, painting the foaming ocean silver. In its flash, Mjiska saw what she'd thought she'd glimpsed before, but now she could be certain.

She turned without loosing her hold on the prow and raised her voice against the storm-fury.

"Land!" she cried. "Land to the west! West!"

The words were, despite her effort, swallowed by the wrath of wind and wave.

Nonetheless, she knew that, far back at the steering-oar, Aerk understood. It had ever been that way with them, in moments of trouble or urgency. He threw his full weight upon the oar-pole.

Some joked that the Norns must have crossed and tangled their life-threads while they grew together in the womb, hence their way of seeming to know the others' mind. This also, some said with knowing looks or sly winks, was why each had been born with traits more befitting the other. It was of no matter to Mjorsk Boarstooth, whose grandfather had followed Erik the Red first into battle and then outlawry and exile.

It was, however, of great matter to Aerk. He was as vain about his reputation as he was about his handsomeness, taking quick offense to any perceived slight or insult. That, in their younger days, his sister had more often than not been the one to wade in fists flailing against the bigger boys that bullied him…well, it was not his favorite truth, but it had made him cunning as well as ambitious.

The ship, their trusty *White-Bristle*, angled westward.

The Boarstooth had been proud of his son and daughter in equal measure, and would be prouder yet of them now. Proudest of all if they succeeded.

To succeed, they must first survive.

And to survive…

A monstrous swell reared up beneath the hull, as if Jormungandr himself meant to surface from the deeps and bring challenge again to red-bearded Thor. But it was surge and not serpent, lifting the ship like a child's boat made of twigs.

More lightning, stark-white and sheeting, tore through the clouds. Land was near, yes, land; Dunvik and Njallan saw it as well and called out.

The *White-Bristle* gave a sickening dip and tilt. Folk screamed, by no means all of them women. So too screamed the horses, tethered close to the mast, the pregnant mares and yearling stallions that were to begin their new herd.

For a terrible moment it seemed they must roll and be capsized, that their struggles would mean nothing, that they would be cheated of triumph as their long journey ended in destruction within the very sight of shore.

Then they crested the swell just as it began to curl into a wild white-maned wave. A dark, glassy slope plummeted away before them. The prow tipped into it and the sleek ship coursed down with such speed that Aerk uttered a loud whoop of exhilaration.

Her brother was cunning, Mjiska knew, but could also be reckless. He had a way with charm and clever speaking that might have well served him as a skald, and there was proof of it in how he'd convinced forty men, some with their families, to accompany him on this brave undertaking.

She herself had needed neither convincing nor persuasion. Where Aerk went, she went as well; someone had to look after him. And the *White-Bristle*, their inheritance, was as much hers by right as his.

It was Vinland they sought. Vinland, which Leif Eriksson had discovered, coming home with such tales of. Lush and green Vinland, where the grape-vines grew in wild abundance and the timber-forests put even those of Norway to shame.

Vinland, which others had subsequently sought but forever failed to find.

Or, perhaps, had found it but never returned.

In the next of Mjolnir's blinding blows, sharp shadows leaped into view between their ship and the land. A black reef jutted up through the seething waters. Surf pounded against it with ferocious force, froth flinging high in tatters and spume.

Mjiska shouted a warning but Aerk had already seen the peril. He strained at the steering-oar with all of his might. Dunvik, who was closest, rushed to help him. But the powerful current and northeasterly gale had seized the *White-Bristle* in an iron grip, hurtling it inexorably toward this unforgiving barricade.

The reef, the deadly black reef...

It formed a long, curving shield-wall lined with spear-points and axe-blades, as if some ancient army waited braced on the battlefield...some ancient and undead army made from slick sea-stone and coarse coral... bony and bleak, disease-raddled with clusters of cankerous barnacles.

Closer now, Mjiska noticed how the reef was pocked with caves and with crevices, how skeins of lank kelp tangled rotting among its spires. Such a stench of dead fish hung around it that not even the incessant waves could wash it away.

The *White-Bristle* would be dashed against it, broken like an egg—

Another swell came, another surge of the ocean. It bore them up and over the reef with a hideous scraping of the hull-planks. The ship shuddered from it but carried on past, then swept in toward the coast.

The jaws of the reef had torn three ragged gaps in the hull. Men rushed to plug the leaks with wads of oakum.

Pretty Eyn, old Ypsvik's daughter, made her way to the prow. "Is it Vinland?" she asked, wiping rain-soaked red hair from her brow.

"I see no grape-vines from here," Mjiska told her. "Not that there's much of anything to see."

Eyn nodded. She stood a time, pensive, peering into the night.

Thor's battle above the clouds had moved southward by then, the bright lightning-strokes and thunder-crashes more distant.

"My father says," said the girl at last, twining her fingers with Mjiska's, "that once our new home is settled, I'll have to marry. He wants grandchildren."

Mjiska squeezed her hand gently. "We must all do our part."

"What about you?"

At that, Mjiska snorted. "Persuading some man to marry me would be the greatest challenge yet to Aerk's silver tongue."

They had no more time then for talking. To the north were the weathered bluffs of a wooded headland and what might have made a good harbor at what might have been the mouth of a river, but the tide carried them past it and ran them aground in a wide, fetid bog.

The hull splashed through sluggish creeklets and squelched to a stop in a gritty salt-mud sand bank. Rain pattered on briny brackenweed. A few stunted, dead trees canted this way and that. Crabs scuttled. A startled bird flew.

Land.

Such as it was.

Here again was the smell of decaying fish-flesh, not as vile a stench as before but a low and seeping miasma that seemed to waft in from all sides.

No one spoke. Even the penned livestock and tethered horses held their silence.

Then Aerk laughed, such a glad and joyful laugh that the others could not help but laugh with him. They leaped ashore, floundering in the silt and sludge, wading in cloudy brine-water. There were hearty embraces, and back-slappings, and cheers.

Whatever else might come, they were alive.

They sacrificed a pig, cutting the beast's throat, spilling its blood in thanks to the gods. By sputtering, smoky torchlight, they beached their injured *White-Bristle* on higher and dryer ground, and made what camp they could for the duration of the night.

Aerk went among his folk at their tasks, jesting, bringing words of encouragement to lighten their spirits.

"All right, I grant you, it's hardly wine-grapes in abundance," he said as they gathered by the cook-fires for a meal of boiled meat, hard bread, harder cheese and ale. "But, by day, this land may show us a fairer face. Let us give it a chance."

Nods and murmurs greeted this.

Aerk grinned. "We are here, and it is ours if we want it. Is that not why we came? To find a new land, claim it for our own?"

"Yes!" cried several.

"We'll build halls and houses, farms and settlements," he went on. "Towns, even cities! More folk will come, our kin and friends, following our bold example. Our names will live on in lore and mens' memories..." Arms outstretched, he turned in a slow and encompassing circle. "Aerkheim, my home will be called!"

"Aerkheim!" they echoed, lifting their cups.

"And who else?" Aerk asked, striding among them. "Mjiska, my sister, would you have a hall or a town with your name? Dunvik, how about you?"

With more jests and laughter, they passed the evening until the fires burned low, then went to their sleeping-places. Notched beams fitted together in frameworks, over which they'd draped the sturdy sail-cloths to fashion long tents to ward off the rain. For beds they had mats of leather, wool blankets, and fleeces or furs.

Most, for added warmth and comfort, had bed-mates as well. Families with children slept all bundled together. Mjiska rested with Eyn's head on her shoulder and Eyn's soft breath on her neck. Only Aerk, wrapped in a thick reindeer's pelt, slept apart and alone.

He often did, Mjiska knew. Not for any lack of lovers, or lack of opportunity…but such encounters were fleeting, never serious in nature. Aerk, she suspected, still blamed himself for Sven's death so many years ago—Sven's murder, gone unpunished and unavenged. Since then, he had contented himself with one sword-brother after another, when the mood so took him.

She wondered, in her last waking thought before sleep fully claimed her, if what she'd said to Eyn—"We must each do our part."—and Eyn's question as to whether that meant Mjiska would also marry…if that further applied to Aerk himself. Unlike old Ypsvik, their father the Boarstooth had not much expected grandchildren.

The rain ended by morning, the sun dawning golden in a fine clear spring sky. It could not shed much beauty over the salt-marsh where they'd come ashore, but the sea rolled dark blue trimmed with white foam. Gulls wheeled and larks twittered. To the west and north, hills climbed toward dense green woodland.

The reef over which the *White-Bristle*'s hull had scraped was all but invisible now, just the tops of its ridges and spires poking up through the high tide like the tines of a black comb. Past it, the sea was an even darker blue yet, suggesting depth beyond measure.

Aerk left a few men to guard the ship and look after the livestock and horses. The stretch of coast might seem deserted, he reminded them, but the tales told by Leif Eriksson and his men had made mention of *skraelings*, strange people who dressed only in animal skins. The rest went out in pairs and small groups to explore. They needed wood and fresh water, they needed a better place to make camp, and they needed to know what resources this new land offered as well as what dangers it held.

Pretty Eyn was the first of them to find the river. "By nearly falling into it," Njallan reported, his teasing tone and his smile making Eyn blush.

"We'll name it for her, then," said Aerk. "The river Eyn, or Eyn's river."

She blushed again, but seemed pleased.

They saw no signs of *skraelings*, and no signs that ships of their countrymen had been here before. There was some game for the hunt and it seemed ample fish for the catching. Both stone and timber were plentiful. Although they found no grape-vines, there were fruit trees and berries. Grasses grew for good grazing, and wild grain grew as well. And where those would grow, so too could wheat and barley be sown.

At the mouth of Eyn's river, where the headland curved to form a natural harbor inside the black reef's palisade, was where they decided to move their ship and their camp.

Then, of a night when a half-moon hung in the sky and the waves rippled silver-sheened far out toward the horizon, young Bari, Bragir's son, raised the alarm.

Bragir, a sailor and good fisherman, a strong back at the oar, had volunteered himself and his wife and sons to sleep aboard the *White-Bristle* and keep watch over the ship until their own house was built.

At the boy's frantic cries, everyone else rapidly awoke. They sprang from their sleeping-furs and blankets, seizing up shields and weapons near at hand. Swords sang from their sheaths.

Few had brought mail-coats and there was no time to don them. Some men grabbed for their helms. Mothers drew their children to their sides. Aerk bade a dozen warriors stay; the rest, Mjiska, Eyn and Geira among them, would accompany him.

Bari's voice was cut silent with violent abruptness.

They rushed out expecting to see the slim shapes of *skraeling* hide-boats on the water, or a dragon-prowed longship, or some other such threat.

Instead, they saw the *White-Bristle* listing, half-submerged in the harbor.

Bragir's boy, they found on the beach. His clothes were wet and sand-speckled, stinking of rotten fish. He sprawled face-down on his belly and when they turned him over his head lolled so loosely they knew his poor neck was broken. His dead eyes stared and his dead mouth gaped with a look of such horror that brave men recoiled.

Bragir himself, they found drowned and floating. His wife Olga and their other son were nowhere to be seen. The *White-Bristle*'s hull was wreckage and ruin, great holes ringed by the sheared-off edges of planks that looked almost gnawed, shark-bitten.

"Who did this?" Aerk shouted. "Show yourselves!"

Eyn pointed and screamed.

Pointed to the sea.

For, from the sea they came.

The stench of them—brine and fish and decay—was revolting.

The sight of them was far more so.

They came hunched and squelching, with clumsy, hopping gaits. The surf hissed and gurgled around them as they waded ashore. Twenty of them, twenty at least, emerged, and more bobbing heads surfaced further out in the direction of the reef.

Moonlight and torchlight showed the creatures well in all their grotesqueness—skin both pallid and greenish, misshapen limbs ending in splayed and webbed extremities more like claw-tipped flippers than hands or feet, thick and flabby necks where gill-slits pulsed and flapped obscenely, the black orbs of eyes bulging.

Some wore scraps of kelp or sea-plants like garments; others were naked, slime-coated and hideous. A few carried weapons of sorts, crude implements fashioned from coral, driftwood and bone.

Fishlike…froglike…manlike…a vile mingling of the three…yet it made no matter.

"Kill them!" Enraged, Aerk charged.

Mjiska was moving almost before her brother, shells and pebbles crunching underfoot. Olaf, Olga's brother, anguished for his young nephew, was close on her heels, shrieking wordless fury.

The rest followed, and they met the advancing repugnant host in the clash and clamor of battle. Blades swung. Whalebone spears splintered on iron-bound limewood. Steel met sharp-edged coral. Sharp-edged coral met leather and flesh. Steel met pallid, greenish skin.

Red blood and watery ichor flowed.

The blood was hot. The ichor, cold.

Aerk's sword, Gore-Tusk, their father's sword, opened a fishman's throat from gill-flap to gill-flap. Mjiska hacked another at the shoulder with such an axe-blow that the slimy arm was severed. She kicked it aside as she stepped forward to bury the curved, honed edge in its inhuman skull.

A driftwood club studded with pointed spirals of shell split the battered bronze of Dunvik's old helm and sent him half-senseless to his knees. A serrated coral knife plunged into Thurvald's chest, grating audibly on the ribs. He coughed his crimson death-breath defiantly into his killer's face.

Olaf's sword was wrenched from his grasp but he, in a near-berserker's madness, went at his foe weaponless. Even as its hook-clawed hands shredded his linen night-shirt, his fingers gouged into its bulbous black eyes and they burst like overripe fruits, popping in sprays of clammy fluid.

A fishman seized Giera by the hair, dragging her toward the water as she thrashed and scrabbled and spat and swore. Eyn threw herself at its legs and drove a long dagger through the webbing of its toes, spiking its flipper-foot to the packed wet sand.

Two of the creatures overpowered Freyulf and bore him to the ground, where he howled in agony as they savaged him with teeth like bent and crooked needles. A third lunged at Aerk, jaws snapping, and earned a mouthful of Gore-Tusk's blade instead.

Njallan, roaring, swept his great-sword in a hewing arc of carnage. Fish-scales and ichor flecked his wheat-colored beard. Dunvik, dazed and with blood dribbling from his ear, shed the remnants of his helm. He tried to rise, tottered, and went again to his knees.

Mjiska and Ypsvik fought their way to where another fishman had hold of both Eyn and Geira, each by an ankle. The one who still had Geira by the hair would not relinquish its prize, tugging her between them as its toe-webbing ripped. Mjiska solved the problem of its pinned foot for it by chopping through the squat, froggy leg. Ypsvik, grey of hair and beard but still a warrior, shield-bashed the other, knocked it flat, stood on its gilled neck, and stabbed it through the guts.

A squalling noise sounded, a shell-horn being blown. At that signal, the surviving fishfolk retreated. Those that were able blundered clumsily back toward the sea as fast as they could.

Aerk and Njallan gave chase, cutting four more of them down as they ran. When Aerk saw that a fifth would, despite its graceless gait, gain the surf's safety before it was within reach of his blade, he stooped without missing a step and snatched up from the wave-strewn pebbles a discarded whalebone spear. He hurled it mid-stride and it did not miss its mark.

Then the battle was done.

Corpses littered the beach. Three of them were men, Thurvald and Freyulf and Hruni the Bald. But they had left many times their number on the wet sand. Wounded fishfolk squirmed, mewling and burbling, until they were bludgeoned to death or beheaded.

Dunvik lay unconscious. Olaf bled freely. Of the rest, some bore slight injuries and some were for the most part unscathed. Bringing the bodies of their fallen companions—including those of drowned Bragir and his boy—they hastened to the place where they'd made camp.

The piles of planks and lumber they'd already cut in preparation of the building of houses they threw together now in a defensive wall. More torches were lit, some on long poles stuck into the ground, and bonfires were kindled until the flames crackled high. Watches were posted. The injured were tended and the dead set aside, covered until they could be decently pyre-burned or buried.

There was much talk, and much desperate debate. They could not simply leave, not with the *White-Bristle* damaged…and, indeed, already the fish-folk had towed the stricken ship further out so that it sank in the harbor. If they fled, it would have to be inland…but that would mean abandoning Olga and her younger boy to a suspected but uncertain fate.

Eyn was the one to ask what they all had been wondering.

"What *are* those foul things?"

"Sea-trolls?" suggested Geira. "Or spawn of Jormungandr, the world-circling serpent?"

"What they are *not* is wave-maidens, Njord's lovely daughters," Njallan said, grimacing.

"I have heard tales of deep ones such as these," said silver-haired Ulrunn, who was besides old Ypsvik the eldest among them.

"Go on," Aerk told her.

"Before Odin cast Jormungandr into the sea, even before the Aesir and Vanir made peace, the oceans were ruled by giants far more ancient than our own gods. They came from a realm beyond Jotunheim, where Yggdrasil's furthermost roots and branches can scarcely span."

"We haven't time for skald's stories!" Olaf interrupted. He sat bare-chested, bloodied bandages bound around the worst of his wounds. The shallower cuts from the fishman's claws looked inflamed from the touch of the slime, the flesh puffing, the skin reddened.

"Let her speak," Mjiska said.

He glowered but gave no more argument, and Ulrunn went on.

"The lord of these giants was called Father Daakon, and his queen Mother

Heydra, and they were Njord's bitter enemies. With Odin's help, and that of all the Aesir, they were banished to the depths, to the black trenches. But there they bred countless hideous children, who defied the gods' exile to seek prey and plunder upon the dry land."

By then the moon had set and the night-time was waning, but the sentries saw strange blue-green glows and movement down by the water. The slumped, froggish shapes of the fishfolk emerged in procession. Some carried in kelp netting the eerie flameless lamps that were the source of the light.

A few ventured forth to retrieve their dead, bearing them into the waves where they vanished from sight. Most formed a line along the surf's edge and stood waiting. Their briny, rotten smell wafted thick in the air.

Five of them came closer, stopping halfway between the sea and the wall of logs and lumber. Of those five, two held lamps and two others held woven baskets. The one in the lead wore some kind of robe or mantle.

Inhuman though they were, these actions seemed familiar.

"They seek a truce," Ypsvik said. "They want to talk."

"Talk?" echoed Mjiska, remembering the gurgles and glottal grunts they had made. "How can they talk?"

"We'll find out," said Aerk.

"Are you mad?" Geira cried. "They're monsters!"

"They killed our folk," added Olaf.

"I know," Aerk said, "but what else is there to do?"

No one had a good answer. Mjiska stepped up beside him. Aerk chose Njallan, Ypsvik and Dunvik to accompany them—Dunvik insisted that he would not let a little bump on the head keep him idle. The rest hung back at a prudent distance, watching in a tense, anxious silence.

Slowly, bearing torches, their group approached that of the fishfolk.

The robed leader, the emissary, lurched another few paces to meet them. The creature's throat swelled like that of a bullfrog. Its gills stretched wide, pink and repellently moist. The tip of a long, thin tongue slithered the rim of its lipless mouth. It uttered a bubbling croak perhaps meant to be speech.

"Aerk..." Mjiska said in a low undertone.

"I feel it," he said.

She felt it, too. A sense of something...a pressure, a presence...a mind...a mind so unlike theirs as to be abhorrent...questing for their own, questing to communicate...

Questing, and because she and Aerk were as they were, succeeding.

Its thoughts came to them not as words but vague meanings and impressions. Aerk, head tilted in curious but sickly fascination, concentrated intently on what the emissary tried to convey. Mjiska murmured to the others to stay their hands, to be patient, Aerk could understand it and so could she, and would tell them what they learned...

"They dwell in the deep trench past the black reef," Aerk said. "They have dwelled there for centuries, in a great city, undying of age or sickness. But they would have peace with us. They would be our friends."

"Friends," muttered Dunvik, rubbing his head.

"They offer us wealth," Mjiska said.

"Wealth?" asked Njallan.

The emissary gestured out across the harbor with an expansive sweep of one web-fingered hand. There, in the blue-green radiance of the strange kelp-netted lamps, the water thronged and teemed with fish. Silver bodies leaping, fins flashing, tails flicking, there were more fish than any of them had ever seen. Fish enough to feed kingdoms.

"The sea's bounty," Aerk explained. "Plentiful fishing. And—"

The two fishfolk with the woven baskets poured out their contents onto the ground at their feet. Metal gleamed on sand and shell...gold, a pale gold, glistening...gold worked into ornaments, circlets and crowns, bracers and arm-rings...the designs intricate yet loathsome...a golden fortune in treasure...

"Gold," Mjiska said when her brother could not finish.

"What do they want in return?" Dunvik asked.

"For us to make sacrifice," she said.

Ypsvik's brows drew in. "Of pigs and goats?"

"No," Aerk said.

"Of our own," Mjiska said as the meanings and impressions took shape in her mind. "Twice a year, in the spring as now and again in autumn."

"For that, they will favor us, and reward us richly." Aerk gazed at the gold strewn before them.

"In exchange for the sea's bounty of fish, and a fortune in gold," said Njallan, thoughtfully.

In what was almost a manner of nonchalance, the emissary croaked again, just to add one more minor detail. Aerk's brows rose.

"And we must each take one of them as a second husband or wife," he said. "Our children by them will live as we are until they grow old, then join the others in the deep city and live forever."

A moment passed as they all considered this.

"Forever," mused Ypsvik, stroking his own grey beard.

The emissary regarded them with its bulging shark's eyes. Behind it, the eastern sky brightened and the stars faded in anticipation of sunrise.

Marry with these creatures…mate with them, breed with them…

"They only can die by violence," Mjiska said.

Aerk smiled. "Then let us not disappoint them."

He drew his sword and rushed the emissary of the fishfolk.

With a fierce war-cry, Mjiska and the men attacked the attendants, who stumbled backward in slap-shuffling astonishment.

Mjiska struck at the nearest, who with a wet yelp of terror blocked the axe-blade with the woven basket. But the basket was sheared into pieces, and Mjiska's next blow split the creature from sternum to groin.

A gush of cold jelly spewed out, a lumpy flood spilling over the sand. It was roe, the thing female and these her fishy eggs. Within the soft, whitish casings twitched and wriggled tiny wormlike forms. Revolted, Mjiska struck a third time. She lopped off the fishwoman's head, sending it tumbling into the sloppy, miscarried mess.

Around her, the battle raged in earnest.

Their violent rejection of terms had caught the fishfolk by surprise. The ones waiting by the waterline had barely begun to react when the rest of Aerk's people charged down to join in. They all came with weapons, the men with swords and spears and axes, the women with knives and cudgels, even the children with sticks and thrown stones.

A curved sliver of light, the sun's shield edged in fire, appeared above the horizon. Dawnlight spread like melted butter across the waves, across the beach where once again blood and ichor rained from deadly wounds.

They fought to the death, Aerk's people, fought for death, to bring it and to obtain it, to die in this way, free and glorious and on their own terms.

The fishfolk, unaccustomed to pain and death, panicked and fled, routed.

One by one, limping, bleeding, the survivors gathered around Aerk and Mjiska. Many had already gone to Odin's hall—pretty Eyn among them, but Mjiska could not grieve for her and knew she would be with her soon enough.

They knew better than to hope they'd claimed victory; their foes were in far vaster numbers and would soon rally.

But the fishfolk did not rally, did not return in force.

Far out upon the reef, a host of shell-horns blew. There was a great and resounding din of slapping, as of flat tails smacking the water. A shrill keening and croaking arose from many pulsating throats.

The sea stilled.

The wind changed.

Beyond the black reef, the water first briefly sank in a rotating depression and then rose in a coursing, bulging bubble as if something immense came up from below.

Something did.

Aerk dropped his sword into the bloodied sand and surf and broken shell. Mjiska sensed her brother's mind fracture, sensed his wits rent from him in a single ripping stroke. He gibbered, he wept, and he laughed a madman's laugh.

She dropped her axe and began to laugh as well.

The shape from the deeps loomed higher still. Seawater coursed from its slumped and massive shoulders. Below its many sunken yellow eyes clumped a mass of writhing tentacles like a nest of immense headless snakes. It blotted out the rising sun.

And over the river Eyn's mouth, a dreadful shadow fell.

RETURN OF THE PRODIGY

T.E. Grau

It was over the "Complimentary Anniversary Cake for Two!" that Gary finally sprang the news.

Minutes before, the Vahlkamps were wrapping up another predictably silent ceremonial dinner at The Drover, where they had memorialized each anniversary for the last thirty-four years. The occasion was once again ushered in with identical iceberg salads, butter-grilled Omaha steaks, and long looks around the room over smeared cocktail rims, searching for familiar faces and forgotten gossip.

But this night was different. This was the thirty-fifth, and after enduring exactly 12,775 days of intermittent harping on the fact that he had never taken his wife Gladys on a honeymoon following their traditional Lutheran wedding, Gary decided to man up and do the right thing, if only to find a little goddamn peace.

You see, Gary was a frugal man, but not inappropriately so, considering the circumstances of his upbringing. Born with the sluggish blood of German stock on the cusp of the Platte River Valley, he wore his innate thriftiness as a badge of honor. It was the right thing to do. It was the *Nebraska* thing to do. Gladys, a former Kansas City socialite and theatre actress of little renown, was quite the opposite, and although she loved her husband as a historian loves a bygone civilization, she always chafed at his chintzy ways. But the heart doesn't deal out fairly, so she suffered his shallow pockets mostly in wifely silence. Mostly. That would be her story, anyway.

But on this night, Gary bit the bullet. He didn't like the taste, mixed as it was with the floury chocolate he was trying to work out of his bridgework, but he understood that men sometimes do things they don't want to do. The burden of the masculine, and all that jazz.

Gary finished his Beam and water, placed his hands on the tablecloth, and made the pronouncement. Gladys was ecstatic, and nearly spilled her Mai Tai as she leapt with surprising speed across the table and planted a series of awkwardly received kisses on her husband.

"Hawaii, right?" she asked rhetorically.

Gary, long since accustomed to her odd fascination with Don Ho, tiki parties, and all things Polynesian, just smiled. "You'll see," he said with one of his patented, ex-jock winks that first wooed Gladys all those years ago, all the while searching his internal map of the South Pacific hard earned back in '68.

Gladys blushed and hugged him tight. Gary inhaled her Avon perfume that always smelled like Raid on her skin. "I love you," she whispered. Gary grunted and patted her arm. Gladys released, and clapped her hands like a schoolgirl, drawing much-needed attention from the room, and trundled off to the bathroom, squealing happily through tears.

Gary sat back, exhaled, and ordered another drink.

***

When they arrived home, Gladys hustled to her laptop to purchase a whole new wardrobe of "nouveau chic cabana wear" from QVC online, while Gary logged onto his desktop, searching out "affordable vacation options in Micronesia." Hawaii wasn't even an option. Fiji and Tahiti were out, obviously. Money-sucking tourist traps lousy with shirtless newlyweds and Eurotrash stuffing their uncut manhood into Speedos. Murderous. Guam would be fitting in a way, as a former Navy man, but he knew Gladys would see right through this, and nag him into suicidal thoughts he'd long since put behind him.

Clicking through various slick tourist sites, Gary finally came upon a promo page for Walakea, a flyspeck peeking up from the water nearly equidistant between the Philippines and Easter Island, which sported "A cozy resort nestled upon a dreamy, secluded island of exotic, black sand beaches." "*Cozy…*" Gary grumbled at the thought of such forced intimacy. Worse, a backwater like this probably wouldn't even serve proper liquor. But before he could move on, his gaze was caught by *The most affordable vacation value in the Pacific!* highlighted inside a flashing gold star. Nice. These islanders were speaking Gary's language, and doing it with class. Cross-checking a few reputable news sites, he discovered that Walakea had experienced a spate of underreported "ecological incidents" that had nearly ruined the local fishing economy late last year. Gary nodded with satisfaction. If he had to hand over his hard earned greenbacks to foreigners, might as well do a little charity work amongst the godless zipperheads while he was at it. Two birds with one stone, moonlighting as a Christian imperative.

Gary now had to sell Walakea to his wife. He whipped up a batch of Malibu Rum Runners and presented them to Gladys as she stood in front of the mirror, going way easy on the condition of her pearish body while babbling about various crash diets "that all the actors do." Gary kept the cocktails flowing, and after less than an hour, his wife was on board.

A belated honeymoon on Walakea. Let the angels sing.

***

The creaky SouthPac Airlines 737 circled the tiny, mountainous island a few times, shedding altitude like a bad habit as it began a tight, controlled corkscrew. Gary, who hated flying with a white-hot passion normally reserved for illegal immigrants and tax hikes, steadied himself as his stomach rose into his throat. He glanced nervously past Gladys, down on the lush greenery below, which seemed to chew its way up to the lip of the pitch-black beach, as if wanting to retake the land from the sea. From above, Walakea looked like a sooty History Channel graphic of the islands of the Pacific theater in WWII. Guadalcanal. Palau. Okinawa. Back when America won its wars.

Suddenly, the plane shuddered, jerked nose down and careened toward the tragically short landing strip. Gary gritted his teeth, tasting the bourbon and club crackers that served as his breakfast after waking up mid-flight, hoping that it was already over.

After a screaming descent that felt more like a free fall, the plane finally skipped, skidded, then thudded onto the asphalt, and wobbled toward the lone gate of the one-horse airport. The AC was cut, and Gary mopped his brow, feeling the creep of the unencumbered sun that beat down on the winged metal cylinder. This was heat without season.

"Wow, wasn't that something!" Gladys chirped, clutching Gary's leg. "What an *adventure*!" Gary was just hoping their baggage had made it into the guts of this rattletrap during their layover in L.A., and that the rooms had central air and plenty of ice. He had vacation drinking to do.

The passengers disembarked across the boiling tarmac, and were met by a garishly painted golf cart that took them to the Sea Pearl Resort, where they had booked three nights of "fun with the sun," as the confirmation agent assured him in choppy English.

The room was modest, and smelled a bit musty, which was odd for the dry, kiln-like conditions of a Pacific islet squatting on the equator. Gladys flopped on the bed with a laugh, and excitedly paged through the various faded brochures left on the nightstand. Gary set about inspecting the room, checking for faulty wiring and load-bearing beams behind the walls. This was earthquake country, and he'd be good god-damned if he'd breathe his last under a pile of cheap roofing smack dab in the lap of slanty-eyed heathenism.

Suitably satisfied that the walls would hold for the next three days, Gary rang down to the front desk while Gladys peeled off her Spanx and launched into a clumsy fashion show, ripping off tags and dangerously stretching new, non-breathable fabric. As she kept calling for Gary to look, he scanned the television, finding nothing but bizarre Japanese game shows and incomprehensible regional news, which seemed to be covering yet another natural disaster somewhere along the dark Indochinese Peninsula. Retribution for the godless Socialists, Pat Robertson always said, before he lost his mind and started talking about legalizing dope. Gary clicked through the channels a few more times, hoping for a different outcome, but found nothing remotely resembling ESPN or Fox News. Hell, he'd even settle for the Trinity Network, just to get a little home cooking. "Jesus Christ," he hissed, hoping to high heaven that they sold Tom Clancy at the gift shop.

There was a knock on the door. Gary leapt up to open it, moving past Gladys, who was in the middle of asking his preference between a Trim-Shaper skirtini and something called a "sarong." Gary opened the door and found a pineapple standing at shoulder height in front of him, decorated with a wispy moustache and mirrored sunglasses. It was the room service attendant, a huge grin etched across his wide, pock-marked face, making it seem wider and more pock-marked than Gary thought possible. Must be some strange genetic quirk, he thought. *Inbreeding*, he finally deduced with a nod of finality, as the walking botany experiment held out a red and white plastic bottle and two Dixie cups.

Gary glared at the label. "The hell is this?"

"Language, Gary," Gladys trilled from the bathroom.

"Whiskey," the attendant answered simply, then smiled again, putting the bottle to his mouth as if instructing this confused round-eye what to do with it.

"I asked for Jim Beam," Gary growled, taking the plastic container of Black Velvet and holding it out in front of him with disdain. The total lack of understanding of decent distilled spirits was worse than he'd feared.

"Whiskey," the Walakean repeated, handing Gary the Dixie cups, and held out his hand, palm side up. Gary looked at him with disappointment and shook his head. "It's already starting," he sighed as he dug into his pocket and pulled out some loose change, which he dropped into the man's gnarled, net-scarred hand. The attendant's smile only dampened slightly. He bobbed his head, and loped away, walking in a manner more accustomed to being on the deck of a pitching skiff than solid land. Gary frowned at the shabby bottle, most likely airlifted in during the Reagan administration. Better than nothing, he surmised, and a definite necessity to survive the next half of the "beachwear for the mature woman" burlesque going on inside their room. When in Rome, drink low.

"He kind of looked like Don Ho, didn't he?" Gladys called out from the bathroom. Gary sighed and closed the door.

***

The sun dropped quickly behind the island's volcanic peaks, and under the burden of jetlag and cheap bourbon, Gary was soon ready for a nap that would hopefully extend into an early bedtime. Gladys had other plans, and finished her fashion show with the grand finale, waddling out of the bathroom in an ill-fitting, matronly nightie cut from way too much shiny material. She slunk over to the bed and shook Gary awake, purring something about "consummating the honeymoon." Gary knew the drill, and got down to business, turning the light off while he fought through his boxers.

"No," Gladys cooed. "Tonight I want us to see each other, like the natives on the Island of Blue Dolphins."

Gary looked for his Dixie cup as her eveningwear hit the floor.

***

In their intertwined, post-coital positions, the couple listened to massive waves crashing down on the beach below. "I think I felt the earth move while we were.... You know," Gladys whispered.

Gary, feeling buzzed, smiled. "Yeah, I have that effect on women."

She giggled. "Can you believe these waves?"

Gary scratched at his jaw. "Must be high tide," he muttered, dozing off.

Gladys listened as Gary began to softly snore. "We could get washed away at any moment," she said quietly, delighting in some imagined danger on this forgotten reef thousands of miles from civilization. Now that he was asleep, she snuggled up close to Gary's thick torso and exhaled happily, running her fingers through his chest hair that always reminded her of Magnum P.I.

***

That night, Gary dreamt that the whole world was heaving and pitching around him, then disintegrated like a sand painting into an endless, howling abyss below. But as everything melted away, Gary stood tall in the middle of nothingness, balanced perfectly on a six-fold circular pattern shimmering bright yellow below his booted feet. He looked down into the void, and found a comfort in the emptiness. He paused for a second, trying to remember his waking life, then leapt off the edge.

Gary fell, but didn't experience a plunging sensation. Instead, he felt himself twirling, tumbling slowly upward amid a cloud of oily bubbles. His body softened, becoming pliable, and finally clove into a double helix. Even through all of this, Gary didn't try to wake up. He just watched, inside his dream, as his body separated into minutia, wondering how it would all end.

***

The next morning, Gary awoke with a start, threw off the smothering covers, and tried to press himself back together. He couldn't remember his nightmare, which was strange. Gary was inclined to bad dreams and cursed to remember them all, filing them away in a dark vault deep inside. He'd seen a lot. In the haunted jungles of Vietnam. In his private, shameful thoughts since then. But this was different. Stark flashes came to him, yet he couldn't make heads or tails of what he had actually dreamt last night. Just fractured glimpses. Suffocation… Choking… Drowning in the sky… Gary blinked his eyes and crawled out of bed, careful not to wake Gladys, who slept with a contented smile on her face. God bless her little mind. She never dreamed.

He pulled on some baggy swimming trunks and padded to the dresser, where he poured the last of the Black Velvet into his limp Dixie cup. Gary took a sip, trying to burn away the strange feeling nagging at him, and looked in the mirror, squeezing a portion of his hardened gut. *Not bad, sailor.* His self-examination was broken up by an unholy racket coming from outside, down by the beach. The frantic squawking of birds.

He walked out onto the patio and looked down at the waterfront, where a jabbering cloud of sea fowl were dive-bombing the sand. Gary reached for his flip-flops.

***

Gary made his way down to the beach, approaching a gathered group of locals helplessly watching the feeding frenzy in silent mourning. A few shooed away birds in hopes of salvaging the fresher carcasses, but most were ruined, chewed up before they hit shore. It was the same scene up and down the beach—black sand hosting a twisting colonnade of the ocean's gleaming dead. Gary examined the heaps as the first squirm of rot began to set in. Amid the mass of dismembered commercial fish and knotted balls of kelp, he spied some very unusual creatures. He'd watched plenty of Jacques Cousteau with his oldest in the '70s, and knew that what he was looking at wasn't your usual collection of supermarket filets. Here and there were the pulpy, many-legged remains of bizarre creatures from the darkest depths, possibly never before seen by human eyes. Whatever violence drove these things to dry land must have dredged them up from somewhere impossibly deep.

Wanting a souvenir, Gary bent down to pick up a bony, rigid specimen sprouting what looked like a dozen eyestalks and feet-like flippers, when a hand stopped him. He looked up, and found a squatty, strong-shouldered Walakean gripping him tightly by the arm. The man just shook his head and pulled him back. Irritated by this close contact but not wanting to make a scene, Gary scowled, stood up and gave ground, while the man shook his head again and crossed his arms, continuing his silent gaze at the unhallowed funeral in front of him.

Suddenly very thirsty, Gary turned and headed back to the room and his deteriorating Dixie cup, passing a rusted front loader belching smoke into the screeching sky as it headed toward the shore.

***

After a continental breakfast of slimy eggs and bacon presumably hewn from shoe leather, Gary took initiative and proposed that they go for a swim, which had the added bonus of allowing Gladys to show off her new "Day One" bathing costume.

Hoping to gain wide berth from the aquatic holocaust that choked their side of the island, Gary and Gladys caught a scooter-drawn rickshaw to the opposite, undeveloped side of Walakea, which, according to the desk clerk—an oddly proportioned man with puffy hair and sideburns who looked like a villain in those knock-off Bruce Lee films—boasted a secluded beach not even used by the locals. That suited Gary just fine. It had been forty years since he swam in the ocean, and he'd be damned if some grinning native or snickering tourist saw him trip over a rip tide or lose his shorts in the undertow.

In a dusty trinket shack just outside of town, Gary picked up some antiquated, Navy-issue snorkeling gear that must have come from a returning

American brother, freshly emerged from the slimy hell of Vietnam, his sanity left behind in a bloody jungle pill box.

The scooter puttered up a bumpy dirt road that meandered into the hills, affording a view of the oblong island and the never-ending water that tried to swallow it every high tide. Even with the underpinnings of black sand, the surrounding sea just beyond the breakers seemed darker than most volcanic islands in the South Pacific, hinting at an unusual depth, positioning the island of Walakea as just the tip of a capacious ebony spear thrust fast and hard from the sea floor.

Gladys slipped her arm under Gary's, interrupting his musing. "Isn't this romantic?" she sighed.

"Yeah, it's something else," he replied.

She rested her head on his shoulder. "I want to be buried here."

Gary knew she was just caught up in the moment, but his thoughts turned to the grim-faced locals gathered on the beach, watching as his wife's swollen, naked body sank slowly to an unreachable ocean bottom. Patting her absently on the head, he surmised that Gladys probably wouldn't find a watery grave, chewed to the bone by unclassified fish, as romantic a notion. Moving his gaze to the hills to his right, he scanned the ridgeline of the leveled-off peaks. He did the same just outside of Da Nang. The zips cut them to fucking pieces that day, raining down hot death for eighteen straight hours. Ghosts of the past never rest, especially in heat like this.

Just then, something not altogether natural in the shadow of the mountains caught Gary's attention. Shading his eyes from the blazing sun, he spotted a ring of tilted, worn statuary on a sloping hillside. Aside from their greenish gray color, they looked similar to those silent monoliths found on Easter Island. But that couldn't be the case, as Easter Island was 4,000 miles away.

"What are those things?" Gary asked their driver. Gladys looked around quickly and fumbled with her camera, hoping to shoot something interesting enough to impress the gals at Sunday brunch. The driver turned around to Gary and motioned to his ears. "What are those things? Up there!" Gary yelled, jutting his finger at the hillside.

The driver just shrugged and smiled, as everyone seemed to do on this goddamn island.

Gladys began snapping pictures at random, not sure what Gary was talking about. "What is it, honey?" she called. The driver glanced up at the hills and made tiny movements with his hands. Gary noticed this, and looked up at the worn, discolored monoliths, sneering at such superstitious nonsense. But just as they rounded a curve and were out of sight, Gary could have sworn that one of the statues looked vaguely amphibian, which would clearly make them *not* like the exaggeratedly human effigies carved on Easter Island. "What did you see?" Gladys asked again, checking her shots.

"Nothing," Gary replied, trying to convince himself by clearing his throat and swallowing.

Every place has its ghosts.

***

Gladys set up a picnic on one of her mother's quilts atop the rocky beach, dotted with large basalt rock formations, polished smooth by endless years of determined wave and weather. It wasn't the most comfortable stretch of sand, but at least the natural bowl of the cove protected it from the fickle tide and the onslaught of dead fish that plagued the Sea Pearl side of the island. After a snack of venison summer sausage and Colby cheese brought from home, lubricated by a clay jug of room temp Jap sake purchased locally, Gary stood and beat his chest, grunting like a silverback, which elicited a giggle from Gladys. He grinned and marched to the water, determined to make contact with this unruly, foreign ocean. Gladys watched him go, trying to remember the exact year when the fullness of his backside suddenly evaporated.

Gary stopped at the lapping water's edge and dipped in a toe. Not bad. Easing in slowly, the water became surprisingly frigid just yards from the beach, much colder than he expected. Shivering, he waded out to his chest, then pushed off and began to tread water, working forgotten muscles. Gary leaned back and kicked his legs, staring up at the infinite blueness of the sky above. For just a moment, floating weightless, he felt like an infant inside an immense, frigid womb of dark fluid. His dream whispered back to him…Gary smiled for a second…before something long and thick slithered between his paddling feet. He froze, allowing his toes to touch sand, bringing the waterline to just below his upturned mouth. Gary hastily tried to recall the list of sharks native to the area. He came up with nothing other than scenes from *Jaws 3D,* his favorite installment of the series. Gary held his breath, feeling the tightness of water around his submerged body. Nothing moved, save the gentle rise and fall of the waves. Maybe he imagined it. This island set the mind to strange things… He was just about to continue his swim, when something large and powerful bumped into his lower back, and stayed there, pressing against him, nuzzling… Gary thrashed his arms behind him, striking something hard and ice cold that shot away quickly, the force of its propulsion dragging him under momentarily. He surfaced and swam/ran with a panicked stiffness to the shore.

Breathing hard, he rushed from the water and jogged toward Gladys, who looked like a bell-shaped porcelain doll lying on a stretch of black nothingness. With leaden legs, he finally made it to the blanket, and collapsed next to his wife, who was "sunbathing" under a thick slathering of 50 SPF. "Jesus Christ," Gary let escape between labored breaths.

"You almost drown again?" Gladys asked without concern behind her absurd sunglasses two generations too large.

"No!" he shot back angrily. She shaded her eyes and peered at him. "No," he repeated, lowering his voice. "I just…felt something out there."

"The ocean is full of all sorts of things, honey," Gladys said simply, putting the issue to rest. "Remember Jonah and the whale?"

Gary rose to his knees and toweled off, keeping an eye on their scooter driver, who smoked and watched them underneath squinted eyes on a cliff above. Gary lay face down on the quilt, not noticing what was higher up, on the sloping hillside in the shadows of the mountains, where a collection of motionless, naked human figures stood and watched the two stark white visitors lie on their black beach below. From this elevated vantage point, the basalt along the shore showed clear evidence of careful cutting and shaping of massive stonework, which lay half buried in the sand. The ruined columns outlined a foundation of an immense structure, as if scattered in a fit of rage by a colossal child in a time when the world was still young and wild.

***

Back at their room, following a silent scooter ride from the far beach, Gary and Gladys showered together for the first time since before their grown children were born, and remarked with laughter at how shower stalls must have been more spacious in simpler times. Their intermingled feet danced over the rivulets of dark grit that collected on the tile, before slithering down the drain, joining their billion-year-old brethren under the sea.

***

Gary found himself inside the same dream, only this time he was an amphibious creature rising from the abyss that had taken him. Higher and higher he climbed, finally to be birthed onto a burnt, sandless shore recently cooled from the fires that raged and smoked on mountaintops looming in the distance a thousand miles high. The domed sky above was copper colored and veined with crimson gold. Triple moons, soft with youth and fat in their close orbit, jockeyed for prominence in the starless expanse of space just above. The Gary creature moved with pain, his soft bones protesting against dry gravity. He struggled for breath, feeling his neck tighten and his chest about to explode. Finally, he coughed, drew air into tiny lungs, and exhaled a roar of victory, declaring himself a prodigy.

Gary awoke from his dream, coughing onto his pillow and scratching at the sides of his neck. He sat up, staring sightlessly at the wall opposite of him. But he wasn't afraid. He felt like a conqueror. Looking down and noticing the bulge in his boxers, he nudged Gladys awake.

***

In an unusually jovial mood that evening as they dressed for dinner, Gary announced that they were to dine away from the resort, finding the finest place on the island that served only the most authentic Walakean cuisine. Gladys was as shocked as she was overjoyed. "You really mean it, Garebear?" she asked.

"Sure do," he replied proudly. "Let's soak up a little local color, huh?"

Gladys squealed and hugged him close. "Yay!" She rushed over to the closet. "Let's *really* have a safari tonight!"

Immediately feeling uneasy, Gary slumped into a rattan chair and waited for it. Sure enough, he regretted his generous idea as Gladys unveiled a gaudy Hawaiian shirt for him, and a matching dress of the same flowery material for her. He knew it was no use arguing, nor fighting it, for it had arrived. They were THAT couple. They'd be power walking in the local mall every morning in matching sweat suits the day after they landed back in Omaha. Gary's mood darkened considerably, and his thoughts turned to whiskey.

"You think we can find a place with a luau?" she asked excitedly. "We can pretend we're Mr. and Mrs. Ho!" "Ho," indeed. Cuckolded by a dead Hawaiian. Again. Gary excused himself and headed for the front desk, praying to the Christian God for the discovery of another plastic bottle of Black Velvet.

Even this far out, no matter how hard he tried, some things would never change.

***

They set out from the Sea Pearl an hour later. Gary walked several steps ahead of Gladys, who was taking pictures of every neon-lit tourist shop and gaudy storefront she came across. Gary scratched at the tag irritating his neck inside the back of his stiff shirt, which still had that hollow, stale smell of a Taiwanese warehouse. He felt ridiculous. Walking about, in this loud, garish get-up that strategically matched his woman's. If he had a tail, it would have been tucked deeply between his chaffed legs. Gary glanced behind him at his wife's enormous purse, wondering if anyone else could hear the clanging of his testicles against her bottle of Avon perfume better suited for pest eradication. Walking alone, wrapped inside the old, comfortable blanket of boozy gloom, Gary searched for the first place that looked presentable, just wanting to get off this strange, black-rimmed island that seemed so at odds with the rest of the civilized world. Honeymoons are for suckers. He was right the first time.

Rounding a corner, Gary came across a glowing sign for the Seven Seas Grill, nestled between two large warehouses. He peered inside, and saw that the joint was sparsely populated and seemed more or less clean. Good enough. Gary prepped his case and turned to find Gladys, but she was nowhere to be found. He darted his eyes up and down the cramped street, feeling an unexpected rush of fear.

Gary headed back around the corner, and found Gladys bent over a legless transient propped up on the curb. She handed the wrinkled old man a few dollars, rewarded with a toothless grin. Gary's face soured. He called out to her, and she trundled over. "That sweet old man just gave me the most wonderful thing." Gladys held up a spiny shell hanging from a hemp string, featuring a six-fold circular pattern shimmering bright yellow.

"Put that away," Gary admonished, a bit too harshly.

Gladys was taken aback. "Why? It's so pretty, and that old man told me that it would protect us on the island. Isn't that *neat*? He didn't even have any legs."

Gary scowled. "It's pagan jewelry. 'Neat' has nothing to do with it. You think Pastor Thune would want you wearing that around town? Come on! Toss it out."

Pouting, Gladys walked to the nearest overflowing trashcan and laid it gently on the pile. Gary was distracted, his mind delving into his memory, trying to uncover his certainty about this cheap trinket. Gladys glumly rejoined Gary. "Party pooper," she mumbled.

Gary pulled at his itchy shirt. "Let's go eat."

***

Gary and Gladys were seated in a corner booth next to a murky aquarium. Cuttlefish swirled along the bottom, hiding from the sputtering light, while tiny eels slithered to and fro, taunting their older descendents. A sea snail clung to the inside of the glass, unable to keep up with the filth, or had merely quit trying.

Gladys read the menu aloud to no one in particular. Gary stared into the tank, once again remembering the death scene on the beach, remembering a tiny sliver of his dream…

"So, what will it be?" The question caught Gary off guard, and he jerked his head to find a tall, darkly handsome Central Asian man who definitely didn't look local standing in front of them. Still Asian, though. Asian enough. Gary glanced at his wife, flexed the faded green anchor tattoo on his beefy forearms and opened the menu.

"What's the best thing in the house?" Gladys asked, avoiding her husband's glare.

The waiter smiled broadly. "Devil Fish, ma'am. Best in all the islands."

Gladys's permed hair seemed to shiver with excitement. "*Oooo*, that sounds yummy, doesn't it, Gare?"

Gary shook his head, squinting at the prices on the right side of the menu. "I don't like the sound of that."

"Oh, *poo*," Gladys chided. "Live a little."

Gary glowered and handed the menu to the waiter without looking at him. "I'll have the special."

The waiter nodded and turned to Gladys, who continued scanning the menu like it was the goddamn Rosetta Stone. "You're supposed to let a lady order first," she said, as if an afterthought, but which clearly wasn't.

Gary cracked his neck. "You have any whiskey here?"

"No sir," he answered coolly. "Only rum."

"Oh goody," Gladys clapped. "I'll have a Mai Tai, AND the Devil Fish." Gladys handed off the menu and smiled sweetly at her husband. A barb dipped in honey.

***

According to Gary's Timex, the food arrived exactly twenty-eight minutes after the waiter disappeared into the silent kitchen. Gladys was already on her third Mai Tai, served in a ceramic cup fashioned into the mouth of an exotic fish. Gary was absently rubbing his stomach that burned with sugary indigestion from nine shots of cheap rum. This is what you get for traveling, he ruminated dourly with a burp.

The waiter set a plate in front of Gary that featured a thick, inscrutable slab of grilled marine life surrounded by seashells and a giant clutch of parsley. "What's this?" Gary demanded.

"Special," the waiter assured him with a pleasant smile.

"I mean, what *is* it?"

"Catch of the day," the waiter shrugged as he set a sizzling plate of braised Devil Fish in front of Gladys.

Gary was about to protest, when his wife cut him off. "Don't complain, Gary. You get what you pay for."

The waiter nodded and bowed slightly. *"Bon appetit,"* he said in a perfect—and perfectly annoying—French accent as he retreated.

Gary frowned at Gladys as he snapped open his napkin. "Can't you be on my side, just once?"

Gladys slurped up the last of her Mai Tai. "Oh, don't be silly." She held up her glass to the waiter hovering by the bar, as Gary picked up his knife and fork and tucked into his meal. The skin was a bit rubbery and tough, resisting Gary's efforts.

"Shark," Gary concluded aloud. "I like shark."

"Of course you do, dear," Gladys said absently as she received her fresh Mai Tai from the waiter with a suggestive smile.

"Gonna need a bigger boat," Gary mumbled to himself with a chuckle as he sawed with his knife. Gladys just hummed tunelessly to herself. Finally, the plated skin parted under the blade and revealed a pinkish flesh underneath. Gary frowned, cut off a slice and put it in his mouth. He chewed hesitantly at first, but found the flavor surprisingly agreeable. "Not bad," he declared proudly. "I guess I do get what I pay for." Gary cut off a larger hunk, smiling as he chewed. "How's Satan's ding dong over there?" he asked, poking his knife at her plate.

"Absolutely *sinful*," Gladys enunciated in that actory way that came out far too often when she drank. She took another exaggerated bite while keeping wobbly eye contact with their swarthy waiter.

***

By the end of the night, Gary felt like he was warming up to the island. The dinner was spectacular, and reasonably priced. Even the bar bill was a pittance, as their waiter seemed to have comped half the drinks poured with a heavy hand. Island hospitality, Gary reckoned. Maybe he was wrong about this place. They left the restaurant and headed back to the resort. Gladys seemed heated up, so Gary let her go on to the room, determined to comb the shops for whiskey.

***

Gary only made it a few blocks before his extremities turned to jelly and he pitched to the sandy pavement, skinning his hands and tearing the knees of his linen trousers. The heartburn had dissipated in his notoriously iron gut, but his head felt like it was packed in cotton. Worse, his heart was pounding like he had shotgunned a pot of Folgers. Sweat coated his brow, soaking through the flowers of his stiff shirt, making it feel like an exoskeleton he needed to shed. He crawled to his feet and clutched a corroded street lamp for support.

He spit something thick and unnatural and looked around, trying to get his bearings. The streets were deserted, but he felt eyes on him, hundreds of them, and not all of them in pairs, peering out through grotesque pineapples from deep in the dark places away from the isolated circles of light and the neon glow of the storefronts. One window display featured naked female mannequins, arms arranged into obscene poses, topped by hideous tribal masks. He hadn't seen this on the way home, but it was all he could see now. Distended necks and tiny breasts with nipples like fingers. Unnatural, primal postures as suggestive as they were threatening. The vacant eyes that seemed to have depth and purpose shot their darkness deep into him, and he reeled, falling backwards without moving. He saw clouds of exploding napalm flatten smears of green, rising triumphant into a mushrooming horror show of angry soot and burned trees and skin and innards and dreams that were no different than his own. White phosphorus melted into the ground, eating up the bones of ancestors and their buried secrets. Gary clawed at his face and blinked his eyes dry, only to see lolling tongues quiver from underneath plastic teeth and lick toward the window, tasting the glass and streaking it with blackish gore.

He turned to flee the other way when he stumbled over something lying in the gutter. At his feet was the body of the legless transient, his skin gray, as if mummified, his mouth wrenched open sideways, gums crawling with insects. A final scream, or a last desperate bite.

Gary careened back up the sidewalk, hoping he was heading in the right direction. Behind him, the poorly lit street narrowed, waiting.

***

After what seemed like hours, Gary threw open the door to their room. Gladys was snoring in a rattan easy chair, dressed in a crooked grass skirt and bunched-up pink nylons, a string of pooka shells balled in her hand, succumbing to the Mai Tais mid-primp. Gary collapsed to the floor, clothing soaked, heaving for breath.

"I'm sick," he wheezed, trying to wake her. "I'm—" His voice failed.

Gary slumped into the bathroom and pawed at the switch, jarring the six walls into painful, sudden white light. He propped himself up in front of the mirror and saw bloodshot, yellowing eyes staring back at him like a demented stranger.

He bent down over the toilet bowl and held on tight. He hated vomiting, but he had to get this liquor out of him. Just like when he was twelve, when he took on an entire fifth of gin for his debut. He had almost died then. That was before he went pro. Maybe he had lost a step. He just had to get through this and start fresh tomorrow. Man up and do the deed, goddamn it.

Gary stuck his finger deep into this throat, which gurgled and contracted, as his stomach prepared to empty against its will. He pushed deeper, eyes gushing tears, until his guts finally seized and pushed upwards. Gary leaned into the bowl, his body clenching as if shot through with a cattle prod. Paralyzed with the effort, he choked a scream into a high-pitched rasp, yet nothing but foamy saliva came out. He tried again, and only quivering drool dripped through his strangled shriek into the toilet water. He sat back, gulping air, fighting back the tremor as his body attempted to resume normal functioning. The ceiling spun, the water stains in the tiles taking on demonic shapes. Goat-faced faerie folk fucking on clouds. A whale swallowing a city. Someone must have spiked his cocktails with enough LSD to melt a buffalo. The waiter. That fucking waiter... Gladys...

Anger burning through his revulsion, Gary bellied up to the commode and jammed his finger down his esophagus, nearly fitting his fist inside his mouth, stretching and cracking the skin around it. Jaw wrenched sideways... Crawling insects...

His stomach convulsed and expelled whatever was left inside, which felt like nothing. This was what Gary feared—the dry heaves, with that endless span of trapped time that never seemed to end, freezing him in panic forever. Veins bulged in his neck and forehead. Blood vessels burst in his eyes. Gary's face turned purple and the light dimmed. Finally, finally...a dribble of black ichor dripped past his lips and dotted the water like ink. In it writhed what resembled a dying tapeworm, but it had tiny legs, like a millipede. Parasite brought up from a tangle of guts.

More suddenly bubbled out of him and everything went dark.

***

Gary woke up on the bed as Gladys was getting dressed in a high waisted denim jumper. It was still dark outside, and the ocean sounded closer than before. Right outside the patio door, underneath the ground. The sheets chafed his skin, the terrestrial cotton strands clawing at him. "Oh, there you are," she said cheerily. "Did you feel that shaking?"

"What—?" Gary said, a deep-body shiver stealing his words that felt rounded and unfamiliar on top of his rubbery tongue. The rest of him felt numb. He tried to move but only quavered like a Mad Dog drunk drying out in an alley after a forty-year bender.

"Between the walls moving and those noises you were making… Scared the *dickens* out of me. I ran into the bathroom and found you on the floor, all frozen and stiff with a bloody mouth. I was afraid you were having an aneurysm!" She laughed, but it came out shrill, like a bird.

"I…" He put the ball of his head to his throbbing head. He felt worse than before. "Fuck…"

"Language, Gary… You should have seen what was in that toilet. All sorts of weird things." She sat next to him on the bed and placed a moist hotel towel on his forehead. "I think all those toxins are leaching out of your system. Must be this fresh air and organic seafood. I told you that we should start juicing. It worked for Jack LaLanne."

"He's dead."

"*Well…*"

"I feel like…" He didn't know how to describe it. Didn't have the strength.

"I know you do. Rest now. You'll feel better in the morning." She bent down, removed the towel and felt his forehead for a fever. It was clammy, cold. She paused for a second, then grabbed her purse and headed for the door.

"Where're…you going?"

"Just out for a walk."

That fucking waiter.

"Be back in a jiff!" The door closed behind her and he heard her mules clatter away faster than he thought possible. Gary closed his eyes and felt a thousand others opening up inside of him. He prayed for no dreams and knew that his mumbled pleas would fall on deaf ears, or maybe no ears at all.

***

Gladys hurried up the deserted sidewalk, an address written on resort stationery clutched in her hand. She peered anxiously at the street signs. Something large and low to the ground shifted back into the shadows without making a sound. She never noticed as she moved on, the lines in her face carved deeper under the cathode lights swaying on poles above. Farther up, amid the jagged shadows that marked where the mountains bit into the sky, tiny fires burned and bobbed like dancing sparks escaping a smoldering log.

She finally arrived at a set of barred windows decorated with a wired plastic sign. The painted cross had faded from red to a pale, unpleasant pink. The bulb was turned off. Gladys banged on the bars. "Hello?" Someone moved inside the clinic. She banged again. "Is anyone in there? My husband's sick. He doesn't…" She didn't continue. Didn't know how. She heard another sound, and peered through the window. A pair of wide, staring eyes looked back at her from the gloom. They were rounded and buggy, not like anything she'd seen on the island. They moved toward her without blinking, or giving away what was attached to them, even as they reached the bars. Gladys stumbled backwards, falling out of one of her shoes. She left it on the sidewalk behind her and hobbled on one heel further down the street.

***

Gary forced himself to sit up. He wanted to be awake when she came home, smelling of garlic sweat and Oriental fuckery. He knew that stink all too well, from Burma to the Philippines. He'd be damned if his wife did too. He'd kill the bitch first.

All of his old impulses born in piles of maggot-choked jungle corpses flowed back into him, firing his limbs and putting salt back into his spine. He stood up and strode to the dresser, taking off his clothes. He flexed in front of the mirror, muscles bulging with a youthful strength and vitality left on the college gridiron. He felt massive, transcendent. He felt like a goddamn monster.

It was then that he saw the tiny black needle poke through the skin just above his unruly nest of pubic hair surrounding his erection. He stared at it, detached, as other spiky tendrils emerged from his rounded belly that swelled by the second.

The room shuddered, or maybe it was his cells shouting out in protest and the walls never moved. A low tone rumbled deep below him like the last bass note on a million-key piano, reverberating from somewhere far beneath the ground. As if breaking a spell, Gary's body sagged, and he puked up blood, holding it in his mouth under glassy, terrified eyes, and then swallowed, taking down skittering chunks that laughed at him...

The island swallowed with him, stealing the air and leaving everything deathly still. The incessant sound of the crashing waves was gone, sucked back home, away from the shoreline that hated it.

Jarred inside a cocoon of profound silence, Gary felt his chin dip and gore leak from his mouth as he looked down at the spreading forest of black writhing spines sprouting from his body. In a moment of instant clarity, Gary then realized that he was about to see exactly what his insides were made of. And he wasn't afraid. He was curious.

***

Gladys was lost, but that was the least of her apprehension. The entire city suddenly seemed deserted. Even the ocean seemed to have fled, as she couldn't hear the surf, just an occasionally creaking, like her grandmother's old porch swing. It was a thick, pregnant silence, amplifying her sobs.

She moved one way, then the other, wiping at her eyes, looking at the mascara that clumped on her fingertips. It was black and runny, like what she'd found in the toilet next to her comatose husband... Her husband. Gary...

She turned to run, then gasped, hope flickering in her face. Gladys kicked off her remaining shoe and ran toward the familiar restaurant. Up on the hills, far above town, thousands of people, not all of them local Wakaleans, stared down at the lone woman running through the street. Their naked flesh was decorated from toe to forehead with Polynesian tattoos of swirls and spirals, meshed with patterns far older and more ominous, of teeth and eyes, twisted geometry and forgotten glyphs. None of them moved as they watched, not even the waiter, who stood taller than the rest, his face painted yellow and green and dotted with black, his protruding eyes following Gladys below.

All the signage was turned off in the window of the Seven Seas Grill, but the front door was open. Gladys ran inside and found it just as empty as the rest of the town, but there was no sign of a hasty exit. Tables were arranged neatly, chairs left on the floor, awaiting business the next day.

"Hello!" she called out, startled by the sound of her own voice that seemed to echo back at her from a soft barrier. She rushed through the swinging double doors and into the overly bright, spotless kitchen that seemed to be missing most of its appliances and utensils. She looked around, not sure what to do. Out of reflex, she grabbed a butcher's knife resting on a white plastic cutting board.

Just then, Gladys discovered an insulated door slightly ajar in a far corner of the room. Moving as fast as her trembling legs would take her, she followed the knifepoint into the walk-in refrigerator, and found that it was more of a corridor, lined with prepackaged and canned food that one wouldn't expect to find on an island surrounded by an ocean teeming with fish.

She emerged from the passageway into a spacious cooler the size of a small plane hangar, her feet splashing in a pool of oily water on the floor. The smell of gasoline mixed with a noxious, heavy odor that stank more like a filthy reptile house at the zoo than the docks at high tide. A generator puttered and smoked just outside a window that provided the only light, blocked by a prodigious bulk that took up most of the room, rising to the high, reinforced ceiling.

At first it looked to be a mound of dirt, or maybe a bus covered in a sprawling tarpaulin, held fast to the floor by small hillocks of melting ice. But as she moved forward, Gladys noticed a glistening quality to the shape in the low light. An almost phosphorescent glow, lined with creases and furrows. The smell was overpowering, and the water deepened the closer she crept, but she was drawn to the enormous mass. Just feet from it, she discerned deep cuts into one side of the deeply wrinkled hulk and large slabs of missing tissue, conjuring images of old whaling footage and the gashes left in the sides of great beasts by blades the size of a man. Gladys reached her hand forward, compelled to make contact with what could only be called wounds, when a shiver seemed to run across the surface of the shape. She froze, just as the colossal thing clenched and thrashed, booming against the corrugated roof.

Gladys shot backwards and landed in the stinking slush. Outside, an emergency warning siren gathered itself into a scream from somewhere high and far away.

"Oh my God..."

***

Gary moved to the bed, his legs somehow still working but disjointed and jerky the way a marionette flails under the control of an inartful puppeteer. He lay back slowly onto the comforter, his skin bubbling like a latex balloon stuffed with beetles. The siren was blaring outside, then wound down to a long, extended murmur. Gary wasn't breathing, just waiting with something resembling a smile pinched under his bloated face. He felt the sudden urge to roar, and did, just as his body imploded, falling in on itself as a mass of writhing creatures emerged from what was once him to feast on what was left, on each other.

***

Gladys ran like she hadn't since childhood, her arms flailing and breath caught in her chest. She moved on instinct, barreling onto a side street that angled downward, taking her to the seashore. Looking up the beach, she spotting the resort with a scream of joy, when her attention was caught by the sinking expanse of pitch black sand stretching out to her left, dropping out of sight where the water once was. The ocean was gone, exposing the lip of the island and nothingness beyond. She was suddenly standing on a box butte in central Nebraska, like the ones she and Gary marveled at outside of Salt Creek on their way to Denver as the pink sun faded to dusk, and the prairie yawned like a brown abyss below.

***

Gladys flung open the door to their room at the Sea Pearl, and found the wall facing the sea eaten away. A trail of blood and debris led down to the ocean. She ran to the patio and saw a twisting mass slink toward the waterless beach, expanding as it went, moving from what looked like a pool of slime to actual shapes, finally growing erect, evolving with every quivering second, worming toward the shadow that was forming high in front of it.

Gladys gaped up at the towering bulwark of water bearing down on the island. It was a mile out, and what looked like a mile high, and it made no sound. It didn't have to.

She turned and walked back into the room, lying in the blood and black-soaked bed, resting her head next to the desiccated eggshell skull that once belonged to her husband, who broke the mold and decided to take her on the honeymoon she always wanted.

Gladys smoothed out the denim of her outfit and folded her hands over her stomach. She began to pray, but forgot the words.

THE CURSE OF THE OLD ONES

Molly Tanzer & Jesse Bullington

Father Randolph Carter's voice rises to a desperate howl as the waters of the faintly glowing pool begin to bubble and roil.

"Say the words!" he cries. Arms outstretched, hands clenched, he beseeches the girl who stands across from him, shivering on the rocky shore. Her spray-soaked white shift reveals just how cold she truly is. "Mary—*say the words!*"

Mary Whatley nods. She clutches an encyclopedia-sized tome with *NECRONOMICON* written in gold gothic letters tightly to her chest; it presses her heaving, spray-moistened bosoms higher. She opens her mouth to speak—relief is evident on Father Carter's face—but then Mary's demeanor subtly shifts. She sensually licks her lips.

"No!" cries Father Carter, stepping back in alarm. The black cassock he wears snaps and flutters with sudden movement. "You have to finish the ritual, Mary! You have to—augh!"

He cries out as snakelike, sucker-lined arms emerge from the pool, thrashing wildly. He looks from them to Mary, and for a moment, it seems as if the frightened girl is back, swaying, close to fainting. Her eyelids flutter, and Father Carter sees her irises have gone milky-white.

"For the love of God, Mary," he pleads, "say the words!"

Mary Whatley tosses her loose hair and laughs, showing that her incisors have lengthened into sharp but rather fetching fangs.

Father Carter clutches his crucifix as he looks back and forth between the horror emerging from the pool and the newly-wanton Mary. It is evident he is unsure which terrifies him more. "No! Jesus Christ, no! Take me instead, ye devils of the sea! Take *me!*"

With the practiced slowness of a burlesque dancer Mary Whatley sets the *NECRONOMICON* on a convenient rock. Her fingers snake toward the laces of her bodice; they are stretched to the limit in their effort to contain her ample charms.

"Take you, little prietht?" Her new-sprouted fangs make her lisp ever so slightly as she undoes the knot. Her heavy breasts spill out. "However did you gueth?"

Father Carter starts to sputter an indignant protest as a loud crack followed by a tremendous splash startles talent and crew alike. It takes everyone a moment to realize a floodlight has fallen into the pool, soaking Father Carter and Mary Whatley. It sizzles there, accompanied by gasps and exclamations of disbelief.

"Cut!" calls Freddie, the director.

Father Carter dabs at his face with a handkerchief as the lights come up, and the subterranean grotto is transformed once again into a kiddie pool lined with painted polystyrene rocks; the wriggling tentacles to wire-strung rubber props. "I say," he says, "that's the third accident this week."

Mary Whatley smirks as she shimmies back into the shoulders of her gown, tucking her breasts away in a perfunctory manner at odds with both the blushing girl and the possessed seductress. "Don't worry, Peter. Ith juth the Curth of the Old Oneth. Thays tho right on the clapper. Haven't you been paying attenthion?"

"Call," says Peter, with as much dignity as he can muster in wet clothes and running stage-makeup. "It's *Call of the Old Ones*, Ingrid."

"Deep Ones," cries the screenwriter, from just behind the director. All eyes swivel to the fellow. August's flat cap is askew and he is clearly furious, red-faced as an apoplectic and clutching the script in his white-knuckled hands like it might try to wriggle away from him.

"You're right, Peter," says Freddie, ignoring the writer's outburst. "This is all getting to be a bit much. I'll just go have a word with the gaffer…maybe the whole production team."

"No!" August stamps his foot like a little boy. "We *must* stay on schedule! There's still so much to be done!"

Silence descends in the wake of the man's outburst.

"I believe *I'll* make those calls," says Freddie. He is struggling to keep his tone friendly, Ingrid can tell. "Everyone, that's lunch. August…" he turns to the writer. "Go wait for me in my camper. There are a few matters we need to discuss. Be back by two, everyone, all right?"

"Shall we order lunch?" Peter asks as he helps Ingrid down from the platform. "I don't believe I can stomach any more of craft service's tuna mayos today."

Ingrid nods. "I'm tho hungry I could eat a horthe," she lisps.

"Not with those fangs," he says, holding the door for her.

***

Ingrid and Peter commandeer the prop camper, sending the make-up artist's assistant off-set to get curry takeaway after the girl removes Ingrid's opaque contacts and false teeth. Sitting in ludicrously uncomfortable folding chairs, Peter pours them both a cup of Harrod's finest tea as Ingrid lights up a joint of Camden's worst.

"Tell me the truth," she asks, her voice strained from holding in smoke as she passes Peter the jay.

Peter daintily takes a hit. "Mmmm?"

Blowing out a rich blue plume, she says, "Is this the most ridiculous production you've ever worked on?"

Peter passes the joint back, shakes his head, then pauses, nods, and then shakes it again as he begins to cough.

"Is that a yes or a no?"

"Difficult to say." Peter smacks his lips and takes a sip of First Blend. "All these accidents! It's enough to make one think the production is… *cursed*."

"Maybe it is." Ingrid ponders the smoldering roach. She's found filming *The Curse of the Deep Ones* or whatever it's called rather trying. The accidents have been bad enough, but the screenwriter and director have both denied her requests to read the whole script all in one go. She feels she doesn't quite have a handle on Mary Whatley yet, but all her appeals for more information have been denied. "This teasing out things one scene at a time. I can't tell if it's mysterious…or worrisome."

"I know they're spinning it as a great mystery, but I think it's just a… hahah, a *smoke screen.*" Peter waves his hand in front of his face. "Andy told me he heard a rumor that this is the second time they've tried to shoot *Call of the Deep Ones.*"

"Which Andy?"

"Keir?" says Peter, blinking his already bloodshot eyes. "You know, your 'father'?"

"Right right right," says Ingrid. "You were saying?"

"I was?"

"The first time they filmed the picture?"

"Oh, I was! Yes, the first go 'round they supposedly let the actors read the full script and they all went *mad* from it." Peter rolls his eyes. "More likely they just up and quit. I never read fruiter lines."

"Maybe they're doing some last-minute rewrites."

Peter nods. "That seems likely. I've heard the studio's in some rather dire straits…perhaps one of the bigwigs decided *this* must be the film that saves them from bankruptcy, God help him. So they need it to be actually good."

"Fat chance." Ingrid leans forward to refill her teacup. She notes how Peter tactfully directs his refined eyes to the mildewed ceiling. Such a gentleman.

"For my part, though, I'd much prefer a script that really would drive us all mad if we read it in one go," he says. "As it stands, the only danger seems to be driving us to the nearest lavatory."

"Why the hesitation, then?" Ingrid asks, leaning back in the chair that simply reads STAR on the canvas backing. "When I asked if this was the most ridiculous production you'd worked on, I mean."

"Hmmm?" Peter stalls, looking sheepish. He seems uncomfortable.

"Out with it, man."

"Queer is the word, really." Peter's eyes won't quite focus on Ingrid as she stares at him, waiting to hear what he'll say. "Not worst, not by a country mile, and maybe not even most ridiculous. But queer…yes."

"*Peter…*"

"All right, all right." Peter leans in, looking to both the right and left before committing to sharing his suspicions. "*Vincent Price,*" he whispers.

"What about him?"

"The make-up artist," says Peter. At first, she doesn't think he's being serious, but something about his tone gives her pause. "It's Vincent in his old Phibes wig and sideburns."

"Oh, Peter," Ingrid frowns as she throws the joint into an overflowing ashtray, "don't tell me this is the first time you've smoked."

"It's him!" Peter croaks, then collapses into a giggling fit. When he's regained his composure, he grins at his concerned co-star. "I'm not *tripping out*, my dear. It's Vincent. Believe you me, after all the work we've done together...well, one ham can smell the other."

"But Vincent's not in this picture."

"Not officially." Peter giggles again. "But then again, we haven't seen the whole script. Perhaps he's got a cameo and it's meant to be a surprise when he shows up."

"Quite the shocker," she murmurs. Peter's bizarre allegation bothers her more than she'd expect.

"Well, why else would he be here?" Peter asks. "We have quite the history, Vincent and I. That's he's here at all is odd, but that he hasn't approached me once, well...it's a rum business, even by Vincent's standards."

"Maybe he's researching for another film. Method acting, or some such?"

"Or maybe he was cast in the first attempt and since it failed, he's sabotaging *this* production for revenge."

This time they both dissolve into giggles, but they sober quickly. For some reason, the idea of sabotage casts a pall over the camper. After what happened to that script girl, it's not something they should joke about. Neither eats much of their curry when it comes.

***

It is indeed Vincent Price. It *has* to be. When she looks carefully, Ingrid can see him beneath the silly wig and chin prosthesis. At first, she chides herself for being so unobservant, but really, it isn't so surprising. It's a damn good job he's done, camouflaging himself.

But the question remains—*why?*

She doesn't want to ask. That would acknowledge she's aware of his presence, and clearly, he has some reason for maintaining his disguise. But the oddness of it eats away at her as they wrap up filming at the London locations and begin the process of moving to Berkshire, where they will shoot the rest of the film.

It couldn't be Vincent sabotaging the production…could it? She asks herself this yet again when a bookshelf nearly falls on poor Ferdy during the scene where Dr. Armitage is giving Father Carter the *NECROMNOMICON.*

But the accidents continue, and still the make-up artist does not reveal his true identity.

***

"Ingrid?"

"Hmm?" She looks over to Pippa as she drives them through pristine countryside. It is a cloudy day, cool with the promise of rain, but they've taken down the top on Pippa's black MGB anyways.

Pippa sighs, exasperated. "Will you take a look at the map, then? We just crossed the river, and I'm not sure where the turnoff is."

"Sorry," says Ingrid. She fumbles with the map, opening it up and scanning it. "I was elsewhere."

"No kidding." Pippa holds out a fag for Ingrid to light. She nearly loses the map to the wind, fumbling with the lighter, but eventually she gets it. Pippa puffs away happily. "You've been elsewhere for weeks."

"Just weeks? Sometimes it feels like my whole life." Ingrid grins at Pippa, a bit guiltily. She had been thinking about the mystery of Vincent Price again. The make-up artist, "Lazarus Brimble," as he's calling himself, was coming with to their next location, apparently some manor house in Earley that belongs to the screenwriter's uncle. The crew had been claiming the dilapidated London studio they'd rented was to blame for all the accidents—she, however, remained unconvinced. They'd just have to wait and see…

"Ah, but I've known you long enough to see a change," says Pippa. "It's something. A friend always knows."

"There!" Ingrid points, relieved to spy the sign for Elm Hill, their destination. Pippa turns quickly, and the beauty of the private drive, and then the views of the stately Georgian manor distract them both from their conversation. Ingrid is relieved. She hasn't discussed Vincent's presence on-set with anyone but Peter, who still believes—or claims he believes—the man is 'just having a bit of a lark, is all.'

As they crunch up the gravel drive, Ingrid whistles.

"Nice pile," she says, gazing up at the dizzying array of windows and elaborate dentilwork cornices. "Here I thought the Whatleys were supposed to have fallen on hard times."

"What?

"It's in the story. I read it, trying to get a feel for Mary as they're being so dodgy about the script. Turns out, she doesn't exist. Wilbur Whatley hasn't got a sister."

"No? That's a shame. It's nice, you being the sort of, you know, virginal maiden, with Sandor playing up Wilbur as some sort of…is he supposed to be a demon, or possessed, d'you think?"

"Something." Ingrid looks slyly at her friend. "You know, you don't exist either, my dear *Jane*."

"Priests always have corruptible young daughters!"

"Yes, but Randolph Carter isn't in the story, either. He's in another, by the same author, but he's not a priest, he's a, whatsit, *antiquarian*." Ingrid shrugs. "Ah, well—it was a fun read anyways."

"Ingrid! Pippa!" They've arrived, and so, apparently, has Freddie. He's waving at them from the front door. "You're here! Good, good, welcome to 'Dunwich Manor!' It's no Moor Park or Down Place, but the price was right," he says. "Come in, come in, I want you to meet someone! He's *awfully* excited to meet you."

"Here it comes," Ingrid says as she clambers out of the car and stretches in the drive. "Hopefully."

"What's that?" asks Pippa, heels slipping on the gravel as she comes around.

"A special appearance by an eccentric guest star," says Ingrid with a wink, taking her friend's hand as they make their way up the stairs. "Come on, I've been waiting weeks for this!"

Except Freddie doesn't introduce them to Vincent Price. Instead, Ingrid shakes the clammy hand of one of the studio's backers. Mr. Leng is a leering old gent who claims to be from Warsaw, too, but his heavy accent certainly isn't Polish. He is apparently the chief financial interest in this project. But mostly, he seems interested in dredging up unhappy memories of Ingrid's childhood. When the creep presses her on which camp she and her family were taken to Pippa intervenes, insisting the ladies are exhausted from their drive and are in dire need of a lie-down.

On the stairway up to her room in the musty manse, Freddie is wildly apologetic, Pippa is irate, but Ingrid is simply in need of a hot shower and a smoke.

When she comes down for cocktails in the once-stately dining room of Elm Hill, everyone in the cast and crew wants to talk about the investor who has already headed back to London. Everyone but Ingrid, anyway. The old codger left a sour taste in her mouth that the flat tonic water does little to dispel.

Pippa is nowhere to be found among the chatty throng, but Peter arrives midway through. As Ingrid hugs him tightly she catches a glimpse of the make-up artist watching them from the doorway of the bustling hall. He raises a glass in her direction and vanishes into the interior of the house. Having had just about enough of all this, Ingrid grabs Peter's hand to follow hot on his heels. Peter protests, but after grabbing a cucumber sandwich from a tray, he's willing enough to toddle along after her into the dank heart of what they're all calling Dunwich Manor.

Away from the brightly lit party the hallways take on a spectral grandeur, especially when Ingrid catches sight of a sinister figure double-timing it up the cotton-cobweb-strewn central stair. The make-up artist swirls a *cape*, for God's sake, as he reaches the landing and darts down another shadowy corridor. Ingrid is halfway up the flight after him, Peter huffing behind her, when her eye is drawn to something hovering above her, something that slams her stock still as though she careened into an invisible barrier. She gasps, Peter bumps into her back, and then he gasps, too.

Suspended on the wall of the landing, just above the portico, is a human body. She seems affixed there by some noxious black resin, the tarry stuff stinking of rotten marine life and bleach, and her shredded dress reveals a bulge in her belly. Worst of all, beneath the crown of seaweed on her brow, her eyes have been torn out and mouth has been stopped with the sodden pages of some blasphemous book. Her exposed breasts, however, are pristine and untouched.

It is Pippa.

Peter lets out a sob and buries his face in Ingrid's bosom, but she does not avert her gaze from her murdered friend. From down the black corridor beneath Pippa's dripping feet comes a gurgling chuckle, and Ingrid puts her arm protectively around Peter as an enormous squelching shape fills the hallway and—

"Cut!" Freddie bleats. "Beautiful! Perfect!"

"What?" Ingrid's head swims, and she looks to Peter for support. His face is grim as he squeezes her arm and then steps back, both of them blinking as they take in the hovering crew, the mid-morning sun drifting in through the grimy windows.

"Is that a wrap?" Pippa calls from her perch. "Was that okay?" And Ingrid's panicked confusion melts into relief at seeing her friend shift from foot to foot on her platform above the door. In the light of day the girl's costume is so shoddy Ingrid wonders how she ever mistook it for...whatever she mistook it for. But glancing down at herself, she sees she is wearing Mary Whatley's shift. She doesn't remember changing into it...

"More than okay!" says Freddie. "I like what you two did there, having Peter turn to you. Good show."

"Show?" Peter looks as peaked as Ingrid feels, the white of his face offset by his black cassock. Had he been wearing that at the party? She can't remember. "We...what?"

"I'll tell you this much," says Freddie, putting an arm around each of his two stars. "If we can nail *every* scene in one take, it'll more than make up for all the time we lost in London! Now let's head downstairs and see if we can't get the ritual murder in the kitchen banged out before lunch."

Too much to drink at the party the night before. A hurried breakfast in bed. A sleepy session with costuming. It's all fragmented, but Ingrid can picture them so well they must be memories. They *must* be.

As the make-up artist's assistant brings a ladder to get Pippa down, Ingrid sees a grinning face watching them from down the hallway. It's not the make-up artist, though, it's August. The screenwriter puts a finger to his lips, and a migraine ambushes Ingrid so quickly she nearly swoons.

***

Quick as it came, the headache is gone...but after the shock Ingrid keeps to her room for the rest of the day, lying on the bed with the curtains drawn, watching dust-motes drift in the lone beam of darkening sunshine as she smokes cigarette after joint and drinks Glenfiddich with fusty tap water. It's only been a day but she misses Steffanie terribly, already regretting her decision to have her daughter stay with friends in London rather than accompany her to Elm Hill.

Then again, perhaps it's for the best Steffanie isn't here, considering how queer things have become: Ingrid cannot reconcile her memories with her feeling of certainty that she'd been at the cocktail party mere moments before.

Freddie comes to check on her as evening falls, bearing a bottle of 'something old and red, courtesy of Dunwich Manor's cellar.' He looks worried as he pours them each a glass, even if he insists that her absence on-set hasn't caused any major delays. They filmed a lot of good stuff that doesn't feature her, and all's well that ends well, eh? And she'll be right as rain tomorrow, he hopes?

She sips her wine, lounging crossways on the creaky, uncomfortable armchair, and glances to where he's sitting on her bed, hands clasped.

"You know," she says, "your teeth look like gravestones. They're all rounded and crooked. And grey."

"Yes, *well*," says Freddie, looking none too pleased by this description of his person, "be that as it may—Ingrid, have you been listening to me at all?"

"Big scene tomorrow, yes," she says. Freddie insisted on opening the curtains, and the hustle and bustle out on the back lawn keeps distracting her. In the gloaming the crew appears to be hauling hay-bales and pitchforks and all sorts of things to a distant bungalow. "What's going on down there?"

Freddie peers out the window. "Oh. They're making the summer-house into a barn."

"I thought you said this dump had a barn?"

"It does." Freddie massages his temples with his knuckles. "I forgot, you wouldn't know. Your little spell wasn't the only incident on-set today…"

"No?" Ingrid's heart thumps and she leans forward. "Is everyone alright?"

"What? Oh yes, of course, everyone's fine, it's just the barn, is all. Apparently, the ruddy thing isn't to be touched. It's some sort of…*historic* barn. I forget what August said about it, but we went down today with all and sundry to find the place locked up tight. Sassy tried to jimmy the lock but just as he'd gotten it August rushed up, screaming bloody murder about permits and regulations and his uncle and I don't even know what. It's not *such* a disaster, we filmed the exterior shots but we couldn't shoot Wilbur's big love scene with Jane. That'll have to be tomorrow, along with a juicy bit where you walk in on them in the barn, *in flagrante delicto*." Freddie rubs his hairy hands together.

"Oh?" This is news to Ingrid, of course.

"Right, of course…you haven't read that far ahead yet," says Freddie.

"I really would like to have the full script, you know," Ingrid says for the umpteenth time.

"So would I," says Freddie with a trace of annoyance. "Between you and me, August is barely giving me more of a lead on the action than he's offering you lot. But," Freddie brightens, "tomorrow's scene is going to be something special, I can tell you that much. Sandor's been really chewing the scenery to pieces, and I know it'll bring down the house when we shoot the *ménage a trois*. He's got this line…how does it go? *To sin with one's own sister…surely this will please my Lord Kootulu, Great Hierophant of Satan!*"

"His own sister…" says Ingrid, breathless. "Wilbur would never! I mean, I don't think he would…then again, he has been so *strange* ever since he came home from University…"

"What's that?"

She looks up into the concerned eyes of her friend. "Oh, *Jane*," she says, leaning her head on her friend's shoulder. They are sitting in her bedroom. Jane is wearing the loveliest frock, low-cut and luridly purple, but Mary is still in just her shift. "Don't listen to me. You know how silly I can get… overprotective. But after Mother died, it was just Wilbur and I looking out for one another, with Papa being away so often in the South Seas. I don't judge him, of course—he wanted to be able to send Wilbur away to study, just like he always wanted…but it's *changed* him…I think."

"Changed, Mary?" Jane puts a concerned hand on her friend's cheek.

Mary shakes her head. "There I go, being silly again." She stands and walks over to her vanity, where a yellow party dress has been laid out. "I'm ever so glad you two got engaged. My best friend and my little brother… you'll settle close by, of course, and we'll be together always, just like when we were young."

"Well, not *just* like when we were young." Jane blushes modestly. "Wilbur's a *man* now. I hardly knew him when he came home, the way he was dressed, how he acted…how he looked at me…" her expression becomes uneasy, "and you."

"What do you mean?" Mary nervously licks her lips. She doesn't like hearing her concerns echoed by her most trusted confidante. "Wilbur's… just affectionate—always has been." She turns around, deliberately makes her voice cheery. "Now, won't you help me into my dress? We should be going. It's your engagement party, after all—you can't be late!"

When they get to the Crown and Devil, it seems as though the whole village is there, drinking, eating, smoking. It is a merry scene, and Mary's rakish brother is lord of the pub, standing on the table, making toasts in an outlandish bottle-green swallow-tail coat and bright blue cravat. For some reason he is wearing a hat indoors. He cries out joyfully when Jane and Mary enter and jumps down to embrace them both. He kisses Jane on the lips and Mary on the cheek, which makes them both flush and exchange a happy glance—though Father Carter, Jane's father, looks a bit sour. But then again, he usually does. All is right with the world.

"Let me get the two most beautiful girls in the world a drink," Wilbur says gallantly. "What'll it be?"

"Champagne!" cries Jane. "Champagne for all of us!"

"All right," agrees Mary.

"My dearest Jane, come get it with me—we'll be right back," promises Wilbur.

The lovebirds scurry off, leaving Mary alone. She smiles as they go, then sobers. The party is crowded and overwhelming, full of Wilbur's friends from school. And others—as she waits, a strange foreign man approaches her.

"You are Mary Whatley?" he asks. She can't quite place his odd accent, but it is hauntingly familiar. "I am Professor Leng—your brother was one of my best students. He told me he had a sister, but not that she was so lovely."

"Thank you," says Mary. She wants to get away from this creep, he smells of mothballs and the Crown's best bitter.

"You're not here *alone*, are you?" He steps closer. "With all these rowdy university students, you'll need some protection. Come, let me—"

"Wilbur!" she cries, pretending to wave at him, and with an insincere apology to the professor, she dashes off. But really, her brother is nowhere to be seen, so she goes out back behind the pub.

Mary takes a deep breath of the fresh air and sighs. But when she turns round to go back in, she bumps into a tall, imposing figure. The man in the cape grabs her by the shoulders.

"Is it true what they say?" His mellifluous voice makes her shudder and squirm. "The sweeter the fruit, the harder the *pit*?"

The sheer corniness of the line is as bracing as a cup of strong black coffee, and Ingrid blinks. Up close the disguise isn't nearly as convincing. Price's patrician nose is not something you can easily hide behind a little make-up and latex. Ingrid crosses her arms. "Careful, *Vincent*. I socked Ollie Reed in the nose at a party for making some horrid rhyme about the state of my Pitts, you know."

"I couldn't help myself." Vincent Price waggles his bushy synthetic eyebrows.

She jabs a finger into his chest. "This is no laughing matter! You've got a lot to answer for! Peter nearly lost his head when that lighting rig swung loose."

"It was his fault," Vincent sniffs. "If he hadn't missed his mark it never would have come close to him. He was supposed to be two steps over."

"You don't deny it, then!" Ingrid advances on Vincent as he backs away across the weedy, overgrown yard. "So all those accidents really were your doing!"

"I deny nothing!" There is a manic gleam in Vincent's eye as he grabs Ingrid's wrist. Inside the summerhouse-*cum*-barn-*cum*-Temple to the Unpronounceable-*cum*-local pub, the party sequence seems to be carrying on well enough without them, and two things occur to Ingrid, then. First, it's not the party sequence that has everyone inside so merry—it's the wrap party. Second, even were she to scream, nobody could hear her.

Vincent's breath smells oddly of lilac as he suddenly pulls her into him, casting his cloak over her back. "Silence, someone approaches—oof!" He staggers back, and Ingrid bounces on her heels, ready to deliver another right hook to his breadbasket if he tries that shit again.

"Ingrid?" Peter calls from the doorway, backlit by the party lights. "Are you sneaking off for a smoke?"

"Petey Cush?" Vincent cackles triumphantly. "Who would have figured *you* for a closet beatnik!"

"Oh, hello Vincent," says Peter, extending his hand. Vincent takes it, and Ingrid notices they do something weird with their thumbs as they shake. "Finally dropping the ruse, eh? Why didn't you come forward from the beginning?"

"After the mess you and Christopher made of things during the *Scream and Scream Again* fiasco, I had to make sure you were playing for the right team," Vincent says reproachfully. "I couldn't risk unmasking myself until I was certain. Now that I am sufficiently convinced, the time is nigh to reveal all."

"Past time, I'd say," says Ingrid. She pokes Vincent in the sternum. "What's your game, Price?"

"Come," he says, taking each of them by the wrist. This time his grip is light as a ladybug. "We have much to discuss, yes, but it would be better… *if I showed you.*"

"Where are we going?" asks Peter as they are dragged across the lawn. "Should I fetch a torch?"

"The last place they want us to explore," says Vincent, "and don't worry, you'll see enough without a light."

"So long as you've got a match," says Ingrid, popping a spliff in her mouth as they approach the hulking silhouette of the ancient barn. Her heart is in her throat, and not just because she's been losing time again, or because she's sneaking off into a forbidden building with someone who's clearly lost his marbles. No, what makes Ingrid's palms sweat is that she can see the landscape as well as day, as though a cheap night-filter were draped over her eyes…she's no longer sure if this is really happening, or if it's just another scene in *Curse of the Deep Ones*. Or whatever it's called.

***

Vincent Price is apparently an expert locksmith, for the padlock falls away after he fiddles with it for a moment. The door moans as he pulls on it, revealing nothing but impenetrable darkness. God knows Ingrid has seen some horrors in her day, on- and off-set…and yet her heart pounds as she contemplates the abyss.

"Ladies first," Vincent burbles.

"Like hell," she says. "You know what's in there—*you* go in and give us the tour."

"Oh all right," he says, stepping into darkness. It swallows him quickly, and Ingrid looks at Peter—bright as the night seems out here, inside it's black as a tomb. The real kind. But they've come this far…

It smells of hay and old dung, with faint notes of leather and the tang of oiled metal. Just a barn. Pigeons coo from the rafters, and there is a rustling further in—Vincent, she hopes. Peter snakes his shaky hand into hers.

"Come on, come in." Vincent's voice comes from somewhere ahead of her, and she takes a few more cautious steps. "Nothing to worry about, I promise you."

"Is he joking?" she whispers. Her eyes have adjusted, and in the dim starlight that penetrates the cracks in the ancient walls, she sees Peter shrug.

"No." Vincent's face is a narrow white moon hanging nearly a foot above her; she gasps, and takes a step back, alarmed. "I know you think me the villain of this drama, and while that is indeed the kind of juicy *rôle* one might sink his teeth into, you may rest assured I am the intrepid hero." He stands aside, his cape billows, as he points to…something. Ingrid squints, but can't see anything.

"What the hell is this, Vincent," she snaps, finally frustrated.

He sighs. "I suppose August was getting sloppy at the party; likely he won't notice if we shed some light on the matter." He casts about and eventually locates a lantern. Getting it going with a match blinds her, and by the time she can see again he's turned down the flame, creating more shadow than light. Once she's lit her joint with a match of her own, though, it's enough illumination for Ingrid to see that someone—August, if Vincent's oblique ranting is to be believed—has created a little office of sorts. A shabby desk slouches in the corner, covered with loose paper, old notebooks, and an encyclopedia-sized tome that says *NECRONOMICON* on the cover in gold gothic letters. But it's not the prop—or is it? Ingrid can't tell.

"See?" crows Vincent as Peter approaches the mess.

"I see the den of some eccentric," says Peter, "but not your angle."

"Look at the walls!" he cries, "and see the doom of humanity writ large!"

But all Ingrid sees is a series of maps. There is Great Britain, with little red flags stuck into various random locations, and the United States, too, with the same. A few other nations are represented as well—China, some Continental countries, and Africa, though fewer flags dot those locales.

"It's their sign," he mutters. "All shall cower before the great old ones once," he says something bizarrely familiar and yet utterly unrecognizable, "is loosed!"

"Yes, well, I really must get back." Peter's clearly at the end of his rope, and Ingrid nods in agreement as Vincent whirls on them, eyes wild.

"See then, and know the truth!"

From nowhere Vincent produces a pen and begins to trace the points between the flags like a connect-the-dots puzzle. But the outline that begins to emerge is not a cat or an ice cream lolly, but something sinuous and strange, a maledictory shape Ingrid can't put a name to, but that appalls her nonetheless. It is an unholy sigil, that's the only thing she can say with any certainty; a precise shape that could not be a coincidence. It pulses and writhes like a living thing, even after she passes Peter the joint and rubs at her eyes.

"Never before has this studio managed such broad distribution for one of their films," murmurs Vincent, "and the film, if played at these crucial points around the globe, shall bring about the end of mankind. It is a key that when turned in these international tumblers will unlock...*doom*. *This* is why I interfered—*this* is why I did what I could to create delays—to destroy the work entirely! But I fear I have failed, and it has all been for naught. They are too strong—those August works for are as powerful as they are keen to see their unholy desires made real!"

All is silent in the barn as they contemplate this. Then a seed pops in Ingrid's joint. Shaking his head, Peter asks, "How in the *hell* did you glom on to any of this?"

"August originally came to an American director with his project, a friend of mine," explains Vincent. "Roger showed me the pitch, and while he didn't see it for what it was, I recognized at once what the madman intended with his little 'adaptation.' I talked Roger out of making the movie, but when I caught wind that August had taken his plot across the pond I followed. Great forces conspire against us, so I knew I had to be subtle in my sabotage."

"So what do we do?" Peter's convinced, strangely enough, and Ingrid realizes she is, too. Or at least, she's convinced Vincent's convinced.

"It's missing a scene," says Vincent. "A small one, yes, but as I understand it, the entire picture must be complete for the ritual to function. All you two have to do is refuse to film the last scene—an elegant solution, is it not?"

"But it's wrap," says Peter, echoing Ingrid's thoughts. "I mean, we're done, Vincent, we completed principal shooting—"

"Impossible!" cries Vincent, gesturing to the cluttered desk. "I've been over his notes and part of the Great Work is missing—just one moment, one brief scene where 'Wilbur Whatley' calls upon," again that strange name, "by its true appellation!"

"But Vincent, we filmed that bit." Ingrid remembers it clearly. "It was one of the first scenes we shot, on the first day, before…" She stares at him. "Before the 'new make-up artist' joined us after the original chap got food poisoning!"

Vincent stares at her. "No," he whispers. "Then we are…"

"Oh dear," says Peter. Wringing his hands, he nearly drops the spliff, but Ingrid gets it back from him in time. "That is a shame. I'm rather unhappy to be part of some film that dooms humanity. Goodness."

"There must be something we can do," says Ingrid. "We can't just sit idly by."

"There's nothing to do," says Vincent. "I've examined the contracts, and the producer has promised August final cut—not Freddie."

The smoke curls through Ingrid's lungs and out her nose like the tentacles of some infernal fiend. She's had an idea that might save them all, or at least calm down her friends.

"There *is* something we can do. Something I bet no actor's ever done, so they'll never see it coming…"

"What?"

"Remember all that hullaballoo surrounding *The Vampire Lovers*?" she says to Peter. "How the censors ruled it obscene, because of my scene with Kate?"

"Yes," he says slowly.

"Well, they ended up allowing it, obviously, but only because all that lesbian stuff was in the Le Fanu."

"The what?" Peter asks.

"*Carmilla*," Vincent intones. God damn, but the way he says it sends a shiver down Ingrid's spine. She could listen to him pronounce things all night. "The novella by Sheridan La Fanu."

"But I've read 'The Dunwich Horror,'" Ingrid says, "and I assure you, there's no threesome with Wilbur Whatley and his sister, or all that weird rutting with fish-people." She shrugs. "I'll make a few calls. Once the Board hears about August's 'creative liberties,' they'll demand edits. There's no power on earth more diabolically powerful than British censors, so there's no way it'll make it into theatres uncut…unless everyone in the government's already fallen to the curse of the Old Ones." She grins. "Though come to think on it, Thatcher seems a likely candidate."

Vincent is staring at her with wide eyes and falls at her feet like she's some radiant avenging angel.

"My lady," he says, grasping her ankle and kissing the top of her foot. "You will go down in history as the bravest, most beautiful, most intelligent woman in the world. A simple solution—so elegant—so perfect…my own genius pales before yours!"

She takes a long drag on her joint and passes it back to Peter. "Oh, come off it," she says, kicking him away. Gently.

***

Curse of the Old Ones, The (1975-British) **85m**. BOMB D: Freddie Francis. Peter Cushing, Ingrid Pitt, Sandor Elès, Pippa Steel, Andrew Keir, Ferdy Mayne. Incomprehensible mishmash of several stories by H.P. Lovecraft. A priest (Cushing) and a young woman (Pitt) wander aimlessly around shoddy sets in an attempt to stop a sinister cult from summoning the devil. Francis is usually reliable and the top-notch cast seem game, but what could have been a fun if predictable entry in the canon of bodice-ripper horror is hamstrung by bad pacing, sloppy editing, and a nonsensical script. Widely regarded as one of the financial disasters that brought down Hammer Film Productions, along with the marginally more watchable **Captain Kronos, Vampire Hunter** (p.47) and the equally inept remake of **The Lady Vanishes** (p.169). Apologists have made much ado over the years regarding the British Board of Film Classification's heavy censorship of the film, but Cushing and Pitt refused to promote the picture, and the screenwriter adopted an Allan Smythe credit. A forthcoming director's cut promises to restore the film to its original vision with recently rediscovered footage that was excised from both the theatrical run and prior home video releases, but in light of the quality on display in all previous versions, this new release will appeal strictly to completionists.

AKA: **Call of the Deep Ones**, **The Evil of the Old Ones, Kootulu is King of Hell**

LOVE WILL SAVE YOU

Cameron Pierce

By Christmas morning, the world was dead.

***

The job offer in Elko fell through before Thanksgiving. A week later, Anna called off the engagement and asked Mark Rothko to move out. Mark packed his few possessions—clothes, fishing gear, a vintage bottle of scotch—and drove away from the one-bedroom apartment where he and Anna had lived for several years. He pulled on to I-80, out of Truckee, intent on leaving his disappointments behind.

California had little left to offer him, and his opportunity in Nevada had dried up before he even arrived, so he headed northwest into Oregon. He spent the first night of his new life in an unheated yurt in the Valley of the Rogue. In the morning, he fished the Rogue River and fought a nice steelhead to the bank, but when he reached down to net the fish, the chrome buck thrashed his head from side to side and dislodged the hook. Mark fished for another fruitless hour before hitting the road. In Medford, he stopped at a gas station for coffee and a pack of powdered doughnuts.

His card was declined and he was forced to put the doughnuts back on the rack. The clerk let him keep the coffee.

Back in the truck, he dialed Anna. She answered after the second ring. "So you cleaned out the account," Mark said.

"Mark, you need to know—" Anna said, but Mark's cellphone died before she finished.

In his rush to leave, he'd forgotten to pack a cellphone charger. He dug in the center console for change, counted up wads of crumpled dollar bills—relics of all the time and money he'd invested in strip clubs east of Truckee—only to realize that he needed every last dollar for gas, if he was going to make it further north.

Mark sat there in his truck, debating something in his mind, before getting out and going into the gas station again to get change for a dollar. He stuffed the quarters in the payphone outside and put a hand to the cold silver numbers. "Shit," he muttered. They'd never gotten a landline and Anna had changed her cell number several months ago. He hadn't bothered memorizing her new number. In his cellphone she was listed under *Honeybee*, but now his honeybee was unreachable. He'd write her a letter when he got where he was going, wherever that happened to be.

Mark continued north. Late that afternoon, he parked his car in a desolate river district somewhere outside Portland and hiked to a beach on the river. He walked along the beach until he came across the graffitied, rusted-out hull of a wrecked ship. It would provide adequate shelter for the night. He gathered twigs for a fire, then sat beside the fire until sundown, when he stamped out the flames to avoid detection. The night was cold and he would likely find sleep hard to come by, but he wasn't ready to be around other people, couldn't admit even to himself that he had nowhere to go. He crawled inside the shipwreck, only to find that at night it did not look as it did in the daylight.

At first the spheres appeared to be some sort of glow-in-the-dark graffiti. The spheres, black yet somehow glowing, were three to five feet tall—and everywhere. Stacked upon each other like the shipwreck was some sort of abandoned, ethereal storage unit. And then all at once, yellow eyes blinked and shark-like mouths opened wide across the shadow-like flesh of the spheres. The eyes floated as if in a jelly, the mouths whispered unspeakable words.

Mark scuttled backwards like a crab, but a tendril with the texture of a fine-haired cactus unfurled from the dark and dragged him closer. In the many eyes of the sphere that held him close, Mark saw puppet versions of Anna and himself playing out the most intimate moments of their lives. Witnessing the puppets act out their obscene domestic drama, their movements so unnatural, Mark understood that love was nothing more than madness—and decided he would do everything in his power to reclaim it.

This discovery made, the world would never be the same for Mark. Not for him or Anna or anyone else.

***

Anna had received no word from Mark in weeks, not since their call was disconnected the day after she broke up with him. She'd called dozens of times a day since then, but his phone went straight to voicemail every time. She'd gone to the police and filed a missing person report. His name turned up in the registration at a state park in southern Oregon. An attempted debit charge had been declined from a gas station in Medford. The bank's fraud department had put a freeze on the card due to perceived suspicious activity. Although Anna sorted everything out with the bank later that day, Mark never ran his debit card again. His cellphone remained off, and no hotels or campgrounds reported anyone registering under his name or matching his description. Mark Rothko had simply vanished.

When she and Mark had had the blowout fight that resulted in him leaving, she'd been aware that her period was late, but only weeks later did she muster the courage to take a pregnancy test. The smiley face that appeared on the pale pink stick confirmed that everything she never wanted out of life was coming true.

Now, on the day before Christmas Eve, Anna sat at the kitchen table after getting off the phone with her sister, who'd offered to fly Anna home to Fresno for Christmas. Anna had declined. She wanted to be home in case Mark happened to return, unlikely considering the severity of their fight, or if any news of him came in from the police.

The knock on the door startled her. Her legs felt weak as she stood. Balancing herself on the kitchen counter, she shuffled to the door. She held her breath, pressed her face to the peephole, and peered out.

She caught the back of the postman as he returned to his mail truck. He waved to her as he drove away.

Anna waved faintly. The postman had left a package on her doorstep.

The handwriting on the shipping label was unmistakably Mark's, but provided no return address.

She took the package inside and set it on the kitchen table. After staring at the package for too long, she sliced the packing tape with a knife and peeled back the flaps of the box, timidly, as if a jack-in-the-box might leap out. Inside there was a gallon-sized Ziploc bag and a handwritten note. The note read: *I miss the feel of your soft skin. Please take me back.*

She pursed her lips into a smile. "Asshole," she whispered, feeling affection for her missing ex-fiancé.

She opened the Ziploc bag. The stench of rot was overwhelming. The bag contained an object wrapped in a handkerchief, which appeared to be the source of the smell. She pulled away the handkerchief, uncovering two human hands.

They'd been severed at the wrists. Bones jagged, as if cut with a dull saw. The hands were clean of blood, as if they'd been bled out and wiped down with a wet cloth before the sender bundled them in the handkerchief and shipped them to Anna.

***

The police came and went, taking the hands with them. They assured Anna that an officer would drive by the house every hour, but without any leads or suspects, there was nothing to be done, no protection offered.

Anna called her sister as soon as they left.

"Are you okay?" her sister asked.

Words did not form easily.

"If you need to be here, just say yes."

"Yes," Anna said.

"I'll book your ticket and call you back."

Anna remained on the line long after her sister hung up. So long, in fact, that by the time her sister called back with the flight information, there was no Anna left at all. In the apartment, a darkly translucent Anna-sized sphere sat in her seat at the kitchen table. Anna's cellphone vibrated on the table in front of the sphere, but the sphere did not answer the phone.

Deep inside the Anna sphere, the embryo formed eyes and mouths. So many eyes and so many mouths that soon the barely-formed baby was little more than a swarming mass of lidless eyes and screaming mouths, trapped in the slime of endless dark.

***

The phone rang and rang before going to voicemail for the umpteenth time. "Dammit, Anna, pick up," Tess said. She texted the itinerary to her sister, then called again, hoping to reach Anna and instead reaching her voicemail.

Anna had been troubled, hardly uttered a word on the phone, but they lived so far away, Tess could not jump in her car and drive to Truckee. She did not know any of Anna's friends, no one in that town. She dialed Mark's number, on a hunch that her sister was upset because Mark had returned. No such luck. His phone remained off.

In frustration, Tess smashed her phone against the tile floor.

She knelt down, tears welling in her eyes, and began stuffing the shards of phone screen into her mouth. The edges cut her tongue, cut her mouth. She wept as she choked down the phone, the sharp triangles of glass sticking in her throat, cutting off her airflow.

When James, her husband, returned from the car dealership that evening, he found that Tess was not at home. He turned on all the lights and called her cellphone. Her ringtone emanated from somewhere in the house. He followed it into the kitchen, where a hollow glass sphere sat upon the floor. The sphere was approximately four feet tall and four feet wide. The sphere emitted Tess's ringtone, the grating jingle of a popular sitcom that James only begrudgingly sat through on Tuesday nights.

Then, as he went to end the call, the sphere spoke.

"Hello?" it said, in Tess's voice.

"Tess, is that you? Where are you?"

"I'm right here, silly. Why don't you crawl inside me?" The voice was almost just like hers, but wrong in a way James could not identify.

James ended the call because what was the use talking to a sphere? Clearly this was some kind of sick joke, or the lead-up to an early Christmas gift.

"This isn't funny," he said.

The lack of response, the silence that permeated the house like a draft of cold air, unsettled him.

"Answer me, Tess. You've had your laugh."

Fed up, he dialed her number again. The sphere rang, then promptly answered.

"Why'd you hang up?" it asked, again sounding like Tess, but not.

"I hung up because you're not my wife," James said.

"Then what am I?"

A red liquid filled the sphere in plumes. The red spread until the translucent sphere was no longer see-through, and then the sphere darkened, flickered at first like an octopus James once saw on the Discovery Channel. Color was the language of the octopus. James wondered what it meant that the sphere was now a shimmering, roiling obsidian, a blackness so complete that he could think of nothing else, eyes fixated, pupils dilating to obliterate the blue irises.

"Then what am I?" the sphere repeated.

"You're my wife," James said.

He dropped his phone and approached the sphere, one shuffling footstep at a time. The sphere appeared to be solid, but this did not prevent him from crawling inside, as if the sphere were a bottomless sea and not a sphere at all.

***

By the early hours of Christmas Eve, the reported missing reached unprecedented numbers. By the afternoon, police stations sat empty. By the time a state of emergency was declared, there was hardly anyone around to listen. The loveless were lucky. Everyone who'd ever loved had become a dark sphere, except for one man, who was still trying.

***

The earth was silent as it snowed on Christmas morning. In California, near the Nevada border, in the town of Truckee, a man without hands stumbled through the forest. He'd walked for many days, maybe a whole lifetime, trying to get back to something he'd left behind. Slung over his shoulder was a knapsack that held a vintage bottle of scotch, but he was incapable of opening it with his scabbed and gnarled nubs.

The man stopped in his tracks. Ten feet away, a doe grazed on a shrub. Somehow he hadn't startled her, but as soon as he noticed her, paused to admire her beauty and grace, she ran off into the wilderness, leaving behind no trace of her existence except for hoofprints and a torn shrub.

The man marched onward through the falling snow. Ahead lay the apartment where he knew he belonged. Night was coming and he still hoped to arrive before the sun vanished. His feet ached from soreness and blisters, but he persisted. The whole world was waiting for him. He couldn't wait to see her again.

ASSEMBLAGE POINT

Scott R. Jones

for Ramsey Campbell

You'll want to know about the body liquescing at the bottom of the stair, of course, and I will get to that, I promise, but first I need to warm up my pen a little, work the kinks of long disuse out of my cursive, and tell you a few things. Three things.

First, I want you to think about predation. I mean, beyond the *Mutual of Omaha* dramatics we all grew up on, beyond plummy British voiceovers on high-def video. I mean *real* predation. The complete slavery that the food chain ensures. First Law of the Universe? It's simple: Everybody Hungry. Doesn't matter how you've incarnated here, whether you're a galaxy or a microbe, or where you are on the chain, top link or scraping bottom, if you want to live to see tomorrow, you'd best have something on your plate tonight.

I've thought about predation a great deal lately, and what makes the perfect predator, and it's not the sharpness of the teeth, or the fleetness of the feet, or the keenness of the eyes, or the brute power of the muscles, although those things help, obviously, those things make for great documentary TV. No. No, it's camouflage. Chasing after your prey is for chumps and show-offs. Waiting quietly, appearing to be what you're not, appearing to be benign, appearing to be nothing at all, even, so that your prey places itself in your mouth all unawares... I've been thinking about that a lot. Ultimate predators. Ultimate camouflage.

See, there's camouflage. And then there's *camouflage.*

And as I sit here writing this, I'm thinking about the old stories, too, that used to amuse me so much. You know the ones. The tales of dark deeds done, awful and rare books acquired, terrible knowledge gained, sanity sacrificed, then lives. As a boy, I'd read those stories and be properly enthralled as any twelve-year-old would be, along for the ride as the tale's contents were correlated towards a mind-shattering conclusion, painfully identifying with the narrator because, after all, he was *me*, wasn't he? A seeker. If not a hero, than at least a quester after lost, hidden things. A sorcerer, even.

You could see it coming, of course. The end of that search. The arrival of the vengeful Thing. The conclusion of the deal with a devil. The narrator would telegraph that final, shattering revelation from miles away, which was part of the fun.

Here's the amusing bit, though: in the face of utter horror, as Death (or worse) loomed from out of the night to greet him, he'd still write out his final moments, our narrator, that dedicated fellow. In a wild and unsteady hand, naturally, but still. As they were happening. A goddamn play-by-play.

That hand! The window! The window!

The three-lobed burning eye!

I am it, and it is I.

Well. It's a cliché, but I found it funny, even at twelve when it was new and I didn't know what cliché was. It should have scared, but I'd laugh instead, taken out of the story by a paragraph of frenzied italics that amounted to little more than a wordy *boo!*

But then, for the reader, I suppose that's the perfect time to be taken out of a story. At the end.

Which, again, I *will* get to. But first, one more item: I should tell you that I'm naked as I write this. You'll find my clothes neatly folded on the desk next to these pages. You're looking at them right now, I'll bet. I half-considered arranging them, on the chair and the surrounding floor, in such a way as to suggest that my body had been spirited away, snatched to heaven "in the twinkling of an eye", as the Rapturous Christians like to say. For a moment, I thought that would be amusing, but then decided that it was too much trouble for a gag. I mean, on top of the hilarity that's about to ensue. Don't think I'm not aware of how funny this is.

Honestly, though, I just don't want to shit in my pants when it happens. They don't tell you about that when you begin these practices, when you enter this appalling lifestyle, but if you're doing things right, or you've read your Castenada, you learn fast. You shit yourself a few times before you get wise.

I got wise. And now I impart this wisdom, and more, to you.

That was the warm-up. I'll begin.

***

It was Castaneda, that old fraud, who brought me to this. Yes, *that* Castaneda. Little Carlos. *The Second Ring of Power. Journey to Ixtlan.* Peyote and mushrooms and oneiric dopplegangers and shapeshifting and the loosest of academic standards.

See, if you've a certain sort of mind, if that early sense of being a searcher after hidden truths is more than just a byproduct of hormones and teenage romanticism, if you are, basically, *me*, then you move on from the old stories with their amusing finales and stumble into fictions more potent and far less trustworthy. The gravity of secret knowledge pulls you from the shelves that hold *Fantasy*, and *Horror*, to the dimly lit ones in the back of the store labeled *New Age Thought* and *Spirituality. Occult. Witchcraft.*

It's a pit trap, naturally, but a poorly camouflaged one. The contents of those shelves are there to put a little numinous thrill into the grasping, sad lives of proto-Crowleys, urban shamans, and menopausal women. And again, if you're like me (and you *are*, aren't you? You must be, to be sitting there, reading this) you don't stay in the trap for too many years. It's long and deep, though, this pit, and occasionally there are jewels embedded in the walls. Ideas that you pluck from the muck and pocket almost without thinking, concepts that stick like burrs to your skin long after you've crawled out of there.

Castaneda was definitely a burr, one that stuck deep in me, even after his dangerous hucksterism was exposed to the world. His three missing-presumed-dead witches slash sexual partners. The suicide pacts. A banal, hushed-up death by cancer: camouflaged cells dropping the act, finally, and killing from within, and not the heroic sorcerer's journey into the Second Attention his followers claimed for him. Yeah, Castaneda. Here was a guy who had sold his humanity, and convinced most of his readers that he'd done it for real knowledge, real power, and not just for a dreary SoCal compound full of witchy pussy.

Still, there were ideas in those books that affected me strangely. Weirdly practical suggestions for practice, like removing your clothes before doing any sorcerous work. That way, Castaneda's teacher don Juan Matus explained, when you shat yourself from fear at the things you were seeing and the deeds of power you were accomplishing, all you'd have to do is go wash up in the river. Pick up your clean clothes on the way back to the house.

Castaneda was all about *seeing,* too. True perception. Shifting awareness from this world to others. Moving what he called the "assemblage point", that focus of attention that builds the human world, to another spot on the "luminous egg" that formed your energetic body, so that you would assemble a different world. A world that was more *true*. Serene and primal and potent. A sorcerer's world.

Well. That was the huckster's line, anyway. He was, maybe, a better sorcerer than he was an anthropologist, at the end. A series of debunkings and high-profile exposures pushed Castaneda out of the spotlight, though his book sales weren't hurt any. Definitely a better writer than anything else.

I wasn't *convinced* or anything. I mean, if you jump from a cliff because a talking eagle tells you that the experience is going to trigger your transition to an exalted energetic state where you will receive special knowledge, then brother, you get what you deserve. I wasn't convinced.

But it was *compelling* stuff, nonetheless. Just practical enough, just strange enough, just a hair on the other side of comprehensible enough to smack of something legitimate. Something truly otherworldly. I got things from Castaneda that I couldn't find in Crowley, or Bertiaux, and certainly not in the standard New Age boilerplate.

A burr, worrying its way inside. An itch to *see.*

Reading about sorcery is like reading about sex. It's not the real thing, but it gets you hot for it, makes you want it more. So, I left the bookshelves behind, and began to move in strange circles. I began to fall away from the human world, waded into the deep pools of night that surround that pretentious little island of grand ideas and goofy hubris.

I don't like to go into great detail about those years. Sites were visited. Temples, ruins, forgotten wastelands. An island off Nan Madol. An abandoned forestry camp in the Olympic Mountains of western Washington. Even visited the Yucatán stomping grounds of Little Carlos, though for a purpose that was not merely nostalgic. Something darker.

Yes. Dark things were done, terrible things, as you no doubt know. Whoever you are, you're sitting here reading this, which means you've tracked me this far, a not inconsiderable feat. Let me congratulate you on your cleverness, for what it's worth. So of course you don't need details; you already know about the things, or some of the things, I've done. The sacrifices made. The ones left behind, damaged. More than damaged. I've hurt a lot of people. Could be you're hoping for answers about one of those people.

I don't know. I don't know anything about you, except that you're here, and have done some things yourself to get here. That's enough.

The things *I* did led me here, to Camside, to this house. There are places where the true world is more apparent. I don't have to tell you this. *Thin spots*, as the menopausal New Agers would say. Which is fine as far as that goes.

In any case, this house is such a place, known only to a few. There was a breakthrough here, back in the Sixties. That magical time, eh? Two enterprising young warlocks had pulled a rookie cock-up, really done a number on themselves in the process. *Do not call up that which you cannot put down,* right? A standard caution, sure, but where would we be without the bold, I say. Without those willing to go that extra distance.

It has a name. All the old ones do, but I won't bother with it here. Names are just more camouflage. The brief waggling of a wad of human tonguemeat cannot fully encapsulate *It*. *It* is what *It* is, this entity, and no more or less than that. A being. An eternal principle of that true world, a facet of how things really are.

How things really are. That, in fact, was what commerce with this old one brought. True vision. A rending of the veils. Pure sight. Few worshipped *It*, for that reason alone. That's what the warlocks were after, though. The stronger one, the bold one, had an idea that our eyes were fooling us, with all those many million rods and cones embedded in a globe of viscous tissue, filtering every particle of light, flipping images on their heads, doing who knows what else. How could anyone be sure that the things seen were in fact how things really were?

They needed items to call the old one up out of the black dimensions which held it. Most importantly, an image of the being: a migraine-inducing metallic sculpture of hemispheres and rods, cylinders and empty spaces. It was the empty spaces that drew the eye, so that to look upon the image of the old one was to not see it at all. There was also a misshapen skull, a "rod with an icon," a "weirdly shaped pentacle," and "obscene candles."

I'm relaying these things to you, as I found them in the scandal sheets and police reports, more for your own amusement than anything else. You and I both know what really calls these things up, and it's the First Law of the Universe. *Obscene candles!* But it was the Sixties. The empty-handed methods such as you and I use were decades away.

And in any case, it worked. The warlocks called, and the old one answered. Did more than just answer, *It* came, and bestowed gifts upon them. Of course they were found dead the next morning, and of course it was ruled a murder-suicide, but oh, they'd left more behind than their mystical, fetishistic paraphernalia! Our boys had *taped* the ritual, on a nice old reel-to-reel unit. Took me a while to lay my hands on the original, but the moment I heard their death rattles, I knew it was no gag, no prank. They'd seen things as they really were, and the sight was too much.

I *knew* they'd been successful. Those last forty seconds or so of the tape? Pure italics.

The veils had been rent for them. The camouflage dropped away and the primal world of Truth, the sorcerer's world, revealed. I wanted what they had, what they had been unable to process, unable to properly endure.

Now, you know what I've done, to become the sort of person who could survive what those two couldn't. I was ready, able, and oh so very willing to look upon the naked heart of the universe. I had *done the work*, and I was ready to have the scales fall from my eyes, ready to *see*.

So I came here, and I called.

It answered, and the veils were rent. Gifts were bestowed. *It* touched me, just once, almost delicately, cracking my luminous egg wide open and permanently shifting my assemblage point to its new position. Castaneda would have shat himself, I'm sure. I certainly did.

And now I *see.*

I see what *It* is, the old one. I see how *It* rests in Time, the way *Its* limbs straddle the dimensions, the way *Its* eye-analogues caress the skin at the back of our reality with fevered intensity, the way *It* rubs up against our false world. My initial perceptions of *It* were a riotous confusion of forms and spastic movement, as *It* cycled through untold manifestations. The vision settled, though, finally, pulsing with the awful slow beat of the eternal, of that which really is.

What *It* is, you see (*do* you see? You will! Soon enough!), is *everything. It* is this room, and my clothes upon the desk. *It*'s the air moving in and out of your quickening lungs, and the rain on the windshield of the cab you took to get here, and your dogged insistence on answers that keeps you reading this through to the end, though your every animal instinct is to run. *It*'s the body at the bottom of the stairs that you had to step over to get up here (did you really check that corpse, I wonder?), and Castaneda thinking about how to make a little money off some soft-headed hippies. *It*'s the chuckle I made the first time I reached the italics at the end of one of those stories (a chuckle mirrored by my own laughter here, years later, as I pen just such a ridiculous narrative), and *It*'s the foolish, malnourished amateur who wrote those stories thinking that would be a decent way to finish, to take the reader out.

It's the young warlocks who died in this house, and the people I used and discarded to get here. *It*'s me, lying to you a few paragraphs back, when I wrote that I didn't know who you are. Because of course you're her father, though you're not unique. There have been so many fathers. Mothers and siblings and lovers, too. Hired investigators. Though none of them ever made it this far. Again, congratulations on your cleverness. On becoming like me, on becoming what you'd revenge yourself upon.

It's that cavern on that island near Nan Madol, and *It*'s her blood on the well-used stone in that cavern, and *It*'s the celebrants I'd gathered there, up to their ankles in blood and spunk. *It*'s these pages you're holding, and the ink that makes the letters you're reading, and *It* is especially the empty spaces between those letters.

It's the shit on that body downstairs, which was mine, caking the inner thighs and back of the legs. *It*'s the body itself, half-dissolved from the old one's touch, and the energetic structure within that body swirling in a mad chaos of anguish as it mutates. Scrambled luminous egg! *It*'s the stirring of that body as the right hand rises from the floor and slaps down wetly upon the first stair.

You really should have checked it, though I doubt there's anything you could have done to stop what's happening, for you have been fooled, taken in, placed yourself within the mouth, as I did.

It's allowed me to see as *It* sees, across the expanse of Time and Space, allowed me to feel what *It* feels, exist as it exists. Even as I sit here writing, *It* is doing its terrible work upon me. I write the words *Nan Madol* and I am there, in the cavern, doing unspeakable things to her. I write *the young warlocks who died in this house* and I am here with them, touching them as *It* touched them, and shaking with glee as they destroy themselves. I write *the shit on that body downstairs* and I am there, at the top of the stairs, a few minutes from now, out of my mind with terror, trying to flee from the liquefying touch of something that's been disguised as *everything,* shitting myself and slipping in it, my head describing an awful, graceful arc in the air before the impact.

I write these words, and experience these things, but it is only the camouflage. There's camouflage, and then there's *camouflage,* and it is *all camouflage*. My life. Your daughter's life. The world. Our reality is nothing but a skin for the ultimate predator, discarded when It is ready to eat. I cannot even guess why *you* are on its plate tonight. It feeds on many things, and its hunger is inscrutable.

Perhaps sorcerers taste better. Less human. We give up so much of our humanity to learn these things, accrue this power, and in the end, we're food. Thanks for nothing, Carlos.

It's at the door now. I'm at the door now, naked and viscous, flesh sliding on supple bones. I wonder how I'll fit into my clothes afterwards. I am changed, made glorious and violent and true, the merest tip of the smallest appendage of *It*. A claw, tapping.

I am It, and It is I, right? Oh, the italics of it all! But I won't burden you with that cliché. I don't find it all that funny, anymore. It's not a decent way to finish.

You might get lucky when that door opens. For a moment, your assemblage point may shift so far that you create a world in which you're just some schmuck reading a pulpy horror story in a cheap paperback. Only for a moment, though. Enjoy it.

Time to take you out of the story.

THE RETURN OF SARNATH

Gord Sellar

The tireless things crept over the vast desert's brutally hot sand, each trailing a miniature pillar of black smoke behind it. As they approached, their myriad forms—endlessly inventive, dreadful, sublimely beautiful—became visible, their steely shells casting off a searing gleam. Ajal squinted beyond them, before nodding to his lady master, Terea.

"The maps were right," she declared, smiling. Ajal stared down at the trails the things had scratched into the dust, marveling.

Terea's caravan was the fifth to cross the wastes of Mnar seeking the source of these iron-carapaced horrors. Back in plague-stricken Celephaïs, tales had spread among the idle and dying of a new horror arising in the distant wilds of Mnar, glimpsed climbing among the ruins of Kadatheron and Ilarnek, teeming across the land's now-dead plains and dessicated marshes.

Ajal watched carefully his zebra's steps; its legs were armored, but he had seen for himself what these things had done to iron-clad Kadatheron. During his wanderings among the factories nestled in the city's ruins, he had even glimpsed several Kadatheroni natives battling the things—some scorpion-shaped, others with dreadful forms akin to human hands, or armored mechanical centipedes. He knew how gruesomely the things performed their slaughter, and their mechanical chittering had haunted him as he'd inspected the ancient, cylindrical stones carved from top to bottom in wind-worn glyphs that few could still read.

The image of the corpses they had had left behind troubled him still, though he was miles away now, in the vast and dusty plain beyond Kadatheron; they haunted him like the memory of a lost lover might haunt a weak and tired man, burrowing through his wits and leaving him a pale, crumbling ruin—shattered like the ruins of once-great Kadatheron, or the fouled countryside of once-verdant Mnar.

Nearby, another pseudo-oasis beckoned from its shadowy hollow. The water there would be foul, Ajal knew, but he longed for the slight coolness the air held in all moist places. The endless dust and scraggy brush of the flatlands of dead Mnar were gnawing at him.

"No, Ajal," Terea said, so softly that perhaps he alone heard her. "We're nearly there, and will reach the lakeshore before nightfall, if we continue."

A murmur spread out among the travelers, masters and servants and slaves both, and even their mounts—the zebras and horned calaphaxes that trudged before the slow, coal-fired landbarges—seemed to bristle at the thought of nearing the lake where lost Sarnath had once stood just as the sun sank down into the umbral earth, and the heavens revealed the trillion distant stars spattered across their cold, black depths.

But Terea was a determined sort, an unwearying adventuress who had crisscrossed the world a dozen times during during her long and colorful life: none dared challenge her. Ajal, the hardiest and most pampered of her slaves, knew all too well what criticizing her plan might incur; he knew, also, that he could never change her mind. Terea was like stone come alive—like willful, breathing granite.

So the group trudged on through the light and dust of the wastes of dead Mnar.

***

The dying light of evening had half-dimmed the colors of world when a young slave hurried back over a nearby rise toward the group, crying out, "The lake! It's here! And the city!"

This heartened even those who feared the ruins of fabled, doomed Sarnath, celebrated as a lost city of once-gleaming parapets, an icon of folly soaked in blood with cries ringing through its drowned streets…lost Sarnath stood in the minds of the world as a warning.

Would they find, too, the ruins of that other city, the one destroyed by the Sarnathans, that fabled grey stone polis of Ib? Would they glimpse the broken towers shrouded in greenish lake-mist? Would unspeakable things emerge to greet them, soundlessly, by the flapping of drooping lips, by a threatening wave of webbed hands?

Ajal rode beside Terea, silent, while those up ahead began chattering loudly, with wonder, as they summited the rise and glimpsed what lay beyond. A curious suspense gripped Ajal, his stomach fluttering; but also a quiet, cold foreboding crouched behind that flutter, a dark whirlpool of dread swirling in the depths of his lean, pale belly.

For her part, Terea, a heroic prodigy of exploration and adventure, remained unmoved by the spreading excitement. She spurred her calaphax up the rise without betraying the merest hint of fear or pride. Her mind was fingertips poised on the strings of a zither, focused and trained solely on the task she had undertaken.

Yet when they reached the peak of the rise, none—not even Terea—could look upon that vista without some sensation, however hidden, of terror. The iron city was so near, below; the lake, so vast, the greenish mist so thick, the oily smoke that clotted the sky so dark. Distant mountains loomed beyond the lake, hunched like enormous black giants posing in the deepening gloom, staring into the chaos of the wriggling, climbing things—visibly frenetic even in the deepening twilight. The city shone, its steel spires lit by thousands of tiny glimmering lights, its walls—like the stony plain beneath them—a mad carpet of endless crawling, tumbling forms, all steely and jittering and entangled, their multiplicity and their variegation shattering something in Ajal's mind.

Sarnath—lost, dead Sarnath.

Rebuilt.

The awe that had filled Terea's face gave way, now, to satisfaction, for Celephaïs's great philosopher Mendt seemed correct: if the things were not designed by men, then they were surely the offspring of such things as man had fashioned. Sarnath's survivors must have, by whatever means, returned: perhaps the city's original denizens had taken refuge in some dreadful corner of the Underworld, or exiled themselves to the terrifying world of dreams? Their hidden secrets, Terea had sworn, awaited only her discovery.

But as Ajal gazed upon the buzzing, shivering hive of activity that covered the city walls and surrounding plain, his natural and wholly explicable sensation of terror gave way to a more poignant sense of foreboding. Terea's quest was utterly foolhardy, on some level; after the mechanized bloodshed they'd glimpsed in Kadatheron, no sane group would have continued the journey… Yet mad though she might be, Terea was a survivor, not an idiot: she was driven, obsessed, and willful, but also successful. She'd traveled widely enough to know whence a man or woman came at a mere glance; had sketched for herself images of all the great monuments still standing, from the descending foothills before the plains of Leng to the greatest temples in the Fantastic Realms south of Oriab. Crisscrossing her arms and back, her belly and haunches, scars and tattoos commemorated the battles and victories and cunning escapes; reminders, as memory itself dimmed across the aeons of her life. The deeds and omnipotent powers of Terea the Wondrous would, she had often proclaimed, never be forgotten.

Some doubted these tales, but Ajal knew better—he had escorted her on many voyages, and had been guarded jealously at her side, for he possessed one skill that great Terea herself lacked… Dreaming. When she slept, her mind was as blank as a fresh leaf of letter-paper—no places of wonder glimpsed from the distance, not a marvelous secret unfurled. For her, sleep was just a kind of temporary death, despite the endless potions, incantations, prescriptions and disciplines she had tried.

And so, Terea had retained Ajal as her chief slave all these long years, as other servants, slaves, lovers, and enemies had each in turn risen up to engulf her days, and then fallen away from her life like the tides of the ocean, slowly but regularly. Throughout everything, Terea had kept Ajal close by her side, watched and flattered, for Ajal was the greatest dreamer ever born into their world, and perhaps even the finest living dreamer in any world, now that Kuranes the Undying's ancient mind had begin to falter at the precipice of eternity.

What if the philosopher Mendt had been correct, and the things had entered the world from the dreaming lands, through a portal that men, too, could traverse bodily? If Terea found that route into the lands of dream, and no longer needed Ajal…would he be freed? Where would he go—in the waking world, or off somewhere in the dreamlands? Would he go alone? These sudden thoughts terrified him more than the roiling vista of deadly, creeping machinery that lay before him.

Then Terea said, "Let's go," and side by side—he upon his zebra, and she astride her weary, growling calaphax—they carefully descended the hillside; not towards the shimmering, noisome polis of steel, but rather into the much smaller, simpler ruin of black stone a few miles eastward, down by the lakeshore. That ruin was thought to be the remnants of once-great Ib—the ancient polis of the voiceless fishlike men who had descended once, long before, from the moon; worshippers, it was claimed, of dread Bokrug, the Great Lizard of the Watery Depths. Terea was eager to venture into Sarnath, but even she realized that a journey into the chaos before them by starlight and torches was suicide.

For his part, Ajal found the strange, squat ruins of Ib no more inviting.

***

He slept poorly, that night, in Terea's steel-skirted tent.

More than mere dread troubled him. The noises out in the darkness had bred in him a kind of insomnia he had never before experienced, for great dreamers are rarely insomniacs. Thence came the chittering, tumbling cacophony of machines, which in their multitudes resembled a vast army of giant cicadas singing death all through the night; but other noises, noises closer by, echoing through the huddled ruins of dark, low Ib, also troubled Ajal.

Finally, he sat up on his mat, glancing briefly upon his master Terea, who slept tangled in the limbs of a pair of nude slaves, one a powerful grey-skinned male, and the other a sallow, slender female with a shaven head and pierced lips. Terea's face was curiously serene, but then, her sleep was never troubled: she apparently trusted both her detail of guards and her steel-woven tent—which, at least, had been tested successfully against the few specimens various adventurers had brought back to Celephaïs. But Ajal worried about those variegated forms that had not been glimpsed before, the new and strange contraptions in the mechanical army that clattered all around. What they might do to the wondrous modern inventions of those in the employ of Terea, he hated to imagine.

When morning came, Ajal rose bleary-eyed, and found he had dreamed, if but little—only enough to wander out of the tent, to glimpse strange lights amid the mildly acrid lake-mists, before running toward the mechanical city and through a horde of little creeping things, all decked in steel, that took no notice of his dream-form's passing. He had hurried through the city's open gates, sprinting along walls and leaping from one steel-scaled roof to the next, seeking some hidden wellspring of dreams from which the things might have emerged.

Then he remembered falling through a high, domed roof, tumbling down onto a great altar of dark yellow-green chrysolite; he recalled rising from it, and at a glance recognizing the famous word scratched across it, faint and faded through many years, but still just barely visible. He'd fled, and somehow finally he had reached a high place, a tower far above the city; and then he had tumbled down, plummeting toward the roiling mess of clattering machines as the breaking dawn had rendered their myriad forms discernible.

He had woken before striking the ground, to the sound of Terea's laughter—at a slave's flirtatious joke, doubtless—and the smell of grilled smokemeats and roasted chical infusion. When he rose, Terea gestured toward a plate bearing sliced bread, fruit, and a few morsels of smokemeats. As Ajal approached, she muttered, "Did you dream?"

"Yes. Fruitlessly," he replied. "But the city…it is Sarnath. I saw the altar where the high priest scratched the word 'Doom.' The whole place… they've overrun it."

Terea popped a spoonful of steaming spelt porridge into her mouth, as she ran her free hand along the shoulder and bicep of the male slave seated upon her lap. As she chewed it, she asked, "And the wellspring of the machines? Was there a…a way through to their world?"

Ajal shook his head. "I saw something, but…then I woke. The city is a…violent place," he said. The words were wrong. Too small, too soft to describe what he'd glimpsed.

Terea only nodded, and urged him to eat.

***

An hour later, Ajal was back outside, under the blinding, broiling sun.

Terea luxuriated high upon the flat roof of her steel tent, where the observation deck stood, sunning herself and sipping chill water tinged with the juice of sorachi-buds. But on the ground, where Ajal stood, guardsmen muttered of the night before: of coldly drifting lights in the mists that shrouded the lake; and of silent, inhuman figures glimpsed creeping among the shadows of broken Ib.

One of the guards, too young for Ajal to have bothered to learn his name, rehearsed his story ceaselessly to whoever would listen. Variations aside, the plot remained consistent: wandering into the darkness to take a piss, something had set him on edge—some breeze or odd noise, perhaps, or some primal, unnameable instinct. When his eyes had adjusted a moment later, he'd seen several hunched, shadowy humanoid figures lumbering toward him, their bulging eyes glowing weirdly. When he'd struck the nearest one down with his blade, and summoned his fellows with a cry, the silent things had fled, abandoning their stricken friend.

Or so the boy claimed. At dawn, a black stain had been found in the sand where he claimed it'd happened, but no corpse was discovered anywhere nearby. Ajal had been inclined to dismiss the claims on first listening, until he'd glimpsed the boy's eyes; there, he'd glimpsed something he had seen once before, in his own father's eyes when the old man had lain on his deathbed: absolute terror. Ajal knew then that the boy had seen something; the exaggerations and shifting details were, he realized, merely the struggle of a mind fighting to explain the inexplicable, to understand its most terrifying experience.

Throughout the day, Terea dispatched parties into the city, with differing commands: the first was sent inside a clanking steam-powered tank to find the temple Ajal had dream-visited; another was driven forth on pairs of greased stilts, seeking of a passage down into the hidden underworld, to hunt for human descendants of Sarnath's ancient natives—the possible authors of this steely return of the ancient city; yet another group was sent upon riding-zebras, straight into the writhing mass of the machines itself, to test how it reacted to foreign bodies. The guard-boy who'd spread his rumor of glimpsed nocturnal Ib-ites was among the latter group, and Ajal wondered whether Terea had sent him to stem the tide of rumor and panic.

But that made no sense: the third party was lost almost immediately, their screams terrifying all who looked on from within Terea's camp. The carnage, though unsurprising, disheartened everyone: even the special armor given to these unlucky men had proven useless. (Terea's reaction to the slaughter did not help: as the air filled with screams, she munched on dried fruit and sipped fruited water, pausing only momentarily to frown.)

But as for the other two parties, Terea patiently awaited their return. Only hours later did she turn to her most-prized slave and whisper, "Go now and find them, my Ajal..."

***

Dreamers, especially those of Ajal's prodigious talents, did not require night's darkness to sleep or dream, yet that afternoon Ajal found his body resisting sleep, despite the weariness that followed the previous night's poor sleep.

It was the noise: the chittering, the hiss, the clatter-jangle, the clanking and cries of those mechanical voices: his thoughts turned constantly to writhing machines, and then from them to the face and voice of the boy, still clear in his mind...and thence, to the shadowy figures that Ajal was certain the boy *had* glimpsed in the darkness.

But after prodigious effort, he managed to descend into somnolescence, and beyond, rising soon again as pure mind, unanchored from body. Then Ajal turned toward Terea, whom he knew could not now see him. She was barking orders to guards, to stand watch over his body, as always. As they saluted her, they seemed little boys playing dress-up, suddenly; certainly not real guardsmen of an important caravan through a precarious waste, in search of occult secrets.

Ajal knew better than to tarry: if he woke without news of the scouting parties' fates, or where a portal might lie, Terea's rage would be hard to quell. He feared that in her frustration she might add to the scars she'd left in his hide over the years, and so Ajal swept from the room, using his powers to hurl himself into the air and out through the wall of Terea's steel tent.

Outside, the mechanical horde still writhed, steam and smoke pouring into the air above it as the things clambered—with chilling *mindlessness*—over one another, bearing bits of metal, colorful wires, the failed bodies of others of their kind, and more. Ajal gaped in horror as he soared above the buzzing horde, sweeping ever nearer to the city, and wondered: when we gaze upon them, do they gaze upon us? Do they *see* us? And if they do, are *they* equally horrified by what they see?

Then Ajal soared over the iron turrets of Sarnath, carefully tracing the human logic of the design below: the roadways lined by windowed buildings, the wells that plunged into the dark depths of the earth and towers that rose above everything. And yet, the place was empty of humans; the only things moving below were mechanical, and numbered in the millions, swarming and crammed upon every available surface. The parties had to be lost, he knew. He needed other information if Terea was to be appeased.

Ajal hurried along those chaotic roadways, slipping through the walls of suspicious-looking buildings and mysteriously retrofitted steel-swaddled ruins. He plunged through windows and steel doorways, into grand halls and underground chambers, always to find only bones and rags and more of the mechanical *things*, but no living human souls. Tracing the paths of several underwater rivers, he found no hidden refuge of humans; twice, he emerged from the depths, swimming up through the earth, passing layers of different-hued stone littered here and there with precious gems and seams of strange metals, glimpsing briefly the immense fossilized corpses of bewildering ancient creatures too terrible to gaze upon longer, until he finally burst up into daylight among the ruins of Ib. And there he glimpsed with his own bodiless eyes shadowy figures that immediately retreated into the waters of the enormous, frigid lake, their passing marked only by faint ripples upon the water's surface.

Finally, Ajal decided to hurry back into the city, to inspect the tower-tops. He knew, as an experienced and lore-versed dreamer, that not all points of world-juncture clung to the ground: some hung far overhead, up in the air where they could be reached only from the spires and towers of temples and fortresses. And so Ajal soared upward, through clouds of black smoke and foul steam, hoping to find some portal above; if this failed, *then* he could conduct a more time-consuming search of the interiors of the city's towers, room by room.

He soared through the thick, acrid fog, searching for any sign of a portal: a glinting light, a strange noise, a particularly unusual, otherworldly aroma. In the end, it was a breeze that caught his attention: a chilly, hard gust of air that seemed out of place in the broiling Mnari desert. He scrambled toward its source, and found a gaping window of blackness hovering amid the thick smog, a few feet above the pinnacle of a flat-topped tower ringed with high stairs.

An ancient window nobody had thought to shut.

Trespass between worlds was dangerous, he knew, but freedom called to him, siren-voiced: his body was safe, and anyway Terea would send him to scout beyond the portal eventually; once she heard of it she would, absolutely, insist on crushing the endless machines, on ascending the tower and plunging through the portal herself.

So, with a glimpse downward, Ajal traversed the dark portal, into the world of deeper slumber.

***

Almost immediately, Ajal realized where he was.

Not, of course, *where* in terms of this dreamworld's geography, but rather *in which world*—and *in which of its ages*—he had arrived. It was the dead dreamworld, the one that had once teemed with humans and a myriad of other wondrous creatures, but was now a universal ruin: the fouled air, damp and hot in some places, and devastatingly frigid in others; the deadly forests teeming with wild, malformed beasts; the great dead cities that dotted the planet in broad, foul, half-drowned ruins…all of it. And though he could not guess this particular city's forgotten name—could it matter now?—this *type* of place was familiar from past dream-voyages through this world. It was a junkyard of abandoned machines, of hopes and triumphs forsaken by the lost race of humankind: a crumbled land of dreams turned nightmarish.

Ajal stood amid a mess of trash and broken machines, piled all around and overgrown with weeds and creeper vines. Enormous wasps' nests hung here and there, the wasps themselves buzzing lazily through the musty, fungal-smelling air. The skies above hung sullen and dark, long ago clogged by the smoke from the steel city by the lake—for that greasy smoke and foul steam poured out through the portal, and had done so perhaps for so long that it had filled up this whole world's airy vaults. The reek of decay and hopeless doom hung heavy here, in whatever city this was. Here and there, on the scattered, ruined machines, he glimpsed a bewildering script, a sort of ancient, non-alphabetical language that he'd seen before in the Easternmost lands of this dream-realm, but could not read.

Ajal concentrated, reminding himself he was dreaming now, and willed himself airborne. Though he could still fly here, his body was no longer ghostly, as it had been during dreams within his own world. His heart could wound, and his neck could snap; perhaps his body knew this, and that was why it seeemed to hesitate before rising up into the air. And yet, when he did rise skyward, he did so rapidly. From high aloft, Ajal searched the cityscape for familiar signs. After all, this could be an abandoned junkyard in an earlier age, during the rule of man rather than during humanity's decline, or centuries after his extinction...all three eras had dreamers visited, and Ajal had witnessed each with his own eyes, each with its own beauties and its own unique dangers.

But he already *knew*: this was that third and final age, the silenced world in which abandoned cities collapsed onto themselves, into the flooded subterranean tunnels that formed their roots. Ajal glimpsed the distant skyscrapers leaning upon one another, on the verge of collapse, dressed in the green of aggressive climbing weeds. Below, cracked pavements led down into drowned roadways. Ajal had dream-voyaged to here before, searching for the secret of the world's demise, this once-vibrant and crowded world of humans and their pet machines; he had slipped beneath the ocean tides to glimpse the strange creatures that dwelt there—at a distance, seeming almost human, and yet utterly alien when examined up close. He had soared across the faces of the oceans, following the swimming forms of great ochre-hued, many-tailed horrors below, until he reached an island missing from all the dead world's ancient maps, one that must have surfaced anew.

But of *that* city, of its bewildering and awful geometries and streets full of terrible noises—those streets that all led to the same black, kelp-strewn palace with its awful god ruling within—of all of *that*, Ajal dared not remember anything at all. He drove the thought from his mind, as panic choked him. Claustrophobia struck, a squeezing tightness within his chest. Was the island only half a world away? Perhaps less? He could almost sense that horrible, distant god-thing groping ravenously within his mind again. He felt sure that it knew he had returned to this world. His only comfort was in knowing that he could escape whenever he liked, through the portal nearby that led back to the light and comfort of home; or, at least, to the sanity of his own world, where the oceans still lived, and cities like Celephaïs and Ulthar still bustled with men and women and cats, and the perils of zoogs and night-gaunts and the mastiff-riders of the south were all known, familiar, and far from insuperable.

Ajal let himself sink back down into the junkyard, now dead certain of the doom that had befallen the world, and turned to a more immediate concern: locating the origin of the mechanical crawlers. He turned first to the portal, and found that it was no longer where it had been when he'd first arrived. Panic set in: he'd heard vague, dubious gossip of one-way portals and stranded dreamers being trapped in one or another distant dreamworld…but had always doubted these tales, never having experienced such a thing himself. What if they'd been true?

Ajal managed to remain calm: one did not become one of history's finest dreamers without a sense of reserve. He crouched for a few minutes, scanning the dim junkyard, before his self-control was rewarded: the portal had simply drifted aside, as if nudged by some caustic breeze toward a pile of old screen-boxes. (Their proper name, Ajal had once learned when journeying through an earlier era in this world's history, where he'd seen people spend whole days or weeks staring into the faces of these machines, and their images of distant people and places…but he had long forgotten that word.) The gateway flickered, shimmering momentarily, and then disappeared as it drifted straight *into* the discarded machines. There followed a curious sound, of suction and then a bang, and the precarious pile of screen-boxes shifted. Several of the relics tumbled to the ground, and one screen even shattered.

Ajal remained still.

Soon, the portal shifted back out of the pile of screen-boxes, shifting direction suddenly and gliding rapidly back toward Ajal himself. He jolted out of its way just in time to see it drift toward a morass of wires and nuts and bolts torn from the guts of some dead machine. Several wires stood on end as the portal approached, shivering in the darkness, and then all at once slipped up toward it, disappearing through it with a flash.

Ajal rushed toward the portal, peeping through it, and caught a glimpse of something falling down from it, onto the lofty tower-top below: a tangle of writhing, unarguably *living* serpent-like things squirmed there, bright as the copper wires the portal had swallowed. He barely had time to glimpse the now-living things slither over the edge of the tower before he felt himself being dragged through the portal as well. The pull homeward was powerful, and to resist it, he had to withdraw his head back into the dark and ruined dreamworld. Though memories of his last visit made him yearn to escape, he knew Terea would only send him back if he did not complete his investigations.

For a moment, he stood perplexed: what would the philosopher Mendt have made of *this*? How, in merely passing through a simple portal between worlds, could scattered trash take on life? Nothing in his studies or journeys had ever prepared him for such a notion...and still, the portal drifted, now gliding past other wreckage, a nearby pile of broken metal vehicles. Ajal knew these things well, recalled seeing them in an earlier age of this world. The roads of the great cities—and the endless roads that linked those cities—had teemed with these things, almost as densely as the crawling things had teemed in the streets of what Sarnath had become...if it could be truly called Sarnath. These machines had linked the world...and now, they rotted by the millions in the mist and rain, the endless gravestones of an ancient, doomed civilization.

He took a seat nearby, and watched the portal draft to and fro, first close and then far, through rusted steel girders, and flood-ruined furnishings, through the hanging wall-hung screens through which people had talked and shouted in their ancient days. And Ajal found a pattern: though the portal drifted ceaselessly, always it returned to a specific point, an empty spot in the middle of the junkyard. It was tethered there, perhaps loosely but also certainly, by some invisible force, he reasoned...and it could be found again when needed.

But what force? And tethered by whom? If the ancient men of Sarnath had opened it, in their city's last days...

Ajal's reveries were interrupted by the clattering of junk, and then footsteps in the mucky soil. He sank from his seat into a low crouch, and crept behind a ruined steel desk. As he peeped from behind it, a group of shadowy figures appeared, silent but for their footsteps and labored breathing. Twilight had rendered their faces indistinct, but when one figure bent down to peer into the gate as it drifted past, a little daylight from Ajal's world was cast into its face. A little, only, but enough: Ajal recognized the bulging eyes, and the pouting droop of its lips, like the mouth a huge, awful fish; he recognized the rippling gills on its throat, and the rotten-grey-green hue of its skin.

Valiant as he was, Ajal gasped aloud at the sight before ducking back down into hiding.

Though he hardly dared move, through the legs of the desk he could see their feet as they turned, hissing softly. They were turned toward him now, he knew.

Listening. Waiting.

One pair of webbed feet approached, sloshing in the mud. Ajal clenched his body and then, with a sudden burst of desperation, he flung himself skyward, ascending rapidly. As he rose, he glimpsed the thing's yellowish bulging eyes, wide and angry, but also full of awe…as if it were astounded to see a living, breathing man at all, let alone a *flying* one. Then Ajal soared off over the towering ruins, toward the glorious pink of the sunset-lit coast. Below, up ahead, a bundle of massive, broken high-rises stood ankle-deep in seawater, leaning upon one another. Lights flicked in some of the upper floors, and Ajal imagined, without thinking, a few desperate humans gathered through fires, surviving perhaps by scavenging the fruits of the poisoned ocean.

He soared toward one of bright windows, gazing into the firelit room beyond the smashed glass. Around a bonfire fed by a pile of shattered furniture, he saw a circle of figures gathered like little puppets set out to cast enormous shadows on the walls behind them. Most were adults but a few children sat scattered among them, all in rags, with matted, greasy black hair. A nasty stink filled the air; it smelled like rotting fish, like a seeping wound, and Ajal shuddered when he made out what they were cooking over the flames: a black snake-like fish, as long as several grown men and studded with dozens of bluish, human-like eyes hung in a metal net over the fire; its open mouth revealed a terrifying set of fangs, and dozens of fins sprouted from its sides, stretching out like enormous great webbed hands, or wings perhaps.

Ajal's stomach churned, and he gagged. One of the figures nearest the window, a child, turned and glanced up toward him. When it cried out, Ajal cried out too, at the familiar, awful visage: the child's bulbous eyes, its gilled throat, the tiny quivering nostrils of its boneless, flat nose. The others swiftly rose, swarming toward him, and Ajal leaped from the window, letting himself fall until a breeze caught him like a dead leaf and bore him off into the deepening darkness. He searched at window after window, but found no humans, only these chimerical horrors that combined the most revolting features of frog and fish with the human form. Out to sea, he glimpsed a rusty-hulled ship drifting through the waters in the distance… a ghost ship, or perhaps it was piloted by these things, these monsters, or descendants of man regressed back into the sea.

An impossible prophecy he'd once read in an ancient scroll—one housed in the now-lost library of Oriab—surfaced from his centuries of memories. It had claimed that all the worlds, one by one, would be flooded by an avenging army of the servants of a mad ocean-god from some other reality. When he'd read it, he'd discounted it as ancient superstition, the blooming of man's natural fear of the sea…or perhaps the sort of thing a god told a civilization in order to call it to heel.

But after the horrors in the ruined towers…it was almost enough to stop his heart, to remember that black city, once-sunken and now ascended from the waves, glistening and laden with kelp and air-drowned deep-sea monsters…and the hungering god at its heart, that had vowed to devour the world…

Ajal's every instinct fought to drive him back to the junkyard, to plunge through the portal and to the safety of his world. Yet the city called to him. Though his hands shuddered, through he soared through the fog-clotted sky with his eyes shut against the whole world, he felt the enigma of the southern city tugging at him. Terea would know, would sense his fears. If Terea were to come to this world…she would insist that he go there, seek out the city.

Ajal had read all he could about that place, since that first, accidental visit of his. He had sought out the accounts of all of the great dreamers in history who'd glimpsed the risen city, in ages past. Not that the accounts made much sense: each had either died, or gone mad, or vanished mysteriously. No account could be trusted. Ajal moaned as all this sensible reasoning filled his mind, though: duty, good sense, investigation…these were not reasons to go to *that* place, that awful-angled drowned aquapolis. The mere thought of returning there filled him with a dread so immense one could not hope even to name it, and yet…the reasoning felt like excuses.

It was the calling that drew him. Some awful part of him hungered to return there.

In the darkness above the junkyard, hovering Ajal looked down to where the portal ought to have been…but what he found was no mere troop of the creatures. This was an army: hunched fish-men pushed and shoved one another, bickering voicelessly as they fought their way toward the slowly drifting portal. Whenever one got close, a sudden jolt drew it silently through with a flash of light. The light was cruel, to Ajal: it revealed the mass of creatures, the hundreds of them gathered in the junkyard, silently clawing at one another with webbed paws as they fought over the entranceway to his world.

Shuddering, he soared away, terror-weakened, a distant, low call echoing once more through him.

***

Ajal found himself soaring through darkness across the southern ocean, drawn along by a force he could neither name nor resist. The voice in his mind, deep and gurgling, communicated only a dim awareness, elusive consciousness. The surface of the ocean was broken by waves taller than any skycraper ruin, somehow unnaturally sustained, that bore somehow still-living victims in their crests, teeming bodies screaming for help as he flew past overhead.

The waves were headed the same place he was going, those waves full of minds to be shredded and savored.

And then returned the groping within his own mind, as a hand might heft an egg before cracking it into a frypan, or pinch at the flesh of some beast being fattened for slaughter. Then the sun rose, a searing eye rising from black water. The waters roiled beneath him, underwater explosions spraying saltwater up on gassy jets from the depths. Ajal's dreamer-eyes discerned the gas as luminous white vapor, and it stank of the sea, of the breaths of living things, of the guts of enormous hidden monsters from below.

The waves—teeming with faintly malignant awareness—seemed almost to steer themselves into those gaseous eruptions, so that their unwilling, terrified passengers were tossed skyward, only to be caught up again when they fell: an exquisitely cruel game formed from the eschatological wreckage of the world.

Then, in the distance, Ajal glimpsed it: the city. Horrible, hazed with green mist, still-familiar and still-terrifying though it had been drowned when last he'd seen it. But now the black polis had risen to the surface, perching upon a monstrous promontory of inky, jagged igneous rock. Chants filled the muggy air above its gargantuan edifices, and as Ajal sank toward its blade-sharp parapets and baffling, alien-geometried roadways, he glimpsed the central mountain shimmering in the searing sunlight… and thereupon, a great black throne of stone, carven from the mountain itself—and upon it…upon that awful throne…

Ajal rebelled, even as he felt the tendrils of that dreadful god's vast feeding maw drift through his mind. He shrieked, and hurled himself up into the air, only to be yanked back down. The thing whispered into his mind, not in words but through notions barely comprehensible. All Ajal truly understood was the most base of them: vague anticipation, half-appetized interest in Ajal's terror, a dull but gnawing hunger, and a terrifying sense of reognition. It had enjoyed the search, the hunt, and even the wait, but now, all that was done.

Poor Ajal fought, as the god summoned him down into the bewildering streets of the city, reaching out past the jagged sills of dark-glassed windows and rusted-iron doors slathered in immense barnacles. His head ached, as if some invisible fishhook had speared him in the brain.

Then the air itself suddenly thickened, hoisting Ajal upward and hurling him toward the gargantuan figure enthroned at the peak of the island's mountain. He saw enormous yellow cats'-eyes buried in a wrinkled wall of burnt-maroon flesh, and then a maw gaping wide, the jagged, long yellow teeth—human-like, chillingly—ringing its interior while from the lips grasping, boneless appendages spread wide. In a blur, they closed about him, forcing him between the gnashing teeth…

By sheer force of will alone, he fought to free himself, even to wake, but the tendrils gripped his mind, digging into him, claiming and marking him. The chanting inhuman voices, the screams, and beneath it all, that rumbling noise that he knew—was absolutely sure—was the sound of the ancient god-thing laughing. A toxin spread within him—not within his dreaming flesh, but rather through his consciousness, and then the hellish maw closed around him, wide as a world and terrifying with its countless barbed teeth curled row upon vicious row. Within the vast throat, a dozen boneless, fingerless appendages wrapped round him, snake-like, shoving him deeper into the crushing darkness, and then—

Ajal woke, dizzy, in Terea's steel-woven tent.

He sat up, and searched his memories, calling for a guard to whom he could relate them before they faded, for dreamers often forget what they have seen when forced to wake this way, but he found nobody nearby. This was…unusual. Terea had always assigned guards to watch over his body during dream-voyages. But now Ajal was alone.

He rose to his feet, eager to find Terea and warn her of what he remembered—of danger beyond the portal, for the vast maw remained terrifyingly clear in his mind. However, at the tent's door, he paused with a shudder. The opening…it appeared to him as another yawning maw. His eyes widened, he shrieked in terror, and he imagined the doorway slamming shut on him, chewing him up and swallowing him into some dark, gloom-filled chamber crammed with lost, mad souls.

Ajal sank into a crouch and shuddered, muttering to himself for hours and weeping, calling out to Terea, and tearing at his own skin in order to stay awake, for he did not dare to sleep. Shuddering, he tested the steely maw with his fingertips, terrified.

It did nothing. It was merely a doorway.

When lucidity returned, he realize the desert outside the tent had grown calm and still. Once again, he was overcome by a burning need to find Terea, to warn her…for he had sensed something within that distant god-thing's hunger, a desire to devour more prey than him alone. Its appetite was for worlds, for whole civilizations…

When Ajal finally tore open the door and stepped out into the deepening twilight, not a single human soul stood near Terea's tent. Even the mechanical things carpeting the walls of Sarnath seemed somehow quieter and calmer now, their riotous activity noticeably diminished. Ajal found there neither corpses, nor any sign of even the mildest struggle.

But then a distant flash caught his eye; it came from above Sarnath's highest spires, revealing the silhouette of a tiny human figure before it. That, he realized to his horror, was Terea! She must have fought her way to the tower-top! As he strained his eyes, he discerned a crowd of tiny figures behind her, their blades flashing and firearms blasting into the darkness, the distant gunfire audible a moment later. A battle raged upon the tower-top, above which he knew the portal hung, spewing mechanical things down into the world. As thick greenish mist rolled in from the lake, Ajal cried out softly, knowing what would happen to Terea if she made the crossing into the other, awful world.

The ravenous, many-appendaged maw yawned immense before Ajal. He was seized by panic, his mind and bladder emptying themselves all at once. He squatted low, cringing in terror through long minutes, and mumbling to himself of doom, and death, and hopelessness, as the cold, sickly-olive mist of the great lake spread out around him.

He was roused from his mental fugue, after an inestimable stretch of time, by the light touch upon his shoulder, of a hand—or what felt *almost* like a hand. Glancing upward, he immediately recognized the figures gathered nearby: bulging-eyed, greeny-gray, the gill-throated horrors of the lake!

When he shrieked, the monsters recoiled, the soft eyes squinting in what seemed almost like terror, and backed away from him.

Ajal fled to Terea's great steel-woven tent, and with a final glance toward embattled, wondrous, doomed Terea upon the distant tower-top, Ajal plunged inside, sealing the entrance behind him. Ignoring the pounding of his heart, and the tyrannical calling of the distant god-thing's endless, constant summons, and the scrabbling of inhuman webbed hands at the walls of the steel-woven tent, Ajal crouched, alone, in the darkness of his master's refuge, his eyes wide.

By the time Sarnath's mechanical monstrosities set upon the fish-men, filling the night with their soft, hissing screams, he was certain Terea had reached the gate, and gone through to the other side...and that she would soon meet the fate that lay beyond, in the belly of that island-god's endless, awful hunger. He fought against his last remaining instinct, to rise again in dreaming form, and go to her, to warn her: he knew she could not hear him in that state, and even if she could, she would ignore his warnings.

So Ajal only rocked back and forth, his eyes wide, the terror of sleep keeping him shivering awake through the night. Whether day might come again, he could not guess, nor whether he would resist the god-thing's awful call long enough to see it come; but he clung to the world, to his body, listening intently to the machines' endless chittering in their vast swath round New Sarnath. If only he could remain wakeful till morning, perhaps he could set back out across the wastes, alone; perhaps, if he found a calaphax, or a hidden cache of supplies...he might not survive long, true, but he would flee the portal, and the still-echoing call from beyond it...Yet to do so, he would have to survive until the day's first light, and resist those strange tendrils that even now tugged within his skull.

Thus Ajal, the greatest dream-voyager in the world, came finally to hate and to fear slumber itself.

THE LONG DARK

Wendy N. Wagner

Pa's secret weighed down Ylie's feet as he ran through the stone tunnels to deliver the week's shift schedules, and it kept him from answering all the curious greetings that came his way as he ran. Usually, he stopped in for drink of water or a bit of bread or just to earn good favor taking someone's message from one end of the underground city to another, but today he ran faster and faster, as if the pounding of his secondhand boots could drown out the urge to spill out his father's secret like a sack of tailings.

It hurt him to ignore the people who called his name. He knew that most people depended on runners like him for news, for entertainment, for the sense of belonging to something larger than their little tunnel and their small work. The people who flagged him down were never miners or the families of miners, but shopkeepers and old women, the kinds of people who had done well for themselves in Patrie's past, but now found themselves alone and isolated in the ever-quieter tunnels. He felt bad, running past them without offering anything more than a smile. He knew his speed gave them false hope. He wasn't carrying some important, exciting message from the mine's head office; he was just trying to keep his father's secret and finding it harder every day.

He lowered his head and ran faster.

A figure stepped out in front of him. "Ylie. A word."

Ylie slid to a stop. "Sister Hauer." He opened and closed his mouth, searching for the appropriate pleasantry. The priest rarely came down from the observatory on the surface, and in her long black robe, she was a formidable figure. "Good dark to you."

The woman did not reply for a moment. The robe's hood shrouded her face in shadows. "It is a good dark," Sister Hauer answered in her dry voice. "My sky eyes have seen lights approaching from Kalifa."

For a second, Ylie was too excited to remember to be nervous of the black-robed woman. "A ship? They're sending a ship?"

"It would appear so. You should return to the office immediately and let them know." Hauer held out a piece of onionskin folded in half. Ink stained her long fingers, so that the nails were like the black claws of the creature in the school kids' whispered stories. "Take this to your father when you have finished."

Ylie hesitated. Paper. He hadn't seen paper in over a year. It was the kind of Kalifan luxury that ran out between shipments from the neighboring planet, and he had never owned any himself. It wasn't for people like him and his pa. They had memories and slates, and that was good enough for them.

But Sister Hauer wasn't folk, he reminded himself. Sister Hauer was a sky-watcher, a priest with book learning, pledged to serve the people of Patrie. Paper was probably ordinary equipment to a priest.

He reached for the folded slip. "I'll go as fast as I can," Ylie said.

She stepped in closer to him, still holding the paper tight. He could feel the rasp of her skin against his and smell a strange scent that seemed to billow up out of her robe, a spoiled metallic smell that made him want to pull away from the old woman. "Don't slow down," Sister Hauer warned.

The paper pulled free of her horrible hand. Ylie spun around without answering and broke into a run.

The mine's office was a long ways away, dozens of levels below this one. He'd be running all night, he supposed—the mining office would be striking new orders for the miners once they got the news. Ylie picked up speed. As he ran, he wiped the sweat off his forehead with the back of his hand and thought that her metallic smell still clung to it, thick and nasty, and just faintly sweet.

***

Ylie's leg muscles trembled as he made his tired way down to his father's workshop in the lowest level of the city proper. Ylie had carried new orders to every miner on all forty of the city's levels. Now the city and the mine below buzzed with activity. The floor vibrated beneath his boots, and the walls shook hard enough that little curls of dust rose up off them. Ylie couldn't remember the last time the mine and the foundries had operated at full capacity. As long as he'd been alive—fourteen Standard years, with twenty-nine Long Darks—Patrie had been a quiet city, growing quieter every year. When he'd been in school, he'd once asked why the population kept shrinking, but the schoolmaster had no answer.

He knew that when ships still came from the other planets, Patrie had been a good place to live. Supplies came in from Kalifa, Valdez, Weyland I, and dozens of worlds whose names he had seen emblazoned on the light murals, but were rarely spoken out loud except in the stories whispered between classes by children who knew no better. He'd been one of them once, but he'd outgrown such foolishness.

Ylie paused at the next-to-last landing and studied the mural on the wall. The bulbs had burned out long ago and no one had seen the need to replace them. Perhaps being reminded of this lost world, Weyland IV, once full of people and now a silent absence in the night sky, was too depressing.

The loss of this mural was sad, Ylie thought. He could still remember this mural, although only vaguely. It had shown such a colorful place, its continents green and pink and gold on a setting of blue sea. If anyone had made a mural out of Patrie, they would have painted the world in steel and dirt.

He brushed his fingers over the dusty surface of the mural. Where had Weyland IV gone, he wondered. The priests said there were no creatures between the stars, that nothing existed that could swallow a world. But no ships came from the Weyland worlds or Valdez any longer, and to even an untrained eye, the sky grew darker every Long Dark. Where did the worlds go? How did the space between the stars get bigger every year?

It wasn't the place of a simple messenger to ask such a question. Ylie turned his back on the mural and pushed on to the door of his father's workshop. He tested the doorknob. Locked, of course. Pa had taken to locking even the door of their living quarters since he'd gone to work for Sister Hauer. Ylie rapped his knuckles against the door and heard the steel echo hollowly.

"Pa? It's me."

The door opened a crack. "Can I help you?" Pa peered out into the hallway. The fluorescent light above the door made the lines of his face deeper, turning him into a little old man and not Ylie's sturdy father. He blinked down at the boy.

Ylie reached for the earmuffs his father wore when he was cutting steel. "Hi, Pa."

Pa rubbed his ears. "Forgot about those."

"You must have been working hard." Ylie pushed inside. His father hadn't always worked in this massive space. Before Sister Hauer and the sky priests recruited him, he had worked in the main machine workshop in the mine, even farther beneath the surface than this place. Pa could have gone to priest school and learned the books to build machines; he had the smarts for it. But priests couldn't marry or have children, and so he'd chosen to just keep learning on his own, working in the machine workshop and handling the repairs the priests thought were beneath them.

The boy walked over to the workbench where a sheet of unpolished steel lay, a long narrow shape grease-penciled along its length. The machine his father was building for Sister Hauer was complicated and huge, the kind of thing he would have never gotten a chance to build down in the mines.

Perhaps that's why he'd decided to help the sky priests. He'd always wanted to learn more and do more. Maybe being just another worker and Ylie's pa wasn't enough for him anymore. Ylie felt his stomach seize up with a feeling he didn't want to name. He took a deep breath and reached out to touch the steel.

The surface looked strange, as if it had been treated with some kind of chemical while the steel cooled. He knew most of the polishing and coloring compounds, but not this one. He sniffed his fingers, but couldn't place it by smell, either.

He studied the shape drawn on the strangely ruddy steel. "This is going to be another support arm, right? It's as long as the one that holds up Kalifa," he said.

"The last support arm." His father patted his shoulder. "The biggest."

Ylie wished he understood how the machine worked, but he was also glad his father hadn't told him more about it. Ylie met too many priests in his rounds of Patrie, and the more he knew about the device, the harder it was to resist telling them about his father's secret project. The priesthood was firm about its central rule: priests specialized. Some studied the stars, some learned to heal, some built and repaired the machines that made the city and the mine work. The priests maintained that if one branch encroached on the other's specialty, it risked diluting the precious knowledge the priesthood had tended for all these centuries.

Then, to Ylie's dismay, his father added: "This is special steel. Fine, fine steel. Sister Hauer, she's looking out for all of us, you know. That's why she makes sure I get the best for this project."

Ylie felt the weight of his father's secret grow heavier. He quickly drew out the folded onionskin. "Sister Hauer sent me, Pa. She saw a ship in her sky-eye. Coming from Kalifa."

Pa clapped his hands. "That's good! That's real good!" He scurried across the workshop fast enough that Ylie had to jog to catch up with him.

The workshop was huge. Broken bits of stone jutted out from the walls at one point, marking the point where a wall had once separated the space into two big rooms. They must have been storage spaces for the mine, once. Ylie wondered if the mine would ask for the space back now that they were picking up production. He doubted it. Even with every worker pulling double shifts, the mine would be running with a skeleton crew. It couldn't produce half as much as it did in the era when it filled these rooms.

And even if the mine needed more warehouse space, Sister Hauer had ways of getting what she wanted. She wanted paper, so she had paper. She'd wanted Pa, and she'd brought him out of the mines to build her secret device. Ylie wasn't sure how Hauer got the council to do her bidding, but she always did.

Ylie squared his shoulders. He was *angry:* that was the feeling in his gut right now. He was angry that his father had chosen to break the rules of Patrie and he was angry that his father spent all his time down here with the damn thing. Pa loved the device more than he'd ever loved being at home with Ylie.

The boy circled the big machine. The orrery. He hadn't been good at school, but he knew what an orrery was. His teacher had used a simple one to demonstrate what made the skies over Patrie go dark for months at a time.

Although maybe if Ylie hadn't gotten a job as a messenger this year, spending his days running past all the old, burnt-out murals of lost worlds and constellations, he might not have realized that what his father had built was more than just a massive model of the sky around Patrie. It was a work of art. His father had found bits of colored glass to add detail to the planets' surfaces: there was big green Kalifa and small blue Shogrin, orange Bijou nearly as big as the Sun itself, and dozens of smaller moons like Patrie. Ylie could even see how they all lined up at different points in their circuit, the planets' shadows sending Patrie into the dark for weeks at a time.

There was something odd about this orrery, something that made it different from the one in the school room, but Ylie couldn't put his finger on it. He had a feeling the device wasn't just a model to help study distances between the planets or better calculate the length of the next Long Dark. It was just too large and too beautiful. Sister Hauer wouldn't have broken the rules of the order to build another orrery. No, she wanted something special from this machine, and Ylie couldn't help but wonder what she would get from it.

"You've got something there, Ylie?"

Ylie blinked at his father. He had almost forgotten the onionskin. It was so light, so delicate, he barely felt it between his fingers.

"You should hurry on home, my boy. Sister Hauer was planning to come down," Pa added. "After star recording."

The plaintive note in his father's voice made Ylie ball his hands into fists, paper be damned. It wasn't bad enough Sister Hauer made his father leave his real job and sneak away to work on some secret machine: it was like she owned the man. When she snapped her fingers, he came running like a man with a double-shift request from the mine office. Something snapped inside the boy, snapped like steel bent past its breaking point

"I guess you'll be missing dinner again." Ylie thrust the crumpled onionskin at his father. "This is for you."

He turned away and stomped toward the door.

"Ylie." Pa hurried to catch up to him. "It's just one dinner. This project is important."

"Yeah? To who?"

"To all of us!" Pa looked suddenly nervous, even though they were alone. He lowered his voice. "The orrery is going to save us from what got all those other planets. Sister Hauer, she's smart. She knows things. She's got books that go all the way back to the first planet, books that talk about the—the world eater."

"The world eater?" Ylie threw open the door. "That's why you're never home? Because of some stupid story kids tell?"

"Hush, Ylie!" His father shook his head. "Be quiet, please!"

"Go piss on yourself, Pa. And your stupid orrery, too."

Ylie slammed the door behind him, rage roiling in his belly, red-hot and fierce. He scrubbed at his face with his rough sleeve and told himself he wasn't crying, that he wasn't sad, not one bit.

***

Ylie lay on his bunk, letting his eyes find patterns in the worn surface of the steel shelf above him. The room smelled of the meal he'd overcooked—algae from the hydroponics facility and bread, the tangy stuff the baker managed to make from Patrie's own breed of wheat. Pa had always made good food, but Ylie hadn't ever learned his father's skill.

The knock at the door echoed throughout the small living quarters. If his father had been there, Pa would have jumped down from his bunk and sprinted to the door, thinking it was Sister Hauer needing his help. The thought made Ylie want to pull the blanket up over his head and pretend he hadn't heard anything. Instead, he rolled over and stared at the door a long moment, his limbs heavy. It was probably a summons to run more messages.

The knocking sounded again, with more urgency.

He forced himself off the bunk and opened the door. He stepped backward, surprised. "Sister North?"

The sister stepped inside as if he had graciously invited her instead of half-stumbling out of her way. He only vaguely knew the priest. Before Ylie had finished school and gotten busy with his own work, he would often stop by the mining workshop to visit with his father, and Sister North's pale shaved head with its orange fuzz had stood out like a beacon from the overseer's platform.

A novice followed at her heels, one of Ylie's former classmates now gone to the priesthood. He caught Ylie's eyes for a second and hastily looked away, ducking his head and frowning. He wore the gray coveralls of a novice of the priesthood, and a tool belt cinched the oversized garment. Ylie tried to remember the boy's name and came up empty.

Sister North pushed back the hood of her coarse brown robe. A smudge of grease ran across her cheekbone, as if she'd absentmindedly scratched at an itch in the middle of some complicated project. She looked from Ylie's face to the still-dirty cooking surface, and then to the empty bunks on the far wall. "Your father isn't here?" Her eyebrows lifted into high arcs of rusty wire.

A sheen of sweat showed on her shaved pate. She had hurried up out of the mines to find Pa, Ylie realized. A mining workshop overseer, a machine priest, had actually run to find him.

"No," Ylie admitted. His voice was squeezed small by the weight of his father's secret. If there was anyone his father wouldn't want to learn about Sister Hauer's orrery, it was this woman.

"There's been an accident," she said. "We need him in the mine. Immediately." She watched him intently. The smell of algae and burnt oil hung heavy over the room, the smell of months spent alone and unhappy with a burden too heavy for a boy fresh out of school. He remembered how angry he had been earlier.

The weight inside him shifted, and he blurted out: "He's working for Sister Hauer." He took a deep breath. "He's building something to save us all from the *world eater*."

"What?" Sister North's hand clamped shut on his wrist.

"He's working for Sister Hauer," he repeated. "He's building—"

"Take me to him," she said. "Right now."

***

The walk felt longer than any message run he'd ever made. Sister North said nothing as they made their way down to his father's workshop. Ylie's palms grew damp as they got closer, and finally, he stopped in front of the darkened mural of Weyland IV. He had to know more before he faced his father.

"Why do the worlds disappear, Sister North? Can Sister Hauer do anything about it?"

Sister North's lips compressed. "If Sister Hauer has an explanation, she has not shared it with me."

"But what do you think?" Ylie pressed. "Is there a world eater? Is that why the worlds disappear?"

"The world eater is a story," said Sister North. "Preparations for the delegation from Kalifa are real. I do not have time to talk about superstition and nonsense. Take me to your father. Now."

He led her to his father's workshop, then. He didn't feel any better, but he didn't know what else to do.

When they reached the door and he raised his fist to knock, the sister pushed him aside. "No warnings," she said. She beckoned for the novice, who produced a slim tool that Sister North wiggled in the lock for a few seconds. The door swung open.

A trickle of smoke curled out of the workshop, carrying with it a smell that made Ylie cover his nose: the metallic smell of Sister Hauer's hands combined with some luxurious scent he had never smelled before. All around his father's machine, oversized metal cups burned, sending up plumes of thick smoke. The flicker of hundreds of candles lit up the space, and at least a dozen black-robed priests moved about the workshop, tending the smoking cups and the candles and anointing the different parts of the orrery with a black and tarry goo.

"Sister North."

"Sister Hauer."

The two priests faced each other. Sister North's head gleamed in the light of the candles, and Sister Hauer was an implacable column of darkness.

"Ylie!" Pa lurched forward. "Why have you brought her here?"

"I made the boy do it," Sister North said. She shook her head. "I am disappointed in you, Larken."

"I had good reason," Pa said. "Sister Hauer is the only one doing anything about the world eater." He clasped his hands as he spoke, as if begging her to believe in his cause. Ylie could hardly stand to watch him.

"There *is* no world eater," Sister North snapped.

"Oh, but there is." A smile spread across Sister Hauer's face, revealing her small, sharp teeth. "Did you ever wonder when we started locking up all the books on Patrie? I always thought it was odd, that the priesthood could have so many and the ordinary folk, so few." She turned to Ylie and said in an amiable voice: "Did you ever have a book, Ylie?"

He opened his mouth and closed it again. He could feel the novice beside him trembling, his arm vibrating through his coveralls and robe.

"I didn't think so. Even in the schools, children only get slates." Sister Hauer's hood obscured all of her face save for that small smile. "But children's stories often contain the seeds of the truth. When I joined the priesthood, I read everything I could, and I was surprised by how many books confirmed the stories."

"Stop it," Sister North spat. "You're twisting the truth. You know many of the books the priesthood keeps are myths and legends, not real science."

"If that's what you want to believe." Sister Hauer snapped her fingers, and her black-robed priests stepped in. Hands closed on Ylie's shoulders, and he heard the novice gasp as someone grabbed him.

Boyd. That was the boy's name. Ylie remembered him suddenly, a quiet boy, good at all his classes. He said the stories gave him nightmares. Ylie could remember describing the claws and the fangs and the evil burning eyes of the eater of worlds, and leaning closer and closer to Boyd as he spoke. It had been fun to watch him squirm. It had been fun to know he wouldn't sleep that night.

Ylie's head spun. Was he really remembering that? His head felt strange and heavy from all the smoke in the air.

"I have a little confession," Sister Hauer said. "There is no delegation from Kalifa."

"What?" Sister North's face twisted. "Why would you lie about that?"

"Because I needed a distraction." Sister Hauer waved her hand to take in the orrery, the candles, the priests, all of it. "I knew my orrery would be ready tonight. I knew this was our last chance to save Patrie."

Sister North struggled, but the priests who held her were strong. "Save it from what?"

Ylie didn't mean to answer, but somehow, even with all his thoughts twisted by the flickering light and the perfumed smoke, the pieces had come together in his mind. "The world eater. It already got Kalifa, didn't it?"

Sister Hauer nodded. "Years ago. I saw it happen and I knew I had to do something."

"What do you mean?" The strength had gone out of Sister North's voice. She believed, too, Ylie thought. She didn't want to, and maybe she couldn't even admit it, but no one who had heard the stories as a kid had ever really stopped believing.

He remembered the way the story began:

"In the darkness between the stars, the world eater sits and waits, sharpening its black claws and picking its black teeth."

"Please stop," Boyd begged. "Please."

"No, keep going," Sister Hauer commanded.

"It sits and waits for dinner time," Ylie whispered.

"It'll eat up all the light," Sister Hauer added, her voice strong and clear. "It'll eat up all the worlds."

"It'll eat up all the stars and all the boys and girls." Ylie's legs shook. He'd told this story so many times before he'd outgrown it, and he had almost forgotten how terrifying it really was. No wonder Boyd had been afraid.

The other priests were doing something, he realized, painting symbols on the floor beneath the orrery in their black goo. One stopped in front of Boyd and painted a line down the novice's face. Ylie could smell it now, the same smell as Sister Hauer's hands and the strange coating on the orrery's steel. This time he recognized it.

"Blood," he whispered. "Where did you get all the blood?"

"You already know." Sister Hauer smiled like his old schoolmaster when he was encouraging the children to solve some simple kind of problem. "Why do you think there aren't enough workers down in the mine?"

Pa shook his head. "No. I won't believe it. You've been killing people?"

A black-robed priest slapped his paintbrush in Pa's face. The black goo ran down his forehead and ran in rivulets down his cheeks and lips.

"We've done what we could to keep the world eater at bay. But it's hungry. And it sees us, the last of the human worlds. A few small sacrifices just aren't enough any more."

Gears ground deep within the base of the orrery, and the worlds began to turn, slowly at first, and then faster. Blue Shogrin sped by, its waters never touched by human visitors. Orange Bijou crawled along behind it, its dusty skies not much different in color from Patrie's, but unbreathable by human lungs. Those worlds were safe, Ylie knew. What the world eater hungered for was not just dirt and minerals and water, but life.

The small steel ball of Patrie began to fall into line.

"I can't stop the turning of the worlds," Sister Hauer said, and for the first time, she sounded sad. "But I can open a door into the darkness and show the world eater we are not just a meal."

"What?" Sister North struggled against her captors, but the two other priests held her fast. "What do you mean?"

"There is a science beyond your science," Sister Hauer said. She took the bowl of blood from her acolyte and carried it to stand before Sister North. "And there are deals to be struck."

The moons and worlds moved slowly above their heads, their colors twinkling in the candlelight. It was both the most beautiful and the most horrible thing that Ylie had ever seen, and he found he couldn't take a deep breath. If no one had held him up, he would have collapsed from the spinning in his head and the thickness of the air.

She began to paint a shape upon Sister North's forehead: a star that was not a star, a shape of such darkness it made Ylie's eyes rebel. He had to look away.

Sister North's scream made him look back.

A length of steel jutted out of her chest. Blood bubbled up out of her mouth and spilled down her chin. Bright blood, not the old black stuff staining her forehead. In the golden light, her blood was very nearly the brilliant auburn of her close-cropped hair.

"No," Ylie whispered, but the life was already going out of Sister North's eyes.

The orrery groaned as it sped faster and faster, and a darkness began to flicker in the air above Sister North's dying body. If darkness could gleam, then this darkness did. It sucked the light into itself with a cruel hunger.

Ylie could feel the wrongness of it weighing down the air like his secret had once weighed down his feet. He struggled against his captor. "No!"

Sister Hauer turned to him. She pulled back the hood of her robe. For the first time, he saw her face fully, the weathered cheeks and the long black-and-gray-streaked hair. He saw the lines pressed into the skin around her eyes, lines made from squinting into the darkness and watching the stars for long lonely years.

And he saw her eyes, huge and dark, deep pits of nothing, like the space between the stars.

"Yes," she said, and the darkness opened.

THE GREEN REVOLUTION

Cody Goodfellow

Sometime after midnight, just before they got thrown off the Olancho bus on the muddy, rutted road to La Colonia, Whitney found proof.

The girl dozed in the seat behind her, beside an old man with a hooded gamecock in a cage on his lap. Emerald sweat beaded on her copper brow, smelling sweeter than cane sugar.

When the girl awoke to find a strange *gringa* collecting swabs of her sweat, she screamed. The other passengers woke up and cursed Whitney in Spanish and Pech when she tried to offer the girl money. When she said *Ciudad Blanca*, hands grabbed her and shoved her out into the aisle.

Beside her, Colin awoke to angry peasants dragging him out of his seat by his dreadlocks. The driver flipped through Whitney's journal as if he could read it, confiscated her seeds and water samples. She tried to catch his hooded, mud-yellow eyes to guess whether he knew what he was protecting.

When the bus limped off down the road, it took the only light, leaving her feeling as if she'd been sealed in a bag of primordial ooze and biting insects.

Flinching and throwing punches at the dark, Colin hyperventilated, "What just happened?"

She started hiking. "We were right to come down here." Even though she felt like she was breathing hot water, she dug in her backpack's side bellows pockets for her cigarettes.

"What were *we* right about? *I'm* down here because I probably can't ever go home..."

"Try to keep up," she called over her shoulder, stifling a hacking cough. He'd tried to complicate things again last night. He wasn't getting over it like she'd hoped. They hooked up once back in Oregon, right after their cell broke up and everybody else got arrested. He just went along with the plan. She didn't even have to ask. He needed to think he was saving her, so she'd let him.

After a few minutes, he shouldered his pack and ran after her, following just close enough to splash mud on her with his stomping combat boots. "If this is the rainforest," he demanded, "where are all the fucking trees?"

Whitney Dirksen and Colin Bushong had warrants out in three states, and the FBI was probably looking for them. They fled the U.S. the same way millions snuck in every year. They rode south through Mexico on the roof of a freight train, swam a river of sewage to reach Guatemala, and stowed away among the freshly cut logs of hundred-foot jungle sentinels on a flatbed semi to get into Honduras. She had told him only that they had to disappear. Only that they were running, never what they were running to.

The burnt-flesh and diesel stink of the capital still coated the back of her throat. They lurked around an airstrip until they got lucky, hitching a ride in a Mormon missionary's Cessna to Catacamas. She thought they were in the clear, but Internal Security goons showed up when she tried to use a stolen credit card to rent a jeep. Running from the banana republic dragnet, they somehow caught the bus. This latest reversal of fortune was all part of the pattern, the agonizing, peristaltic pull that had drawn them into the jungle.

Aside from package tours and charter flights, there was no direct route into La Mosquitia. Before today, hiking the undeveloped jungle would've sounded like magic, but she knew they were being tracked and blocked, and she'd tipped somebody off to their location, if not their intent. They could be waiting in La Colonia, at the end of the road. Or they could find no trail, no sign, nothing, and she'd have to decide if she was hardcore enough to go into the jungle on foot, chasing a ghost.

Eastern Honduras had no railroads except for a few broken-down relics built by the fruit companies, and more canoes than cars. The roads all ended at the edge of La Mosquitia's thirty-two thousand square miles of wilderness, or veered around it to reach the coast.

When United Fruit turned every other country in the region into banana plantations in the 1890s, Honduras proved too wild to bother with. In Guatemala, the first railroad they built to connect the plantations with the Mosquito Coast cost four thousand lives for the first twenty-five miles of track. Honduras was so much worse, they never really tried.

It was exactly the kind of place *he* would hide. If he was really alive...

Her lighter reflected off flurries of glossy wings. She had to hide the cherry of her cig from suicidal insects.

The largest primary tropical rainforest in Central America, La Mosquitia had been subdivided into a host of national parks and nature preserves, but the ecotourism revenue Honduras hoped to steal from Costa Rica failed to bootstrap the country into the new millennium. Honduras was still second poorest in the hemisphere and number one in murders, a fine conduit for cocaine traffic, and a bivouac for Contras—too passive, backwards and dangerous to become a resort destination. The poverty and lack of basic healthcare were extraordinary. She never thought she'd feel bad to see humanity losing to the jungle.

But the war was far from over. As their eyes adjusted to the dark, they saw high grass and blackened stumps stubbling the hills, cattle starving on ruined pasture land. They set up their tent under a stand of breadfruit trees filled with birds that sounded like Verizon cell phones. She didn't sleep.

"We have a chance to find something better than what we've been doing," she said to the dark. "Burning, blowing up and sabotage are *their* games. We don't have to play them anymore. We can help build a new way... something *truly* sustainable..."

Colin didn't answer, but she saw him blinking away mosquitos that tried to drown in his tears.

Just after sunrise, they came limping into a village that wasn't on the map. Little more than a few rings of cinderblock huts with tin or thatched roofs that might have been slapped together yesterday, the village was already overrun by strangler figs and broadleaf cheese vines. A white ceiba tree towered over the village square like a huge, half-melted candle, elephantine roots plowing up the granite paving stones and vast, parrot-infested canopy draping nearly the whole village in green shadow.

"D'you smell that?" Colin asked. She shook her head. "Yeah, me either. There's no meat cooking, no fossil fuels. It's a vegan village. This might be the place…"

"Go find us something to eat," she said. He gave her a dark look, but plugged in his earbuds and disappeared.

Hurt to admit it, but he was right. She saw no power lines, smelled no burning diesel, heard no motors, and saw none of the clearcut subsistence farms that pit Indians against their own forest.

A line of Pech and Tawahka women carrying sacks and baskets brimming with unidentifiable fruits waited outside a hut on bowed stilts. A crowd of men and boys gathered around a rusted storage shed that somebody had tried to use as a church. Some were Miskito or Pech Indians, while others had grotesque gang tattoos on arms, necks, faces. Sitting or standing, they remained frozen as she walked past. Not drugged or exhausted or weary or drunk—frozen. Their broad, bronze faces turned to the rising sun, their eyes closed, like a patch of sunflowers.

She looked in vain for the Coca-Cola sign that always denoted the local market. Almost out of cigarettes, damn it. Usually, she tried to blend in and observe, but a tall, green-eyed redhead in hemp fatigues, carrying a huge backpack, usually sparked at least some reaction, greed or lechery, raw curiosity or the silent shunning born of jealousy and superstitious fear. She'd never felt more out of place, or more invisible.

A squat, spiny tree squeezed out between two collapsing shacks, brimming with star-shaped burgundy fruit. She picked one and walked away eating it—something like a fig, but smelling like floor wax—and noticed people watching her. They seemed to scowl at her like they knew she was a thief; then it dawned on her that they were looking at her the same way she and her comrades looked down on anyone they saw eating meat.

She paced the square, circling round the trunk of the tree, when he came out of the chapel shed. In a spotless white shirt and pressed slacks, he looked like a missionary. His white beard and shoulder-length, carelessly tousled silver hair set off his piercing black stare and red-gold, acne-scarred complexion.

He hadn't aged. As he walked through the motionless crowd of human sunflowers, touching their heads and smiling, he looked like an artfully aged actor playing him in a Hollywood biopic.

Then he looked at her, bowed his head and came ambling towards her as if she were expected.

To call Silvio Aguirre an environmentalist would be like calling John Brown a civil rights leader. The closest this apathetic backwater ever came to a true revolutionary, Aguirre was a Honduran ecology professor who joined the Sandinistas and was educated in Cuba. He soon renounced all human politics and returned to Honduras as a rogue "deep ecologist." A gallant fusion of Che and Hayduke, he coordinated peasant revolts and sabotage campaigns to protect virgin rainforests in Guatemala, El Salvador and Honduras from '87 to '98. Because he was apolitical, shunned media and never directly took a single human life, he never became an outlaw celebrity like Che, Chavez or Subcommander Marcos, but North American corporate interests were terrorized, and he had more than a little to do with United Fruit pulling out of the region altogether.

Aguirre's lectures read like metascientific love poetry—Castro's bottomless spleen shot through the Gaia-philic poetics of Thoreau—perfect for Yanqui fundraising and capturing the hearts and minds of college coeds like Whitney Dirksen. His words somehow unmasked everything else the world said as a lie. "Always when they talk of human history," he wrote, "they start with Man coming down from the trees, and everything since an inevitable improvement. Our whole journey began with a wrong turn."

The Earth could not sustain the gluttonous orgy of modern human society, which he described as a global machine for making shit. "Renounce the machine," he proclaimed, "and return to the trees before the Mother awakens." When U.S. Rangers out of Panama were covertly deployed to snatch him, he and his guerillas vanished into the Nicaraguan cloud forest.

By the time Whitney left school and plunged into environmental activism in '98, Silvio Aguirre had gone missing. Two of his old compañeros surfaced to claim he was murdered by a roving CIA-trained death squad and left in an unmarked grave in the heart of La Mosquitia, before they themselves disappeared.

She modeled her own mission on Aguirre's teachings, but she was surrounded by fair-weather activists who quit or got picked off for less idealistic crimes and turned snitch. When there was nothing left for her in the States, she turned to her initial inspiration, to Aguirre's writings, to learn what she should do next. And within a week, the world sent her marching orders.

One of her old message boards buzzed with a slew of uncorroborated reports of radical ecoterrorism in Honduras. Twenty-two men from an illegal logging operation on Rio Patuca all went missing; evangelical missionaries disappeared or found dead, attacked by wild animals. At the same time, a couple grainy pictures and rumors surfaced suggesting that Silvio Aguirre had been spotted in a village on the outskirts of La Mosquitia, and was linked to a group called Ciudad Blanca. Peasant stories of *la gente de árbol*, wandering *curanderos* who healed the sick and in whose wake fruit-bearing trees sprouted, became urban legends with the speed of a new messianic faith. They were either murderous ecoterrorists, a humanitarian aid group or an evangelical cult, from one web page to the next.

"Good morning," he said with a tired smile. "You are American, yes?"

"Yes, I'm afraid so…" She choked up, it *was* him! "But…we're not tourists. We came a long way, actually…to find you."

"You need a doctor? I have many patients to see, but if it is an emergency…"

She tried to get in front of him as he moved, tried to trap his eyes. "No, please. We—I—have followed your work for years. We came to join the struggle. I know who you, um…who you really are."

A stormy, Mosaic frown. "I apologize for your difficult journey, but you must have mistaken me for someone else…"

"What do you think you know about me?" This was not the way to start. "I've proved myself—"

"This is not about you. Many Americans come looking for the last wild rainforest, searching for something they invented in their heads…"

"I'm not a goddamn tourist. We came down here to—"

"You came here to hide, and perhaps to burn and break and kill to purge your guilt."

"You were the one who opened my eyes. Loggers and missionaries have gone missing down here. The government militias are killing your people on the road. There's a war on, whether you're fighting or not."

He shook his head, touched her shoulder with a hand lighter than a leaf. "This is not a safe place to chase fantasies. Now, if you are not sick…" He turned to leave.

She caught his arm and dragged him to a halt. "We came to find Ciudad Blanca."

He stopped and shook his head, came close enough to whisper. "Who knows you are here?"

"No one. Like I said, I came here to help, however I can…"

"What can you do to 'help,' pale, soft thing that you are? What do you even know about the true struggle, or who is fighting, or what the stakes? You don't even know what you are chasing."

"You don't know—" She blinked back tears. "We have nowhere else to go. We want to fight to save the forest, just like you."

Smiling sadly, he threw up his hands to the vast ceiba canopy. "The forest needs no one to fight for it. *Men* fight. Nature wants no revenge. She wants harmony, where every species thrives in its place."

She nodded, but he kept staring at her as if she hadn't understood.

"What?" she finally snapped. "I'm sorry…I…" She could not bring herself to say, *I'm dying for a smoke.*

The one horrible habit from her death-culture youth that she'd never been able to shake. She knew some kind of chemical imbalance in her brain kept her smoking, but she couldn't function without it.

He reached into a pocket in his baggy white shirt and pressed a small handful of berries into her hand. So purple, almost true black, like ingots of tar.

"This should cure your craving," he said. He watched until she ate one, then said, "Forgive me." He moved off to join a Tawahka hunting party which came roaring down the street bearing a prize out of the jungle.

Whitney reflexively looked away from the expected sight of blood and dead flesh, but their trophy appeared to be some kind of huge fleshy bean pod, over twenty feet long and draped over their shoulders like a sea serpent. Those not paralyzed by the sun gathered around the party to touch the trophy as it passed.

It was here, she realized. Ciudad Blanca. *Here.*

From Chiapas to Cali, there was talk among the Indian underclass of a small, anonymous group led by a saintly doctor, dispensing miraculous medicines. The rumors surfaced in a suppressed WHO report indexing infant and adult mortality among Honduras's Miskito and Pech Indians, but few others connected the dots.

What it said—and what ruined the career of the Scottish epidemiologist who wrote it—was that all health and nutritional indices for indigenous people living in the region had rocketed past most urban working class conditions in North America in the last ten years. This unlooked-for miracle had occurred even as missionaries reported that more of their charges had stopped coming for help, and Tegucigalpa's oligarchs phased out basic state medical programs and were accused of burning down overcrowded prisons to cut costs. His spitball hypothesis for the miracle? He pointed to the stories of *la gente arboles* and Kao Kamasa, as the Pech called Ciudad Blanca. Legends persisted that somewhere in La Mosquitia was a lost pre-Mayan ceremonial center greater than Copan, which had been reborn as the home of the Tree People.

She expected crowds. She had eavesdropped on suspicious whispers among the packs of drifters waiting for the next northbound trains to Mexico, but no one would talk to her. Only the most desperate still sought Ciudad Blanca.

The pilgrims who'd left their homes in hope of a new life had come back disappointed, if they returned at all. Paranoid rumors that the government was rounding up the pilgrims for deportation or worse met with stony denials from the capitol. Mass graves had been found in the jungle near Catacamas and Wampusirpi, but none of the dead could be identified. Even in poor, tightly-knit societies, these were invisible people. Whitney was sure, now, that she had found them.

Her mouth tingled with the quickening tartness of the berries, a metallic tang like smart drinks loaded with neurotransmitter precursors. She'd chewed coca leaves before and thrilled to the rush, but this was much more than a stimulant. It was the catalyst for a neurological sea change cascading through her system. The rusty keyholes in her brain that she'd clumsily pried open all her life with street and prescription drugs turned inside out, the convoluted knots of anxiety that twisted her gray matter suddenly unwound, leaving her mind a sea of ecstatic bliss. She felt not just faster and happier, but *perfected*, and knew as her shaky steps began to become surer, that this was not just a drug. This was permanent.

She couldn't stop grinning. When Colin came up and asked for a cigarette, she said, "Try this." She gave him a berry and ran down the street after Aguirre.

The crowd pushed her back, only to split open and suck her deeper, until she was pressed against him.

She caught his arm. "Show us more," she said.

His smile was sad. "Open your eyes, and see."

The crowd seemed to multiply, the noise to build, until it was Times Square and Mardi Gras and then blinding green light and a sustained shriek like dry ice on steel. A smiling, toothless old woman took her by the arm and led her off the street. She became heavier and slower with every step, until she sat down in a small clearing under a twisted *guanacaste* tree crowded with chattering scarlet macaws. Colin sat across from her, slack-jawed, oblivious as a couple kids rifled through his bush vest and fanny pack.

She reached out to stop them, but they disappeared. Colin started to smile and say something, but before he could open his mouth, the sun fell out of the sky. Colin was still as stone, but the jungle quivered and screamed and turned to a roiling wall of emerald fire.

She had tripped on acid, psilocybin, mescaline, DMT and even taken the Yage sacrament, but nothing like this…

Leaves and tendrils quivered and throbbed with the breeze and the light. They were not moving but *growing*, seeking light and space and Colin.

Rain fell in a single, devastating slap. Clouds of mosquitoes and flies descended on her exposed skin like a shotgun blast, but her sweat exuded a thick, astringent citrine odor that drove them away. She lifted a hand to swab her brow and taste it (was it green?), but before her hand had stirred in her lap, night had fallen.

The moon rose and fell and the sun climbed into the trees and the plants commenced a polymorphous orgy with sexual fireworks that blossomed and exploded in extravaganzas of flower and fruit.

Seeds fell all around them like wedding confetti and some took root and unfolded into tender green appeals for earth and water and sunlight. An unlovely, odorless flower loomed before her nose, and then she realized it was her hand, come at last.

The sun went away when she blinked and came back before she opened her eyes. The flowers yawned and ate daylight, twisting eager, beaming faces to follow it across the sky.

With no visible animal life, yet there was endless, mindless violence. A cowering berry bush was dismantled by golden streaks that must've been leafcutter ants, its leaves and fruit vanished, leaving only a few gnawed stalks. She watched in horror as a strangler fig sent up questing tendrils that thickened around the slender neck of the young *guanacaste* tree and throttled it with all the ferocity of a murderer taking the life of a child.

All around her, cheese plant vines climbed helpless trees and unfurled broad, elephant-ear leaves and ejaculated packets of seeds that erupted in green Catherine wheels of unbridled avarice. Orchids and bromeliads and pitcher plants seduced insect suitors and swooned and rotted under the weight of their own beauty.

The state of harmony she imagined reigned over the vegetable kingdom was an illusion. Observed from within, the jungle was in a constant state of war, not just with humanity and animals, but with itself. All growth and reproduction was an act of desperation and bravado. All of nature seemed to tear itself apart in its sleep. Underneath the perfume of seduction and rot, she began to perceive the constant olfactory screams, the chemical expressions of hunger and pain, fear and fury, of every plant in the jungle.

The sun rose and fell and rose and fell and at last she could hear it behind the unfathomable din of animal life, under the rustle and thrust of growth and fertilization and domination that was, if anything, more brutal than the animal kingdom...under it all, she could hear their respiration, their millions of stoma gasping and flexing in unison, and whispering Her many, Her million names.

She opened her eyes to see the sun looking back at her through a perfect curtain of green. When she moved, dead skin split and peeled away in long, fibrous strips from her wooden flesh. *A cocoon*, she thought, looking at Colin.

He was petrified, a bony Buddha in a neglected garden. White as a slug's belly underneath a shaggy shell of roots and mosses, opportunistic fungi and lichens, many of which appeared to be growing under his skin. A tiny orange frog leapt out of a pool in his slack, half-open mouth.

She inhaled to scream and choked, gagging and coughing until she expelled something solid into her hand. A mass like a generous steak of pinkish black flesh studded with tumors like tiny pearl onions.

A gentle hand, thorny with calluses, settled on her neck. "Not all who come survive the loss of their sickness. For many, the shock is worse than losing their name."

Breath came in deep, stabbing seizures. Her chest felt empty, her lungs scraped clean. Everything burned…

Aguirre knelt beside her. "You did not know you were dying?" He looked grave, like he was sending someone to war.

She made herself get up and crawl towards Colin. His eyes were closed, his mouth quirked, just starting to smile. "He's dead…you killed him…"

"No, girl. He sleeps, as you did. In his dream, he still seeks the door to awakening. When the Mother finds a purpose for him, he will be harvested." Running a gentle hand over Colin's petrified face, he added, "He must be planted, and allowed to ripen."

Standing, he turned and walked down a trail out of the grove where she'd sat for—a week? A month? A season? She felt stiff and dehydrated, but no more so than if she'd hiked all night. Her clothing had rotted to colorless rags. Patches of furry moss and a few puffball fungi grew on her skin. She wondered if it was growing inside her, as well. She felt hollowed out and unable to take any initiative.

"Stop! Wait!" she croaked, but he only nodded and disappeared into the overgrowth. Two Indians uprooted Colin and carried him down the trail after Aguirre.

Before, she realized, she had seen only the undifferentiated mass of the jungle, an idealized state of nature less real than Disneyland. Now, she saw every one of the millions of plant and animal organisms that made up the jungle, even as she saw the whole of the great, green thing that was their collective face.

Finding words was like rummaging through a junk drawer packed with broken, alien tools. "Hey, goddamn it… Stop! Stop and look at me!"

Aguirre paused on the trail and turned. His patience was not so saintly now, but something cold and stiff. "Your friend will be taken care of. You have seen what you came to see. If you learned from it, you will go where the wind blows you…"

She rubbed her eyes very slowly. She felt like she should be hysterical.

Aguirre gave her a green waterskin. It was a huge, bloated flower, like a pitcher plant. The water from it was cool and infused with nectar that burned her lips and warmed her throat like brandy as it went down, but charged her muscles with a weirdly serene strength.

Staring out into the jungle as he walked, Aguirre said, "We have been blinded to our true wealth. Man is like a rat that has just discovered it has sprung a trap. And its only thought, when it has one, is whether it can eat all the cheese before the bar crushes its head."

"You're not a fighter, anymore."

"It is a different fight. We don't wage war upon human society, for it must destroy itself. Our true enemies are the domesticated crops that rule their lives. Before nature can be saved from man, humanity must be delivered from the Cavendish banana, the Red Delicious apple, the Russet Burbank potato, from patented Monsanto corn.

"Think of it. Mankind has domesticated plants for ten thousand years, changing them to suit his desires. But plants emerged on land millions of years before the first walking fish, and they have had two hundred million years to learn to make animals serve *them*.

"All of humankind is enslaved by grains, fruit and livestock. All these species drove men to reshape the world to spread their genes. At the behest of corn and bananas and coffee and cocaine, man has cut down nearly all of the forests. They have cut out their lungs to fill their bellies. They mutilate DNA to produce sterile 'terminator' seeds, to protect their monopoly. It would take only a simple further twist of the genome to make them pass the terminator on to its consumers. It would be a mercy."

He caught her eyes glazing over and laughed. He could still lecture like Castro. "I assure you, I am still a fighter. But in the plant kingdom, warfare is slower and subtler. We have found something better than endless conflict and destruction. We have found the path to a true and final peace."

He pushed aside a curtain of fleshy leaves and stepped down into the shovel-shaped bow of a thirty-foot dugout pitpan nosed into the red mud of a sluggish river.

Colin's pallbearers gingerly settled him in the middle. Stringy, trailing roots like the eyes of an overripe potato dangled from the rotten rags of his shorts.

She was parched. Staring longingly at the muddy water, she sat down in the tail of the dugout. The Indians pushed them out onto the water, but only one waded in after and climbed into the stern to fire up an ancient outboard motor.

The shovel nose of the mahogany pitpan slipped into the sluggish red river, into a darkness deeper than night. They meandered through stagnant swamps and forced their way up rock-strewn cataracts between white limestone cliffs like towering teeth. Howler monkeys and iguanas watched from the trees on the right bank, but she saw nothing larger than insects on their left. The density of plant life was maddening to her raw senses, its endless profusion, its subtly veiled violence. When she was tripping, she had felt its blind, inwardly curved antagonism. Now, she seemed to smell a sour chemical condemnation in the air. Nature was not asleep, out here. It was awake and aware…and angry.

She looked everywhere but at Colin, whose wooden, half-lidded smile looked more content than he ever had when he was alive.

When the dugout finally beached on a mud bank in the grip of a mangrove tree like a giant, greedy octopus, Whitney was loath to climb out. The Indian lifted Colin out of the canoe by his shoulders. Aguirre took his legs. Hesitant, she followed them up the bank and into the deep forest.

The game trail was crowded with thorny nettles and more vicious plants. Huge spiderwebs stretched between the trees. Skyscraper trunks festooned with pitcher plants the size of washing machines crowded close. Stray sunlight passing through the veiny gullet of one specimen showed her the half-digested silhouette of a howler monkey floating inside. Every known vegetable barrier had been deployed to deflect animals from the glade in which they emerged. They set Colin down on a hillock of ferns. Aguirre took up a shovel.

"You're just going to bury him out here…?"

Aguirre walked out into the shafts of sunlight penetrating the triple canopy as if crossing a minefield. He wandered over the broken ground, bending to smell the riotous grasses, to pick up a fruiting body or an insect and taste it. "This is not a graveyard, *señorita.* It is a garden."

She looked around and realized that the earth was turned in tight rings of elliptical furrows beneath the thriving beard of secondary growth, like the regimented lines of a plow. Dozens, hundreds of delicate green saplings stood knee-high out of the tilled earth. Their tightly coiled, fleshy leaves looked like human ears.

"There are five million Maya alive today," Aguirre said, "more than at the height of the empire. This is a surplus of people created by monoculture and urban crowding, and we would not see them wasted. We plant them here and elsewhere, so that whatever comes to pass, true humans will not pass from the earth."

As he talked, Aguirre dug a hole in the earth. It was soft and fine as cheese, but choked with roots like veins and arteries, like a dense net of capillaries that gushed strange syrup when severed by the blade.

"They only see us as cut flowers or fruit rotting in their homes, so most humans dismiss plants as fleeting, temporary things, but the oldest living things are trees. Man must see that he is not the gardener. He is, at best, only the fruit."

"But when you dig them up…they're fit to join Ciudad Blanca? Is that what you're calling the new movement?"

"Not a movement. *Uno crecimiento.* A growth. We care for the people's health and education, and we try to offer what their old leaders could not." He swept the field with his arms as if to embrace a cheering crowd. "We are building a new way to live. They might try the old ways of fighting, but it will come to nothing."

"You accept everyone who comes to join you? You don't just…bury all of them?"

Aguirre was already knee-deep in his hole. "Most go in the ground. They sleep and dream of the green world to come, but they also share their old lives, their knowledge and languages and memories. Most will sleep and germinate for the Long Count, but some will be needed to go forth and heal and lead, when the changes overwhelm the old brown world."

Aguirre laid down the shovel to pry clumps of rootbound rocks from the hole. The Indian stood over him, chanting and bowing to the four points of the compass.

What they believed…it was wonderful and pathetic and insane, a grotesque sham. But could she really say it was impossible, after what she'd already seen? *Put away your prejudices,* she ordered her reactive mind. *This is their world, and they know best how to survive in it.* It could just be the miracle she'd dreamed of.

"So…you worship Mother Nature?"

He laughed. "No more than any child worships its mother. It is not an act of faith. She has opened Her arms to embrace us, kindled the dead seeds in us to bear much fruit. She is not our mother. She is motherhood itself. We are not so much her children as the extension of Her indivisible body. She is all of us, all life on Earth, the force that drives us to adapt, to conquer and create.

"Even the seed feels terror. Even the egg knows despair. Without Her love, all life is an empty machine. The only crime, the only sin, is in believing oneself a separate entity. Anyone who can accept that is one of us..."

At last, he stopped digging. At the bottom of the hole, a convex green-black bulb jutted out of the compacted mesh of rootlets. Aguirre took out a knife. "A Christian missionary at Wampusirpi was killed last week by the narcos. The children must still be educated, the sick must still be treated, and the people must be fed in a way that will not make them despoilers and slaves. This one will help them."

Stabbing at the hard green wood, like an enormous, whorled walnut shell, Aguirre cracked it open and peeled it back, like shucking a seedpod. Inside, packed tightly in a bed of roots, Whitney saw a jade green human face.

Eyes opened. Rigid muscles twitched in slow motion like a flower opening to the dawn. The man in the ground smiled.

The Indian knelt beside the hole and spoke in a proto-Mayan dialect and then listened, smiling at the whispered news from beneath the earth.

"Your friend," Aguirre said. "What was his dream? What would he become, if he had his heart's desire?"

Colin Bushong wanted to be an ecowarrior and torch Hummers and ski lodges, and Colin wanted to love me and he came here to be my protector... Colin wanted...

"A teacher," she murmured, looking in vain for the sky. "He wanted to be a teacher."

***

The jungle grew thicker and the trees grew taller—over two hundred feet by her best guess, though that was impossible. The thin, rain-leached topsoil should not support such giants, let alone so many giant hardwoods, some clearly thousands of years old. This was not just a primary growth rainforest. It was primordial, and yet they passed underneath a military jeep lodged in a tree, forty feet above the forest floor, and it wasn't thrown or blown up there. The tree had grown up under it.

Aguirre walked even faster with no trail, threading a path between monolithic trees draped in lianas and broadleafed saprophytes, leaving her to stumble and fight. Roots and vines tripped her; thorns and poisoned nettles carved livid stripes in her arms and legs; hummingbirds plunged at her like ruby-throated knives, intent on drinking her eyes.

She heard a cacophony of insects, birds and frogs, but no larger animals. The trees and even the vines bore flowers and fruits that defied everything she knew about rainforests. An abundance of health and freakish variety was garishly displayed in orchids like gigantic genitalia and clusters of fruit that glistened like fire opals with an eerie phosphorescence. Not one species in a hundred was identifiable.

Butterflies and bees the size of canaries made their rounds of the blinding riot of flowers. She was watching them admiringly when she tripped over a vine and fell into a patch of overripe melon-shaped fruit. Bursting under her touch, they unleashed a stench worse than durian and swarms of enormous gold-headed ants that ran up her sleeves to sink their mandibles in her arms, neck and chest.

She rolled in black rot until the biting stopped. He helped her to her feet and looked away modestly as she shed the last rags of her shirt. He offered her a pale fuchsia cloak that felt like the skin of a kiwi fruit. It was a single leaf.

Ahead of them loomed a white limestone stela, twelve feet tall and slightly tilted, settling into the soft earth. Here and there underfoot, the white remains of a Mayan *sac be*—a paved road—held back the encroaching roots.

Even faded by rain and shrouded in lianas and morning glories, the stone was of exquisite workmanship, the bas-relief carvings seeming to dictate the floral overgrowth's bizarre animal motifs. Intricate ideograms and calendar calculations crawled over it like moss-encrusted ants. The goddess in the central image had an obscene flower for a head, from which spilled a host of twisted chimera that partook equally of animal and vegetable symbols.

Aguirre bowed his head as he approached the stone. "The Mayan empire reveled in its decadence for centuries, but it was drought and famine that undid their hold upon the land, long before the Spaniards came. Ix Chel, the mother of all, had forsaken those that forgot her true name.

"Ciudad Blanca was the first city, and the last stand of the Maya against the fall of its empire in the Petén. Their chroniclers erased it because they could not accept the peace that the priests of the White City had come to offer. And when they would not yield to the new way, they went into darkness. The calendar has turned to the year 8 Ahau again. This is the apocalypse, the fork in the path, that confronts us again."

Once, there was a city here, more ornate than Copan and reaching higher than the pyramids of Tikal. The jungle had all but devoured it. Now, it was a green cathedral.

Now, it was a city of trees.

The rootbound ruins of a colossal step pyramid loomed at the north end of a vast, quarter-mile square plaza. The white limestone steps and combed roof were split apart and dwarfed by a skyscraper of bone-white trunk that emerged from the summit, stretching another two hundred feet into the sky to form an unbroken canopy of perfectly interlocked leaves with its four cardinal rivals. Many of the leaves in the green roof were transparent prisms, which allowed scattered rainbows of broken sunlight to fall upon the plaza floor.

Crumbled white paving-stones and bas-relief monoliths reared up everywhere under garlands of flowering creepers. From ruined pyramids and temples at each of the compass points another monolithic tree grew, each larger than the largest Sequoia redwood. A gnarled black tree emerged from the forest of crooked columns around a goddess's temple, dripping rain from clouds trapped in its branches. A red mahogany grew from the sundered dome of an observatory at the east end, its gnarled, blistered surface flowing and folding upon itself like a glacial geyser of lava. A yellow, thorny tree, shorter than its siblings but forking into hundreds of sprawling horizontal trunks, grew out of the cloistered remains of a nunnery in the west.

And in the center of the square beneath the pillars of the Earth, a monstrous green-barked *ceiba* at least three hundred and fifty feet tall, thrusting out aerial prop roots like a herd of daughter trees, and flinging out an impossible tangle of branches like a naked circulatory system that terminated in a labyrinthine canopy, rife with huge, woven nests like giant cobwebs.

And everywhere in its branches, she saw people.

They lived in the tree, and they *were* the tree. Some ran up and down the trunk like squirrels, or brachiated from branch to branch like spider monkeys. Others were tethered to vines that joined seamlessly with their spines, playing out like extension cords as they snatched flying prey from the air, only to snap taut and retreat back into the green.

Others were little more than tumors on the trunk and branches. Their green skins were scaly and infested with fibrous growths, their bodies bloated to translucence, converting sap and nutrients by some weird internal alchemy into nectar for endless lines of thirsty workers.

They climbed a ladder of shelf fungi up the flank of a spreading root the size of a subway car to behold the vertical gardens of the trunk. Close up, the tree was a forest unto itself, shaggy with orchids, staghorns, bromeliads, pitcher plants and stranger flora that reminded her of an old European satire about a place called the Island of Tools, where the trees grew weapons and other useful human artifacts.

He led her up onto a horizontal branch as wide as an avenue ending in a cluster of galls hollowed out into huts. A naked old woman whose whole face was one great, glistening black eye sat before a hut. Her engorged, tuberous breasts drooled syrup into cysts that she pinched off into discrete pods at a twitch of her long, splendid spider-fingers. Wriggling masses in her drooping apron of a belly like unfinished babies that never reached escape velocity, unformed things yearning to be born.

Smiling with dangling onion root teeth, the cyclops drained violet milk from one of her dugs and rubbed it into Whitney's seething insect bites. As the pain turned to an equally unsettling euphoric glow, she went stupid with gratitude.

Their society was everything she was fighting for. Harmony with nature… it should feel wonderful, it should be heaven…

Nothing was wasted. Passing on a low branch over a compost heap, she nearly slipped from the wash of steam as well as the shockingly potent stench of vegetal carrion. Hulking, faceless workers turned the compost and tended gardens of bloated luminescent fungi among the tree's enormous roots. The gardeners' stunted heads bristled with outsized tongues like the sticky tendrils on sundew plants, attracting and trapping flies and other insects by the fistful to feed as they worked.

Her repulsion metastasized into panic, threatening to send her running off into empty space, which only drove the screws deeper. "It's just like a *maquiladora*. They're slaves!"

"Aren't we all?" he chuckled. "To our bodies, to our minds. They are doing the work of the forest. Synthesizing the compounds, poisons, and medicines that sustain life. The jungle has always produced a bounty, and it can serve man, if he will but serve the Mother."

She saw birds, some bigger than she was. She really thought they were birds; they glided on the winds over the roof of the rainforest, circling and sporting on the updrafts like eagles. Their iridescent green plumage left sparkling trails against the setting sun. They were women.

"They are seeds," he told her. "When the season comes, the right wind, they will fly away."

"The people in the mass graves…turn into these?"

"No, my girl." He sat beside her, his hands kneading and stroking the waxy green bark of the branch between his feet. "These are the children of the forest. My first group became so adapted that they entered into a deep symbiosis… The forest bore all of our needs…and our children…are they not beautiful?"

"So…they killed you. And you got buried in the ground. And when you woke up…you were…"

Where he touched the bark, it had become softer…fleshy. "A part of the forest," he smiled, "a fruit of the Forbidden Tree."

"Are you in charge, here?"

"I told you. We are not the gardeners, my girl. We are the fruit." Under his fretful hand, the wood formed unnervingly familiar shapes. An anus became an ear, then an eye… "Men have called Her Ixchel, Coatlique, Kali, Astarte and Demeter and Gaia. Her true name…only the so-called lower animal kingdoms can even speak it. Under Her reign, the forest will spread over all but the deserts. The coastal cities will drown and billions will die without a choice. But they don't have to. The world could become a garden…"

She did not notice his hand moving up her arm until it was working the knotted muscles of her neck. She felt hot and giddy, and barely even outraged at the crude methods by which her own body was manipulating her.

He took her by the arm and led her up a coiling spiral branch to an aerie high inside the leafy canopy. The floor of the plaza and the sprawling roots of the tree were misty with distance, far below.

The spherical nest had portholes looking out into the jungle, a knothole filled with fresh water, and a pallet of furry leaves.

She felt a queer heat in her guts and just under her skin. He watched her expectantly as she paced the pod. "Perhaps you need another lesson," he said. "We are nothing, if not patient." Smiling, he turned and began to disrobe.

She had allowed herself to be seduced when she needed to feel wanted, or when she wanted something done she could not do herself (sorry, Colin), but now she quivered with rage. Her body was not *her*, and now it was not even hers. "I don't—listen, stop, okay? I don't think, right now, it would be right for us to…"

"But my dear, in the only meaningful way there is for such as we…we already have."

He turned around and moved into a hazy green bar of sunlight. His naked body was lithe and muscular for a man Aguirre's age. It was also covered in burgeoning encrustations that looked black in the green light, yet glistened like jewels, like clusters of ripe, purple berries…

"What I freely gave you, you took and ate. Your chemistry and ours have become…entangled…"

In thick clusters and clumps from the spread of his pectoral muscles, the tiny bitter berries gave way to larger and more varied fruit until they reached his groin, where a grotesque cornucopia of gourds and fungi erupted from the otherwise featureless fork of his crotch. Like some horrid Arcimboldo portrait, the cunningly disguised flesh of his body underwent a dizzying metamorphosis in her tearing eyes as she realized what he was, all along.

The berries he fed her, that she fed Colin…weeks ago? Months? It was too late to feel disgust. Far too late to vomit it out of herself.

Gentle hands roaming over the shiny growths on his body, he plucked a twisted root from his groin and offered it to her. "All that I am, all that I have, I have shared with you…"

"You're not…him…"

"I never claimed to be. I was the first seed, properly fertilized by the man you wanted to find. Through his ambition, all this came into being, but only because She willed it. She will not abide the ruin of Her body. I became Silvio Aguirre to serve the people and spread Her seeds, and who can say if it was not true? However…"

He sat at ease on the branch, his hand slowly growing towards her like a strangler fig. He seemed to sag into her like a passive dance partner when she twisted his arm, kicked his feet out from under him and sent him out the window and plummeting to the plaza floor.

He burst like a pumpkin on the white stones, spraying seeds and spores and nothing remotely human inside. No organs, no bones, no brains…

She stood looking down, waiting for sirens or irate jungle drums, but nothing changed. The sound of birds that were not really birds at all thickened, maybe talking about her. The walls glittered like stars, she realized. Hundreds of tiny eyes looked at her out of the wood.

Branches that seemed as wide as a crosswalk when they'd climbed up now seemed like greased slides as she tried to run on them. She passed a few arboreal Indians like giant spider monkeys stained deep green with chlorophyll. They looked at her quizzically as she pushed past them and jumped down to a broader branch. It was their screams that she heard first, that told her something was chasing her.

Clinging to the bark like a three-toed sloth in severe cardiac distress, she looked back and nearly flung herself into thin air.

The *tree* was coming after her.

The branch she'd leapt from flexed, shedding massive shreds of rigid green bark. Underneath, shiny as new snakeskin and so green it glowed, twisting around as fluidly as a gigantic tentacle, shaking off green people like aphids in its eagerness to smash her.

Whitney crawled almost faster than she could run down the unfathomable girth of the trunk, trying not to panic and throw herself away from this thing, trying not to think, *it only looks like a tree!*

Nets of creepers closed like fists around her and she began to ascend faster than she'd fallen. Her knife came out and slashed through the vegetal straitjacket, making her sick at the blinding stink of chemical agony that was louder than any scream.

Falling, she passed two tiers of branches and crashed into a dense crowd of bloated bodies, crushed several of them into a soup of human rinds and mildly electrified plasma.

Packed cheek by jowl on a wide branch under a patch of naked sunlight, they were like human solar panels, making sugar and electricity that flowed up the umbilical vines snaking between their vestigial feet. Like leaves shrinking from a browsing cow, they shriveled against the bark floor into fetal bumps. The coiling vines dangled overhead. She ran to the edge and leapt off without looking. She fell nearly fifty feet and plunged into a compost mound.

Walls of putrefaction closed over her head. Stunned, she held her breath and struggled against the undertow pulling her down into the hot, homogenous depths of the heap. Kicking and clawing, she struggled to bring herself horizontal and swim, as if she were caught in quicksand.

Hard objects—plastic, metal, bone—jabbed at her body. The stench flooded her lungs. Black slime clung to her face and plugged her nostrils. Buried alive like a lost skier in an avalanche, she felt an oppressive languor seeping into her muscles, a longing to lie down in the warmth and let nature take its course.

She broke the surface and was sick. The whole compost mound rose up under her, turned over in a rolling wave. Whitney paddled and kicked and swam just ahead of something ripping apart the earth to get at her, the rumble of seismic violence sending her rolling head over heels across the broken flagstones of the plaza. The roots of the great green tree churned the earth to black foam and sent yawning cracks racing across the plaza beneath her drunkenly stumbling feet.

She could not look back, could only see directly ahead. If she paused to look, if she even cast a glance at the massive cords of drill roots ripping up the Mayan flagstones to either side, she would stumble and fall and never get up. It was bigger than the biggest tree, but it wasn't a tree at all. Its seed was a man. Its roots went down into the seething womb of the Earth, where the Great Mother dreamed of a new order for Her children… And Whitney had awakened Her.

Her body wanted to crash in a heap when she passed the great white stela and staggered into the flowering garden, but the ground still trembled beneath her, so she kept running.

Now the game trails were vividly clear. She ran and ran until she broke through a wall of vines and cobwebs and stumbled into the clearing where they buried Colin.

Two men in jungle camouflage fatigues pointed rifles at her, screaming in a language that sounded like German after extensive oral surgery. She threw up her arms and collapsed, trying to catch her breath to beg for help, but a third man came up behind her and clipped her across the top of the head with a shovel.

She woke up in a dank canvas sack in the back of a Land Rover. Hogtied, hands behind her back, ankles curled up almost to meet her wrists. She should scream, panic, struggle, but she knew there was no use, and a weird, mellow calm welled up in her chest. The last thing she wanted was to be let out of the bag.

Inside, she could hear their angry, unhinged screaming, smell the poisoned sweat and fetid breath of her captors, their cigarette-ravaged lungs and the red meat rotting in their guts. A certainty that all was right kept her from trying to communicate with the foreigners who shouted at each other in Spanish and Dutch as the Land Rover bounced and skidded up winding roads. Drifting in and out of sleep, she wondered where they were going, but only as a way of passing the hours. When she slept, it was dreamless, perfect blackness, the muted, protean dreams of a seed sleeping in the earth.

Awakening to find the Land Rover sitting idle, she stretched her arms and was surprised to feel the ropes snap from her wrists. She untied herself and tried to find her way out of the bag. It was tied shut, but it tore like wet paper. Her muscles felt soft, feeble, but the material was rotten.

Only the dimmest, dull green light filtered through the coating of scum on the windows. All three men sat in their seats with their heads tilted back. Their faces were lush carpets of moss with curling, questing vines spilling out of their nostrils and gaping mouths.

Whitney climbed over one of them to get to the door. His body squelched and settled under her weight, reminding her of the compost pile.

Outside, the air was cool and clotted with smoke and petroleum fumes. A rutted, muddy alley between ramshackle tenement towers of cinderblock and corrugated tin, purple hills studded with whitewashed shacks like mushrooms feeding on vast, festering corpses.

Catacamas. She was in the city. She felt dazed, unconvinced by the reflexive need to find an American business, a way home. There was no going home, now.

Walking the streets, she burned with hunger. Men whistled at her but backed away from her heat, from the way she looked back at them. Wandering from alley to alley until she found a paved street teeming with pedestrians and choked with idling, honking traffic. She fought the urge to sit down and regress, to take root… If she used her new eyes, all of this would disappear…

But she couldn't rest. She burned with thirst and a strange, nameless hunger. The corner *panaderia* was redolent of PCB's and heavy metals baked into its products, but she craved sugar. She went in and touched the countertop glass. Like frost or Kirlian emanations, delicate arcing fans of fungi spread out on the other side of the glass, mirroring her hand. The room grew hot and damp. The woman behind the counter swore at her. The mounds of parti-colored cakes swelled with fermenting gases, then melted into a soup of black rot.

She ran out of the bakery and into a maze of produce stands. Bananas dominated in their polymorphous perversity, from familiar fat yellow Big Mikes to bunches of purple ladyfingers alongside pineapples and potatoes, mangoes and bins and barrels of exotic fruits she couldn't identify. Her throat burned. She longed to devour all of it, and when she took a mango from a neat ziggurat of tightly packed fruit, she did.

The fruit shriveled in her hand. The whole pyramid subsided with a horrible sigh of decay that sent droves of customers to their knees in vomiting seizures. The black blight settled on the produce in a visible mist and reduced them to clouds of spores and pools of noxious ooze. Mangos, papayas and breadfruit blackened and burst like grenades as she passed.

Only one stout old farmer could stand up to the wave of sickness. He shoved her out into the street, screaming for the police.

She started to run, but the creeping languor claimed her legs and made her stagger through the crowd and in between taxis, looking for a place to lie down. She had to get to the airport. She could beg a ride from a missionary or some drug smugglers. Or she could get to a computer and have her parents wire her some money to get home—

A car stopped in front of her. Two cops jumped out. The old farmer screamed in Spanish that she had the plague. She turned and ran through the traffic. They shot her in the back once and hit a car and two other pedestrians before they gave up.

She ran across a lot choked with exotic weeds from every corner of the globe and down a steep, unpaved alley, running like the tree was behind her again, until she no longer heard screaming.

She stopped in a courtyard between two cinderblock buildings sagging towards each other like waterlogged stacks of cardboard boxes. The gray mud underfoot was seeded with dead batteries and cigarette butts. Somewhere nearby, she heard the rumble and blare of lumber trucks.

She lay down against an overflowing trash dumpster—just long enough to catch her breath, then she'd get some fresh clothes and some medical attention for the bullet that never found its way out of her chest.

Bright green sap bubbled out of her mouth when she tried to get up. Her feet and legs clung to the mud with millions of microscopic fingers, boring like drills into the polluted soil. If she dug deep enough, she would find what she needed. *These bones are seeds—*

The rain pelted down and flooded the slums for a solid week. Black water swirled and stagnated over the spot where Whitney lay.

After the floodwaters receded, a gang of hungry children found her, but they didn't know what she was. She had nothing worth taking, and they argued over whether the strange white things were branches or bones. They dared each other to eat the black-red berries that clustered on the hollow cornucopia under the dumpster, so like a ribcage. When the stupid wall-eyed boy who took the dare went into a seizure, the rest of them wanted to try it, too.

DON'T MAKE ME ASSUME MY ULTIMATE FORM

Laird Barron

POLYCHROMATIC MERCY

Before you become Dee Dee Gamma, before the Black Kaleidoscope takes over your existence, you are Delia Dolores Andersen and you specialize in knocking over jewelry stores. Today will be your last day on the job. Your head swivels and that serves nothing, spares you nothing as your partner, a brute, points her gun at the jeweler and squeezes the trigger. A bullet punches into the jeweler's forehead. The pistol vibrates. The frame drags, almost disintegrates into cigarette burns, and then steadies. Words and sound synchronize

What you're thinking at this moment is primitive and inchoate as the explosion of chemicals and electrified neurons through your system. The thought is as elastic as all of time and space, and like the contrail of the reflexive act, it hangs in your mind in the gulf between, *Don't touch that alarm, you stupid sonofabitch,* and, *Sweet Jesus, oh, fuck. Willa killed him.* That's right, you forgot for a moment, your partner's name is Willa. An Iowa girl, a Star Wars action figure collector, overweight and undereducated, childlike in her emotional incapability. She appears baffled at the report and the jeweler sprawled on the floor.

Now you've got the case with the diamonds and you're cat-footing through the ghost-lighted lobby for the doors. You stepped in blood to collect the prize and you leave a trail.

The driver rolls up to the curb in a Maserati. She pegs it zero to sixty before you get buckled. The vista of glass shop fronts, sidewalk cafes, alleyways, and cross streets blurs, reverses into sequoias, swamps, the mists of prehistory and bubbling lava. Keep rewinding. An old star burst into a fountain of gamma rays about a hundred million years ago. That cosmic lance has crossed an infinity of cold and darkness to pierce the sunroof, the dome of your skull, and your brain. Cells roil and transform in squamous panic. Decades of your allotted mortal span are reduced to a handful of years. Every tick of the second-hand is emphasis.

Your consciousness untethers from its flesh and rises above the car for a fraction of a millisecond that lasts closer to an eon. The universe fractures into a blizzard of eternally replicating slivers of ice. Images are imprinted within the slivers. You see men with automatic weapons. A wound drips in a magenta sky. You behold with the searing clarity of an X-ray the new ravenous companion that has taken root in your gray matter.

You will never be alone again. That realization is terrifying. You feel nothing, however. You remain numb, even when it all begins to come true.

MRS. SHRIKE

Seven months into a twenty-year stretch in a Spanish prison, a chick from way back in high school visits your cell. She apparates between skull-shattering migraines.

Norse: "Hi, I'm Indra Norse. Mrs. Shrike thought a friendly face might cheer your gloomy ass up." Afro, shooting glasses, gold jumpsuit, utility belt with a black sunburst buckle, and combat boots. She looks different than the demure schoolgirl you knew in Alaska. Faster.

You remember her instantly because she'd been the smartest girl in the room. Her names fascinated you. Indra is a male god and Norse seems an odd surname for an African American family. You also recall that speculating on the subject is a sure-fire way to get punched in the mouth.

Norse: "Two options, Dee Dee. Run away with me to the circus or rot here. Option one, I return in twenty-four hours with all the papers to make you a free woman. Only catch, you gotta repay the debt. We'll talk about that later. Option two, I hope you are happy with the roaches."

You don't require twenty-four hours to weigh the merits. She gives them to you anyway. She asks how the migraines are as she watches you dress in clean traveling clothes. No fancy jumpsuit for you. Later, perhaps. Your own questions are deflected—who, what, why?

Norse: "The spirits aren't cooperating? Ask the magic eight ball again later. Eat these. Take the edge off those headaches."

Clean clothes, clean record, passport, and tickets home. Norse's reference to your heightened powers of perception, which is a secret you've not bothered to share with anyone. The FBI is running a game, has to be. *Somebody* is running a game. Life is rigged.

It's true—pain pills are addicting when you gulp them in bunches. An inoperable brain tumor grows fat and you've resigned yourself to the worst. The pills fog your mind too often. Although once matters begin to reveal themselves, you're actually grateful for the respite from reality. What passes for reality, at any rate.

You: "Where are we going?"

Norse: "The Nest."

THE NEST

The Nest is located in western Washington. *Mrs. Shrike's Home for Wayward Girls* is how it hits you after you mingle with Norse and the others at Liz Lochinvar's Bellingham residence. Set among old-growth fir trees and straight out of the 1960s with lots of glass and lots of shag. Jacuzzi, steam room, a wet bar, etcetera, etcetera. Lochinvar, another of your long-lost high school comrades, inherited it from some rich relative and this is where

Mrs. Shrike keeps you sharp and ready as a box of knives. You have access to food, weapons, and discretionary funds. Everything except capes and domino masks.

Several women form the heart of the sorority itself. Introductions occur around a coffee table while a grand Pacific Northwest thunderstorm rumbles overhead.

Norse: "Naval Intelligence. Profiler. Authority doesn't give a damn about ridding the world of evil. I want to burn things down."

Lochinvar: "Ex-Army. Olympic Judo champeen. Too many rules. Wasn't suited for it. Not at all." She smiles at the knife in her callused fist.

Sloan: "Ex-housewife. Alcoholic. Addict. Antisocial. Shrike taught me how to manage my assets. By the way, fuck Judo. Krav Maga all day and all night." She smiles at Lochinvar. A couple of sweet-faced calendar girls who can tear phonebooks apart with their bare hands.

Mace: "Professional final girl." Her voice is rough, her neck is scarred. She smokes the living shit out of cigarettes. She wears a bunch of fighting rings. A tattoo of binary code runs along her left forearm. The Zeroes and Ones spell REX. He's dead.

You: "I'm a career criminal. I'm dying."

Norse: "Dying? Dying? Bitch, we're survivors."

Sloan: "Survivors—for now."

Lochinvar: "It doesn't matter a rat's ass what we *were*. Now we're the point of the spear. Now we are the first cohort. What scales you ain't shed from your old life, will fall real soon."

Sloan: "The legionary first cohort of ex-girlfriends." She whacks her bottle of Rolling Rock against Norse's.

You: "Groovy digs, to be sure, and the company is pleasant—"

Mace: "She wants to know why we've been gathered here today..." She's half in the bag, which proves to be a routine condition.

You: "Point of the spear? That's not phallic or anything."

Sloan: "We're down with phallic metaphors, and phalluses."

Norse: "*Some* of us are down."

Lochinvar: "We are a privately funded clandestine civilian agency. Certain elements within local and federal law enforcement and military organizations are aware of our existence. Some of these tolerate us, assist us on occasion. Mostly we're on our own."

Norse: "We fight evil."

You: "Specifically?"

Norse: "We rescue kittens from trees."

Sloan: "We help old ladies cross the street."

Norse: "No job is too large, no need too small."

Lochinvar: "The other day I personally annihilated a cult that wanted to revive mass sacrifice to open a wormhole to deep space in somebody's basement. Next week it could be some asshole has figured a way to construct a pocket-sized death-ray."

Mace: "Or the kitten will be up another tree."

Sloan: "We ennoble the downtrodden and defame the wicked. We set fires, we bat our eyes, and we get the last word. Whatever it takes."

Norse: "You just never know what will happen when you jump out a bed in the morning. Shrikes have all kinds of fun."

You nurse your near-beer and search their faces for the joke or the con. None of them give a damn about your skepticism. The easy camaraderie and devilish smiles aren't the kind a woman can fake. Their gallows humor and haunted glances are sharp enough to cut right through your cynicism. These are condemned souls hatching doomed escape plans while the firing squad assembles. If your foot wasn't already in the grave you might worry more. You wonder about frying pans and fires.

Norse squeezes your hand and your apprehensions are overcome.

X

The stories are similar for the others who inhabit the Nest, the girls who come and go on mysterious errands and sometimes disappear without a forwarding address. Each of you has a purpose, a function within a great complicated pattern. Nine is the current magic number of the roster of your all-girls club. There were eleven as recently as last week; circumstances are such that membership fluctuates. Although the core of the team hails from Alaska, none of you calls it home for one reason or another. The last frontier is a magnet that draws against the metal in your blood and you'll head back soon enough, ready or not.

Cryptic histories and gallows humor to the contrary, not all of you are damned. Far less melodramatic. However, *you* are and that's why everybody smiles like you're a puppy with cancer, except you're a thirty-something ex-con with cancer. You're happy to have a job. Each of you has one individual to thank for this newfound lease on life.

You refer to your benefactor as The Old Woman in the Mountain. The connotations are evident upon consideration of your group's favorite problem-solving methods. You also refer to her as Mrs. Shrike because that's the long-defunct company name graven into the serial plate on the underside of the midnight-blue phone. Shrikes are beautiful and cruel. The universe, blind, insensate, and implacable, understands perfectly.

The Old Woman represents an enigma. The fact you can't turn the Black Kaleidoscope her direction is troubling. Who is she? A do-gooder tycoon? The mouthpiece of a multinational corporation? A government shill pulling strings for murky objectives? Lochinvar and Mace allegedly have the most insight. Too bad they aren't talking. The name of the game is trust, although blind faith seems more apt. Bottom line, you placed your bet. Let it ride.

You and Norse aren't present when Lochinvar unlocks the sacred gun safe (a rusty and verdigris-stained Diebold hulk with skulls and crossbones painted on the side) and makes the ritual call on the midnight-blue rotary. You get an earful soon after. Lochinvar convenes an emergency session to discuss the options. She drops the blinds and puts on the lamp with the crimson shade; transforms the furnished basement into a bunker where generals have gathered to decide between DEFCON 2 or DEFCON1.

Word is, X must be retrieved or else. *Or else* could indicate the assassination of a world leader, the end of an era, or the fiery demolition of planet Earth. *Or else* covers a spectrum of unpleasant possibilities.

Once X is secured, further instructions will follow. The main problem confronting the group is that none of you know what X represents. The basic idea seems to be this person or item currently resides in a ghost town in Alaska and that you'll recognize X when you see it. Are missions always this ambiguous? That would explain why Lochinvar brought you into the fold despite your violent misdeeds and how much fixing it took to cover your tracks.

The other girls want to draw lots, throw dice, or knives, go two out of three falls. This case is special. *You* are uniquely suited for the business at hand—the mind control lessons are paying off. Most importantly, the Old

Woman in the Mountain informs Lochinvar and Sloan that it must be you, no substitutions. This is your trial by fire, Gamma. The first mission is a blooding and it is traditionally done solo. Mace and Lochinvar explain that they'll run interference and direct the opposition's attention elsewhere and give you the best chance possible. However, this first go-around, you're on your own with everything to prove.

To be accepted by the team, to become part of something larger than yourself… You need it to fill your hollow core. Time surely isn't on your side. In the face of imminent extinction, no risk is too great for a shot at redemption. Whatever threat lurks in the great white north can't be worse than the miserable existence you've put in the rearview nor the malignancy of your traitor cells. The others laugh at this naïveté. Mace and Lochinvar, despite their scars and their notoriety, laugh the loudest. Their bitterness raises the hair on your neck. In that moment your friends aren't soft or warm or jocular. No longer are they sarcastic ex-college girls gone a little wrong, lounging in bathing suits, indolent from wine. They are druidesses, naked but for antlers and red ochre, obsidian daggers raised high against the black supermoon, as they loom over the sacrificial slab and you squirming there.

You smile as the fantasy bursts. A weak smile because you're never sure anymore. Could be in another reality, a previous incarnation, wherein Mrs. Shrike's crew ate human hearts and trilled Aztec death whistles.

Sloan believes the effort is fruitless and that it will end in all your deaths. She's a gleeful pessimist. Mace says it doesn't much matter, win or lose. She's even more of a pessimist. Neither of them are talking about your impending trip into the north, they're referring to the big picture.

Norse: "May as well be me. Spare new girl the pain."

Sloan: "Nuh-uh." She flexes her biceps. "It should be me *and* thee. Could be an occasion for violence. Home girl's soft. We're the violent ones."

Lochinvar: "You smack-talkin' bitches need to stifle yourselves." Her cool glare shuts them right down. She takes her orders directly from the Old Woman. The Old Woman calls the shots and she has spoken. That makes you the It Girl.

Plans are laid. The point of no return zooms past.

LAIRD BARRON

GO NORTH, YOUNG WOMAN

The going-away ceremony is a barbeque on a beach near the Nest. Lochinvar's a disco fanatic. She lugs a record player and a portable generator to the event; broadcasts the hot '70s beats on scratched vinyl. Neither KC nor his entire Sunshine Band help to dispel the mood of impending doom. The driftwood blaze isn't merry either, it's a Roman Legion bonfire on the eve of a massacre.

Everybody kisses your cheek, except for Norse who goes for a little more. Mace hugs you and whispers to check the drop box in Palmer; she's sent ahead her second-favorite holdout knife. In the morning you're gone and the cabal of kick-ass bitches, the voice on the midnight-blue rotary in the gun safe, and all the rest, recede into the province of dream and delusion.

There's a three-and-a-half-hour flight from SeaTac to Anchorage, Alaska. The easy part. From Anchorage, you drive. The rental is dinged in all four panels, its windshield is cracked. Duct tape on the gear shift. You swing through Palmer and visit the apartment of your contact, a sympathizer. A bland woman in a red bathrobe with a heron stitched to the breast mutes her soap opera to answer the door. She doesn't ask questions. She hands you a key and points to a metal box in her shoe closet. Inside that box there are three burner cell phones, an atomizer of compressed acid (with Mr. Yuck stickers plastered to the barrel), a set of topographical maps, and, tucked into a manila folder, fifteen hundred dollars in assorted bills and a nine-inch commando knife attached to a sticky note emblazoned by a lipstick kiss. Thanks, Mace.

The real driving begins.

Alaska is emptiness ringed in prehistoric fangs. This is the season of mosquitos and thunderstorms. The sun never completely sets. Red skies. Wetlands, peckerwood forest, and mountains keep going and going whichever way you turn your head. The sea gleams harsh as chipped glass, but you haven't seen it since you pushed inland. Mace claims sleeping on a boat brings the weirdest dreams. She'd know.

Green earth gives way to tundra and shale. Towns lie in strips. Roads are geometric slashes radiating from the carven visage of a forsaken god's skull. Summer is eighty-seven days long. Dust cakes the windows of the shops and of the cars. Beams of sunlight and headlights through the dusty windows intersect as rays of mud.

You pop a ball of chocolate caffeine. Trucker-strength, goddamnit. Onward and onward.

Poor men are made of mud. Said Tennessee Ernie Ford. He also said a rich man has blue in his blood. When the blue is black and black is mud that pours from incandescent clouds and caged filaments and oozes like tar from opened flesh, you will have arrived at the great X burned into the map. You will stand in the mud-light, buried like a flint arrowhead, in the heart of the X. Eventually the habitations of men fall away and there are no other vehicles. The land aches. It doesn't want you around either. You're the grain of irritating insignificance in the flesh of the oyster.

Onward and onward until the radio grinds static and ravens glide overhead. Signs warn against trespassing before they disappear.

Murdockville is the ghost of a mining town a corporation laid out seventeen years ago at the height of a boom. No one has lived here in fourteen. Sadly, the mine went bust and the brand spanking new facilities were evacuated overnight. Tundra and earthquakes and relentless north winds are returning the place to dirt, one roof tile, one brick, one smashed window at a time. Summer, and thank the powers for that much. This will be no place for a human being when winter howls down from the snowy range.

You've traveled through dust and darkness to claim your prize, to grasp Fate by the throat. Yours is the gift of second sight. Premonition, clairvoyance, telepathy, woman's intuition. Whatever it is, it's not reliable enough to break the bank in Vegas. Weak and intermittent as a radio broadcast that can only be received under perfect atmospheric conditions, it has led you in fits and starts to these modern ruins lost within the ancient wilderness.

The Old Woman in the Mountain says the prize will be subtle, yet obvious. Your choices inside this shelled-out room in an abandoned rec center boil down to either a jukebox, a buckshot blast pattern through a corkboard bulletin board, or the bundle of rags and wooden sticks cast aside in the corner. The bundle proves to be an Edgar Allan Poe puppet. Two feet long; the puppet's colors are faded bronze flecked black, its skull is deformed, and its prim black suit hangs in cerement tatters. Its strings are clipped and its mustache is clotted from a nosebleed. One cockeye peers, cold as the permafrost. The other eye is a ragged hole. Behold a simulacrum of Poe, dead from booze and rabies and after the vermin have had at his face.

You don't want to believe that you've seen this puppet. Your sister, Harmony, owned several marionettes when you were girls. Poe, an astronaut, a Punch puppet, and others. Harmony wasn't skilled in puppetry; she enjoyed flailing her troupe across makeshift stages in skits she learned while watching *Mr. Rogers' Neighborhood.* Teen years (boys, cliques, and a new car!) arrived and those puppets went into a Salvation Army bin. Yet here Poe is, the once pallidly morose creature who resided on a shelf above Harmony's bed. Pallid moroseness has progressed to disease and horror.

First prize, indeed.

POE BOY

Poe says, "Humans are not inevitable, Annabel. You used the Black Glass to find me. An unwise course. Exceedingly." The puppet's voice is cultured, yet rough, and far from the mannered Victorian accent your subconscious might be expected to affect. This is closer to your grandfather's voice, or how you imagine it after these many years.

A lesser soul would scream and hurl the puppet aside. You are made of heavier metal; one flinch and a strangled cry of surprise is the extent of your concession to civilian frailty. The puppet's lips don't move, the first clue this is a hallucination or a miracle. You would love to believe you've acquired super powers manifesting as psychokinesis or full-on telepathy, however it seems more probable that the brain tumor is finally impinging upon something vital, as promised. Migraines, nosebleeds, hallucinations; none of it is promising. Puppets don't speak of their own accord and that means you've elevated the art of the interior monologue to a new level.

You: "The Old Woman says that." You set Poe in the passenger seat. The trunk would seem more plausible, except you decide to keep the puppet near, like a proper enemy.

Poe: "Does she? Lochinvar *claims* to speak to her."

You: "Maybe I should tape your mouth."

Poe: "I've seen hell, Ann." He pronounces *Ann* with a sneer.

You: "My friends will want to hear all about it."

Poe: "It is not inevitable that you will meet them again."

You turn the key in the ignition and nothing happens. You unwrap another caffeine pill and eat it, slowly crumple the foil and its hornet graphic. Wind pushes against the car. Directly before you, the skeletal frame of a radio tower trembles. To your left lies a row of low buildings with boarded windows and tan doors, sealed tight against the elements. On your right, across a tussock field, spreads a disjointed landscape of alder thickets and marsh. Hills rise and rise. It is late afternoon and the sun is a blade stabbing toward the mountains. You dial the special number and let the machine record, then disconnect. Waiting is the hardest part is right.

The burner phone hums. It's Lochinvar.

Lochinvar: "What you got, girl?" After you describe the situation and your acquisition, she says to hang tight. Minutes pass. "Has it said anything?" Her tone is different.

You: "The puppet?"

Lochinvar: "Has it spoken? This is important."

You: "It's not that kind."

Lochinvar: "All puppets are that kind. This...puppet was abandoned in New York State ten years ago. Now it's hiding out in Tumbleweed, Alaska. Hell of a migration."

You: "Someone obviously—"

Lochinvar: "Someone obviously my ass. Has it spoken or not?"

You: "No." You massage your skull even though the pain hasn't started. You don't need second-sight to detect the edge in her voice. She's been on the horn with the Old Woman, getting the signals.

Lochinvar: "All right. Thank god."

You: "Why thank god?" You straighten in the seat and regard your little buddy.

Lochinvar: "Mrs. Shrike says if it's quiet, you're still in the green."

You: "Oh. I probably don't want to explore the implications."

Lochinvar: "Correct, you do not. Keep X under direct supervision. Get home."

After Lochinvar has gone you chuck the phone and hit the ignition. No joy.

Poe: "Scary music and car troubles mean only one thing."

You study the surroundings. The hand of darkness is slipping ever closer.

You: "We've got the place to ourselves, Eddie. We're in the green."

Poe: "Why'd you lie to your pal?"

You: "I didn't lie."

Poe: "You lied your lips off."

You: "We aren't having this conversation. You're an aural hallucination precipitated by my terminal decline. And shut up."

Poe: "Please, put me back." The puppet's head slips, so its remaining eye fixes on you.

You: "I've driven all this way. C'mon."

Poe: "You've never killed. You're not the same as the other girls. You don't have the guts. Please put me back. It's going to get me. You led it here. Please, please, please."

You: "Nevermore."

Poe: "Fool! The car isn't going to start. I'm dead. The Eater of Dolls is coming."

You: "Shut up, Eddie." After a deep breath, you try, try again and the engine catches, praise the powers above and below.

Poe: "Oh no oh no oh no." Then the puppet laughs.

You've heard that sound. Once when the doctor called to say your mother's cancer, and now *your* cancer, had done its work. You heard it again when your old golden retriever cried once in the night as she was going, gone. You heard it during an adventurous youth, moments before the thin ice of a lake cracked beneath your boots. You heard it last when a kid from Indiana, a Star Trek fanatic, cocked the hammer of a pistol.

You rev the engine and roll.

BLACK KALEIDOSCOPE

Chocolate speedballs can only take a woman so far and no farther. Pricks of fire float upon the eternal Alaska summer twilight and resolve to the streetlamps and illuminated shops of a town. You fuel the car at a Tesoro and roll into a flophouse motel. Your watch says it's a quarter until nine. Exhaustion weighs your skull like an iron ball. Three or four hours sleep to recharge the batteries, then you'll hit the trail again and press on to Anchorage. Food can wait, a shower can wait. Sleep is what you yearn for.

Poe: "Dear Ann, this isn't a good idea." The puppet tries to sound reasonable, avuncular. "Keep trucking, sister. It wants you to stop. It wants to catch us."

You tuck Poe under your arm and go into the cheap, claustrophobically narrow room. Mold, sweat, smoke, a hint of whorish perfume. Water stains and AC on the fritz. TV works fine, though.

You: "Hey, *Lamb Chop* reruns!" You click and click the remote, hunting for some porno.

Poe: "Stopping is bad." The puppet lies primly in its nest on the opposite bed. The table lamp bathes it with a cancerous glow. "In these situations, stopping is always the worst thing you can do."

You: "Short of fucking outside of wedlock, right? Does masturbation count? Because I plan to rub one out and cash in for the night. I can't see straight enough to avoid the ditch. Free skin flicks and a soft mattress win."

Despite your bravado, you lock the door and block it with a coffee table. A peek through moth-eaten blinds apprises you that the parking lot is mostly empty, and no one stirring except a drunk in shredded fatigues collapsed near the PEPSI machine by the manager's office.

You: "There. You're safe from The Eater of Dolls. Wake me up if he, er, it, comes knocking."

You swallow pills to dull the spike traveling through your skull, dim the lamp, and lie propped against the headboard while spray-tanned actors undulate perfunctorily on the television screen. The next click of the remote takes you back and back to a shirtless Danzig performing "How the Gods Kill."

Poe: "You're a doll." Its tone is petulant and sinister. "It will like you too."

You: "Be quiet. You're pissed because somebody snipped your strings. For a marionette that's like getting turned into a eunuch, right?"

Poe refuses to dignify that crack with a reply. You feel the puppet's anger seething, nonetheless.

You haven't dreamed in years. When your eyes close and your consciousness dissipates, it funnels into the barrel of what the eggheads, Toshi and Campbell, who work for Mrs. Shrike, call the Black Kaleidoscope. Quantum location and temporal fragmentary acquisition and dilation is a mouthful. Itty bitty time molecules get snagged in the sieve of your ultra-powerful, ultra-sensitive subconscious and translated into occasionally useful psychic imagery. It feels a hell of lot like astral projection from the way generations of hippies and crystal-loving earth mothers have described gliding along at the whip end of a silver cord. The main difference is, you don't zoom through a gulf of mist and light; you submerge into the black tar between blazing stars, the infinite Lagerstätte where consciousness goes to die. The ichor of the cosmos drowns your senses.

...Your father folds his arms and stares into the sunset. He never hugged you, never hugged your mother or sister. He backhanded you once, for coming home after curfew with your hair mussed and lipstick smeared. He apologized and apologized and pressed an icepack to your cheek. Last time he ever touched you...

...The Maserati careens into a cow pasture. Spanish cops with automatic weapons fill the car with holes, your accomplices with more holes. You surrender peacefully, like the coward you are... A Spartan cell, iron cot, a corroded toilet, trained cockroaches to keep you company...

...Norse caresses your cheek. "Did you have the sight when you were small, or did it develop after you got sick?" *You can't remember not possessing some form of the sight. You don't know if non-memory is true memory. The Black Kaleidoscope has a tendency to overwrite your mind. For example, it helps you forget that Harmony was driving the getaway car and how, after the third or fourth bullet, her face relaxed until it assumed a puppet's perfectly lifeless expression.*

...Lochinvar drags on a joint, although her expression remains severe. She struggles to explain how the team receives assignments; it's cryptic—Mrs. Shrike is a facilitator; she doesn't tell her girls everything. Some of it they must learn for themselves. "We use auguries," *Lochinvar says.* "Tea leaves, pigeon guts, the stock market. Tarot cards. Fortune cookies. Crazier than that."

"Brute force," *you say and decline the joint when she tries to pass it to you.* "What's it all about?"

"Survival. Living to fight another day. We'll see where it goes from there..."

...Ants mobilize in the depths to invade rival colonies. The quiet slaughter that ensues dwarfs all the wars of men combined... Giant wasps float down from the spreading shadows of the canopy to assault a honeybee fortress, and again, the carnage is numbing...

... In the rearview as you bail out of Murdockville, the doors of the deserted buildings swing open, one after another in a domino chain...

...Poe tumbles through darkness, limbs jostling, wrapped in a feeble halo of

light, dissolving. "Oh dear Annabel. It's your fault she's dead. She was the good girl." *You want to defend yourself. Harmony was a grown woman. She chose to roll the bones and they came up snake-eyes. Words remain impossible. You howl in grief instead. Poe can't hear you. Your sister can't hear you either. They're out there, zipping farther into the great dark…*

…Meanwhile, something is coming up from behind. You glance over your shoulder…

THE EATER OF DOLLS

You come to around midmorning. No one murdered you in the night and that wipes the slate. You check in with Lochinvar. She's unhappy, says to decamp and get driving. Pain pills and breakfast are in order. Your head and stomach conspire to heap misery upon you.

There's a lounge three blocks from the motel. The lounge is arranged similar to those rococo establishments that were popular in the '60s and '70s when your parents dragged you along for breakfast before church. Heavy paneling and dark, heavy furniture that invite gloom. Thick glass ashtrays. The host herds you into the smoking section despite your muttered protestations. He seems fearful.

Pancakes, eggs, coffee. Your waitress is haggard. You wonder if she stayed up late watching porn too. You have to wonder because your talent is more remote-viewing than ESP. Her nametag says CRO. She stares at your forehead, your shoulder, Poe canted against the opposite side of the booth, everywhere but your eyes.

The coffee is bitter. It's daylight, barely, and the place is half full of truckers and the jocular plaid and Carhart workaday set.

Two young women occupy a booth closer to the entrance. Tourists like yourself. Unlike you, the pair wear slinky dresses glittering with sequins, long white gloves (more sequins), and expensive hairdos. The brunette faces the door. The nape of her neck curves most shapely. The blonde is sharp-featured in a way that some women find repulsively attractive. Her lipstick lends the illusion she's been sipping at the neck of a slaughtered gazelle. She smiles and sips orange juice, extra-large. She isn't wearing jewelry. Hmm. What to make of that?

The Black Kaleidoscope grinds inside your skull. Crystalline flakes of potentiality quiver, seeking to coalesce into concrete knowledge—all the knowledge that exists exists in the cosmic tar of your subconscious, if only you'll stare deeper... You fight the compulsion. Too much pain this early in the morning.

Poe "Oh." It has remained inert until this moment. "No. No."

The blonde peels the glove from her right hand. Her hand hasn't seen the sun in a while. It belongs to an older, emaciated person. Still smiling (the painted sneer of a manikin), she reaches under the table and you freeze with a premonition of impending awfulness—she's going to whip out a gun or a bomb or some other lethal device. If only you'd brought one of your own; if only Norse or Sloan were here. Either of them would be ready for an action scene. Mace would've, as the group's wise Odysseus figure, plotted an escape route and a plan to burn the lounge to cinders in her wake.

Instead of a submachine gun or a grenade, the blonde retrieves a dummy clad in a lumpy silver spacesuit and balances it on the edge of the table. The dummy's face is white and mottled as boiled flesh, lacking ears, eyes, and nose. Of course the dummy is faceless; without a helmet, one unguarded glance at the sun burned it away. Its mouth makes a tiny sphincter about the size of a woman's fingertip. Its left arm rises and gauntleted fingers waggle a greeting.

Poe: "The Eater of Dolls." The puppet speaks with awe.

You: "What the hell is going on?" Surely it would be nice to ask someone other than a puppet. The waitress moves among the tables, she and her patrons apparently oblivious to the Moulin Rouge hot chicks and the world's most hideous dummy.

Poe: "As You Know Bob. What in the name of the Dark have they done? Bob used to be a marionette. Bob was my friend."

Bob: "Edgar. Edgar. Edgar. Edgar. Edgar. I'm still your friend. Edgar." Bob's sucker mouth dilates. Its voice is husky and feminine and carries intimately—or, as must be the case, the blonde's delivery is theater-caliber. "I've searched and searched for you. I'm your friend, Edgar. I'm." As the dummy speaks, its soft material bulges and darkens where the eyes should be. Yes, darkens like blood seeping through cloth.

Poe: "Oh no oh no oh no." Again with the jagged laugh.

Bob: "Oh yes, Edgar. Together. You and me. Me."

You're impressed. The dummy's voice is in your ear, yet the blonde's lips don't twitch. She's a master of ventriloquism.

The waitress's head snaps around. She lurches to a halt near your booth. Her expression is going through changes.

Waitress: "Yes, a master of ventriloquism. Yes." Her voice too is husky and feminine and soothing. "Dee Dee Gamma. Leave. Leave the puppet. Leave."

Bob: "I want Poe, only Poe." Its voice harmonizes with the waitress's. "You may leave unharmed if you leave at once. Thank you, Mizz Gamma. Thank."

Patrons continue their routines. A trucker tries the door handle several times before he unravels its mystery. Three burly dudes who've traded raucous insults for the past twenty minutes lapse into meditative silence. Two of them are poised, cups raised midway. The third drools through a grin, enchanted by some vison.

You intuit what they're experiencing. The pressure in your head changes. Your nipples stiffen. Warmth suffuses your belly. The harsh dimness of the lounge softens as your mind softens. Your tumor responds to the siren call. That insensate malignancy wants to enter the blonde.

Poe: "—in your mind, Ann!" The puppet's voice cuts through the drone of your colliding thoughts.

It is enough to snap you back to earth. Around the room, glasses and cups shatter. Cutlery and fragments of porcelain levitate and drift in counterclockwise spirals. The floor trembles. A low rumble begins in the earth.

You rise and snatch Poe and stride toward the entrance. Bob and his two bimbos are between you and the door. The blonde manipulates the dummy, or maybe the other way around. The brunette rises to block the way. She's as pretty as a rabid fox. You palmed the atomizer in your left hand. She's wearing sunglasses, but her nostrils flare when you jam the nozzle in her face. She sits again, with alacrity. Good girl.

Ten steps gets you inside your car and the doors locked. As the key turns, you sense a malevolent presence traveling through the wires. You exert your will. The engine fires on the first try.

You: "Ed, what do I win if I get you back to civilization?" You drive across a concrete divider and smash through a ditch onto the road. Your mother raced Baja in the late '70s. She taught you how to handle a car.

Poe: "A tattoo of a shrike somewhere inconspicuous and the satisfaction of a job well done."

Ninety degree left, and you sideswipe a street sign. The passenger window cracks. Needle pegs eighty-five.

You: "Satisfaction, huh? Well, I always meant to get a tat before I died."

Poe: "Your girls think I know details about the enemy. They're wrong. Bob can't be stopped. Bob's master can't be stopped. I can't save any of you. I'm sorry, Annabel. I'm sorry it's going to eat us."

You: "The dummy isn't going to eat us."

Poe: "Bob isn't a dummy. Bob is a shell that contains awfulness."

You locate the last burner phone and dial Lochinvar. Ring, ring, ring. You attempt to project your mind's eye three thousand miles east where your comrades doubtless gather at the Nest. Two problems—first, serious meditative concentration is difficult under these circumstances; second, poisonous psychic vapors roil around the car. You own personal acid rain cloud, courtesy of the dummy and its girls.

Full tank of gas, mountains on every side. You're traveling through a valley, perhaps the original Valley of Death the Good Book made famous. Inside an hour this surface road will intersect a major highway and from there it's three hundred and twenty miles to Anchorage. At the moment, those times and distances feel as if you're in a space capsule plotting a course for Alpha Centauri. Long, long way and the landscape creeps by too slowly.

You make it another seventeen miles.

KISS OF THE PSYCHOPOMP

Every light and dial on the dashboard goes bonkers. A whisper tickles your inner ear. Marilyn Monroe speaking from the grave? Guttural and alluring and incomprehensible, although the sense of threat is plain, the voice initmates you should pull over before it's too late. *This* is why the Old Woman sent you. She'd known the tricks the enemy would deploy. The other Shrikes possess a capacity for violence that dwarfs your own. You're a thrill-seeker, not a killer. Yet, you are the only one who can access the Black Kaleidoscope, and that is the ace of spades in your back pocket.

The devil's breath is hot in your mind, but you push the whisper aside and block the image of a giant silver figure striding across the hills to squash the car into a blob. You also block corresponding images of everyone you've ever loved dying hideous deaths, of the Earth blackening as a leaf blackens in a flame.

Your enemies decide there are other ways to skin a cat, obviously.

The radiator boils over. You forge ahead in a cloud of steam and smoke. The trunk springs open, then shears away and bounces on the pavement. The rear passenger door goes next. The rear passenger tire blows and you do some fancy steering to keep from wrecking. You know it's over but for the crying.

So does Poe. The puppet moans prayers in what you guess to be Old English.

A metallic glint appears in the rearview and begins to chew the gap; it's a black Lincoln roaring at one hundred and twenty, easy. Late '80s model. Heavy as a tank. Intuition suggests the blonde is driving, sneering as she closes the distance.

That last high-speed pursuit in Spain is on your mind. It didn't end well. They seldom do. You grit your teeth and spin the wheel until the other vehicle is in the bull's-eye of your hood ornament.

You: "Guess what, bitches? I'm the last person on Earth you want to play chicken with." You drift into the left lane and gradually press the pedal to floor. Euphoria, better than any dope, carries you away in the split instant that the enemy driver loses her nerve and tries to veer aside and your bumper annihilates everything in its path.

Hell of a crackup. The airbag does its thing, although there's a lot of blood leaking through your pants leg and from your busted nose. Your car lands in the ditch. It's totaled. You escape the wreckage, Poe tucked under your arm like a football. The black sedan has flown off the road and flipped onto its roof near a deserted T intersection. Pieces of metal and glass are scattered along the road.

Poe: "Run run run." It chants in a monotone. "Run, your sister is not far ahead."

Flight is not an option. You're light-headed from blood loss. You hobble to the centerline and take a stand. High noon without a six-shooter. Mace's knife is strapped to your ankle. The thought of bending to draw the blade wearies you. You've misplaced your purse and the atomizer. A tiny part of you dares hope someone will drive by and report this clusterfuck to the cops. Waves of psychic static break against the bulwark you've raised to protect your will. Animals within the radius of that emanation are curled whimpering their burrows; any human approaching within a mile is sure to find themselves parked and missing a block of time. Whatever Bob and its bimbos are, they've cleared the decks to ensure this is a private affair. It's down to you and a maimed puppet here at the crossroads.

The driver door crushes outward until it clangs wide. The blonde unfolds (you think of her as Betty) and shuffles toward you. Same routine on the other side, and here comes the brunette (Veronica). They stand shoulder to shoulder, twenty feet from where you and Poe grimly await what must transpire.

Their dresses are perfect—the blonde in black, the brunette in white, neither so much as smudged. Dresses perfect, hair un-mussed, the duet did not escape unscathed. Their sunglasses are lost. Both women are lacerated and bruised. The blonde's left leg is shattered. Bones protrude. The brunette's lower jaw hangs by bloody strands. She sways as her comrade sways and that gory jaw is a slow-arcing pendulum across her chest.

This should surprise and horrify you. You chuckle and maybe that's the same.

The Brunette: *Leave the puppet, Ms. Gamma.* Her whisper scratches at your brain. She winks. *Don't make him come out of the car.*

The Blonde: "Leave the puppet, Ms. Gamma." Chipper as hell.

Bob (muffled): *Give me the puppet, Mizz Gamma. Give.* It murmurs these sweet nothings into your other ear in the blonde's voice except accompanied by a split-second image of a thorn tree upon a blasted field beneath a carnivorous red sky. Many severed heads dangle from the tree, their many mouths dripping crimson pulp, the hideous red light of the sky reflecting in their eyes.

The offer is tempting. Hand over Poe, turn away, and limp across the tundra toward the sun that never completely sets during this time of season. Demonic smirks to the contrary, possibly the Muppet sisters are on the level and you'll actually go free. Your mother didn't raise a sucker and it doesn't matter. Walking away is a fantasy. In a few seconds you'll keel over like road kill. Suck it up, Gamma, this is your moment of truth. You're standing in the fire.

You: "Poe, this is the end of the road, I fear."

Poe: "Gamma, don't. I was born in a studio in New York City in 1929. My father was a carpenter. He emigrated from Poland. He had many children and grandchildren. I was the only marionette he created. His daughter carved Bob in 1970."

You allow Poe to slip from your hand. The puppet goes quiet. Its expression is inanimate. There is nothing of your sister nor yourself within the eroded face, nothing of life in the tangle of disjointed limbs. Still, a pang shoots through you as your boot descends on the puppet's cranium. You stomp twice, to be certain. Murdering the final vestige of your childhood, or brutally putting it out of its misery. Either way, the act drains most of what's left in your tank. You crumple and your pose isn't much different from the ruined marionette.

The women exchange a glance. The blonde covers her mouth. Her grin slides past her fingers. The brunette makes claws of her gloved hands and rakes her hair. Hanks tear free and she gesticulates. She hisses and burbles. It dawns upon you that they approve of your choice.

The Blonde: "There are mistakes, then there are colossal, life-altering blunders." She lowers her arm to reveal a cold, dead expression. "Guess which one you have made?" She gestures at her partner.

The brunette walks to the upended car. She crouches and disappears inside. You think, how phallic, how quiet it is without Poe's company. You wish you weren't falling asleep. Seconds pass. The sky shifts magenta; swaths are rapidly melted through by undulating cigarette burns. Your hands are magenta and covered in amoeba shadows. Your vision grows fuzzy. You rest your head on the centerline, watch the stripe stretch into the magenta gloaming. The asphalt is as soft as that goose-down pillow you had as a kid.

You mistake the screams for a siren. Soon, the screams end and a figure slithers from the wreckage. The figure reflects the colors of this subarctic wasteland and hurts to gaze upon. It expands and contracts, dragging itself across the road to where you are pawing, too late, for the commando knife. The brunette follows closely.

Bob is missing parts; its mantle is perfect. Bob is coming for you with what it's got. The dummy is no longer a dummy, it has evolved into something old and unspeakable to match its skinned and boiled visage. Right arm torn off in the crash, the sinuous left works fine to lever itself over your body until its sucker lips are poised near your own. You fight. The blonde and brunette step on your wrists.

The Blonde: "Inoperable isn't an obstacle for Bob. He'll fix you, good as new. Ever had psychic surgery, little girl? Get ready."

Bob: "My brother iz spared the worzt. Worzt." Fingers grip your chin and tilt your head. "Inside you iz what I really want. Want. Alwayz wanted *you*, Mizz Gamma. Gamma. Iz why we brought you here. Here. Away from your nest. Nest."

Its mouth opens like an iris and a blood-slick tendril uncoils and descends and penetrates the corner of your eye. Bob licks your right eye out of the socket, crushes and devours that mashed red grape. Magenta brightens and incandesces in a blast of white phosphorous.

Your mind leaps from your thrashing self, breaching sunward. Gravity seizes you, drags you backward. Voices call to one another from the distance, *Inbound, weapons hot.*

—*Too late, goddamnit.*

—*Ninety seconds. She's alive.*

—*Remember, concentrated fire on the visitor. Burn him down, everybody survives.*

—*If the dampeners hold. If she's alive.*

—*Cut the chatter. Eighty seconds.*

A wave of screeching static overwhelms your fleeting escape and you plummet to earth.

The wriggling, piercing tongue burrows. The real delicacy is your faithful tumor, uprooted and teased into daylight and sucked segment by necrotic segment into an eager maw. The dummy whipsaws its head, attacking the extrusion of malignant flesh as if it were a string of saltwater taffy. At last the tumor pops free and is devoured. Bob relaxes its death grip on your jaw and your skull bounces on the pavement.

Bob: "Fear. Guilt. Pain. Ecstazy. Your strength. Your weaknez. Manifezt in cannibal organizm. Thank you, Mizz Gamma. Thank."

You aren't fully conscious for this experience. Unfortunately, the Black Kaleidoscope spins wildly of its own volition and you witness these horrors from multiple perspectives.

The blonde lifts Bob into her arms and cradles the dummy with mechanical tenderness. The brunette extends her index finger and examines the long, sharp nail. She smiles and leans toward you, and her torso disintegrates and the rest of her is batted away. The blonde says something to Bob. The dummy is sated and sluggish and too slow to respond.

The blonde inhales to scream. Bob's mouth dilates. Several laser dots flicker against their bodies, then those bodies are shredded to sawdust and a mist of scorched blood.

A half-track clatters through the hills and rolls up. Sloan is on the .50 caliber gun. Norse and Lochinvar emerge. The women are clad in jumpsuits and headsets. Lochinvar carries a heavy rifle with a scope. She inspects the remains and nods with satisfaction. Apparently, this is a triple-cross. The dummy and its entourage were the targets all along—the Black Kaleidoscope confirms this, a day late and a dollar short, alas. You'd applaud Lochinvar's ruthlessness if you could muster the strength to raise your voice.

Norse presses her cheek against yours. She smells of grief and adrenaline, but she hasn't shed a tear. She says she's got you, that it's over. You laugh because you know the secret. It's always only beginning, always only transforming into something worse.

SHRIKES

There's a video locked inside the Diebold gun safe. The video features various Shrike women in candid shots. An off-camera voice greets each woman by name and asks, "Why? Why have you come here? Why have you pledged yourself to Mrs. Shrike?"

You: Pale from months in the cell, scrawny, apprehensive. You wince and rub your temple. Pain radiates from your eyes. "Time is short. I want to make amends. Redemption? Yeah, sure."

Liz Lochinvar: Surrounded by evergreens, her nose broken and bloodied. Her left forearm is slashed vertically to the crook of her elbow. Exposed metal glistens within the wound. A broadsword rests across her thighs. "Revenge. Man."

Robin Sloan: Luxuriating in the Jacuzzi, fine as a movie starlet in her string bikini and sunglasses. She raises her left fist to reveal raw and swollen knuckles. "I pulverize cinderblocks with my bare hands. Mrs. Shrike lets me pulverize faces. Boom!"

Indra Norse: Leaning against the hood of a '68 Mustang. Her jumpsuit is crimson. "Because there's a war on. It's as tiny and savage as colonies of insects going at it. I'd rather not be on the side that gets annihilated. But yeah, we're gonna lose. Wanna fuck?"

Jessica Mace: Bruised cheek, blazing eyes, wild hair, torn jacket. A car is on fire in the background. Instead of speaking, she takes a long, insolent swig from the neck of a whiskey bottle. Her glare holds until the video cuts to black.

ACKNOWLEDGMENTS

Many people figure into the creation of a book, and no list is ever complete. But with that in mind, I'd like to single out a few people who have helped make this book—and other Word Horde books—possible:

Jennifer Lockhart, for being there for me no matter how crazy my ideas might seem at the time, and the voice of reason in my crazy world.

Justin Steele, for keeping a constant finger on the pulse of Weird Fiction.

Scott R. Jones, for helping establish the visual aesthetic of Word Horde and for continually coming up with alternatives when I complain that a typeface "isn't quite right yet."

Shannon Page, for copy editing this (and other) Word Horde books. Thanks for making me look good!

Jan Frost, for being "Crazy Aunt Jan," a wonderful neighbor for many years, and the best Realtor in town.

Randall Ingalls, for being a resonant sounding board.

Raymond Lawrason, Amber-Rose Reed, and Grace Bogart, for all you've done in getting Word Horde books into the hands of readers.

Gwen Calahan, Brian Calahan, and Aaron Vanek for inviting me to be a part of the H. P. Lovecraft Film Festival/CthulhuCon community, and making me feel welcome, even though my "movies" take place on pages instead of a screen (for now). Mike Davis, Joe Pulver, Kelly Young, Jordan Krall, Arthur Graham, and Shamus McCarty for publishing my weird fiction.

All of Word Horde's authors, in this book and others, who represent one seriously kick-ass assemblage of talented individuals. You rock!

And everyone who has asked me when the next volume of *The Book of Cthulhu* is coming. Needless to say, this one's for you.

COPYRIGHT ACKNOWLEDGMENTS

Titles Available from Word Horde

Tales of Jack the Ripper
an anthology edited by Ross E. Lockhart

We Leave Together
a Dogsland novel by J. M. McDermott

The Children of Old Leech: A Tribute to the Carnivorous Cosmos of Laird Barron
an anthology edited by Ross E. Lockhart and Justin Steele

Vermilion
a novel by Molly Tanzer

Giallo Fantastique
an anthology edited by Ross E. Lockhart

Mr. Suicide
a novel by Nicole Cushing

Cthulhu Fhtagn!
an anthology edited by Ross E. Lockhart

Painted Monsters (October 2015)
a collection by Orrin Grey

Furnace (February 2016)
a collection by Livia Llewellyn

Ask for Word Horde books by name at your favorite bookseller.

Or order online at www.WordHorde.com

Photo Credit: Raymond Lawrason

ABOUT THE EDITOR

ROSS E. LOCKHART is an author, anthologist, bookseller, editor, and publisher. A lifelong fan of supernatural, fantastic, speculative, and weird fiction, Lockhart is a veteran of small-press publishing, having edited scores of well-regarded novels of horror, fantasy, and science fiction.

Lockhart edited the anthologies *The Book of Cthulhu I* and *II*, *Tales of Jack the Ripper*, *The Children of Old Leech: A Tribute to the Carnivorous Cosmos of Laird Barron* (with Justin Steele), and *Giallo Fantastique*. He is the author of *Chick Bassist*. Lockhart lives in a state of quantum flux in Petaluma, California, with his wife Jennifer, hundreds of books (currently residing in boxes), and Elinor Phantom, a Shih Tzu moonlighting as his editorial assistant.

Visit him online at www.haresrocklots.com

www.ingramcontent.com/pod-product-compliance
Lightning Source LLC
LaVergne TN
LVHW041112080826
845145LV00007B/1787

* 9 7 8 1 9 3 9 9 0 5 1 3 0 *